I Shall Not Want

I SHALL NOT WANT

JULIA SPENCER-FLEMING

THORNDIKE PRESS

A part of Gale, Cengage Learning

GALE
CENGAGE Learning™

Detroit • New York • San Francisco • New Haven, Conn • Waterville, Maine • London

GALE
CENGAGE Learning

LIBRARY OF CONGRESS CATALOGING-IN-PUBLICATION DATA

Spencer-Fleming, Julia.
  I shall not want / by Julia Spencer-Fleming.
    p. cm. — (Thorndike Press large print mystery)
  ISBN-13: 978-1-4104-1032-0 (hardcover : alk. paper)
  ISBN-10: 1-4104-1032-3 (hardcover : alk. paper)
  1. Fergusson, Clare (Fictitious character)—Fiction. 2. Van
Alstyne, Russ (Fictitious character)—Fiction. 3.
Episcopalians—Fiction. 4. Women clergy—Fiction. 5. Police
chiefs—Fiction. 6. Adirondack Mountains (N.Y.)—Fiction. 7.
New York (State)—Fiction. 8. Serial murderers—Fiction. 9.
Large type books. I. Title.
  PS3619.P467I35 2008b
  813'.6—dc22   2008026519

Published in 2008 by arrangement with St. Martin's Press, LLC.

To the librarians and libraries who have taught me, shaped me, befriended me, and recommended me, including: The Alfred C. O'Connell Library, Genesee Community College, Batavia, NY; Baldwinsville Library, Baldwinsville, NY; Bangor Public Library, Bangor, ME; Berwick Public Library, Berwick, ME; Beverly Public Library, Beverly, MA; Boothbay Harbor Public Library, Boothbay, ME; Clifton Park–Half Moon Public Library, Clifton Park, NY; Crandall Library, Glens Falls, NY; Delaware County Library, Delaware, OH; The Dwight Foster Memorial Library, Ft. Atkinson, WI; Edwardsville Public Library, Edwardsville, IL; Exeter Public Library, Exeter, NH; Falmouth Public Library, Falmouth, ME; Gorham Public Library, Gorham, ME; Huntingdon College Library, Montgomery, AL; Kennebunk Free Library, Kennebunk, ME; Lee-Whedon Memorial

Library, Medina, NY; Liverpool Public Library, Liverpool, NY; Lucius Beebe Library, Wakefield, MA; Lynn Public Library, Lynn, MA; Mackinac Island Public Library, Mackinac Island, MI; Manhattan Public Library, Manhattan, KS; Nevins Memorial Library, Methuen, MA; Normal Public Library, Normal, IL; North Conway Public Library, North Conway, NH; Norway Public Library, Norway ME; Patten Library, Bath, ME; Perry Public Library, Perry NY; Portland Public Library, Portland, ME; Puyallup Public Library, Puyallup, WA; Richmond Memorial Library, Batavia, NY; Rockland Public Library, Rockland, ME; Romeo District Library, Washington, MI; Scarborough Public Library, Scarborough, ME; South Portland Public Library, South Portland, ME; South Windsor Public Library, South Windsor, CT; Tuftonborough Free Library, Center Tuftonborough, NH; Vose Library, Union, ME; Warren Memorial Library, Westbrook, ME; Warren-Trumbull Library, Warren, OH; Waterford Public Library, Waterford, NY; Wells Public Library, Wells, ME; Wetumpka Public Library, Wetumpka, AL; Wood County District Library, Bowling Green, OH; and the Argyle Free Library, Argyle, NY.

ACKNOWLEDGMENTS

Thanks, as ever, to everyone at St. Martin's Press, at the Jane Rotrosen Agency, and at the Hugo-Vidal house. I couldn't do it without you — literally.

Thanks to the friends and family who hosted me in my travels; Jamie and Robin Agnew, John and Lois Fleming, Jon and Ruth Jordan, Dan and Barbara Scheeler, Neil and Tammy Lynn, Calvetta Spencer Inman, Mark and Laura Hubbard, David Lovett and Meg Ruley, Gordon and Rebecca Scruton, James and Mary Ellen Harris, and especially Rachael Burns Hunsinger, who turned her home into a writer's retreat so this book might get finished.

Thanks to those who gave me information, inspiration, and edification: The Reverend Mary L. Allen, Dr. Michael Brennan, Roxanne Eflin, David Garza, Timothy LaMar, Albert A. Melton, Dr. Parker Roberts, Lieutenant Colonel L. R. Smith (USA Ret.) and the Very Reverend Benjamin Shambaugh.

Finally, thanks to singer/songwriter Bill Deasy, whose CD *Good Day No Rain* was the perfect soundtrack to Russ and Clare's story. (He even looks like Russ Van Alstyne!) Go to BillDeasy.com and give it a listen.

My Shepherd will supply my need,
Jehovah is his Name;
In pastures fresh he makes me feed
Beside the living stream.
He brings my wandering spirit back
When I forsake his ways,
And leads me, for his mercy's sake,
In paths of truth and grace.

When I walk through the shades of death,
Thy presence is my stay;
One word of thy supporting breath
Drives all my fears away.
Thy hand, in sight of all my foes,
Doth still my table spread;
My cup with blessings overflows,
Thy oil anoints my head.

The sure provision of my God
Attend me all my days;
Oh, may thy house be mine abode

And all my work be praise.
There would I find a settled rest,
While others go and come;
No more a stranger or a guest,
But like a child at home.
— Isaac Watts (1674–1748) paraphrase of
Psalm 23, The Hymnal, 1982,
The Church Pension Fund

ORDINARY TIME
JULY

When she saw the glint of the revolver barrel through the broken glass in the window, Hadley Knox thought, *I'm going to die for sixteen bucks an hour.* Sixteen bucks an hour, medical, and dental. She dove behind her squad car as the thing went off, a monstrous thunderclap that rolled on and on across green-gold fields of hay. The bullet smacked into the maple tree she had parked under with a meaty thud, showering her in wet, raw splinters.

She could smell the stink of her own fear, a mixture of sweat trapped beneath her uniform and the bitter edge of cordite floating across the farmhouse yard.

The man shooting at her turned away from the porch-shaded window and yelled something to someone screaming inside. Hadley wrenched the cruiser door open, banging the edge into the tree. She grabbed for the mic. "Dispatch! Harlene? This bastard's shooting at me!" Some part of her knew that wasn't the right way to report an officer under fire, but she didn't care. If she lived to walk away from this, she was turning in her badge and her gun and going to work at the Dairy Queen.

The radio crackled. "Hadley? Is your eighty still the Christie place?"

She could barely hear the dispatcher over the shouting and swearing from the farmhouse. She thought she made out two masculine voices. "Yes," she yelled, getting a squeal of feedback from the mic. She tried again, forcing herself to speak in something like a normal tone. "He's got a .357 Magnum." She had recognized the sidearm. Hot damn. "There may be more than one of them. Men, I mean. Not guns. Although there may be more guns." She could hear herself, close to hysteria. "For God's sake, send help!"

There was a pause. *The hell with this,* she thought. *The hell with it. I've got two kids at home who need me.* As if invoking Hudson and Genny cleared her head, she suddenly realized the highest-pitched shrieking wasn't coming from a woman. *Oh, my God. Oh, shit.* She squeezed the mic again. "Dispatch, it's not just the sister and the caseworker. The kids are in there, too."

This time, Harlene's reply was instant. "We've got cars on the way and the state sharpshooter team is scrambling. See if you can keep him talking until backup gets there."

Hadley stared at the mic. "Keep him talking? About what? Jesus H. Christ, I'm not a negotiator! I haven't even finished the Police Basic course yet!"

"You talked to angry guys in prison, didn't you? Think of something. Dispatch out."

Talk to angry cons? Hell, yeah. The difference was, they were behind bars, weaponless, powerless, while she walked around free, armed with baton and taser. Cons didn't shoot at you from a house full of hostages.

The kids were screeching, a woman sobbing, the man swearing. *Think of something. Think of something.* Hadley slithered out of the squad car and crouched behind the open door. She raised herself up until she could see out the window. "Hey!" she yelled. "Hey! You!"

The end of the .357 Magnum swung out of the farmhouse window, knocking a few more shards of glass onto the front porch. Goddamn, that thing looked as big as a cannon. She inhaled. The July sun beat down on the dirt drive, throwing up waves of heat.

13

It was like breathing in an oven. "How 'bout you let me take those kids off your hands?"

"How 'bout you come up here and —" He launched into a graphic description of what he wanted her to do for him and what he was going to do to her. She hoped to God the children didn't understand.

"Let the kids go and we can talk about it," she shouted. "You want money? You want a ride outa here?"

"I want what's mine!" the shadowy figure with the gun yelled. "It's got nothing to do with you, bitch. Leave me alone and nobody will get hurt!" Something from the interior of the house caught his attention. He swiveled around. Yelled something she couldn't make out. Then the gun went off again.

Hadley was up and moving without thinking, running toward the house, her Glock 9mm awkward and slippery in her hand. If she had any plan at all, it was to get past the end of the porch to the corner of the house, where he couldn't see her without opening a window and leaning out. He turned back toward her. She could see the outlines of his face now, his eyes glittering in the dimness of the front room. He brought up the .357. She heard the breath sawing in and out of her chest, the howling of women and children, the susurration of tires on dirt and gravel, and she knew she wasn't going to make the shelter of the house in time.

Oh God oh God oh God oh God — she heard the shot, higher and keener than the last two, and dove toward the hewn stone foundation, rolling hard into its cool dampness. The blow stunned her, numbed her, and she beat against herself with one hand while trying to raise her gun to a defensive position with the other, all the while wondering, *Where is it? Where am I hit?*

Then her head steadied and she looked back across the dooryard. A big red pickup straddled the drive — defensively sideways, not head-on like her cruiser. Russ Van Alstyne, the Millers Kill chief of police, had his arms braced on the hood of the truck, his Glock .40 tight in a two-handed grip, pointing at the porch. The gun, she realized, that she had just heard discharging.

"You okay, Knox?" Van Alstyne didn't take his eyes off the window.

"Yeah." She struggled to sit up. "I mean, yes, sir."

"Stay right there. Don't move." She glanced up. Some four or five feet above her, a closed window reflected the maple facing it. Hadley squeezed against the edge of the house, drawing her knees in close, doing her best to disappear.

"You shoot one more time and I swear I'll cap one of 'em here," the man screamed. "I'll blow one of these bitches' heads off!"

The chief raised one hand, showing it was empty, and carefully placed his sidearm on the hood of the truck with the other. Hadley heard the crunch of more tires. Another squad car pulled in, flanking the chief's. The door popped open on the far side. She caught the glint of bright red hair and then a bristle brush of gray. Kevin Flynn and Deputy Chief MacAuley. MacAuley and the chief had a short and inaudible conversation.

"What's going on?" the gunman demanded.

The chief had a way of making his voice big without yelling. "My deputy here says the state SWAT team is on the way. They're not interested in *talking* to you. But I am."

"Screw you!" the man yelled. His voice, so near, made Hadley's skin crawl.

"C'mon, man, talk to me." The chief sounded like he was about to buy the shooter a beer. "Whaddaya gonna do, shoot one of them? Shoot one of us? They'll send you up to Clinton, life with no chance of parole. For what? Is one of those bitches worth the rest of your life?"

Hadley felt the shock of the chief's words sizzle up her spine. Was this the same guy who said "Excuse me" when he accidentally swore within her earshot?

"C'mon," the chief went on. "You put your gun down, I put my gun down, we'll call it drunk and disorderly. You'll get thirty days on the county, watching cable TV and sitting in air-conditioned comfort."

"I don't want no trouble," the man yelled. "Me and my brothers just want what's ours. You hear?" his voice shifted, as if he had turned away from the window and shouted to the people inside. "Yeah, I'm talking to you, girlie! You been holding out on me?"

In the drive, Flynn and MacAuley had taken up positions ranged to either side of the chief. Van Alstyne pointed at Hadley, then toward the back of the house, then at his eyes. *See what's around in back.* She nodded. She rolled belly down on the ground and crawled knees-and-elbows toward the rear of the house. It reminded her of the funny salamander-style crawling Hudson had used when he was a baby, except he hadn't been saddled with a bulky belt and an increasingly heavy gun.

The chief was going on about the weather and the heat, and — Jesus Christ! — he actually offered the guy a cold one. Hadley crawled out from beneath the maple's shade, the sunlight pressing on her back like a hot iron taking the wrinkles out of her blouse. She paused at the corner of the building, wrestled her gun into a half-assed shooting position, and peeked around the side.

Peeling white clapboards. A wheezing air-conditioning unit dripping water on the ground. Five steps leading up to a narrow roofed porch. A rusty wheel supporting a clothesline bolted next to the back door . . . the back door that was half open to the room inside.

"Hel-lo, momma," she whispered. If the chief could keep the guy in the front room distracted, she could sneak in and try to get the kids out. There wasn't much cover — the land sloped away from the house, the clothesline running maybe fifty yards over open grass until it connected with a lone birch tree. But if she could get them down the porch steps and around the corner, she could keep them against the foundation, out of the line of fire.

She crawled forward, one foot, two, then raised herself up to get a better view of the door.

Hadley was staring into the eyes of a dead woman. She was half in, half out of the

18

doorway, mouth still open from her last word, her blood soaked into her shirt and puddling beneath a plastic laundry basket filled with towels.

Oh, my God.

Hadley collapsed back onto the ground, squeezing her eyes shut like a kid hiding from the boogeyman. She swallowed, dry-mouthed, against her rising gorge. *I'm not going to throw up,* she thought. *I'm not going to throw up.* With her eyes closed, she noticed the things she should have earlier: the bright copper tang of blood, the nose-wrinkling suggestion of human waste, the buzzing of full-bellied flies.

She could hear the timbre of Van Alstyne's voice floating on the heat-saturated air. *I have to let the chief know about this.* Of course, to do that she was going to have to move, which she didn't want to do, not now, not maybe ever. She didn't want to deal with yet another dead person. What was this? The fourth? Fifth?

With that, she had another realization. The chief's promise of thirty days in the county jail — a lie to begin with, since the guy had shot at a cop, for God's sake — wasn't going to seduce this man. He wasn't going to give himself up. He was already headed for Clinton. He had nothing to lose.

Hadley reversed herself, staying as low to the ground as she could, then belly-crawled back around the side of the house. The chief was focused on the man with the gun, who was ranting about getting ripped off and not being able to trust anyone. Hadley ignored him. She stuck her hand up in the air to get someone's attention. The chief's eyes never wavered from the window where the shooter was hunkered down, but behind the squad car's tail, Kevin Flynn poked his head up and nodded once. He had been the MKPD's least experienced officer before she was sworn in, and his persistent attempts to be helpful and friendly didn't lessen the gall of playing catch-up with a guy eight years her junior. She hoped he was good at charades — there was no way she could use her radio this close to the house — as she laid her gun on the grass next to her.

First she jerked her thumb toward the rear of the farmhouse: *back there.* She used two hands to make the universal feminine shape, out, in, out: *a woman.* She drew a finger across her throat: *dead.* She held one hand like a pistol and "shot" herself in the chest.

Flynn shook his head as if to clear it, then nodded again. His red hair disappeared, to pop up again moments later, behind the chief. The chief heard whatever it was Flynn said to him. His eyes narrowed and his skin seemed to stretch across his cheekbones. He murmured something to Flynn, who slid into one of the cruisers and grabbed a mic.

"What's going on?" the shooter asked. "What's he doing on the radio?"

"I just told him to ask the state troopers to stay back a ways." Van Alstyne held up one hand. "I want you and me to have the time we need to talk our way out of this thing. Can't do that with a bunch of staties with guns hanging around."

More likely Flynn was telling the SWAT team to detour its sharpshooters farther along the road leading to the Christies' half-mile drive. If they went the long way around and stuck to a narrow approach through the sheep pasture, they could make it to the barn without being seen. Once inside, they would have an ideal vantage point through the haymow and upper windows.

The same idea seemed to occur to the gunman. "You tell those bastards to stay away from us," he shouted. "Anybody tries to mess with us, they gotta go through one of these kids to do it." Within the house, a woman cried out. Hadley didn't realize the man had left his defensive position at the front window until the chief shouted,

"Knox! What's he doing in there?"

She scrambled to her feet and peered into the window she had been crouched beneath. She got a beautiful view of the front hallway and the stairs. Useless. She covered the eight feet to the next window in two long strides. The sill was just low enough for her to see into a room in chaos, children scattering, a teenager clutching an infant, a woman struggling with the man as he yanked a little boy off his feet.

"He's holding a kid," Hadley yelled. "He's — oh, shit, no!" She watched, helpless, as the man clubbed the woman in the face with the butt of his gun. The woman dropped to the floor.

"Are there other shooters?" the chief yelled.

"I can't tell!" she screamed. "Maybe in the front —"

The man holding the squirming child turned toward the window, aiming the revolver at Hadley. She ducked and covered just in time. The window shattered. Shards of glass sliced into her hands, stabbed the back of her uniform, caught in her hair.

The chief was yelling for her and Flynn to get to the back door. She heard the muffled thud of footsteps against grass and then Flynn was beside her. He tossed her a Kevlar vest identical to the one he was wearing. She caught it, rose, and took off for the rear of the house, glass tinkling as it flew off her like water off a shaggy dog. She struggled into the vest as Flynn rounded the corner, taking the steps up to the porch in two bounds. He went high, holding the door open, while she crouched low, stepping over the body of the murdered woman — *I'm sorry, ma'am, so sorry* — shouting, "Police! Put your weapons down!" to the empty kitchen. She moved aside for Flynn to pass through and almost fired when a straggly boy appeared in the doorway. "Porsche!" he bawled. From unseen rooms beyond she heard Van Alstyne bellowing, a girl shrieking, and then, Holy God, the sound of gunfire, one, two shots and the .357 Magnum going off.

"Get in here!" Hadley shouted at the boy, as one gun and then another gun fired, and fired, and fired, too many shots, way too many. She and Flynn pushed past him into the doorway, low, high, her heart beating so fast she thought she was going to die.

She thought she was going to die.

The teenager screamed, yanking one of the kids out of the way. They rounded the big table dominating the space and approached the front room. Through the doorway, Hadley could see the other woman, out on the floor, bleeding from a vicious cut in her forehead. Beside her, the gunman was sprawled half on and half off a sofa, his eyes staring unseeing at the ceiling, his chest a bloody mess. A second man slumped in the far doorway, folded over like a stringless marionette.

Hadley thought she might collapse on the spot from relief. Instead, she and Flynn fanned into the room. She froze. Flynn let out a keening sound like a banshee. Omen of death. There was another body crumpled on the wooden floor.

Russ Van Alstyne.

Lyle MacAuley looked up from where he knelt beside the chief. "Call nine-one-one," he snapped at Flynn. He looked at Hadley. "Get me something I can use for compresses." His voice was as sharp-edged as ever. She and Flynn stumbled into the kitchen, where Flynn whirled and ran out the door, while Hadley stood stupidly, thinking, *Compresses?* Then she remembered the basket of laundry. She stepped over the dead woman, dug into the basket, and emerged with two bath towels.

"Hurry, Knox!"

She dashed back to the front room, holding out the towels. MacAuley snatched them out of her hands. While he folded them into thick pads, she looked down at the chief.

"Oh, Jesus," she said.

"Shut up!" MacAuley nodded toward the dining room. "Get these civilians out of here."

Hadley turned around. The door between the two rooms was crowded with crying kids. The teenager with the infant stood weeping — the scraggly boy's Porsche, she supposed — rocking the red-faced baby back and forth while it screamed. Best to start with her. Hadley stepped through the doorway, forcing the girl to retreat.

"Porsche? Are you Porsche?"

The girl nodded, openmouthed with crying.

"Is this your baby? What's her name?"

The girl gasped. "Amari." Her voice was wet and shaking.

"Why don't you let me hold Amari for a sec while you catch your breath." Hadley scooped up the baby and ran her pinkie knuckle over its toothless gums. The baby stopped wailing, a startled look on its face. Then it clamped around Hadley's knuckle and began sucking with a vengeance. An old ploy, but it still worked. "Porsche." Hadley moved her face so she blocked the girl's line of sight. "Let's get these little ones out

of here. They don't need to see this anymore."

"M-m-my aunt."

"The ambulance is on the way. The best
thing you can do for her is help calm the
children down."

The girl nodded. Wiped her eyes with the
back of her hand. Let Hadley slide the baby
back in her arms. The girl copied her pinkie-
nursing trick. "C'mon, everybody," she said,
in a fake-calm voice that Hadley herself
used when she was trying to keep it together
in front of her kids. "We're going outside."
She stepped into the kitchen, saw what was
blocking the door, and whirled around.
"No, Aston! Not that way! Out the front
hall."

Hadley helped steer the kids toward the
mercifully blood-free front hall. The little
boy she had seen in the kitchen stopped
beside the door to the front room, his eyes
fixed on the unconscious woman. He looked
up at Hadley. "Is Izzy gonna die, too?"

Hadley scooped him up in her arms. "An
ambulance is coming to help her, sweetie.
She'll have to go to the hospital, but she'll
be fine." She prayed she wasn't lying. She
took the last child's hand and followed
Porsche out the front door and across the
drive, to where a small grove of large maples

cast a deep shade over the grass.

Kevin emerged from one of the squad cars. "Ambulances coming." He headed for the house. "Harlene called them in before we got here. Support team from emergency services and Children and Family, too."

Hadley shot a glance at the traumatized family, then followed Kevin.

Without the crying children, the farmhouse sank into the deep dreaming silence of a hot July afternoon. The only sounds were the clunk and rattle of cubes falling from the icemaker and a hoarse, wet churning as Russ Van Alstyne tried to breathe. MacAuley had folded one towel around the wound in the chief's thigh and cinched it tight with his belt. As Hadley watched, a pulse of blood appeared on its white surface. MacAuley pressed the other towel, already sodden, against the chief's chest. Flynn was dragging cushions off the couch, wedging them beneath the unconscious woman's legs, getting more blood flow to her injured head. Hadley scooped some ice cubes out of the freezer, knotted them into a dishrag, and laid the improvised ice bag over the woman's eyes and nose. None of them said anything, as if a single word would break open their pretense at composure.

A wracking, phlegmy sound split the silence.

"Can't . . . breathe." The chief's voice was a whisper. Flynn nearly tripped over himself getting to Van Alstyne's side.

"I think you've punctured a lung," MacAuley said. "The EMTs will set you to rights. Listen." Far away, a faint siren sounded. "They're almost here."

The chief inhaled. It was liquid, choking, horribly wrong. Hadley looked down. The towel around his thigh was crimson. *Almost here,* she realized, would not be fast enough.

"Lyle . . . tell Clare . . ." — the chief breathed in again — "tell her. . . ."

"You can tell her yourself when you see her."

Hadley's stomach turned. She looked at Flynn. Tears smeared his sunburned cheeks. Without thinking, she reached over and grabbed his hand. The siren was louder now.

"Russ?" MacAuley sounded panicked, which was almost as scary as the chief's struggle to breathe. "Don't you die on me, Russ!"

The sucking, gurgling sound was louder, accompanied by a hiss, as if Russ Van Alstyne's air was pumping out of him along with his life's blood.

"Clare," he said. And then there was silence.

■ ■ ■ ■

SIX MONTHS EARLIER

■ ■ ■ ■

The Season After Epiphany

JANUARY AND FEBRUARY

I

Hadley pulled into the parking lot across the street from the church with a sense of relief she hadn't felt since she delivered Geneva. Maybe more. Three and a half days on the road with two kids under ten easily matched twenty-plus hours of labor in the awfulness sweepstakes.

She twisted around to check the backseat. Genny was asleep, her booster seat almost lost in a litter of stuffed animals, crayons, water bottles, and picture books. Hudson looked up from his Game Boy, his face pinched and tired. "Where are we, Mom?"

"We're here, lovey. Millers Kill. This is the church where your grampy works."

His eyes widened, giving him the appearance of a starving orphan. She kept stuffing food into him, but his jittery energy seemed to burn it all off before he could put any meat on his bones. The climate here was going to be hard on him.

"Why aren't we at Grampy's house?"

"I don't have a key to get in. We're here sooner than I thought, so Grampy's going to be surprised. C'mon, pull on your sweater and let's go say hi."

He looked doubtfully at his sister. "Are we gonna wake Genny up?"

Hadley unbuckled herself and twisted around to get a better look at her six-year-old. Out like the proverbial lightbulb. In LA, she wouldn't have even considered it — she never would have left one of the kids in the car. Here . . . she glanced at the ice-rimmed snowbanks framing the parking lot, the lead-colored snow-heavy clouds. Air weighted with chill slid in through her partly open window. "It's too cold," she said. "She'll have to come with us."

"Mo-om," he protested. "You could leave the car running. Nobody's going to steal it."

Wasn't that the truth. She opened her mouth. Transformed *I've been smelling something since we left Ohio, and I'm afraid we have another exhaust leak* into, "Fresh air will do her good."

"Fresh air," Hudson said, with all the scorn a nine-year-old could muster. "We've had two windows wide open since we got into New York."

"They're an inch open. Stop complaining." She leaned over the seat and shook Geneva gently. "Wake up, baby girl." Considered, as she wrestled her groggy daughter into her sweater, how much time and effort she took, every day, to avoid saying *We can't afford that.* The bag of toys and books from Goodwill. The Styrofoam box of sandwich fixings and no-name sodas. The tote filled with books on CD — which she had to mail back to the Glendale Public Library. All so that when she heard *Can we go to Toys 'R' Us? Can I get a book? Can we stop at McDonalds? Can we rent a DVD player?* she had a plausible answer. Something that wasn't *we can't afford it.*

For a moment, the outside didn't feel too cold. Then, as she waited for Hudson to finish saving his game, she could feel it against her bare skin and her hair, seeping in through her jeans and her sweater. She wondered if the frog-boiling analogy worked the other way. If you started out at normal temperature and it gradually got colder and colder, would you even notice when you froze to death? She shivered. This was where she had brought her children to, this cold place her own mother had abandoned at eighteen, never to return. Now she was doing the opposite, turning her back on the world and everyone who knew her.

Hudson spilled out of his door. Finally. "Close it!" she reminded him, then lifted Genny onto her hip. She hustled them across the street toward the church. Hadley had at least one parka stored in Granddad's house that would still fit her, but the last time the kids had visited in the winter they had been one and four. She would have to get them coats. Hats. Gloves. Boots. She hoped there was a Goodwill around here somewhere.

The interior of St. Alban's was marginally warmer than the outside. She had been here before, of course, over the ten years Granddad had been its caretaker, but the richness of the place, the stone pillars and the wood carvings and the elaborate stained-glass windows, always gave her goose bumps. Like walking into the Middle Ages.

Geneva lifted her head off Hadley's shoulder. "Momma, is this a castle?"

Hadley laughed. "No, baby, it's a church. C'mon, Hudson, this way." She headed for the door leading to the offices.

"Can I help you?"

Hadley choked back a screech of surprise. Beneath a window where stained-glass children were forever led toward the Throne

36

of God, a woman emerged out of shadow and stone. Black shirt. Black skirt. It took a second before Hadley realized she wasn't wearing a turtleneck but a white clerical collar.

"I'm Clare Fergusson." She moved close enough for Hadley to make out her face, cheekbones, chin, and nose, all points and angles. "I'm the rector here at St. Alban's." She smiled a welcome, but there was a bone-deep sadness about her that the smile couldn't dissipate.

"I know," Hadley said. "I mean, I've heard about you. My grandfather's Glenn Hadley."

Reverend Fergusson's smile tried to brighten. "You must be Hadley Knox. Mr. Hadley's been talking about your visit for two weeks now." She glanced toward the church door. "Um, if you're looking for him, I'm afraid he ran out to grab lunch and go to the hardware store. He'll be another hour, I'm guessing."

Hadley let out an, "Oh, no," before she could catch herself.

Reverend Fergusson looked at her. Then at the children. "You've been traveling a long way." It wasn't a question. "How 'bout you come with me. You can wait for your grandfather in the Sunday school room.

We've got a comfy sofa and some squishy chairs — and," she said to Hudson, "a TV with a VCR."

"Do you have movies?" Hudson asked, as they entered the hallway leading to the church offices.

"Yep. But I have to warn you, they're all religious. We've got *Veggie Tales,* and *The Prince of Egypt,* and *Joseph and the Amazing Technicolor Dreamcoat,* and the *Star Wars* movies."

"*Star Wars* isn't religious!" Hudson said.

"It's not?" Reverend Fergusson paused at the head of the stairs, her mouth open. "Darn it, why doesn't anyone ever tell me this stuff?"

It did Hadley's heart good to see her son's tentative smile. Divorce, disruption, relocation — these past months had been brutally hard on her little boy. She followed him down the stairs to the undercroft, watching him stick close to the rector.

"Next you're going to tell me *Power Rangers* aren't religious."

Hudson giggled. "They're not."

"Dang it, somebody is going to have to answer for this. Who bought these unsuitable movies?" Her eyes widened, and she pressed her fingers against her mouth. "Uh-oh."

Hudson laughed openly, guessing the joke. "You did! You did!"

The Reverend Fergusson's whole body sagged as she plodded down the dimly lit hall. "I'm so ashamed," she said. Hudson giggled again. "And here we are." She opened a door. She switched on the light to reveal a room that had been made as cheerful as a windowless fluorescent-lit space could be. Hudson ran to check out the low bookcase filled with toys, and even Genny wiggled out of her mother's arms to explore the play kitchen set in the corner.

Reverend Fergusson rolled the television, on its stand, away from the wall and plugged it in. "We don't get any reception down here, so it's already set to play videos," she explained. "You just turn it on and press the PLAY button." She straightened. Looked at Hadley again, the same way she had upstairs, as if she could see beneath her skin. "What can I do for you?" she said, half asking, half musing to herself.

The answer popped out before Hadley could help it. "Tell me where I can get a job around here." She wanted to call it back as soon as she had said it. The rector had meant something like *Can I show you the bathroom* or *Can I get you a drink of water.* Acting the hostess. Cripes, she thought

Hadley was here for a *visit* with Granddad, not to repackage her life.

Except her eyes narrowed and she got an abstracted look, as if she was thinking hard. "What are you looking for?"

Something where I don't have to speak to another human being. Yeah, that sounded great. "Anything that doesn't require college. I only have a GED."

Reverend Fergusson, who probably had degrees up the wazoo, didn't blink. "There's a lot of seasonal work come summer. Agricultural work, construction. All the places in Lake George hire waitresses and chambermaids. But right now?" She frowned. "Shape's not hiring. The Reid-Gruyn mill is letting people go, now they've been bought out. Let me ask around and see if anyone I know has a position open. What did you do in . . . where are you from again?"

"California. LA."

"Ah."

"What?"

The Reverend pinked up. Embarrassed. "I was thinking you don't look as if you come from around here. Your tan, for one thing. And your hair."

Hadley ruffled her short hair. "What about it?"

"Well, it's . . . trendy. We don't have a lot

of trendy here in Millers Kill."

Hadley almost laughed. "It's a cosmetology school special. Fifteen bucks. Twenty if you want the shampoo and blow-dry. Which I didn't."

"Were you" — the rector paused, as if she were searching for the tactful word — "an actress? Or a model?"

Hadley thought for a moment before answering. "I wanted to be when I first went to California. I discovered when I got out there that gorgeous girls are literally a dime a dozen." There wasn't any bitterness in her tone anymore. It had been so long ago, it seemed as if those days were something she had seen in a movie rather than something she had lived. "The past few years I worked for a company that took inventories, I waited tables, stuff like that. Before that, I worked for the state department of corrections."

"As a secretary?"

"As a guard."

The reverend's eyebrows shot up. "Well." Her mouth stretched, as if she was smiling about something not very funny. "I know one place in town that has an opening. One of their officers has left for the state police in Latham. The police department's hiring."

II

Clare sat mesmerized by the falling snow. With her sermon outline cooling on the desk in front of her, she watched the flakes float past the diamond-paned window, each one a spot of brilliance against the soot-gray sky. *Flick. Flick. Flick.* She had been like this all morning. Unable to focus on her tasks. Unable to care about them — or about much of anything.

Mr. Hadley stuck his head in the door, bringing with him the odor of furniture polish and cigarette smoke. "Mornin', Father." His usual address for her. She figured he thought of it as a gender-neutral honorific — like Captain, her other newly resumed title. "Thanks fer takin' care of my granddaughter yesterday." Mr. Hadley's North Country accent made the word come out *yestiddy.*

"How're they doing?"

He grunted. "They'll all be better now she's left that turd of a husband floatin' in the bowl. Sorry, Father."

"Mmm." She squelched her smile. "It must be good to have her back home."

" 'Tain't really her home, though mebbe it comes as close as never no mind. My daughter, God love her, dragged the girl all over the country. Never was able to settle,

42

my Sarah. The only place Honey ever came to twice was here. Sarah used to send her to me an' my wife every summer."

Clare had lost track of the players. "Honey?"

"That's her christened name. She changed it to Hadley when she was in her teens."

I can see why.

"Anyhow, I was just checkin' to see if you wanted me to get you a fire goin'."

Clare looked at her hearth, the best thing about her mid-nineteenth-century office. On cold winter days, she could warm herself in front of its brick and iron surround. Now it lay dark and ashy. There was a metaphor there for her life, but she was too flat to pursue it. "I don't think so, Mr. Hadley. I'm leaving for an ecumenical lunch in Saratoga soon."

" 'Kay. I'll stock your wood up some, though. S'posed to be colder'n a Norwegian well digger's you-know-what the rest of this week." He withdrew, leaving the scent of lemon and tobacco to mark his passing. She heard him addressing someone in the hall — " 'Lo, Father" — and was therefore unsurprised when her lunch date appeared in her doorway a half hour early, tall and gaunt and hunched forward like a fastidious vulture.

"Father Aberforth." She got up from her desk to greet the elderly deacon, best known as the bishop's hatchet man.

"Ms. Fergusson." He surprised her by trapping her hand within his much larger ones. He studied her with his penetrating black eyes. "How are you?" he asked. It was not a pleasantry.

"I'm sorry. Were we doing a session today?" The diocesan deacon had fallen into the role of her counselor and confessor. It was not a comfortable relationship. Their talks were like scalding showers: cleansing but painful.

"Sarcasm ill becomes you. How are you?"

She let her eyes slide away to the vine-and-fruit pattern of her carpet. "Okay. Good enough."

He let her tug her hand free. "Good enough, hmm?" He lowered his towering frame into one of the two admiral's chairs fronting the empty fireplace. "I suppose it's always a relief to know one isn't about to be dragged off and tried for manslaughter." Willard Aberforth was nothing if not blunt.

She turned to her desk. The letter from the District Attorney for the state of New York, Washington County, was still there, half covered by the sermon draft.

Upon hearing evidence in the matter of

the death of Aaron MacEntyre, the grand jury has declined to indict. Therefore, in accordance with the Medical Examiner's testimony, the state of New York rules your participation in the events leading to said death is consistent with self-defense as defined in N.Y.S.C Sec. II, p. 1–12.

"Oh, yeah," she said. "I dodged the bullet on that one." She could hear the bitterness in her voice.

"You were justified, girl. I know it and the bishop knows it and the state of New York in its magisterial wisdom knows it. Let it go. You saved three lives. Perhaps more." He paused. "Have you heard anything from this police chief of yours?"

"No." Her tone would have warned off a lesser man, but the deacon, a survivor of the Battle of Cho-San Reservoir, wasn't deterred.

"He is newly widowed," he said reasonably.

"Yes."

"Grief takes time."

"Yes."

"Perhaps you might approach him in a month or two."

She folded her hands over her chair back and watched her knuckles whiten. "He isn't going to want me to approach him in a month or two — or four. I'm the reason his wife is dead."

There was another pause. "Would you do me the courtesy of turning around so I can talk to your face instead of your scapulae?"

She turned around.

Aberforth was looking at her through half-closed eyes. "Do you believe that?"

"Yes."

He shook his head, sending his blood-houndlike jowls swaying. "Good God, girl, your pride is truly monumental."

"My *pride?*"

"Your pride. Did you or did you not make a full confession and repentance to the bishop?" He folded his black-coated arms.

"You know I did."

"Did he, in the name of our Lord, absolve your sins?"

She knew where this was going, and she didn't like it. "He did."

"Then who are you to presume that *your* errors, *your* mistakes of judgment, *your* faults are so grievous that they stymie God Himself? Do you think your ability to sin rises above God's ability to forgive?"

She blinked hard. She shook her head. "I can't —"

"You cling to your faults like a woman

clinging to a lover." He leaned forward. "A lover who has betrayed her."

She shook her head again.

"Are you angry with your police chief?"

She set her jaw. "Of course not. He's the one who's suffering."

"I seem to recall that he entertained the possibility that you may have been responsible for a murder."

"For an hour! God, why do I *tell* you this stuff?"

"Who else can you tell?"

Russ. But that time was gone. Now there was no one else.

"He chose his marriage over you," Aberforth went on.

"*I* chose his marriage over me, too."

"But as soon as he was in crisis, he was back at your door, asking for your help. *Then,* in his moment of deepest need, he turned his back on you."

"His wife had just died!"

"And since then he has steadfastly ignored your existence. Yet you harbor no anger toward him. None whatsoever."

She turned back to her desk. Gripped the back of her chair again to stop the shaking. Breathed in. Breathed out. Waited until she knew her voice wouldn't crack. "You're right. I need to let go of . . . my sense of complicity in her death. I'll focus on that."

"Oh, my dear Ms. Fergusson."

She turned around at that.

"You are a very good priest in many ways. And someday, if your self-awareness approaches half your awareness of others, you might be an extraordinary priest." He folded his hands. "I do not think that day will be today, however."

III

Clare was profoundly grateful the ecumenical luncheon was arranged mixer-style. After the strained ride from Millers Kill — not eased by the fact Father Aberforth insisted on driving his Isuzu Scout a conservative ten miles below the speed limit all the way to Saratoga — she didn't want to deal with any more togetherness with her spiritual advisor for a while. The deacon was seated at the other end of the Holiday Inn's Burgoyne Room, while Clare was ensconced at a table with a nun, a Lutheran pastor, a UCC minister, and an American Baptist preacher — all of whom were a good twenty-five to thirty years older than she was. The only other person attending who was close to her age was Father St. Laurent, a devastatingly good-looking Roman Catholic priest who made the RC's vows of celibacy seem like a crime against the human gene pool. He had glanced at Clare with a sympathetic smile from the middle of his own collection of fossils. *Experienced clerics,* she corrected herself.

The blessing was given by a rabbi from Clifton Park, and the three men, who all seemed to know one another, fell into a discussion of their grandchildren before Clare had even buttered her roll. The nun rolled her eyes at Clare.

"This is just like the get-togethers in my town." Clare kept her voice low. "Dr. McFeely and the Reverend Inman always wind up getting out their brag books."

The sister laid her hand over Clare's. "I can guarantee you I don't have any grandkids. That I know of."

Clare almost expelled her bite of salad.

"Sorry," the nun said. "My favorite soap opera just managed to introduce a secret-baby story line where the father knew but the mother didn't."

Clare had to ask. "How? Amnesia?"

"Split personality." The nun speared a cherry tomato. "So I figure, you never can tell."

Clare's laugh drew attention from several tables away. She covered her mouth with her napkin and coughed. "I'm Clare Fergusson. Rector of St. Alban's, in Millers Kill."

"Lucia Pirone of the Sisters of Marian Charity." She nodded as the waitress reached for her salad plate. "I'm guessing from your accent you're not from this neck of the woods. North Carolina?"

"Close," Clare said. "Southern Virginia. Then around and about a bit with the U.S. Army before seminary."

"Really? One of my brothers was career army. He's retired now, of course. What was your MOS?"

"I flew helicopters." She caught herself. "I fly helicopters. I've just recently reupped with the National Guard."

"Really?" Sister Lucia leaned toward Clare, heedless of the silverware in her way. "With a war on? And you say you're a rector?" The nun's sharp eyes seemed out of place on her wrinkled face. Clare suspected the sweet-old-thing look was a clever disguise. "Whatever did your bishop say about that?"

"It was . . . he supported my reenlistment. He felt it would help me clarify . . . where my vocation lies."

"This is supposed to help you see if you have a true calling?" The sister's glance went to Clare's white collar. "Bit late in the day for that, isn't it?"

"It's not my calling that's in doubt. Just . . . what it is I'm called to *do.*" She dropped her voice. "I think the bishop's hoping Uncle Sam will take me out of his hair."

Sister Lucia's eyes lit up. "Ah. You have *bishop* troubles."

"I'm sure the bishop would say he has Clare Fergusson troubles."

"I'll drink to that." The nun lifted her water glass and looked at it. She sighed. "That's the only problem with these ecumenical things. No wine." She glanced meaningfully at the Baptist preacher before swigging her water. "At any rate, my sympathies to you. I have bishop problems as well, and he's not even *my* bishop."

Clare leaned back to let the waitress deposit a chicken breast on a bed of wild rice in front of her. "Not your bishop?"

"Are you familiar with the Sisters of Marian Charity?"

"Sorry. I'm not as knowledgeable about Roman Catholic orders as I probably should be."

Sister Lucia thanked the waitress for her salmon. "The order was founded in 1896 by a pair of rich sisters who wanted to better the lives of impoverished immigrants in Boston."

"You mean like Jane Addams and Ellen Starr in Chicago?"

"Exactly. Over the last century, the order's mission became focused on the plight of migrant laborers. The motherhouse relocated west during the dustbowl, and the bulk of our work has been in California and Arizona. I'm here as a missioner, the first one in the northeast dairy country."

Clare paused before forking a bite of chicken into her mouth. "Why? I mean, Washington and Warren counties are whiter than mayonnaise. Shouldn't you be in — I don't know — Albany or somewhere?"

"What would you think if I told you there were upwards of three hundred year-round Hispanic farm workers in Washington County alone?"

Clare blinked. "Three hundred?"

"Or more. Some with guest-worker papers, most illegal. The number may double in the summer."

"I'd say . . . that surprises me. I didn't think this part of New York had the kind of large-scale agriculture that requires importing labor." She stabbed several green beans, wondering, for the first time, whose hands had picked them.

"It's dairy farming country," Lucia said. "Hard, thankless work. Dairymen have to be able to fix machinery, repair barns, bring in crops, deliver calves, and, most demandingly, milk. Corn or soybeans or wheat can wait twenty-four hours for attention, but cows have to be milked, morning and evening, three hundred and sixty-five days a year."

"You sound like someone speaking from experience."

"I grew up on a dairy farm in Vermont. Last year, I went back to Rutland for a family funeral and discovered my brother's neighbor had six Guatemalans working for him. That's when I realized we were needed back East again."

"So you got your superiors to send you." She cut a slice off her chicken breast. "But they must have had to get the diocese's support."

"I have my superiors' blessing. I have the Diocese of Albany's *permission.* They weren't too wild about giving it, either." Lucia gave Clare a dry smile. "Caring for illegal aliens is Christian, but it's not very convenient. Especially when you have a large conservative element in your diocese that believes everybody without papers ought to be rounded up and sent back to Mexico."

"So what is it you do?" Clare wiped her

mouth. "I mean, it sounds as if you're shooting for more than getting these people to a Spanish-language Mass."

"We start with basic services, like transportation away from the farms and translators to help them deal with government bureaucracies. Then we act as advocates. Guest workers don't have the right to disability or unemployment insurance, to overtime, or even to a day of rest. The men who are here without papers won't seek health care, won't report safety violations, won't complain if they get stiffed on their pay, because they're scared of the authorities. They keep their pay in cash because they don't have the ID to open bank accounts, and if one of them is the victim of a crime, he won't go to the police. Some of them live in appalling conditions, in ancient trailers that wouldn't have passed safety inspections in 1958, eight or nine men sharing a space."

"Wow." Clare pushed her plate away so she could prop her elbow on the table, a bad habit she had never gotten rid of. "That sounds amazingly challenging. And worthwhile."

Sister Lucia nodded. "I'm glad you see that. Now I just have to find some congregations to partner with me."

"Doesn't your order support your mission financially?"

"I get a modest amount. And by modest, I mean it's swathed in a burka, unseen by human eye."

Clare laughed.

"No, the problem is, we're stretched thin up here in the North Country. Small parishes, every priest responsible for two or three of them, donations down . . . Without the bishop behind me, my tiny little mission's needs get squashed on the bottom of the pile every time."

"Let me help you."

The nun sat back in her seat. "I beg your pardon?"

"I have some friends at the Episcopal Development Fund. This sounds like just their sort of thing: small, grassroots, helping individuals in a tangible way."

Sister Lucia's face was a mixture of interest and doubt. "There is a spiritual component to the work, you know. It's definitely Catholic. Spanish-language Masses and all."

Clare grinned. "Not to worry. In the Episcopal Church, we are all over the ecumenical like white on rice. In fact, we *are* kinda the white on rice."

The waitress replaced their empty plates with fat slices of cheesecake. "Coffee?" She held up a pot.

"Absolutely," Clare said. Sister Lucia demurred, then watched with amusement as Clare emptied packet after packet of sugar into her cup. "I may be able to round up a few bodies for you as well." Clare reached for her spoon. "We've had an uptick in our membership over the past year, younger people —" they could hardly be older, since the average age when she arrived at St. Alban's had been fifty-seven — "who haven't found a spot in our current volunteer programs. I think your mission might be just the thing." Her spoon *ting-ting-ting*ed in the cup as she stirred clockwise, then counterclockwise. "When I started my ministry, I was worried I wasn't going to be able to get anyone to reach out to the marginalized among us. But I've come to believe it's not that people are unwilling, it's that they just don't see them. Look at me. I've lived here over two years without knowing about any of these workers." She looked at the nun confidingly. "I didn't really want to come to this luncheon. Now I'm so glad I did."

Sister Lucia smiled. "Do you always leap into things so . . . ah . . . decisively?"

"You bet," Clare said. "I'm not sure if it's a virtue or a flaw, but after thirty-six years,

I've come to accept it's who I am." She took a sip of her coffee and sighed as the heat and sugar and caffeine hit her. "And thank you."

"For what?"

"For calling it *decisiveness* instead of 'jumping in without thinking things through.' "

"Oh, I see it as fearlessness." The nun glanced at Clare's left hand, bare of rings. "You're not married."

Clare shook her head.

"Partnered?"

"No! I mean, no. . . . I'm not."

Sister Lucia patted her hand. "Not meaning to be nosy. It's just that I've found one of the great benefits of the celibate life is fearlessness. Especially for women. You can see what needs to be done and do it, without fear of how it's going to affect your family or your reputation." Where she had been patting, she squeezed, hard. "Don't let anybody convince you it's a flaw. We need more fearless women following Christ, not less."

IV

On the way back to Millers Kill, she and Deacon Aberforth had to stop at a Citgo station to gas up. When she went inside to pay — leaving the deacon muttering about the wasteful extravagance of the tricked-out Hummer taking up almost two spaces at the next pump over — there were five young Hispanic men getting sodas in the back. Five. Bumping into each other, joking around in Spanish, underdressed for the weather in sneakers and the ripstop jackets she saw kids in her congregation wearing. She shook her head.

The people we don't see.

Feeling well justified in her decision to aid Sister Lucia, she returned to the deacon's Scout. "Father Aberforth." She willed her eyes away from the speedometer as he more or less accelerated up Route 9. "Would you describe me as impetuous or fearless?"

He glanced at her. "I would describe you, Ms. Fergusson, as the vehicle through which God shows me He still has a great deal of work for me to do."

LENT

MARCH

I

"Father? I'm finished up. Them floral guild folks are still puttin' up palms for the service tomorrow, so I'm not locking the sanctuary." Mr. Hadley hovered in the doorway to the church office. Unless he was cleaning, repairing, or tending, Clare never saw him go into the offices. Fair enough. He had his own kingdom in the boiler room and the furnace room and the mysterious Sexton's Closet.

Lois, their church secretary, glanced at the clock. "School bus time?"

"Honey's out on another interview." Mr. Hadley sounded out of breath. He clapped one meaty hand against his chest. "Sorry," he said, panting. "Guess I come up those stairs too fast. Anyways, I don't want them grandbabies of mine comin' home to an empty house."

"Absolutely not. When my children were

small, I was always there when they got home. Give them a good snack, make sure they've started their homework, and then you can have Happy Hour in peace."

The Reverend Elizabeth de Groot looked scandalized. She had been assigned as St. Alban's deacon in January, and two months sharing an office had not accustomed her to Lois's sense of humor. Clare was beginning to suspect it wasn't going to happen.

"How's Hadley's job search going?" she asked, before Elizabeth could say anything.

"I don't mind tellin' you, it's been disappointin'. Used t'be plenty of good jobs for a body not afraid a hard work. Now what the Mexicans don't come up and take, they ship overseas." He made a gesture that said *what ya gonna do?* "Eh-nh. She'll find sumpin' sooner or later. She's at the police station today."

Lois and Elizabeth did not look at Clare.

"Hard to picture her in uniform," Mr. Hadley went on, unaware of the charged atmosphere. "Allus wanted to be an actress when she was little. Pretty enough for it, too. But I guess it's hard to make a livin' at it."

"I'm praying for her," Clare said. "Let me know if there's anything more concrete I can do."

"Eh." He fished a less-than-clean handkerchief from his pocket and mopped his face with it. "If you know anybody in the police department, you can put in a good word."

Lois choked, coughed, and grabbed for her water bottle. "You okay?" the oblivious sexton asked.

Red-faced, Lois waved him off. "Fine," she gasped.

"You'd better get going if you want to make that school bus." Clare glared at the secretary, who was thumping herself on the chest. "We'll make sure Lois doesn't swallow any more words the wrong way."

" 'Kay. See ya tomorrow. 'Bye, Father." Mr. Hadley thumped off up the hall.

Lois blinked several times, then ran her fingers through her strawberry-blond bob, restoring it to its usual razor-cut perfection. "Let's see. Where were we?"

Clare decided discretion was the better part of valor. "Holy Week. We need three more readers, and somebody has to let the AA group know their meeting is going to conflict with the Stations of the Cross."

"Why do you let that man call you Father?" Elizabeth smoothed her Chanel-style jacket over her woolen shift. She was the only woman Clare had ever seen who managed to turn a Little Black Dress into clergy wear. "Don't you worry he's being satiric? Denigrating your authority?" Elizabeth was big on clerical authority.

"People can call me what they want. At least it's grammatical, which is more than you can say about *Reverend.*"

"How about *Mother?*" Lois suggested.

"Only if followed by *Superior.*" Clare shook her head. "The only gender-neutral title that's both proper and traditionally Anglican is *bishop,* so that's what I'm going to shoot for. How do you think I'd look in a purple shirt, Elizabeth?"

A shout down the hall saved the older woman from coming up with a tactful lie.

"Clare! Reverend Clare!" Laurie Mairs appeared in the doorway. "It's Mr. Hadley! Come quick!"

Clare pelted down the hall, the flower guild member close behind her. The door to the sanctuary had been left open, and as she burst through into the church, she could see Mr. Hadley collapsed near the center aisle, his face half in a puddle of vomit.

"Oh, my God," Clare said.

Delia Hall, the other volunteer, was dancing back and forth, unable either to go to the fallen man's aid or to back away. "Oh, Clare, thank heavens! He sat down on the pew, like he was tired, and then he simply toppled over! Do you think he's — could it be —" She tipped an invisible bottle to her mouth. The Sexton's Closet was rumored to have its own stock.

"No." Clare knelt by the sexton. His face was pale, damp with sweat where it wasn't smeared with vomit. She touched his cheek. "Mr. Hadley?" He was clammy beneath her hand.

He pawed at his chest. "Heavy." His gravelly voice was so low she could barely hear him. "Can't . . ." He worked like a baby with croup, struggling for each breath.

"Clare?" Elizabeth's voice was calm. Clare hadn't seen her come in. "What can I do?"

"Call nine-one-one. I think he's having a heart attack." She glanced up at the flower guild ladies. "Delia, get a wet soapy towel. Laurie, something to dry him with. We can at least clean him up."

The fifteen minutes before the Millers Kill Emergency Squad arrived was one of the longest in Clare's life. She thought every heave of Mr. Hadley's chest was going to be his last. The whoop and clatter of the ambulance was like the sound of an angelic host, and she could have kissed the paramedics when they hurried through St. Alban's great double doors.

"Heya, Reverend Clare, whatcha got?"

Duane Adams, who cobbled together a living as a part-time cop, part-time firefighter, and part-time EMT, didn't spare her a glance in greeting her. He and his partner knelt by Mr. Hadley.

Clare backed out of their way, bumping into Elizabeth, who had returned to keep watch with her. "His name's Glenn Hadley. He's — um, seventy-four."

Duane's partner was strapping an oxygen mask over Mr. Hadley's face, sliding a blood pressure cuff on his arm.

"Any history you know of?" Duane asked.

"He smokes. He's got diabetes, but he doesn't take insulin shots for it." She rubbed her arm. "I didn't know what to do for him, other than try to make him comfortable."

"You called us," Duane said. "That's what you do." His partner unslung a radio and was rattling off a string of jargon and numbers. The only thing Clare recognized was "MI."

"They're calling it in at Glens Falls," the EMT said.

"Okay." Duane stood. "Let's get him on the stretcher."

"Glens Falls Hospital? Why not Washington County?" As soon as she said it, she knew. It was serious. Too serious for their small local hospital to handle. The bad stuff always went to Glens Falls.

"They'll want him straight to the cardiac cath lab. Any next of kin?" Duane asked.

"Oh, my Lord, his grandkids." Clare looked at Elizabeth. "I don't even know how to reach Hadley."

"You go get the children," Elizabeth said. "I'll follow the ambulance to the hospital."

"Good." Clare didn't wait to see the paramedics remove Mr. Hadley. She dashed back to her office and grabbed her coat and keys. "Lois," she yelled, "call the police station and see if they can pass on a message to Hadley Knox." She stopped in the door of the main office, shrugging into her coat. "Mr. Hadley's had a heart attack. He's headed for Glens Falls. I'm picking up her kids and bringing them back here."

"I'm on it." Lois reached for the phone.

As Clare slopped across the tiny parking lot, wet from the melt of the last stubborn snow piles, she heard the ambulance siren rise like a screaming bird into the air. *Lord, be with them,* she prayed. *Be with us all.*

II

Hadley picked a fuzz ball off her wool skirt. It was an old A-line, left behind in the closet of her grandfather's house from a Christmas visit. She had needed something to go to Midnight Mass in, and back then she had enough money to buy something she was only going to use once. Well, she'd gotten her dollar's worth from it now. She had worn it on every job interview in the past two months. Too bad the only thing it had gotten her were a few long looks at her legs.

The man scrutinizing her paperwork had certainly checked her out, coming up the hallway to the squad room and going toward his desk at the far end of the room. She hoped it was because he was a cop and not because he was going to be trouble. She eyeballed his desk. A mug with a bunch of pens. A brass nameplate: LYLE MACAULEY, DEPUTY CHIEF. No pictures of the wife. Not that that always meant anything.

Being a good-looking woman in a male-dominated field was tricky. She had always been able to handle her co-workers okay, but catching the eye of a superior meant trouble for everybody. There wasn't going to be any privacy here; it looked like everyone on the force worked out of this room. Five desks, a bunch of chairs, and a big old wooden table. File cabinets, whiteboard, and maps squeezed in between tall, elegant windows from another age. *We're not in*

California anymore, Toto.

"You've got great scores here." Lyle MacAuley held up the results from her NYS Police Test.

"Thanks." She shifted in her sturdy metal seat.

"And your scores from the California Department of Corrections are good, too. You worked for them two years?"

"Three." She knew what was coming next. "I got laid off in a budget cutback. If you look on my résumé, you'll see my supervisor is one of my references."

"Mm." He glanced at the paper on his desk. He had bristly gray hair and bushy eyebrows that looked like they came out of a Halloween disguise kit. "You have a gap of almost two years between the end of your DOC job and now."

"I was a stay-at-home mom for a while." She had been a frantic paddling-to-keep-their-heads-above-water mom. The crap jobs she had been forced to take — scooping ice cream, handing out brochures, walking around in high heels and a bathing suit at a car dealership — weren't worth putting down on paper.

"How come you're applying for a position as a patrolman? I mean, patrol officer. I'd've thought you'd be looking for a job with the

New York DOC. The pay's better."

She shook her head. "The nearest correctional facility they're hiring women guards for is Dannemora. I need to stay in this area."

"Because of the kids?"

She shrugged.

"Look, I'm not supposed to ask this, so if you get pissed off you can report me to the EEOC, but have you thought about what you, a single woman, are going to do about your kids? We can't guarantee mommy hours, you know."

He was right. He wasn't supposed to ask her this, and it did piss her off. She tried to keep it from showing in her voice. "We're living with my grandfather, Glenn Hadley. He has a part-time job with flexible hours."

The deputy chief slitted his eyes. Hadley could almost see a list of names clicking through his mind. He might look like an over-the-hill hayseed, but she suspected it wouldn't do to underestimate MacAuley's smarts. She wondered if the illegal question was just another kind of test.

"Glenn Hadley." His eyes popped open. "Works at St. Alban's?"

"Yeah. He's the sexton. That's what they call the custodian there."

"Don't mention that when you talk to the chief."

The surge of hope — she was going to talk to the chief! She was a serious candidate! — almost made her ignore MacAuley's weird advice. Almost.

"What, that granddad's a janitor?"

"Just don't mention St. Alban's or anything to do with it."

She frowned. "He doesn't have something against Christians or something, does he? Because I'm not super devoted or anything, but I do go to church."

"No, no, no, nothing like that." MacAuley compressed his lips. Thought for a moment. "The chief lost his wife this past January."

"I'd heard that."

"He was . . . with the minister of St. Alban's when it happened. Not *with* her like there was anything funny going on," he added, so quickly she couldn't help but think there must have, in fact, been something funny going on. "It's just that he feels if he hadn't been with Clare — with Reverend Fergusson — he could have saved his wife. So now, being reminded of her bothers him. Being reminded of Clare. Reverend Fergusson. You understand?"

"Uh-huh," she said, not understanding. Not caring. "I won't mention St. Alban's."

"Okay." He shoved his chair back. Stood up. "Let's go see the chief."

Hadley stood, working her face into the right expression. Ready, willing, and eager. Not desperate. She couldn't afford to look desperate. The prisons were out of commuting range. The private security firms had turned her down. There were only a handful of places where a high school grad could make a decent living, and not one of them was hiring. If she couldn't land this, it was going to be waitressing in Lake George or Saratoga, living off tips and praying nobody got sick or broke a leg. The MKPD had dental. Dental! It had been more than two years since she and the kids had seen a dentist.

MacAuley led her down a short hall, through the dispatcher's station, and rapped on a door with a pebbled glass window and CHIEF RUSSELL VAN ALSTYNE painted in gold. "C'min," a voice said.

She followed MacAuley into a messy office, heaps of magazines and papers piled on a battered credenza, the walls covered with posters and bulletins and a huge map of the tricounty area. A leggy philodendron was dying atop two old file cabinets.

The chief was on the phone, one hand cupped over the receiver. "Hang on," he said. MacAuley tossed her folder onto an equally messy desk. She watched as the chief picked it up one-handed. Long, square fingers. Brown hair with an equal sprinkling of blond and gray, as overgrown as the philodendron.

"Yeah," he told the phone. "Okay. Put us on the list if you find out anything." He laid the folder down without opening it. "No, but send us any prints. We'll run comparisons when we do the ground search in August." Looking at Russ Van Alstyne, she found it hard to picture August. His face was winter-pale, with deep lines etched on either side of his mouth. Ice-blue eyes. She figured him to be about her dad's age, although there was a solidness to the chief that her dad, the king of adult ADD, had never had.

Van Alstyne hung up the phone. "Chief, this is Hadley Knox," MacAuley said. The chief nodded to her. "What's up?" MacAuley went on.

"The rental truck." He glanced at Hadley, including her in the story. "Somebody abandoned a Ryder truck last week at a local farm stand that's still closed for the winter." He looked at Lyle. "Stolen from Kingston. We're getting copies of any prints CADEA pulls."

"Cad-dee-ay?"

Both men looked at Hadley. Uh-oh. Maybe she was supposed to know what that was?

"Capital Area Drug Enforcement Association. It's a sort of regional cooperative, with investigators from departments all over the area." The chief handed another folder to MacAuley. "Their lab tech agreed with your theory that the bales were shrink-wrapped. They didn't find a trace of plant material or THC on any surfaces."

MacAuley tapped his sizable honker. "They don't have this."

"Mmm. Maybe we should hire you out."

"What was it?" Hadley asked. In for a penny, in for a pound, she figured. "In the truck, I mean."

"Marijuana," MacAuley said.

"Pot?" She didn't mean to sound so disbelieving, but pot? Who cared?

"Ten million dollars' worth." Van Alstyne tapped the paper on his desk. "If the truck was full."

"Holy shit!" The second it was out of her mouth, she wanted to call it back. Swearing on a job interview. Genius. "Sorry," she said.

MacAuley looked amused. "I'll just leave you both to it, shall I?"

"Thanks, Lyle," Van Alstyne said. MacAu-

72

ley exited the office, leaving the door ajar. "Sit down, Ms. Knox."

There was only one chair that didn't have junk on it. She took it.

For a minute, he studied her. If it had been someone else, she would have been getting the creepy vibes that came with unwanted sexual interest. But Van Alstyne wasn't looking at her like a man looks at a woman. It was more like a doctor examining an X-ray. Diagnostic.

"You ask questions," he said.

Was that a complaint? A compliment? She swallowed. "I have two kids, and I'm always telling them there's no such thing as a bad question. I guess it's rubbed off on me."

"Why do you want to be a cop?" His question caught her off guard. Damn, she had prepped for this. What had she been going to say?

"I worked as a prison guard for three years in California." She nodded toward the folder still lying on his desk, unopened. "I found it challenging and fulfilling —"

"Why do you want to be a cop?"

She was left with her mouth half open from her incomplete canned response.

"Just give it to me straight."

She shut her mouth. "I've got a family to support. I need a good-paying job here in

Millers Kill. I don't have any college, but my DOC training in California means I already qualify as a probationary peace officer, if I'm enrolled in the Police Basic course."

"What about administering justice? What about getting the bad guys off the street and behind bars?"

She let out a puff of air. "When I was working as a prison guard, I met a lot of guys who claimed they were innocent. I don't know. I figure, administering justice is somebody else's job. As for getting — uh, the bad guys . . ." She trailed off. "I suppose everybody wants that."

He tilted his head to one side and gestured for her to keep going.

"I'm sorry, sir, but if you're looking for Robocop, I'm not the right person. I guess I see policing as sort of like being a mom. I don't want to catch my kids doing something wrong. I want to stop 'em *before* they do it. Or head them off before a little problem becomes a big one." He was looking at her with an expression she couldn't define. She snapped her mouth shut. Policing is like being a mom. Great. Maybe she should tell him she wanted to knit scarves and serve hot cocoa.

"If you're hired, you'll be the only woman

sworn into the department. The first woman, actually." There was an edge of discomfort in his voice, but she couldn't tell whether it was from the prospect of letting a girl into the club or embarrassment that they hadn't integrated the force up to now. "Have you thought about how you'll handle that?"

He had said he wanted her to give it to him straight. "Are the men in your department likely to require handling?"

"No. Well . . ." — he pinched the bridge of his nose beneath his steel-rimmed glasses — "not most of 'em, of course not. I was referring to the job itself. It's not like guard work. You'll be doing traffic stops, pulling apart guys who've had too much to drink, walking into houses where the husband and wife have been beating up on each other. You'll be shorter and lighter than any other officer here. How do you deal with that?"

That *was* a question she had prepped for. "Just like I did as corrections officer. The trick is to never, ever, let them think you're vulnerable. That means controlling the situation, and that starts right up here." She tapped her temple. "It doesn't matter how big you are if you can't project control. And if it comes down to using force, I have an advantage your other officers don't. The drunk guys see these" — she thrust her forearm beneath her breasts and hoisted them, and sure enough, his eyes followed — "and they don't see me coming in with this." She touched the side of his head lightly with the magazine she had picked up with her free hand.

He let out a short laugh. "It's not always that simple."

"Nope. But men still tend to underestimate women."

His smile changed to something wistful. "Yeah. I know — I *knew* — a woman who used to take advantage of that fact."

"Did it work for her?"

"Yeah," he said. "Yeah, it did. . . ." He shook himself. "Okay." His voice was once again no-nonsense. "If you want it, you've got the job."

"I do? I mean, great! Yes! I do want it."

"You'll be on probation until you've completed the Basic course. I don't want to throw away the time and money we're going to spend training you, so I expect you to pass. With high marks."

"I will. I'll be in the top ten percent. You won't be disappointed."

"Plus, you'll have to put in some serious time on the firing range." He tapped the folder, which he still hadn't opened. "The scores from your shooting test are way too low."

"Absolutely," she said. "That won't be a problem."

Van Alstyne stood up. Hadley stood up. He held out his hand and she took it. "Welcome to the Millers Kill Police Department, Officer Knox."

A rap on his door kept her from gushing her thanks. The dispatcher, a square stack of a woman with an iron-gray perm, stuck her head in. "If you're all finished, Ms. Knox has a phone call."

"Me?" She looked at Van Alstyne. He waved her off.

"Go ahead. Harlene here can set you up with the paperwork."

Harlene closed the door behind them and surprised Hadley by dragging her past the dispatch room into the hallway. "You don't actually have a call. It's a message. From St. Alban's." As she said this, she glanced around, as if ensuring no one could hear her. "It's your grandfather. He's been taken to the Glens Falls Hospital with a heart attack. Reverend Fergusson's going to fetch your kids over to the church."

Hadley stood there. "I'm sorry. Did you say —" and then her mind caught up to Harlene's words and her eyes flooded. "Oh, shit," she said. "Oh, shit."

Harlene was saying something about Glens Falls not necessarily meaning it was bad, and that she wasn't to worry about her children, and all Hadley could think was that she had uprooted their lives and come three thousand miles and now her grand-dad was going to die and she'd be on her own again. All on her own. Again.

III

"Don't take your coat off. We're going to your sister's for dinner."

Russ paused by the coat hooks in his mom's kitchen, halfway out of his jacket. "That's okay," he said. "I don't feel much like socializing."

Margy Van Alstyne marched out of the tiny dining room. Cousin Nane must have been over with the home perming kit — her white hair was curled so tightly it looked as if it could power the entire North Country electrical grid if you could figure out a way to release its chemical energy. She braced her hands on her hips, increasing her resemblance to a fireplug. "It in't socializing when it's family."

"I'm tired. It's been a long day. Give Janet my regrets." He shrugged the jacket off and hung it on a hook. His mother grabbed its

78

collar and thrust it back at him.

"Mom!"

"I want you to drive me. It'll be dark coming back, and I don't like to drive in the dark."

"Since when?"

"A woman of seventy-five has the right to develop a few little quirks. Now, are you going to take me, or are you going to sit here in my house, eating food I've made, with your big feet up on my hassock watching my television?"

He glowered down at her. "Now you're trying to guilt me into going."

"You're darned right I am. Is it working?"

He took the jacket. He had been living at her house since his wife died. No, since before. He had moved in with his mom when Linda had thrown him out of their house in what he had thought was going to be a temporary separation. It had become a permanent and irrevocable separation two weeks later, with her death. Her stupid, senseless, preventable death.

He couldn't stand to go back to his own house, and he couldn't stand to sell it, so he puttered along in limbo, buying groceries, fixing odds and ends, paying Mom's bills when he could get hold of them before she did. She hadn't asked him how long he was staying or what he was going to do. She hadn't asked anything of him.

"All right." He jammed an arm back into his jacket. "I'll take you. And I'll pick you up. But I'm not staying for dinner."

"We'll see about that."

In his pickup, she chattered on about Janet and Mike's girls, and about Cousin Nane, and about the latest meeting of her antiwar group, Women in Black. He let her words wash over and around him, as unnoticed as the late-afternoon sun slanting through chinks in the clouds or the faint green traces of spring emerging from the last clutches of winter's gray and brown tangle. It was all part of a world that kept moving and changing, and he didn't want anything to do with it.

They passed an enormous Hummer, pimped to the nines and radiating a bass line that rattled his windows. "Those vehicles ought to be illegal," his mom huffed, and then she was on about greenhouse gases and blood for oil and American entitlement. Same-old same-old. In the dips and hollows, where snow still covered the ground, a thick white mist hovered knee-high, like a company of ghosts unable to break the bonds of earth.

He was startled into awareness by guitar

strings thrumming their way out of the cab's speakers. "What are you doing?" he asked.

"Well, since you weren't listenin' to me, I thought you might like to hear some music instead."

He reached over and snapped the CD player off. "No," he said. "No music."

His mother looked at him. "No music."

"I don't like listening to music."

"Since when?"

Since my life went straight into the crapper. Since every other goddam song makes me think of Clare. He did not say what he was thinking. He had a great deal of practice, each and every day, in not saying what he was thinking. Instead, he said, "A man of fifty has the right to develop a few little quirks."

"Huh," his mother said, but she left him alone as the county highway twisted and turned through densely packed trees, skirting the mountains to the west of Millers Kill. Eventually, the forest gave way to a broad valley, the road falling away like a fast-moving stream to run up and down the gentle hills between one dairy farm and the next.

They were closing in on Janet and Mike's quarter-mile-long driveway when his mother said, "Go on past. We're meeting them at

81

the neighbor's."

Russ took his foot off the gas. "Mom. This isn't some sort of setup, is it?"

She looked — not guilty, she never looked guilty as far as he could tell — but like a kid caught with her hand in the cookie jar. "I'm not sayin'. It's a surprise."

"Listen, Mom. If they're fixing me up with some sweet little widow woman or divorcée, I'm turning this truck around and heading home right now."

His mother made an exasperated noise. "It's not that sort of surprise. Honestly, Russell, it's not all about you all of the time."

There wasn't any good reply to that. He mumbled something that might have been either an apology or an accusation and accelerated up the road.

The neighbor's place was a pretty bungalow, probably bought in kit form from Sears, Roebuck back in the twenties. He started to turn up the short drive. "No, not there." His mother pointed. "The *other* side of the road."

"The barn?" Like many of the newer farms in this part of the world — *newer* meaning one century old instead of two — the barn and outbuildings were across the two-lane highway instead of attached to the house, giving some breathing room, literally, to the residents. Between the main building, the double silos, and the cow byre stretching out toward the pasturage, the neighbors' barn took up four or five times the space of their house.

"Just pull into the drive."

Russ obeyed, parking his truck on the least-muddy section of the short wide road leading to a pair of tractor-sized doors. "Mom, what's this about?" he asked.

His mother, ignoring him, slipped down from the cab and squelched toward the double doors. He jumped out and hurried after her. "Open this for me, will you?" she said.

A vision of hordes of well-wishers waiting inside, balloons tied to the rafters, filled his head. But there wasn't any occasion for a surprise party, was there? His birthday was five months gone. It wasn't the anniversary of his joining the MKPD.

"Criminy's sake, Russell. You going to make a poor old lady haul this back by herself?"

He snorted. Margy Van Alstyne was about as weak and feeble as a steamroller. But there wasn't anything to be gained by standing out in the cold and gathering dark. He wrapped his fist around one curved handle and rolled the door open.

They were greeted by the familiar farm smells of machine oil, hay, and manure, nothing more. His mother strode in, turning pale beneath the cool fluorescent lights dangling from the three-story-high ceiling. "Huh." She put her hands on her hips. "They must be in with the cows." She threaded her way between a tractor and a baler and disappeared through a small door beneath the haymow.

"Who? Mom, what's going on?" He rolled the door shut behind him and followed her, dodging a conveyor belt that led from a hay cart to the mow above. Overhead, Russ could see a few scattered bales in the shadows, ready to eke out the five or six weeks remaining until the arrival of the tender grass of spring. He ducked his head and entered the cow byre.

It was long and low and bright and modern, and it made his heart start to pound. He found himself looking left, right, past the rows of neat stalls that stretched out and out, one silky black-and-white back after another, trying to pinpoint an exit. He took a deep breath to steady himself, but the smell of warm cow and wet straw stuck in his throat as if it would strangle him.

"There you are!" His sister's cheerful

voice focused him a little. Janet and Mike waved from halfway down the center aisle. They looked impossibly far away. A clank to his left made him jerk his head around, and he found himself face to face with a marble-eyed, wet-nosed heifer, staring incuriously at him while chewing its cud.

His brother-in-law laughed. "Look at him. He's gotten all wide-eyed." He spread his arms. "It's pretty impressive, isn't it?"

No, it pretty much reminds me of the cow barn I nearly got shot in two months ago. Where the best person I know had to kill a sociopathic monster to save my life.

It reminds me of where I was when my wife died. He wanted to say it, so they'd have some idea of who he was and what was going on in his head. But he couldn't. His mother would get scared and his sister would spend the rest of the evening being forcefully jolly. Trying to "make him feel better." They didn't want to know crap like that.

Clare would understand.

As always these days, the thought of her brought with it a wave of longing and loss and guilt and self-loathing. For once, he welcomed the acidic brew. It blew away the fog of fear and made this barn just another barn, just another place he had to be before he could climb into bed and achieve his fondest desire: total unconsciousness.

His relations were looking at him expectantly. "Yeah," he said. "Impressive."

Janet and Mike beamed at each other. "I knew you'd think so," Janet said. "It's ours."

"Well, ours and Mom's." Mike put his arm around his mother-in-law.

Margy grinned. "Surprised ya!"

"What?" Russ stared at them. "Yours?"

"The Petersons wanted to sell out and retire," Mike said. "It was the perfect opportunity to expand our operation."

"We're doubling our herd to two hundred and forty head!" Janet said. "Plus an additional fifty acres with hayfields —"

"We'll be able to grow most of our own feed corn," Mike broke in.

"— and produce three million more pounds of milk a year!"

Russ held up his hands. "Wait a minute, wait a minute. I'm no farmer, but even I know doubling the size of your herd means a big jump in expenses. Not to be nosy, but how are you swinging this?"

His brother-in-law grinned. "Well, we thought first we might raise a cash crop of wacky weed, but we figured that wouldn't fly so well, with you being the chief of police and all. So we got a loan from the bank of

Mom." He put his arm around Margy's shoulders and squeezed.

"Not all Mom," Janet added. "We took out a mortgage on our place."

"I'm a partner." His mother beamed. "It's an investment."

"An investment?" Russ gaped at the trio. "In a dairy farm? There's been at least one farm closed in this county every year for the past twenty years!" He rounded on Janet. "You think that's a safe investment for a seventy-five-year-old woman on a fixed income?"

"Russell!" His mother sounded shocked.

"Mom, I can't believe you'd do something so irresponsible."

"It's my money," she said, at the same time Janet said, "Who are you to tell Mom what she can and can't do?"

"I'm looking out for her future. And if you thought a little bit more about her and less about yourself —"

"Oh!" Janet stepped toward him, her eyes — the same eyes he had inherited from their father — blazing hot blue. "All those years you were gallivanting all over the world in the army, who was looking out for her then? I was! I was the one who stayed here in Millers Kill and spent every Sunday with her year in and year out when the only thing she'd see from you was a postcard!"

"And that gives you the right to get her involved in this idiotic — ow!"

Janet let out a similar screech of pain. Margy had reached up — way up, since they had also both inherited their dad's height — and pinched hold of their earlobes.

"Ow! Ow, Mom, stop it!"

"Not until you two stop behaving like a pair of brats fighting over a lollipop."

Russ hadn't heard that voice from her in years. He had no doubt she would tear his ear half off if he didn't back down. He raised his hands in surrender. Janet did the same. Their mother let go. They both stumbled back a few steps, rubbing their respective injuries.

"Russell, I'm sorry you don't approve of my investing in Janet and Mike's farm, but I've been handling my own money for nigh on thirty-five years, and I'm not about to start having somebody else make my decisions now." Janet's tense shoulders relaxed until Margy turned on her. "Janet, if you're trying to tell me the reason you stayed in Millers Kill after you graduated was to keep me company —"

"No! I mean . . . no."

"Good. Didn't think so. One of you stayed and one of you went and it never made no difference in how I felt about you. So don't start with that now."

Janet shook her head.

"Russell?"

"Yes, ma'am."

She sighed. "I think you better go on home, after all. Give us all a chance to cool off. Mike'll drive me back after supper."

"Yes, ma'am." Jesus. Fifty years old, and she could still dress him down like he was a kid. He glanced at Mike, who had gotten very interested in one of the heifers during the argument, and then at Janet. She looked at him warily. He knew he ought to apologize, but he couldn't. It *was* selfish and stupid to drag Mom into such a risky venture. "I guess I'll see you later," he said.

Janet nodded. He beat a retreat, out the byre, through the barn, into the frosty evening. Opened his truck door and stood for a moment, trying to settle. Across the road, a car had pulled into the bungalow's driveway. A woman got out.

A woman in black clericals.

Oh, no. Not this on top of everything else.

But a second later, he realized the woman was too short and slight to be Clare. She turned, maybe attracted by the light spilling out of his pickup, and he could see she was the new deacon from St. Alban's. What was

89

her name, Groosvoort?

"Chief Van Alstyne? Is that you? Is there some trouble?"

"Uh, hi" — the name came — "Deacon de Groot. What? You mean because I'm here? No. No trouble." He kept his voice neutral. "My sister and her husband — uh, farm around here."

"Well. How nice to see you again." She pushed at her immaculate mass of ash-blond hair. "Excuse my appearance. I've been at the Glens Falls hospital since this afternoon."

She didn't do hospital visits, did she? Wasn't that Clare's job? Had something happened to — "I hope everyone's all right," he managed to squeeze out.

"Our sexton, Mr. Hadley, had an acute myocardial infarction." She said it with the careful pronunciation of someone repeating what she was told. "Poor man had to have a quadruple bypass. I stayed until he was moved to the ICU. No visitors there, so I figured it was time for me to come home."

"Home?"

Even in the half-light, he could see her charmed smile. She pointed to the bungalow with pride. "No more commuting down to Johnstown for me. I've just bought the Petersons' house."

EASTERTIDE

I

Kevin Flynn was checking himself out in the mirror. He tried combing his hair down flat, then dragging his fingers through it until it stood up in spiky chunks. Flat? Chunks?

Behind him, Lyle MacAuley finished his business and zipped up. "For chrissakes, Kevin, it's the morning briefing, not a beauty contest." He went to the sink beside Kevin and turned on the water. " 'Sides, either way you wear it, kid, it's still red."

Eric McCrea emerged from one of the stalls, singing, "It's Howdy Doody time!"

"Like you ever saw *Howdy Doody*." MacAuley shook off his hands and yanked a paper towel from the dispenser.

"Just trying to provide a reference you could get, Dep. If I compared our young officer here to one of the Weasley twins, you wouldn't know what I was talking about."

"I knew a couple strippers called themselves the Beaver twins, but no, I never heard of any Weaselies."

"*Harry Potter?*" Kevin said. "Everybody's heard of that."

MacAuley made a face. "Kids' books."

"I like 'em." McCrea twisted a faucet on. "Last one came out, I read it before my son did."

"Grown-ups reading kids' books," MacAuley said with disgust. "It's no wonder we're importin' men from Mexico to do our work for us. We're all getting too dumb to know one end of a hammer from the other." He reached for the men's room door handle, only to be squashed against the wall when Noble Entwhistle pushed it open. Kevin, doing a last check to make sure none of his breakfast was on his teeth, grinned.

"Chief says, where'n the hell is everybody?" Noble reported.

McCrea twisted the faucet off and dried his hands. "If you step back from the door a ways, Noble, I think Lyle might be able to get out."

Noble shoved his wall-like frame through the door. "Sorry, Dep."

Kevin and McCrea snickered as MacAuley and Entwhistle did the doorway dance. Finally the deputy chief squeezed past Noble and disappeared into the hallway, a string of profanities marking his passage.

"What's taking you guys so long?" Noble asked. "You know what they say. If you shake it more'n three times, you're playing with it."

"Nah. We're just giving Kevin some beauty tips. Much better now the fuzzy thing on your chin is gone, Kevin."

"Goatee," Kevin muttered. It would have been a good one, too, if the chief hadn't squinted at him in the dispatch room last week and barked, "No beards. Shave it off."

Noble rolled his eyes. "I got a tip for you. Don't be late. If the chief don't notice *her*," — he wagged his head toward the hall, where the former public restroom had become the women's room — "he sure ain't gonna care how pretty *you* are."

In the mirror, Kevin could see himself blush. Everyone teased him about his freckles, but they didn't bug him. The bright, spotty ones of his youth had almost faded away, leaving him with just a scattering across his nose and cheekbones. But God Almighty, he hated his fair skin! It was like a fricking mood ring.

"We'll be right there," McCrea said. Noble grunted and lumbered into the hallway. When the door had shut behind him, Mc-

Crea said, "I have a tip for you, too, Kev." His voice was light but serious. "It's an oldie but a goodie. Don't shit where you eat."

Kevin looked down at the sink. "Whaddaya mean?"

McCrea sighed. "Kev, you didn't give a rip what you looked like until last week, when Hadley Knox started showing up for the briefings. I admit, she's a total babe. But you do not want to be fishing in these waters. I'd think everything that's happened between the chief and MacAuley would have taught you that much."

"That's different," Kevin said. "MacAuley" — he dropped his voice involuntarily — "nailed the chief's wife. I'd never put the moves on a married woman."

"It's not about married or not married. It's about sticking it to someone you're going to have to see at work every day."

"I'm not —"

McCrea held up his hands. "I don't want to get into it with you. Just think about what I'm saying, okay?"

The door thumped open. "Are you two waiting for an engraved invitation?" MacAuley said.

They followed the deputy chief out, Kevin, as always, bringing up the rear. He kept his eyes fixed on MacAuley's grizzled head until he had taken his usual seat in the squad room, an irregularly shaped space that had been knocked together out of several small offices about twenty years before Kevin was born.

"Nice of you gentlemen to join us." The chief sat on the scarred wooden worktable, his booted feet braced on two chairs.

"Sorry," McCrea said. If it had been, say, last November, he would have cracked a joke about them running a salon, or a book club, or something. But that was before the chief's wife kicked him out. Before she died. Before the department imploded in a smoking mess of old wrongs and betrayal.

None of them joked around within the chief's earshot now.

Kevin flopped his notebook open, and as the chief launched into the bulletins and BOLOs, he snuck a look at Hadley Knox. Eric McCrea had called her a babe, but that didn't do her justice. Kevin had never seen anyone like her, with her perfect skin and her huge brown eyes and her round, pouty lips. Even in a tan poly uniform with no makeup on and her dark hair cut like a boy's, she was better-looking than 99.9 percent of the other women in Millers Kill. McCrea had another thing wrong, too. Kevin knew he didn't have a snowball's chance in hell with a woman like that. If he had swapped more than six words with her since she started patrolling last week, he'd a been surprised. He just wanted . . . to admire her. And to think that when she happened to look at him, she wouldn't think he was a complete geek.

". . . with Kevin," the chief was saying.

He jerked to attention.

"You think that's a good idea?" MacAuley said. "I mean, isn't that like the blind leading the blind?"

"It's a routine traffic patrol," the chief said. "And I want Knox to get as much time behind the wheel as she can. Eric can't take her, he's working the Christie break-in."

"Paul?" MacAuley asked.

The chief gave him a look.

"Ah," the deputy said. Kevin figured Paul Urquhart had made yet another dirty joke about the new recruit. Or did something inappropriate. Whatever it was, the dep had gotten it.

Everything that's happened between the chief and MacAuley. It was a waste and a shame, as his dad would have said: two old guys who worked so well together they could have a whole conversation with a word and a look. Now, those were the only conversations they had.

"If Kevin runs into anything heavy while he's out with Officer Knox, he'll call it in. Right?"

In like Flynn. "Yessir." Kevin glanced toward her again, this time smiling reassuringly. Her face, looking back at him, was blank. What did that mean? Was she nervous about riding with him? Pissed off because she wasn't going with one of the more experienced guys?

"Eric, catch us up on the Christie B and E." They were up to the current investigations. Kevin returned his attention to his notebook.

McCrea flopped open the case folder and began to recite. "Saturday, April six, at five thirty p.m., Bruce Christie reported returning home to find his trailer in the Meadowbrook Estates trailer park had been broken into. The interior had been trashed, as near as Noble and I could tell" — there was some snickering on this — "but he *said* nothing was missing. The manager reports seeing a vehicle speeding out of the park entrance at approximately five thirty p.m. No description, other than it was 'big and expensive.' " He glanced up from his notes. "That might mean any pickup or SUV with more steel than rust. Christie suggested it might be someone his two brothers owe money to and gave us a list of names." He pulled a short stack of papers from the file and tossed them to Kevin, who took one and passed it on. "The manager suggested it might have *been* the two brothers." McCrea looked up. "I tend to discount that. Whatever else you can say about the Christies, they hang tight together."

"If that's what you wanna call it," MacAuley said, under his breath.

"What do you think they were looking for?" the chief asked McCrea.

He shrugged. "Money? Pot? Neil Christie was up for distributing a few years back. Got it knocked down to possession."

"Sheep?" someone said. There was a snort of laughter, stifled.

"Why did he report it?" The question was out of Kevin's mouth before he remembered he was trying to appear cool and knowledgeable in front of their new officer. "If the intruders were looking for something illegal, I mean." God, he sounded lame.

The chief swiveled toward him. "You tell me."

"Um . . . he's genuinely clean?"

MacAuley snorted, but the chief gestured for him to go on. Kevin thought furiously. "He was lying about nothing being missing. He's counting on us to lead him to the guys who took whatever it was."

The chief tapped his nose. "Something to consider, isn't it?" He looked at McCrea. "And, of course, it could be someone with a grudge, looking to beat the crap out of Bruce Christie and settling for wrecking his place. Between the three of 'em, the Christie brothers have a record as thick as the Cossayuharie Directory. Assault, possession —" He glanced at MacAuley. "Didn't one of them do time for resisting?"

"Donald. Got five in Plattsburgh, out in three. Tried to run over the state trooper who was taking him in for D and D."

"So, be careful." The chief pointed at McCrea. "Anything strikes you funny, ease off and call for backup."

"Will do, Chief."

The chief pushed the chairs away and slid off the table. "That's all." He gathered up his folders and stalked out of the squad room. Through the doorway, Kevin could hear Harlene telling him about his calls.

"Christies. They put the dirt in dirt poor." MacAuley shook his head. He squinted up at McCrea from beneath his bushy eyebrows. "I've been to Bruce Christie's place. How did you tell where the deliberate trashing ended and the usual trashing began?"

McCrea snorted. "I wouldn't have wanted

to stay there any longer than absolutely necessary, I'll tell you." He jerked a thumb toward Entwhistle. "Noble here was freaked out by the great big googly-eyed Jesus tapestry he had tacked to the wall."

"It was creepy," Noble agreed. "Its eyes followed you around. Like in that Stephen King book."

"*Carrie,*" Kevin supplied.

"Thank you, Kevin." McCrea smiled at him. *Shit.* There he was, doing it again. He had to stop trying to be so damn helpful all the time.

"You know how you know if a Christie girl is still a virgin?" MacAuley grinned. "She can run faster than her brothers."

McCrea looked at him meaningfully and nudged his head toward Hadley Knox.

"Uh —" The deputy chief was seized with a convenient coughing fit.

Hadley rose from her seat. Looked at MacAuley. Looked at McCrea. "The way I heard it, it's if she can run faster than the sheep." She tucked her folder beneath her arm. "You coming, Flynn?"

II

Clare was three miles out of Millers Kill, at the end of a five-hour drive from Fort Dix, when she realized she was out of booze. She groaned, thinking of returning to her cold house — when she was away for Guard training, she turned the thermostat down to fifty to save on oil — and facing the evening with nothing but some undoubtedly sour milk and a two-day-old Thermos of coffee. No wine. No sherry. No scotch.

No way. She cruised up Route 57, watching the river that gave the town its name running brown and gold beneath the long rays of the setting sun. Driving past St. Alban's, she continued on toward Main, then crossed over the river, headed for the town line. She'd been doing her shopping in Glens Falls, the better to avoid running into Russ Van Alstyne. But Napoli's Discount Liquor ought to be safe, seeing as the chief of police was a nondrinking alcoholic.

In the parking lot, she unfolded out of her seat and stretched gratefully — up, down, and side to side. The breeze from the west was still cool with the snow lingering in the mountains, but the warmth thrown off by the asphalt testified to the power of the spring sun. Winter was gone, and good freaking riddance to it. If she never saw another snowflake in her life, it wouldn't be too soon.

She pulled her cell phone out of her pocket and checked her messages. One from her parents touching base, one from Deacon Elizabeth de Groot, assuring her that they were all doing splendidly without her, and one from Hugh Parteger. "Vicar! Thanks for stopping by for lunch on your way to that pestilent place south of the Palisades." She assumed he meant New Jersey. Hugh may have been born in England, but he was a true New Yorker at heart. "Next time" — his voice dropped — "why don't you just *tell* your congregation you're reporting for duty and stay the weekend with me? I promise I can show you maneuvers the U.S. Army has yet to think of."

"Not happening, Hugh," she told the phone. She erased the message, laughing.

Checking out her order, Mr. Napoli kept peering at her, frowning a bit as he placed the Macallan's and the Harveys and the bottles of Shiraz in their narrow paper bags. It wasn't until she produced her driver's license and checkbook that he smiled at her. "Reverend Fergusson!" He clutched her license with both hands, his eyes shifting from her picture, to her, and back again. "I didn't recognize you, with all these soldier clothes on." He gestured up and down, taking in her desert camo battle dress uniform. "We haven't seen you in here lately! Now I can tell Mrs. Napoli why." He took her check, *tch*ing. "The army. Is that any place for a sweet girl like you?"

Clare remembered, too late, that she had also been avoiding appearing in public in uniform. Too many explanations. She smiled flirtatiously. "Now, Mr. Napoli. You've seen my birth date." She slid her license off the counter. "I'm hardly a girl anymore." While he was gallantly defending her right to be juvenalized two months shy of her thirty-seventh birthday, she extricated herself with a promise not to be "a stranger." Bumping out the door with a bagful of booze, she reminded herself to take her civvies with her next time she reported for Guard service, and change *before* she got in her car to go home.

Russ Van Alstyne was standing beside his big red pickup in the parking lot.

Staring at her.

She swallowed. Hugged her paper sack closer to her chest. Her first thought was, *Was he always that tall?* Her second thought was, *He's lost weight.* He was in his semi off-duty uniform, tan MKPD blouse tucked into a pair of jeans that had seen better days, an official windbreaker balancing his salt-stained hunting boots.

Then she realized where he was. Her eyes widened. His did, too.

"What are you doing at a liquor store?" she asked.

"What are you doing in uniform?" he said simultaneously.

They both paused. His dismay — at getting caught? — was plain on his face. "Are you drinking again?" she said. Her clashing emotions — concern, not wanting to be concerned — made her voice harsher than she intended.

He blinked. Frowned. "What?"

She waved a hand at Napoli's plate glass windows, advertising specials on Dewar's, Bombay gin, and all Australian wines. "What are you doing at the liquor store?" She took a step closer, not wanting to shame him by shouting his problem to any shoppers within earshot. "Please don't tell me you've started drinking again."

He closed his eyes for a moment. Opened them. When he spoke, his voice was tight with control. "I am not drinking again. I'm here to get Napoli's latest bad check report."

Her mouth formed a silent O.

"Now, would you mind telling me what the hell you're doing in BDUs?"

She shifted one shoulder so he could read her New York State Guard patch. His hand came up and touched his collar, where, like her, insignia told the world his rank.

"Where's your chaplain's cross?"

She mirrored his movement, touching her captain's bars. "I'm not in the chaplaincy. I'm in the 142nd Aviation Battalion. Combat support."

"You're what?" He crossed to her in three sharp strides. "You're in combat support? Are you insane? There's a goddamn war on! Who the hell volunteers for front-line duty with a war on?"

She looked up at him. "I don't know. You, maybe?"

He hissed through his teeth. The secret he might have taken to his grave, if he hadn't shared it with her. Suddenly, she felt ashamed, as if she had used a cannon to counter a flyswatter. "Don't worry," she said. "I haven't told. I wouldn't ever tell." That, contrary to what everyone else believed, Russ Van Alstyne had not been drafted to serve in the Vietnam War. He had enlisted — volunteered.

"Christ, I know that. You think I worry about that?" He shook his head. "At least I had an excuse. I was eighteen and dumb and desperate to get out of town. What possible reason could *you* have?"

She shifted the paper sack on her hip. "The bishop and I had several lengthy conversations after . . . after . . ." She was searching for a word to pretty up what she had done. She shouldn't do that. She *wouldn't* do that. "After I killed Aaron Mac-Entyre."

"That was self-defense, not killing. You saved our lives in that barn. His punk-ass friend's, too."

"I resigned my cure, but, strangely enough, he didn't accept it."

"You what?"

She ignored his interruption. "Ultimately, the bishop didn't think what I had . . . done . . . was the problem. He thought it was a symptom. Of me not knowing if I was a priest who used to be an army officer, or an army officer who happened to be a priest. He suggested" — she looked up at him, her mouth twisting — "he *strongly* suggested the National Guard as a solution." She shrugged. "So I joined up. At the end of January." She paused. "You hadn't heard?"

"No, I hadn't heard. Your name hasn't come up. . . ." His blue eyes unfocused. She could see the lightbulb come on. "No one talks about you anymore." She wasn't sure if he knew he was speaking aloud. "No one ever talks about you to me."

Another brilliant piece of deduction by the head of the Millers Kill Police Department. Idiot. She dug her fingers into the paper sack to keep from smacking the surprise off his face. A Pontiac pulled in the lot, parking beside her Subaru. Automatically, they each stepped back. Away from each other.

His gaze sharpened again. "Your bishop pushed you into recommissioning. Knowing you might well be deployed."

"I wasn't pushed. I had my own —"

His snort blew away her rationalization. "Because you took out Aaron MacEntyre."

"Because I have a record of —"

"He was going to gut-shoot me. He was ready to do it."

Clare compressed her lips into a thin line. She didn't want to stroll down that particular memory lane. Then she realized where he was going. "No," she said.

"Because of me."

"No." She was louder this time. The older gentleman getting out of the Pontiac paused and looked at them nervously. Was the chief of police about to haul some belligerent soldier away?

"We are not having this conversation." She turned toward her car. Russ caught at her sleeve, and at that moment, her phone began playing "Joyful, Joyful, We Adore Thee" in her pants pocket. Proof, if ever she needed it, that there was a merciful God.

"Yes, we are," he said.

She fished out the phone and opened it. "Hello?" She twisted, more firmly this time, breaking his hold on her.

"Clare? This is Sister Lucia. Lucia Pirone." The sister's voice was thready. Clare backed toward her Subaru, keeping her eyes on Russ. He took a step toward her. Then *his* phone started ringing.

"Lucia? What is it? I'm sorry, I can hardly hear you." She bumped up against the car and set her sack on the hood. Russ took another step toward her. She pointed at his jacket pocket. *Your phone,* she mouthed.

"The hell with my phone," he said.

"There's been an accident," Sister Lucia said. "My van —"

"An accident?" Clare jabbed her finger at Russ again, then made a face. "Are you okay?"

He opened his jacket and retrieved his phone. Checked the caller ID. Frowned. He retreated to his own vehicle to answer it.

"No, actually, I don't think I am." Clare realized the weakness in the nun's voice had less to do with signal strength than with injury.

"Lucia. Have you called nine-one-one?"

"Yes." There was a noise, as if the older

woman were gasping for breath. "There are two officers here. An ambulance is coming."

"How can I help?"

"I was —" Her voice faded away.

"Lucia? Lucia? Where are you?"

"Sorry. I'm off Route 137 in Cossayuharie. The van — a tire blew. We went off the road."

"We?"

"Some of the men are hurt," the nun said. "They're afraid. They're running off into the woods — please, Clare, please —"

"I'll be right there. I'm getting into my car right now. You sit still and do whatever the EMTs tell you to. I'll take care of everything else."

"Thank you —" The call went dead. Clare dropped the phone back into her cargo pocket. Swung open the back door and dropped the bag of booze on the floor. She paused, hand in pocket, fingers curled over her keys. She could just get in and drive away. She didn't have to say anything to Russ.

Cowardly, Master Sergeant Ashley "Hardball" Wright, her survival training instructor, sneered.

Rude, Grandmother Fergusson chided.

She turned back to him and was startled to find he had recrossed the parking lot and was a scant few feet away from her again. "I've got to run," she said. "This missioner nun I've agreed to help, Sister Lucia, she's —"

"Been in a single-vehicle accident. It's a bad one. I'm headed there."

"Oh." His phone call. Of course. "I guess I'll see you there."

"I guess I'll take you there." He turned toward his truck, beckoning her to follow him.

"I don't think that's a good idea."

He turned back toward her. "Do you even know where it is?"

"Off the Cossayuharie Road . . ." Her voice sank as she realized Sister Lucia's description covered a lot of ground.

"I guarantee I can get you there ten–fifteen minutes faster than you would on your own." He shrugged. "But it's up to you." He strode toward the pickup.

She stood, paralyzed, for a second. *Don't be stupid,* Hardball Wright said. *Just walk away,* her grandmother urged.

"Wait!" She dashed across the lot. "I'm coming with you."

III

He let out a breath he hadn't realized he had been holding, but kept the same steady pace toward the Ford F-250. By the time he crossed to the driver's side, she had climbed into the cab and was buckled in, staring straight through the windshield as if the Napoli's Liquor sign were the most interesting thing she had seen all day.

He fired up the truck. Unclipped the light from its mount and, rolling down his window, slapped it on the roof of the cab. "Hold on," he said.

He pulled onto Route 137, accelerating until he was roaring down the county highway at a good twenty miles above the speed limit. He took his attention off the road for a split second, just long enough to glance at her. It was funny. When he'd thought of her these past months — when he'd let himself think about her — it was always as she was the day Linda died: white-faced, bruised, bloody-mouthed. Her eyes going green with horror as she stared at her hands. *Oh, my God,* she had cried. *What have I done?*

This Clare's pointed nose and high cheekbones were flush with health. She radiated energy, from her crossed arms to her boots, planted square and firm against the floorboard. Whatever was making her eyes glint brown, it wasn't horror.

"Well?" she demanded.

"Well, what?"

"Aren't you going to tell me it's your fault I'm going into harm's way? That if it hadn't been for you, I'd be in prayer and meditation right now instead of waiting to hear if I'm called up? Aren't you going to take responsibility for me screwing up my pastoral duties, and Linda and her sister dying, and every person you work with and every crime ever committed under your watch and" — she waved a hand at the coffee-colored fields unfolding all around them — "and global warming? Didn't you say we had to have this conversation?"

He did. Except he was going to look like an idiot if he just repeated everything she'd said. Christ, what did he think he was going to achieve by getting her in the truck with him? He should have left her there in the parking lot, her and her spiffy little Subaru and her grocery sack of liquor.

"Don't you worry *you* might be drinking too much?" he said, seizing on another topic as a man who's run out of ammunition might lay hold of a stick.

"Oh, for —"

They sailed over a rise to face a line of brake lights stretching down to the bottom of the valley. "Shit!" he said. "Hang on!" He stood on the brakes. The pickup skidded, slewed sideways in a shower of gravel and old salt, and came to rest three inches from the back end of a Toyota Corolla, whose driver was watching him with terrified eyes through her rearview mirror.

He turned to Clare. "You okay?"

"Yeah." She patted herself on her chest. Took a breath. "Yeah."

He switched on the siren and inched into the oncoming lane. He could see the obstruction now — some farmer's disk harrow had decided to break down, half on, half off its trailer, and the two pieces of machinery were blocking most of the road. The farmer, who had been shoving fruitlessly at the rear wheel of the harrow, turned to glare at them when Russ rolled to a stop. He turned off the siren but left the lights. Powered down the window on Clare's side.

"Don't you have a hand to help you with that thing?" he said.

"No, I don't have no goddamn hand to help with the goddamn mess! Can't get no goddamn help for love or goddamn money. Goddamn sumbitch a-hole —"

"I'll send somebody from Fire and Res-

113

cue." Russ closed the window over a steady stream of profanity and inched past the unsteady tangle, forcing the nearest car to roll most of the way into the drainage ditch to avoid getting clipped. Clare pointed to its driver, who was using body language to let Russ know what he thought of him.

"Another satisfied customer," she said.

"Idiot shouldn't have gotten so close to the accident." He gave the accelerator a little kick. "You got John Huggins's number in your phone?" John Huggins headed up the volunteer Fire and Rescue department.

"Just at home."

He pulled his cell phone out of his pocket and handed it to her. "He may already be at the scene of the single vehicle. Tell him he needs to get a couple of his guys over here to direct traffic and help Farmer Greenjeans haul his machinery off the road."

Clare examined his contacts list. "Got it." She dialed, and held the phone to her ear. Once past the remaining stalled cars, Russ sped up. "Uh — no," Clare said, beside him. "It's Clare Fergusson." She glanced at Russ. "He gave it to me. He asked me to —" She sighed. "He's fine. He's sitting right next to me. He handed the phone to me so he could concentrate on his driving."

There was a pause.

"Yes. Is that a problem?" Her voice was sharp. "No, don't answer that. Listen, there's a farmer with a broken down —" She looked over at Russ.

"Disk harrow," he said.

"Disk harrow, about two, two and a half miles east of Napoli's on the Cossayuharie Road. Russ — the chief wants you to send over a couple of men to help with the situation." With her free hand, she poked at one of the bobby pins that was trying, and failing, to keep her whiskey-and-honey hair in a twist at the back of her head. "I know about that. We're on our way there now." She rolled her eyes at Russ. "Thanks, uh — Mr. Huggins." She thumbed off the phone. "I never know what to call him. He always refers to me as Fergusson."

"I'm sure he'd answer to Chief."

She crossed her arms over her chest again and made a rude noise. "There's only one chief in this town, and he's not it."

He blinked.

"I mean, you can't hang a name on yourself and think it makes you a leader," she said quickly. "You have to make yourself a leader, and then the title just comes naturally. I mean, I can call myself the Grand Duchess Anastasia, but it doesn't —"

"I know what you mean."

Her mouth clicked shut. She made a little hissing sound.

"You know, you can't lead men and women without making yourself responsible for them."

She turned her head away. Looked out her window. The road rose up to meet them, carrying them up into one of the mountainous fingers that pierced the rolling farmlands of Cossayuharie. The air around them darkened as the trees closed in. When she spoke, her voice was almost inaudible. "I never wanted you to lead me," she said to the glass. "I just wanted —"

He didn't get to hear what she wanted. They curved in a long arc down and around a steep cut in the hillside and there was the accident scene, at the point where the forest once more shaded into farmlands, laid out in front of them like a set of toy vehicles that some giant kid had played hard with and then abandoned.

"Oh, my God," Clare said.

A large white van lay, overturned, among the trees, its crumpled side panel showing where it had rolled. More than once — it must have done a complete 360 and then some to be that far from the road. Only one ambulance, from Corinth — he frowned — but he could see two EMTs, bent over somebody at the side of the van. The Volunteer Fire Department's pump and hose trucks were angled off to the side, with Huggins's SUV parked tight behind. He pulled in behind Huggins. Clare had unbuckled and was swinging the door open before he had killed the engine. She dashed toward the ambulance. "Stay out of the way!" he shouted. She waved one hand in acknowledgment.

He found Kevin Flynn arguing with John Huggins, Hadley Knox close by, her arms wrapped around herself. "You okay?" Russ asked. She nodded.

". . . how much assistance could they need?" Huggins was saying to Flynn. The fire chief's shoe-leather face and squat four-by-four body made Flynn look even more like a junior varsity basketball player than usual, but the kid wasn't backing down an inch.

"We won't know that until your guys get out there and find them!"

"Settle down, Kevin. Give me a report."

Flynn shot him a frustrated glance. "The driver says she heard a loud noise and then lost control. It looks like the left front tire blew. She went — well, you can see where she went." He flung his arm out to where tender new grass and delicate maple saplings had been torn raw and crushed. "No witnesses to speak of. The driver said she saw a big boxy vehicle, maybe an Aztek or a Humvee or Jeep Cherokee, but it didn't stop." He sounded disgusted. "Didn't call it in, either. The driver's complaining of chest and shoulder pains, difficulty breathing, difficulty moving her legs, dizziness. We've got one guy unconscious, one guy with a broken arm, and one more banged up pretty bad."

"That it for injuries? One driver, three passengers?"

Kevin blew out a puff of air. "I don't know. Officer Knox and I responded with lights and sirens. Like we're supposed to."

Russ nodded.

"So when we come over the hill, we see guys running into the woods; I can't tell you how many. They just scattered." He glanced past Russ to where the long shadows of the mountains were darkening the woods and fields. "Some of them may be hurt."

"As I was telling the kid, if they're well enough to evade arrest, they're well enough left alone." Huggins removed his helmet and scrubbed at his bald spot. "I don't see any need to send my guys chasing after them."

"Evade arrest?" Russ's question was aimed at Flynn, but Huggins answered.

"Illegals. Gotta be. Not a one of the ones left behind speaks a word of English. Probably one of them whaddayacallits. Where they smuggle 'em in."

"The driver is a nun!" Kevin said.

Russ pinched the bridge of his nose beneath his glasses. "John, we're not working for the Border Patrol. We're working for the town, and the town doesn't want injured people wandering around the woods in Cossayuharie, even if they don't speak English. Get your men walking a search pattern. Tell 'em to shout *No soy del I-C-E. Estoy aquí ayudarle.* Can you repeat that?"

Huggins screwed up his face, as if he were swallowing something nasty. "No soy del I-C-E. Eztoy ackee a-you-darrel."

"Close enough."

"Don't know why they can't just learn English," Huggins said, stomping back to the pump truck.

"I didn't know you speak Spanish, chief."

"The army likes its warrant officers to have a second language. Got the chance to polish it up in Panama and the Philippines."

Flynn looked impressed. Of course, it didn't take much to impress a twenty-four-year-old who had never been out of New York State.

"C'mon, let's see if we can sort out these

people." He headed toward the battered van, Flynn falling in beside him. After a beat, so did Knox. "You see or hear anything that might make you think they had another reason to flee?"

Flynn shook his head. "Nope."

"Well. . . ." Knox sounded hesitant.

"What is it?" Russ stopped and faced his newest officer. She was biting the inside of her cheek. "Listen," he said. "You know how you tell your kids there aren't any dumb questions? Well, there aren't any dumb details. Noticing things around you, at an accident, on a crime scene, patrolling, making a stop — someday it could make the difference between life and death. *Your* life and death."

She nodded. "Okay. Yeah. Two of the guys left behind were talking about the accident. One of them was saying he heard two pops, you know, two noises like the tires were blowing out, and the other guy said he heard three." She looked up at Flynn. "But Officer Flynn said it was one tire blown out. When we got here."

Next to him, Flynn stiffened. "You speak Spanish, too? Why didn't you tell me? We coulda questioned those men!"

She shrugged. "You told me our job was to secure the scene."

Russ sighed. "Hadley. We're a small department. We can't afford to have anybody sit on his ass and say, 'That's not my job.' Pardon my French."

"I didn't —"

He held up one hand. "We work as a team. If you have anything to contribute to the team, whether it's an observation, or a skill, or a piece of knowledge, I expect you to put it out there. Got it?"

"Yes, sir."

He resumed his path toward the overturned van. Just outside his peripheral vision, he could feel Knox glaring daggers at Flynn. He decided to let it be.

He heard a distant whoop carried on the cooling air, and a moment later the Millers Kill ambulance crested the hill. It swung in as close to the van as possible, its EMTs on the ground and headed for the injured before the siren had died away.

No . . . that wasn't the echo of the ambulance. Far down the valley, where the road ran out of sight between the next mountain gap, he saw a whirl of red-and-whites, following the blazing headlights of a speeding vehicle.

"Christ on a crutch," he said. Just what he needed, some jacked-up idiot thinking he could give one of their cruisers a run right through an accident site. "Get back!" he bellowed to the Corinth paramedics, who had strapped a man onto a pallet and were now angling for the rear door of the ambulance. He turned back toward where Huggins was huddling with his volunteers. "Everybody away from the road!"

IV

Where was — ? He stalked toward the ambulance, his chest tightening, until he spotted Clare kneeling beside someone on another pallet, her BDUs pale in the gathering dark. Well away from the edge of the road. Okay. He saw a flicker of red hair out of the corner of his eye. "Kevin, get on the radio," Russ said. "I want to know what the hell —" He broke off.

The speeding car was slowing down. Way down. Dust plumed beneath its tires as it veered onto the opposite shoulder and skidded to a stop. The MKPD cruiser rolled into place behind it.

Two men emerged from the car, a souped-up GTO that seemed too small for the size of its driver and passenger. Their dark-blond hair and long-limbed, powerful bodies were similar, although one had a russetty beard swallowing half his face and a couple inches on the other.

"Who're they?" Knox asked.

"Bruce Christie and his brother Donald," Russ said.

"What're they doing out here?" Flynn said.

"Well, that's a question, isn't it?" Across the road, Eric McCrea was getting out of the squad car and settling his lid on his head. He was frowning at the Christies, but made no move to stop them. "You two get over to the remaining passengers," Russ said, without turning. "Take their statements. Knox?"

"Yes, sir?"

"Remember what I said."

"Yes, sir."

The Christies struck out toward the van. Russ lengthened his stride, wanting to intercept them, wanting to appear casual. "Can I help you two?" he asked, pitching his voice to carry above the babble of questions and complaints and radio reports filling the air.

The brothers stopped. Looked his way. The last time he had seen this pair, he had had his baton in his hand and was threatening to bust Donald Christie's kneecaps if he didn't back down and let his brother drive him home from the Dew Drop Inn.

Bruce, the smaller one — inasmuch as any

of the Christie boys could be called smaller — laid a steadying hand on his bearded brother's chest. "Chief Van Alstyne," he said.

"Bruce." Russ tipped his head toward their overheated muscle car. "You two were in one all-fired hurry to get here."

"Your guy was over to Donald's place when the call came in. We heard it was a van got rolled." Bruce glanced over to where the van's undercarriage lay exposed. "We got a van. Wanted to make sure it wan't ours." Like all the Christies, Bruce had a strong up-country Cossayuharie accent.

Russ shook his head. "Not unless you loaned it out to a nun."

"A nun!" Donald Christie's eyes went wide over his red-gold beard. "Hell, no. We don't know no nuns." Russ caught a whiff of sheep and manure as the big man scraped his boots against the pavement.

"He knows that, Donald." Bruce, widely acknowledged as the brains of the family, rolled his eyes. "What happened?"

"Tire blew. She lost control." Russ shrugged. "We've got three or four injured but nothing life-threatening."

Bruce gestured toward the pump and hose trucks with his squared-off chin. "Is it likely to blow? Cast off any fire?"

"Nah."

"Then why's the fire department trampin'
around all over the place?"

Russ twisted, to see a line of Huggins's
volunteers disappearing between the trees.
He turned back to the Christies. "Why so
interested?"

Bruce nodded toward the woods. "This is
Christie land. All up and down this part of
the mountain and the pasturage below." He
pointed to where, in the distance, house
lights could be seen twinkling through the
dusk. "That's Donald's place, there. If
there's gonna be a fire, we want to know."

"Fair enough. No, your property's safe.
The nun — the sister — was driving a
bunch of — ah, migrant laborers. Some of
them ran off when they saw my men. My
officers," he corrected.

"Migrant labor? You mean Mexicans?"
Bruce frowned.

"The ones left behind are Spanish-
speaking. I don't know where they're from."

"Mexicans. Running loose through our
woods." Donald looked to his brother, who
thumped the larger man on the chest before
turning to Russ.

"You gonna catch 'em?" Bruce demanded.

"We're going to try to round them up,
sure. See if any of them need help."

"If they need help" — Donald sounded as

if he wanted to spit — "they get a free ride to the hospital and the all-you-can-eat buffet. *We* get sumpin' wrong, we gotta go to the clinic and sit for an hour to get some woman who ain't even a doctor. And we're Americans! There's been Christies here since 1720!"

Probably interbreeding the whole time.

"Hush," Bruce said. "Anything we can do to help? Round 'em up, I mean?"

"You . . . want to help?"

"I wanna get them off our land." Bruce looked up, to where the first star glimmered in the pink and indigo sky. "When it gets cold tonight, they're not gonna stay freezin' in the woods when they can stroll right 'cross the pastures and take shelter in one of Donald's barns."

"Stealin' stuff," Donald added.

"We should turn out the rest of the boys." Bruce turned toward his brother. "Where's your phone?"

"Whoa up, there." Russ held up one hand. "I'm not sending anybody out as a searcher whose got a hair in his ass about immigrants."

Donald stepped toward him. "You think you can keep us off our own property?"

Bruce thumped him again. "Hush." He looked at Russ. "We don't want anything different than you do, Chief. Get these guys off our land. Take 'em to the hospital or send 'em back to Mexico, dun't matter to me what you do with 'em once we've cleared 'em off. Hah?" He glanced at his brother. "Hah? Play nice?"

Donald rumbled deep in his chest but nodded.

"Okay," Bruce went on. "We can call up some of our cousins and they can help look. Or if you don't want 'em to help that way, they can camp out on the other side of this forest. That's Donald's place, off'n Seven Mile Road. Head off anybody who comes outa the woods."

Russ took off his glasses and polished them on his blouse front. Seven Mile Road was a hell of a long way away by car. This stretch of the mountain's spine was bigger than he had thought — a lot bigger. "Okay," he said, replacing his glasses. "You can assist. You and your cousins." He knuckled his hands on top of his rig, making himself larger and emphasizing his sidearm. "But I'll warn you. Once. If there're any problems, if it looks at any point like one of you messed with one of the missing men, I'm rounding you *all* up. And we'll let the DA sort out who did what to whom. Shouldn't take her more'n a couple weeks."

Donald rumbled again, more threateningly this time, but Bruce nodded. "Deal." He held out his hand to his brother. "Gimme your phone." The larger Christie reached into his side jacket pocket, a movement uncomfortably reminiscent of someone going for a shoulder-holstered firearm. "How many of these guys you got missing?" Bruce asked.

"That's a good question. Let's go see what my officers have come up with." He took a step back, swinging wide so the Christies would walk beside, rather than behind him. To his left, he heard the solid *ca-chunk* of a door's closing, and the rear lights of the Corinth ambulance flared red and white. It crawled off the crushed patch of ground it had been parked on, paused at the shoulder, and then, blue lights springing to life, surged onto the road. Leaving behind a solitary figure in desert camo, who turned, spotted him, and jogged over. "Russ," she called.

"In a minute," he said. They all converged on the Millers Kill ambulance at the same time. Karl and Annie, the paramedics, were positioning an inflatable cast on the arm of a young Latino, whose closed-off expression may have been due to pain, or to an extreme reluctance to engage with Knox, squatting

128

on the ground next to his pallet.

"Por lo menos dígame si cualesquiera de sus amigos estuvieron lastimados," she was saying. The injured man ignored her. She stood up, turning to Russ.

"Hel-lo, baby," Donald said. He sucked and smacked his lips. Kevin Flynn, standing spread-legged behind Knox, flamed up. He opened his mouth.

"If I *were* your baby, asshole, I'd probably be stupid enough to find that flattering. But I'm not, and I don't. Get lost." Hadley looked at Russ. "The only thing I can get out of him is that his name is Amado and he claims to be legal. He's got some sort of guest-worker permit thing. He's happy to flash that around, but anything else, forget it."

Kevin was staring at her, his expression a mixture of admiration and shock. Russ kept his mouth in a straight line. "Thank you, Officer Knox." He got down on one knee — squatting had gone out of his body's vocabulary four, five years ago — and looked at the kid. He was young, barely out of his teens, and his scraggly beard and patchy mustache made him look like a boy made up for a high school play.

"Amado." He tapped his badge. *"Yo no soy del ICE. No cuido sobre su estado."*

Clare's voice. Surprised. "I didn't know you spoke Spanish."

He gave her a look. Turned back to the injured man, who was wincing as Annie finished Velcroing the splints in place. *"Amado, charla a mí."*

"Yo soy Amado Esfuentes. Soy legal."

"No cuido. Deseo encontrar a sus amigos y ayudarles. ¿Cuántos de ellos están fuera de allí? ¿Cualquier persona estuvo lastimada?"

"What's he saying?" Flynn asked.

"Same thing I was," Knox said. "How many are there, is anyone hurt."

"Russ." Clare's voice was insistent. "I know how many men there were."

Of course she did. He was surprised to find a part of himself amused. Smack-dab in the middle of police business. *Just like old times.* He braced his hand against his thigh and stood up.

"Sister Lucia said there were eight men in the van. They were headed for Michael Mc-Geoch's dairy farm."

He pinched the bridge of his nose beneath his glasses. "Mike McGeoch's farm? On Lick Springs Road?"

She shook her head, loosening more strands of hair. "She didn't say where." Donald Christie was looking at her, curious about her BDUs, maybe, but he didn't show

130

any signs of trying out his charm offensive. Of course, she didn't have everything out there on a platter, like Knox. A jackass like Christie wouldn't know how to appreciate a woman like Clare.

He turned to the injured man. Karl and Annie were helping him to his feet. In the light from the ambulance's interior, the kid's face was gray beneath his caramel skin and thin beard. Annie frowned. "You'll have to ask the rest of your questions at the hospital, Chief. We need to get this guy and the other one back."

"Okay. Thanks, Annie." Russ pointed toward the Christies. "You two. Get to the pump truck and get briefed by John Huggins about the search before you call in any of your family." Thankfully, they shambled off without protest. "And remember what I said!" he called after them. "Knox. Kevin."

"Yes, sir."

"Yeah, Chief?"

"You two keep the van secure until the tow truck gets here. Kevin, show Knox how to write up the accident report."

Out of the corner of his eye, he saw desert camo sidling past him. "Where are you going?" he asked.

"To help with the search." Clare's expression said, *What did you think I was going to do?*

Help with the search. Of course she was. It was too much to hope she might stay out of it for once. "I'm taking off *now*," he growled.

"Oh, I'll get a ride."

He sighed. Motioned to his junior officers. "I want you two to see that Reverend Fergusson gets back to her car. And then that she goes *home*."

"You want us to stay for the search, Chief?" Kevin sounded as if there was nothing he'd rather do more. Hadley Knox, on the other hand, looked appalled.

"Yeah. I do. Knox, you're the only other Spanish speaker here. Make yourself available as necessary."

"Yes, sir."

"Are you headed for the hospital, Chief?"

He shook his head. "I'm going to the Mc-Geoch place and let them know all their farmhands have run off."

Clare's face, outlined in the gathering dark by the flash of red-and-whites, changed. She got it.

"You know him, Chief?" Flynn continued.

"Oh, yeah." He sighed. "He's my brother-in-law."

V

Amado heard him before he saw him. One of his own, no flashlight, no badly accented shouts of, "We are not I-C-E! We want to help you!" Just the thudding of footfalls and the whipping, crackling sounds of someone running through the forest. *Idiot.* There was a little moonlight shafting through the bare branches and pines, but not enough to make it safe to race all out as if you were sprinting down a street. He had spent enough time hiding in the dark. The trick was to go slowly. To let yourself see where you were headed and then to move like smoke, silently, safely.

Thank God it wasn't his little brother thrashing through the trees. In the confusion after the accident — men swearing and groaning, Sister Lucia insisting she was all right despite her bloody head and shallow breath — he had seen Octavio's arm. Known at once the boy would have to go to the hospital. Where, without papers or a green card, he faced deportation. Amado had stuffed his own GW-1 permit and identity card into his brother's pocket. "*You* will be Amado," he had said. "*I* will be Octavio." Octavio looked at him blankly, eyes glazing over with shock. "Just keep saying it over and over," Amado had urged. "You are

Amado Esfuentes. You are Amado Esfuentes."

"I am Amado Esfuentes," Octavio parroted.

Amado had stayed as long as he dared, until the lights of the police car came over the hill. Then he, along with the rest of the able-bodied, fled into the woods. His ID would ensure his brother's safety. They resembled each another, and the pitiful excuse for a beard Octavio was growing blurred the differences between their faces. Anglos had a hard time looking past the color of a man's skin, anyway.

A loud thud, followed by a grunt, brought him back to the present: Esteban. He was the only one stupid enough to blunder through the dark like that. Amado debated, for a moment, staying put in his half-hollowed log. Then he heard a faint whimpering noise. Mother of God. Why his family had ever let the boy out of the house, let alone sent him north, was beyond Amado's understanding. Resigned, he heaved himself out of the shadows and headed — slowly, silently — toward the snuffling sounds.

The poor kid was sprawled out on the forest floor, trying to stuff his weeping back into his mouth. It took some of the younger ones that way. Amado had seen it before.

Tell a boy he's a man and carry him two thousand miles away, into a cold and alien place. He misses his mother, he misses his girl, he misses his home. He swaggers around like a fighting cock, to hide his fears, and cries in the dark when he thinks no one can hear him.

Amado had been that boy — once. He paused behind a cluster of pines and coughed, to give Esteban the chance to set himself to rights while he still thought himself unseen. "Is someone there?" Amado said.

The figure, anonymous in jeans and a quilted jacket, shoved up abruptly and scrambled backward, face pale and terrified. *Shit! An anglo.* He faded farther back into the shadows, ready to disappear, when the boy, still moving backward, slammed himself into a tree, making Amado wince. He wasn't Esteban, but he certainly moved with the same grace and coordination. His baseball cap flew off, revealing a tumble of long blond hair.

Not a boy, then. Not a boy at all. The girl held her hands up in front of her and whispered something in impossibly fast English. Pleading, he could tell by the tone of her voice, but for what? Help? Amado stepped into the shaft of moonlight so she could see him, his hands out and open, his arms relaxed. "I won't hurt you," he said, but of course, she couldn't understand him. She balled her hands up into fists — badly — and said something, a thread of defiance over her fear. He recognized one word: police.

"I'm not the police," he said. Slowly, keeping his arms spread wide, he sat on the rusty mat of pine needles beneath them. Making himself smaller. "No police."

"No police," she said in English.

He nodded. "No police." He smiled at her. "I milk cows for a living." He mimed the old-fashioned way of milking teats. "I pitch manure." He flung a few invisible loads with an imaginary pitchfork. "And I roll hay" — no way to indicate that — "and I wipe the shit off my boots at the end of the day." He wiped the soles of his boots on the forest floor. Quiet talk, the kind of nonsense he murmured to the stock while he worked. All the words that, together, meant *I'm no threat to you.*

She stepped away from the huge pine that had been holding up her backbone. She bent a little, getting a closer look at him. In the moonlight, he could see she wasn't a girl, either, but a woman, around his own age. He also got a clue as to why she was

136

hiding from the police in, presumably, her own country. She reeked of marijuana.

She said something. He caught the word *Mexican.*

"Yes," he said. "I'm Mexican. Oaxacan." Not that she'd know where that was. He pressed one hand to his woolen jacket. "Amado Esfuentes, at your service." He bowed as best he could while sitting tailor-style on a cold patch of ground.

"Amado Esfuentes," she repeated.

He nodded. Wondered if he ought to have introduced himself as Octavio. He ought to get into the habit. On the other hand, it wasn't as if she was about to turn him in to the authorities, was it?

She smiled, a bit, and edged an inch closer, like a new calf examining him around its mother's hindquarters. She mimicked his motion, flattening her quilted jacket, revealing she was most definitely a woman. "Isabel," she said. "Isabel Christie."

English vowels always sounded so flat. "Isobel Christie," he said.

She smiled, more broadly. "Yeah, Isobel."

Slowly, one hand still raised where she could see it, he reached into his coat pocket. She shrank back. "It's okay," he said, in the same voice he used to soothe a skittish cow or a frightened horse. "It's okay." He pulled out a king-sized PayDay bar and held it out toward her. "Are you hungry?" He waggled the candy. "Go ahead. You can take it. I have more."

She stretched her hand out and grasped the chocolate with the very tips of her fingers, and it was gone, out of his hand and into hers faster than the eye could follow. He nodded again and dug out another candy bar for himself.

She tore open the wrapper and downed the confection as if it was the only meal she had had all day. He had guessed, when he smelled the pot on her, that she'd be hungry. She eyed the candy bar in his hand. He pulled out another PayDay — his last — and handed it to her. This time, she took it, rather than snatching it, and sat down facing him. She consumed the second one almost as quickly as the first, watching him all the while as he ate his more slowly, crunching the peanuts between his teeth.

"Well," he said in Spanish. "Now I've introduced myself and talked about my work and my home, and shared a meal. The last time I did that, it was a setup with my friend Geraldo's sister-in-law. Now I suppose I'll have to walk you home and introduce myself to your parents."

She drew her knees up and wrapped her

arms around them. She said something to him in a tone of voice so pleasant he wished he knew what it meant. Then she smiled, full on.

"Maybe this is the secret to maintaining good feelings between a man and a woman," he said. "Not understanding a word of what the other is saying."

In the distance, he heard a high, thin voice. "Izzy!" it called. "Izzy!"

The smile vanished from her face. Her eyes went wide and white-edged. He didn't need to know English to translate her frightened whisper. *Oh, God.*

They both scrambled to their feet, as the voice continued on, wheedling, cozening. It reminded him of the way his grandfather would croon lovingly to the chickens right before catching one and putting the hatchet to it. The woman was looking wildly around her, long blond hair swinging through the moonlight. Too bright. Amado snatched her hat off the ground and handed it to her. She twirled her hair into a rope and stuffed it beneath the cap.

"Isobel," he said, softly. She looked at him, on the verge of panic. He held his finger to his lips and pointed, through the trees, toward his earlier hiding place. He held out his hand to her. *Come with me.*

139

She took his hand. *Yes.*

He turned and traced his way through the trees, taking his time, seeing where he wanted to go and then moving. She shoved against his arm, pushing, trying to hurry him, a whimper trapped in her throat. He squeezed her hand and patted her arm, once, twice, turning the pat into a gesture that took in the woods stretching out in front of them. *Slowly. Silently.*

He stepped over a fallen pine and around a dense thicket of sharp-thorned scrub that had sprung up in its place. Hard on the other side of the thorn, a massive maple had split from age or lightning or ice, leaving one half upright and budding, the other angled against the trunk. The dead branches were weighted down with a decade or more of maple leaves, pine needles, tiny twisting weeds, so that the forest floor itself seemed to rise up in a swell. He pointed toward it.

She turned her hands up in puzzlement. *What?*

He angled his body, making himself as flat as he could, and slithered past the spiny brush. Small branches shook and flexed as the thorns caught his woolen coat, but then he was through, ducking down, squatting in the opening of the leaf-mold-and-tangle tent.

She nodded. Followed his path, stepping where he had stepped, her arms outstretched to give herself a flatter profile. The thorns zizzed over the nylon of her jacket.

"Izzy? Izzy!" The voice was louder, nearer, meaner. He — it was a he, Amado was sure of it — had stopped pretending he wanted to feed the chickens. Now they could hear the hatchet in his hand. The woman froze for a moment, her face puckered in fear, but before Amado had the chance to whisper courage to her, she opened her eyes and took another step. One, two, and then she was through, reaching for him. He took her hands and held them, tight, before pointing into the hide.

She crouched, twisted about, and scooted in on her backside, deeper and deeper, snapping off tiny twigs that sounded, with the voice raging in the air around them, like rifle shots. Amado crawled in after her, as far as he could go, and they sat, face-to-face and knee to knee, in a dark so profound all he could make out was the pale blur of her face. The smell, mold and rot and marijuana, made his head swim.

"Izzy! Goddammit! Get out here, you bitch!"

Her hands fluttered against his, and he caught them, squeezing hard. She had calluses, as he did. A woman used to hard work, as he was. Even in his tight grip, her hands shook. He tugged her, gently, firmly, until she leaned forward, and he could wrap one arm around her shoulders and press her head into the crook beneath his neck. She shuddered and breathed deeply. Stopped shaking. He held her, this stranger, against the voice, raging and snapping and threatening things he could not begin to know.

VI

The Washington County Emergency Department charge nurse did a double-take that would have been funny, if Clare hadn't been so tired.

"Reverend Clare? Is that you?" Alta came around the intake counter, her eyes never leaving Clare's uniform, whose coffee-stain design now also sported several streaks of crushed-grass green and leaf-rot brown after almost two hours spent crawling through the woods, searching in vain for the missing men. "Good lord, you haven't left the ministry, have you? Weren't you just on call last week?"

Clare held the rotating — and unpaid — post of hospital chaplain, along with the Reverend Inman of High Street Baptist and

Dr. McFeely of First Presbyterian. She sighed. "Hi, Alta. Yes, I was here last week, and no, I haven't left the ministry. I'm a weekend warrior."

Alta looked dubious. "It's Tuesday night."

"I'm a weekend warrior who is way, way behind on her flight hours. I've been heading to Fort Dix or Latham on my days off to get in more air time."

"Flight hours? You're not a chaplain?"

"Nope. They've got me in the pilot's seat again."

"Well. God bless you." Alta, for the first time in their almost-three-year acquaintanceship, hugged her. "Stepping forward when your country calls." She held Clare out at arm's length. "I'm proud to know you."

Clare made a miserable attempt at a smile. "Yeah, thanks. Look, I'm here to see Sister Lucia Pirone. She was brought in —"

Alta stepped back behind the counter. "Broken hip and internal hemorrhage of indeterminate origin, ayeh. She's been transferred to Glens Falls for an MRI." Evidently, the special tribute was over.

"How about the injured men she was driving?"

Alta bent over her computer. "The unconscious-with-contusion's been admitted for observation overnight." She looked up at Clare. "Routine. Checking for symptoms of concussion." She straightened up. "The abrasions-and-contusions got patched up and was R.O.R. 'bout half an hour ago. I have no idea where he is now."

"You just let him go?"

Alta looked over her shoulder and beckoned to Clare. Bemused, Clare moved in closer. "An agent from Albany showed up."

"An agent?"

"ICE." Alta rolled her eyes. "Formerly known as INS. Some twenty-five-year-old with an MBA probably told them to *rebrand* themselves." She dropped her voice. "So, anyway, I gave the guy ten bucks and the homeless shelter pamphlet. Don't know if it'll do him any good, since he didn't speak English, but —"

"The hospital reported these guys?"

Alta drew herself up to her full five feet two inches. "Of course not! Someone at the accident site called it in, apparently."

One of the MKPD? No. None of Russ's officers would make a call like that without his say-so. Now John Huggins — that was a whole 'nother kettle of fish. "What about the third man?" she asked Alta.

"The broken arm? He's getting casted. He'll be ready for release as soon as Dr.

144

Stillman clears him."

"So soon?"

Alta gave her a glance that said, *And your medical knowledge is . . . ?*

"It's just that when Chief Van Alstyne broke his leg last year, he went into surgery and had to stay overnight."

"The chief" — was it her imagination, or did Alta put a peculiar spin to those words? — "had an open fracture requiring pins. The illegal has a plain-as-vanilla greenstick fracture. Slap some fiberglass on it and he's done."

Clare found herself looking over her shoulder just as the charge nurse had. "What's going to happen to him? When he's discharged?"

Alta threw up her hands. "Lord knows. The lady from the ICE already looked at his papers." She shook her head. "All the way up from Albany for three farmworkers. I wish the government had moved that fast when my ex-husband was skipping out on child support. Their sponsors are on the way over to talk with her."

"Their sponsors?"

"The folks who hired 'em. They're responsible for their work permits. Leastways, that's how it was explained to me."

Sponsors. Would that be the business that

arranged the paperwork and the transportation? Or would that be —

The Emergency Department's old-fashioned swinging doors thumped open, admitting Russ Van Alstyne. He didn't look happy, and his frown grew even deeper when he caught sight of Clare.

He strode up the institutional green hallway toward the waiting room. An anxious-looking man with more hair in his mustache than on his head entered in his wake, along with a rangy blond woman who looked enough like a female version of Russ to be his —

— sister. Oh.

"What are you doing here?" Russ demanded. "I thought I told Knox and Kevin to take you home after the search."

She squelched the first reply that came to mind: *You're not the boss of me!* "Don't blame them," she said instead. "They tried."

The doors to the examination and treatment area clunked open. A white-coated doctor stepped inside, headed for Alta's desk. He paused when he saw Russ, and opened his mouth, but the chief of police went past him without a second glance and stopped in front of Clare. "Oh, I don't blame *them,* believe me."

Clare did a lot of counseling as a priest,

146

and she was good at it. She recognized the weapons of grief: anger, lashing out, keeping the world at bay. She knew the postures of guilt: bending over, ducking away, doing almost anything to avoid confronting the festering wound to the heart. She recognized. She knew. And it didn't do her a damn bit of good, confronted by Russ Van Alstyne acting as if *she* had somehow done him wrong.

"If you have a problem with me, spit it out," she snapped. "Otherwise, get out of my face."

"A problem with you? A problem with you? How about the fact that you're once more elbowing your way into police business that has nothing to do with you —"

"I am here to visit Sister Lucia! It has nothing to do with you."

"— despite the fact that the last time you decided to get involved —"

"Don't you say it."

"— it ended in a bloody mess, you —"

"Saving your life, you —"

"— idiot woman!"

"— overbearing jerk!"

They both stopped at the same moment, breathing heavily. If this were a movie, they would have grabbed each other, but Clare had never felt less like throwing her arms around Russ Van Alstyne. Unless it was to knock him to the floor.

Someone coughed.

Oh, my God. She saw realization replacing rage on his face. They had played the whole scene out in front of an audience.

"Chief Van Alstyne?"

Russ closed his eyes for a moment, then turned. The doctor who had come in earlier was looking at them with one hand resting on Alta's desk phone. Ready to call security, no doubt.

"Dr. Stillman." Clare could hear him forcing his voice into its normal channels. "Hi."

"Uh . . . hi. How's the leg?"

Russ looked down at his ancient jeans, as if it hadn't occurred to him before now that there was something holding him up. "Fine. Just . . . fine."

"Great. Uh —" The orthopedist's gaze strayed to Clare. He stared. "Reverend Fergusson? Is that you?"

She smiled weakly. "Nice to see you again, Dr. Stillman." He let go of the phone and crossed to her, peering at her patches in the same way she had seen him peering at Russ's X-ray last year. "National Guard? Great! Me, too. What unit?"

"Uhm . . . the 142nd Aviation Battalion."

"Are you their new chaplain?"

Russ rolled his eyes.

"No," she said. "I'm their new Black Hawk pilot."

"Excuse me." A new voice, from behind her, startled Clare. She and Dr. Stillman both turned. A very tall and very erect older woman had emerged from the hallway leading to the elevator banks. She had silver hair cut towel-dry short and the professorial air of someone who has been telling people what to do without much back talk for the past forty-some years. "I'm Paula Hodgden, from Immigration and Customs Enforcement." She folded her hands over a clipboard. Her measuring gaze took in the whole waiting-room tableau. "Is one of you the sponsoring employer of the nonresident aliens?"

"Oh!" The mustachioed man tore his eyes away from the Russ-and-Clare show. "That would be me. I mean, me and my wife." He nudged the woman by his side, who was still contemplating the two of them with a look of deep amusement.

"ICE?" Russ said. "Not to be rude, but what are you doing here?"

"And you are . . . ?"

"Russell Van Alstyne, Millers Kill chief of police."

She flipped her clipboard open and made

a notation. "Ah. It must have been your department that handled the accident."

"An accident in our jurisdiction. Why are *you* here, Ms. — uh —"

"Hodgden," Clare said under her breath.

"I received a report that a vanload of possible undocumented aliens had been in an accident."

Russ frowned. "Who reported it?"

Ms. Hodgden looked at him evenly. "I don't think you expect me to divulge that, do you? I will say it was not, as it should have been, your department."

Russ crossed his arms, a move that emphasized his departmental hardware and patches. "We don't go around checking people's papers here in Millers Kill. It's not a damn police state."

Clare had to hide her smile.

"But you and I are in the first line of defense against possible terrorists, aren't we?" Ms. Hodgden gestured toward Clare and Dr. Stillman. "Surely, we do our job so they might not need to do theirs."

Russ glanced at Clare, and she knew, without a doubt, what he was thinking: *This lady has read too many official government pamphlets.*

Their mind-reading moment was broken when his sister shouldered him out of the way. "Hi, I'm Janet McGeoch." She shook Ms. Hodgden's hand. "Is there a problem with our workers?"

"How do you do, Mrs. McGeoch. Let me ask you, did you use a service to facilitate the H-two A permits?"

Janet glanced at her husband. "Yeah. Is that a problem?"

"It was Creative Labor Solutions," Mike McGeoch said. "They came well recommended. We went to this seminar about getting workers, over to Amsterdam? Couple folks there had used them before. We've kept all the paperwork and copies of everything we signed off on." He patted his plaid wool jacket, as if the documentation might be hiding inside somewhere.

Ms. Hodgden made another notation on her clipboard. "Creative Labor Solutions. I'm not familiar with them. I'd like to see any correspondence you have from them."

"Why?" Janet said pointedly.

The ICE agent sighed. "Mr. and Mrs. Mc-Geoch, I suspect you've been stung by a not-uncommon employee scam. Obtaining an H-two A permit costs an employment service time and money, and, as it's designed to do, retards the movement of labor from the resident country to the United States. You follow?"

Janet frowned. Glanced at her husband. "Yeah, I follow."

"Some so-called employment agencies try to make a deeper profit by charging clients the cost of fully legal H-two A employees and then supplying undocumented nonresident aliens instead."

"You mean, like a dealer selling a dime bag for a full ten bucks, but giving his customers baking soda?" Russ said.

Ms. Hodgden raised her eyebrows. "That's not how I would have put it, but yes."

"And we got the baking soda?" Janet looked from her brother to the ICE agent. "What's that mean, exactly?"

"Two of the three men who were admitted here had forged H-two A permits. Not, I should add, very good forgeries, either."

"Oh, shit," Mike McGeoch said.

Janet reached behind her and squeezed her husband's hand. "And the third?"

Ms. Hodgden consulted the clipboard. "Amado Esfuentes. His employment authorization documentation is correct."

"Well, there! There's nothing to say the rest of the men don't have the right papers, too."

"Mrs. McGeoch." The agent's voice had the professional sympathy of someone used to telling the same bad news, over and over again. It reminded Clare of her insurance adjuster. "Properly documented migrant workers don't usually flee after being injured in a car wreck. Yes, it's possible the two who were unable to run away were the only two undocumented aliens, but it's not likely."

"What about this Amado guy?" Mike sounded hopeful. "Why would he have papers and the others not?"

"In all likelihood, Esfuentes has worked in the U.S. before. That makes it easier for him to obtain an EAD on his own, rather than through an agency. It's not uncommon for an experienced guest laborer to serve as a sort of leader or guide for work gangs from his village. I'd be willing to bet everyone in that van tonight came from the same hometown."

"An experienced worker? The one with the broken arm?" Russ shook his head. "I spoke with him. He was barely out of his teens."

Dr. Stillman, who had been listening at the edges of the discussion, broke in. "I agree with Chief Van Alstyne. He's twenty-one, tops."

Ms. Hodgden made a *well, what can you expect?* gesture. "These people go to work when they're thirteen or fourteen. You can't rely on age as a guide."

153

"These people?" Clare propped her hands on her hips. She opened her mouth. Russ laid a hand on her shoulder. She shut up.

"What does this mean for us?" Janet asked. "Bottom line."

"It means the two undocumented nonresidents will be returned to their country of origin." Ms. Hodgden looked back down at her clipboard and frowned. "I'm having some difficulty locating one of them," she admitted. "No one here seems to know where they've placed him. Sloppy work for a hospital."

Clare studied her boots.

"What about the money we've paid to Creative Labor?" Janet asked. "What about us having enough hands to manage our herd?"

"Whether you can recover the fees paid to the agency is between you and that agency." Ms. Hodgden gave the McGeochs another professionally sympathetic look. "My suggestion would be to contact another, more reliable service and have them get started fulfilling your labor needs."

"Another six weeks!" Mike McGeoch jammed his hands in his pockets and stared at his boots.

"In the meantime, your other employees' papers will be examined as soon as they —

ah, turn up." She gave Russ a look indicating this was his responsibility. "Mr. Esfuentes can remain in this country legally, so long as he is employed."

"Employed by us," Janet said.

"Yes."

"As in, paid, and everything?"

Paula Hodgden pierced her with a gimlet eye. "Mrs. McGeoch, one of the reasons we *have* work permits is to prevent employers from exploiting employees from another country."

"I didn't mean it like that. I meant" — Janet splayed her hands wide — "he's got a broken arm! On a dairy farm, that makes him about as useful as . . . as . . ."

"Teats on a bull?" Russ offered.

Janet slugged his arm. "How long is he going to be laid up?" she asked Dr. Stillman.

"Four weeks in the heavy cast and another four in a lighter version. After that, another few weeks in a removable brace, just to ensure he doesn't reinjure it. No weight-bearing exercise for the first month and very mild exertion for the second."

"Mild exertion? What's that mean?"

The orthopedist shrugged. "He could pick up a couple of books. His clothing. For most of my patients, it means you can start to perform normal household functions for yourself."

"We don't need someone for normal household functions," Janet said. "We need someone who can unspool thirty pounds of hose and pitch manure and drive a stick-shift truck!"

Stillman shook his head. "You're talking early July before this young man will be cleared for that sort of work."

Janet McGeoch's eyes met her husband's, and Clare could see them speaking to each other without a word, in the way of long-married couples. Mike nodded.

Janet turned back to Paula Hodgden. "I'm sorry, but we just can't afford to keep him on the payroll for two months or more."

"I understand. I'll arrange for him to return with the other two."

"Wait!" The word was out of Clare's mouth before she had a chance to stop it. "What if he gets a job?"

Paula Hodgden looked at her and then at the rest of them, clustered among the JFK-era chairs of the ED waiting room. Clare could see her assigning everyone a status — employers, investigating officer, treating physician, and . . . woman in a grungy undress uniform.

"I'm sorry," the agent said. "You are . . . ?"

"The Reverend Clare Fergusson, rector of St. Alban's Church."

Ms. Hodgden's eyebrows went up. She looked at Russ.

"Yeah," he said. "She really is."

Dr. Stillman grinned. "I can vouch for her authenticity, too." He glanced toward the admissions desk. "But that's all I can do. I see Alta's waving me down. Excuse me, folks. Reverend."

Clare raised her hand in something that might have been either a wave or a blessing. Then she zeroed in on Ms. Hodgden again. "What if this Amado had a job for the next two months? A legal, paying job? Could he stay then? And work for the McGeochs after his arm healed?"

Russ pinched the bridge of his nose beneath his glasses. "What are you thinking of?"

"We need an interim sexton at the church. Mr. Hadley had open-heart surgery in March, and he hasn't been able to perform his duties since then. He's going to come back this summer, we think, but in the meantime we've been plugging the hole with volunteers. This guy could take the job." She smiled, pleased with herself. "It's perfect."

"Wait just one minute —" Russ began.

"What do you think, Ms. Hodgden? Would that be legal?"

"Well . . . if you're willing to fill out the paperwork."

Clare turned to the McGeochs. "Would you consider taking him on when he's recovered?"

Janet and Mike gave each other another speaking look. "Okay," Janet said.

"Clare. For chrissakes, you're going off half-cocked again." Russ shoved his thumbs under his belt and tightened his hands over his rig. "He could be anybody. He could be wanted in three countries, for all you know."

Paula Hodgden shook her head. "Mmm, no. In order to obtain an H-two A permit, the applicant must have no criminal record in either the originating or the host country."

Russ glared at the ICE agent, then returned his attention to Clare. "He's not going to be able to do custodial work with a bum arm. And what if he boosts the silver and takes off?"

"Most of Mr. Hadley's work is stuff like vacuuming and polishing the woodwork. You can do that with one arm as well as two. As for the silver, I keep it locked away except when it's in use." She let her usual light Virginia accent deepen into molasses. "I am a Southerner, after all. We know how to preserve our silver from depredation."

"Where's he going to stay? Hmm? Are you going to pay for a room for him?"

She bit her lip. As much as it galled her to admit it, she hadn't considered that issue.

"You see?" Russ went on. "You can't —"

"There arc two extra bedrooms in the rectory," she said, thinking out loud.

"No." The word was like a lodge pole driven into the ground. Immovable. She looked up at his grim face.

"No," she agreed. "That's not the best idea, is it."

"Why can't he stay in our bunkhouse?" Mike's voice startled her. She had tuned the rest of them out. She looked at the dairy farmer. "Well, it's not a — you know — western-style bunkhouse." He smiled shyly. "It's the original house on the property. Way back from the road, down by the stream. Hadn't been lived in by anything but squirrels and chickens for the last hundred years, and let me tell you, it was a job making it habitable again."

"Honey." Janet laid her hand on her husband's arm. She smiled apologetically to Clare. "We have the house all cleaned and repaired for the new hands. He would be welcome to stay there, but I'm afraid he'd have no way of getting to work."

"No, no, that's what makes it perfect." Mike beamed at Clare. "The lady who bought the Petersons' house, the house across the road? She works at your church. Her name's Elizabeth de Groot."

Clare felt her jaw unhinge. She stared up at Russ. "My deacon lives across the street from your sister?"

He shrugged. "I told you it's a small town."

The agent held up her clipboard. "This is all very interesting, but perhaps, while they hash out the housing arrangements, I might have a word, Chief Van Alstyne?" She retreated toward the admissions desk.

Russ looked at his sister, then at Clare, then back to his sister. "Don't agree to anything," he said to Janet. "You have no idea what you'll be getting into." He stalked off like a mood-reversed Cheshire Cat, leaving his frown hanging in the air between them.

"I can get Elizabeth to carry Amado back and forth if you'll let him live in the bunkhouse," Clare said, hurrying to close the deal before Janet decided to take her brother's advice.

"What do think, honey?" Janet asked her husband.

Mike shrugged. "Not like it's going to be too full now, is it?"

"Okay, then." Janet held out her hand to Clare.

"Great." They shook. Janet laid her other hand atop Clare's, trapping her in a warm grasp. "Honey?" She kept her gaze on Clare. "Could you go get me something from the cafeteria? I'm starving."

"Uh . . . okay." Mike bumped off down the hall. Leaving Clare alone with Janet Mc-Geoch, née Van Alstyne. Clare swallowed.

"I've heard a lot about you." Janet's eyes were the same blue as Russ's.

Oh, God. Better take the bull by the horns. "I bet you have," Clare said. "Some of it's probably even true."

Janet nodded. Released Clare's hand. "I have to apologize to you."

Now *that* was surprising. "To me? Why?"

"When my mom told me about you and Russ, I sort of mentally cast you in the role of bimbo home wrecker. You know, the much-younger seductress who wears Victoria's Secret thongs and nails the middle-aged idiot by massaging his ego. Among other body parts."

Clare thought she might spontaneously

161

combust from the heat in her face.

"But it's pretty obvious you're not like that."

She didn't know whether to laugh or cry. "No. No thongs."

Janet smiled slyly. "And I don't see you spending a lot of time massaging my brother's ego."

Clare laughed. And then Janet surprised her again by catching her in a hug. "My mother likes you," she said in Clare's ear, "and I think I like you, too." She moved a little way apart, creating a space between them. "And if you can rescue my brother from this pit he's dropped himself into, I swear, I'll love you forever."

VII

It was close to midnight, and he was halfway back to his mother's house, when Russ realized he hadn't thought of Linda in hours. Since . . . since when? This morning? This afternoon? Panic, like a meaty hand, gripped his throat. Since before stopping at the liquor store. He hadn't thought of her once since then. He had forgotten to remember. He steered the pickup to the shoulder of the road and got his four-ways on before the tears blinded him and he buckled over, hacking, the steering wheel cutting a groove

162

in his forehead. He wept for his wife, and for forgetting, and for all the things he had loved and damaged.

PENTECOST

MAY

I

Her car gave out on the Schuylerville Road. At night, of course. At least five miles from the Stewart's on Route 117. No, Stewart's didn't have a garage, did they? Just pumps.

Hadley tipped her head back against the seat and breathed slowly and deeply. *I am not going to fall apart.* She was going to count her blessings. It was a 45-degree night in mid-May, instead of a 15-degree night in mid-February. The kids were safe at home, hopefully, please God, not harassing their great-grandfather into complete exhaustion. She was — her mind went blank. She couldn't think of anything. She tried again. It was —

Nope. That was it. She ran out of blessings after two. She opened her purse and dug out her cell phone — prepaid, thirty cents a minute — and dialed home. It picked up on the fourth ring.

164

"Knox and Hadley household Hudson speaking may I help you please," her son said.

"Hey, lovey, it's Mom. Can you put Granddad on?"

"Okay, Mom. How was police school?"

"We learned about crime scenes tonight, just like on TV. I got some yellow tape from the instructor for you."

"Cool! Are you coming home soon?"

"As soon as I can." In her rearview window, she saw lights. She leaned over and locked the passenger and driver's doors. This is what becoming a cop was doing to her. Nowadays, she assumed every car on the road held a potential threat. She hadn't been that paranoid in big bad LA.

"Hey, honey, what's up?"

She sighed. "My car's not working. Can you call someone to give me a tow? I'm on the Schuylerville Road, about a mile from Route 117."

"Are you okay? What happened?"

"I don't know. All the warning lights came on and then it just sort of . . . lost power. I'm fine, I just glided off the side of the road."

"Humph. You stay put. I'll pop the kids into my car and we'll come and get you."

"No, no, no." *God,* no. Her grandfather

had terrible night vision. Not to mention the assorted drugs he was taking. "It's already close to nine. It's a school night. I don't want Hudson and Genny up late. Call someplace in town. I'll wait here with the car and get a ride home on the tow truck."

They argued about it back and forth for a while, with Hadley mentally tallying up each thirty cents as it vanished into the airwaves. Eventually, she had to threaten to get out and walk toward town if he and the kids came. That shut him up, except for the grumbling. He promised to call for a tow, and was starting in on a list of things she should do to check the car, when her phone ran out of minutes, right in the middle of ". . . spark plug connectors. . . ." She was almost grateful.

She sat back, resigned to the wait, letting herself drift in the cooling dark. She tried to recall the last time she had time to sit, nowhere to go, nothing to do. She could remember times when she was pregnant with Hudson. She'd be so tired after getting home from her receptionist gig that she'd sprawl out on the sofa, not eating, not watching TV, not doing anything. Dylan would come home from whatever party he had been working and ask her how the hell she could waste an entire evening doing nothing. She always figured she *was* doing something. She was growing a baby. Not that he would've given her credit for that.

Lights coming toward her, this time. She sat up to see if it might be the tow truck. It slowed down, its high beams making her squint, then crawled past, a bass line vibrating right through her closed windows. A jacked-up, giant, my-penis-isn't-big-enough Humvee. Or were they Hummers? She couldn't remember. God, she had a test on car recognition next week. She was going to flunk for sure.

Red brake lights bloomed in her rearview mirror. Then white, as the SUV backed up, returning. She sat up straight again. It parked on the opposite shoulder. The back door opened, illuminating the interior, showing her a brief glimpse of four men.

Oh, shit. Why her? Why now? Why couldn't it be some elderly couple on their way home from a revival meeting?

The guy who had exited the back sauntered across the road, the headlights outlining the fluid roll of his hips. Hadley reached inside her purse and grabbed the inactive cell phone. She held it up to her ear and began chatting animatedly with dead air. "So, you'll never believe this, honey, but there's an SUV stopped right across the

167

road from me. A young man's gotten out. I think he wants to help me. No, no, I'll just let him know you're almost here."

He *was* a young man, maybe Flynn's age, but pimped out in an exaggerated hip-hop style that would have worked a lot better if he had been seventeen. And black. And somewhere else besides the cow country outside Millers Kill. He bent down and smiled at her through the window, and she saw he was Latino. He had three studs spaced along his upper lip, and for a second Hadley forgot to be scared, thinking, *How the hell do you eat with that?*

"Having car trouble?" His voice sounded flat and faintly accented through the glass.

"I'm fine," she said loudly. "I'm on the phone with my husband, and he's headed over here now." She smiled like an idiot.

"Pop the hood, I'll take a look."

"No, no, that's fine —" He strolled to the front of her decrepit car. Her flashers cycled him from light, to dark, to light again.

"Open the hood!" He smiled while he shouted. It reminded her of Dylan, the way he'd yell, "What's your problem? We're having fun, goddammit!"

She put on her best hapless female look and shrugged. He just smiled again, fished something long and flat out of his com-

168

modious cargo pocket, and leaned against the hood. The car dipped. Hadley heard a metallic *clunk* and the hood flew up, hiding Stud Boy, who, for all she knew, was stripping down her engine.

For the first time since she had been issued her service piece, she wished she had her gun. For two months, it had been too heavy, too alien, too intimidating. Now she wished she could pull it out from the lockbox under her passenger seat and rap on her window and see the look on this guy's face. Not, despite her firing instructor's gung-ho pep talks about "yer best friend," that she'd ever use it.

But, oh, she wished she had it now. Then maybe she wouldn't feel so scared.

Stud Boy ambled back to her door without bothering to replace the hood. "I hate to tell you, but it looks bad. Your alternator belt's broke."

She had no idea if he was bullshitting her or not.

"C'mon, we'll take you where you're going. Pretty girl like you shouldn't be all alone out here." His smile made her flesh crawl.

She held up the useless cell phone. "Thanks, but my husband's already on his way."

He rapped her window with a silver ring in the shape of a skull. He held it out, as if she ought to admire it. He had letters printed over each of his knuckles. Jailhouse tats, inked in with a sharpened pen and a homemade hammer. *Oh, shit.* His smile grew broader. "If you have a husband, how come you don't have no ring?" His fingers slid down, out of sight, and she heard the *click-click* of the door as he tried the lock.

She dropped the little-wife routine. Hardened her voice. "I'm not going with you. There's a tow truck on the way . . . and the man I live with knows where I am." She considered telling him she was a cop, but with nothing to back that up, she figured it would just make her look more scared and desperate.

He kept smiling. He released her door handle and let his fingers glide over the window, creating shapes. She realized he was miming touching her and her stomach flipped over with a nauseated lurch. With his other hand, he beckoned to the Hummer. Across the road, doors swung open and men got out.

Oh, shit, she thought. *Oh shit, oh shit, oh shit.*

"We don't have to take you anywhere," Stud Boy said. "You can just hang out with us in our truck." A short, broad Latino pressed up against her door next to Stud Boy. He had a nervous ferret face that made him look like Peter Lorre.

Click-click. Click-click. He was trying the rear door. Out of the corner of her eye, she saw the two others, dark shapes on the passenger side.

Click-click.

"You must be getting cold, stuck out here," Stud Boy said cheerfully. "You come with us. We'll let you warm up." One of the ones on the opposite side of the car said something, and they all laughed.

"You like to party?" Stud Boy asked. "We'll have a party. We'll make you feel real good." He said something over the roof that she couldn't make out, and one of the shadowy figures detached himself from her car and meandered across the road. Back to their SUV. He flung open the driver's door and reached under the dash. Their rear hatch popped open. She thought about the handy do-it-yourself hood opener Stud Boy had produced from his pocket and knew, with the horrible sinking certainty of someone whose luck always ran bad, that the one across the road was going to pull a jimmy strip out of the back of that truck, and she was going to be screwed. In every sense of the word.

She eased her key ring out of the ignition and folded her right hand around it, letting the keys jut up between her fingers. If she pretended to play along and acted scared and helpless — God knew, that wasn't going to take much effort — she figured she'd have one good chance to catch Stud Boy off guard. Keys in his throat, knee in his balls, then the flat of her foot to his kneecap with her weight behind it. If she could put him down — put him down *hard* so he wasn't getting back up again — the others might back off. She swallowed. Laid her hand on her door rest.

In her rearview mirror, she saw the flash of red and whites.

Oh, God, thank you, God, thank you!

The cruiser rolled in tight behind her vehicle, flooding her interior with the brilliant white light of the kliegs. She couldn't tell if it was a state trooper or the MKPD, but whoever it was, she prayed he was big, hairy, and heavily armed. Stud Boy and his ferret friend stepped away from her window, and the guy on the far side vanished toward the front of her car. A moment later, her hood thunked into place.

Through the glass, she heard the crunch of boots on gravel. "What's going on here?"

a man said, his voice hard with suspicion and authority. She could see him outlined in her rearview mirror, tall, big, one hand resting on the butt of his service weapon.

Stud Boy raised his hands placatingly. "*Nada, nada.* We were just stopping to see if the lady needed any help."

"Yeah? Well, she's got help now. Clear off."

The smaller, weaselly guy scuttled across the road, but Stud Boy hesitated.

"Either you're in your vehicle, or you're facedown in the dirt with my boot in your back. Your choice. You got ten seconds."

Stud Boy glanced at the guy who was still hovering just out of reach at the front of her car, then gestured toward the Hummer. "We don't want any trouble," he said, smiling. His lip piercings glittered in the cruiser's cold white light. He glanced down at Hadley. "Later, pretty girl."

She wrenched her eyes from his and focused on her hands. Holding her keys. Her knuckles were white. She heard the thudding of overengineered doors, and then the Hummer roared to life and, in a spatter of gravel, pulled into the road and vanished.

The boots crunched toward her. The officer squatted down. "Hey," Kevin Flynn said. "Are you all right?"

II

"Your granddad called the station." They were sitting in Flynn's cruiser with the heater on high. Flynn had complained of the cold when he snapped it on, but she knew it was because she was shaking. She couldn't seem to stop. He had kept up a steady flow of chatter, walking her to the cruiser, grabbing her notebook and her criminal justice text, toting the two bags of groceries she had picked up at the Sam's Club down in Albany. It was almost like the way she'd hear him rattling on at the station, except he kept sneaking glances at her when he thought she wasn't looking. Taking her emotional temperature.

"Of course, dispatch isn't manned, most nights. Womanned? I bet Harlene would like *womanned.* Anyway, his call shot off to the Glens Falls board, and they gave me a squawk, and here I am."

"Thank you." She sounded like Hudson, when she made him thank his little sister. She took a deep breath — it was getting easier the longer she sat in the self-contained world that was the squad car — and tried again. "I mean it. Thank you. They . . . I was . . ." She shook her head.

His hand touched her shoulder, so tentatively she might have imagined it. "You

174

don't have to say anything," he said. "And you don't have to thank me."

"You don't understand," she said. "I didn't — I just sat there. Like a victim. Like a babysitter in a horror movie."

"Naw. They scream and run around a lot."

She looked at him.

"Sorry," he said.

"I'm used to taking shit from men, you know? They trash-talk at me, and I flip it right back to them. But these guys . . . I didn't even tell them I was a cop. You know why? Because I'm not. I'm just a woman who gets dressed up in a costume five days a week and pretends to be one." She leaned forward, bracing her arms on her knees, and his hand fell away instantly. "I am such a failure at this. A failure and a fake."

"What, because you didn't get out of your car and mix it up with four bad dudes? That's just being smart. Hell, if it'd been me in that car with no weapon and no radio, I would've done just what you did. Stay put and keep my mouth shut."

She shook her head again. "You don't need a gun. You have that thing, you know, that cop thing going on. With the hard voice and the take-no-shit attitude." She looked at him again. Eyeing his frame. "You looked huge. I mean, you're tall, but you're not —"

She curled her fists and shook her arms in an iron-man pose.

He grinned. "It's a trick I learned from Lyle MacAuley. He leaves his bomber jacket unzipped and kind of spreads his arms out. Makes him look twice as wide as he really is."

She let her mind wrap around that one. "There are tricks to it? As in, performing?"

He twisted in his seat so he could face her. "Sure. Like what you were just talking about. The voice? And the attitude? I just copy the chief. Nobody gives him shit." He paused. "Well, nobody except for Reverend Fergusson." He smiled a little. "Look, when I started at the MKPD, I felt exactly the same way you do now. It was, like, the day after I turned twenty-one. I was sworn in before I'd had my first legal drink. *And* I was even skinnier than I am now, if you can believe that." He held his arms open, inviting her to gaze upon his skeletal thinness. She didn't see it. He was lean, all right, but in a good way, the way of a healthy young man who hasn't quite finished fleshing out.

"I felt like somebody's little brother, getting to tag along with the big boys. I kept waiting for . . . I dunno, some TV moment, when I would suddenly stop being Skinny

Flynnie and start being bad-ass Officer Flynn."

"Skinny Flynnie?"

He blushed. "That's what they called me in high school."

"Hah. They called me —" She stopped. "Never mind. High school sucks."

"Oh, yeah." He reached out to turn the blower down a few notches, and the way his wrist bones poked out of his shirt cuff did make him look like a teenaged boy. "Anyway, I was working this case last year, interviewing a witness, and she lied to me. She and her husband. I had to go back with the dep and reinterview her. I was really pissed off, thinking about how she'd played me, but then, it suddenly struck me; it was my own fault. Because up here" — he tapped his temple — "I was still Skinny Flynnie. I knew the rules and regs, I had learned the tricks, but I didn't *believe*."

"Believe." This was starting to sound very California. "In what, yourself?"

He shook his head. "In the power of the suit."

"Okay, you've lost me."

"You know that movie where the dad puts on the Santa suit and he turns into Kris Kringle?"

"*The Santa Clause*? Oh, yeah. I know it."

Hudson and Genny had watched it approximately eight hundred times last December.

"Okay. All this" — he waved his arm around, taking in the computer and the mic and the racked and locked shotgun and his hat balanced on the dashboard — "is the suit. You put on the suit, and you become The Man."

She thought about that for a moment. "I don't know. I've got the uniform and all that, and I still feel like a fraud."

"Just give it time."

Her mouth crooked up. Words of wisdom from a — "Flynn," she said, "how old are you?"

"Twenty-four."

From a kid who was eight years younger than her. She curled into the seat. "I think you may have more time than I do."

Spinning yellow lights appeared on the road ahead of them, resolving into a tow truck. She stirred, ready to get up, but Flynn's hand was in the way. "Gimme your key," he said. "I'll take care of it."

She stripped the key off her ring and dropped it onto his open palm. She watched through the windshield as he spoke with the tow truck operator, handed over the key, and shook the man's hand. Weird. Considering what almost happened with the freaks in the Hummer, she should still be jangling, jumpy, coked up. Instead, she felt as relaxed and boneless as she did in the shampoo girl's chair at the salon.

Letting someone else take care of her.

Huh.

Kevin climbed back into the cruiser and tossed his hat back on the dash. "All set." He turned off his light bar and shifted into gear. "He's taking it to Ron Tucker's garage. Best mechanic in town. He'll do you right." He pulled onto the road. She let the rolling fields and farms slip past them, almost invisible in the darkness.

"Flynn." The question popped into her head from nowhere. "Did you run the plates on those guys?"

He grinned.

"What?"

"There you go. That's thinking like a cop."

"Did you?"

"Of course I did. When I pulled in behind you. The truck's registered to Josefina Feliciano, DOB 7-25-61, POR Brooklyn, New York. Three points down for passing a school bus, no record."

She shook her head. "Did you see the guy who was hassling me? With three studs in his upper lip? He looked like he escaped from an S and M convention."

"Maybe Ms. Feliciano likes to hang out with rough trade."

"You sure the vehicle wasn't stolen?"

"It hasn't been reported. Maybe one of them was Feliciano's son?"

"God. Can you imagine? If my son ever gets anything other than his earlobe pierced —" She pictured the pumped-up SUV and the young men in their city clothes. "What were they doing up here, anyway? It's a little far for a ride in the country. And it's too early for people coming up to do Lake George."

"Hikers? White rafting? Bird-watchers?"

She opened her mouth to shoot him down, then noticed his grin.

"Mexicans and Jamaicans control the pot trade up through the North Country," he said. "Mexicans, for the most part. They bring it up out of the Caribbean and Central America, funnel it through New York City, and distribute it up here."

"You think maybe they were here on business?"

"What do you think?"

"I think we should flag the car. Send out its plate and description to area law enforcement."

"I think you're right, Officer Knox." He

grinned again.

"What?"

"Who's The Man? You're The Man. Say it with me now. Who's The Man?"

She mumbled.

"I didn't hear you!"

"I'm The Man! Idiot." She shook her head and looked out the window. Her own reflection, limned by the computer lights, looked back at her. She thought it might be smiling.

III

Amado Esfuentes wiped the sweat from his forehead before tugging his work gloves back on. He reshouldered the spool of electrical cable he had set against the fence post. "Ready?" he asked Raul. Raul groaned as he picked up the buckets of porcelain conductors and screw plates.

"If this was barbed wire, we'd have been done by now," Raul said.

"If you worked as hard as you complain, we'd be done by now." Amado wished, as he had every day in the month since the accident, that his little brother was toiling beside him. Octavio worked more and talked less than any other man on the crew, and when he did have something to say, he didn't whine like Raul. But Octavio was in town, sweeping and polishing for a lady minister and answering to the name "Amado." Meanwhile, Amado was the Mc-Geochs' foreman "Octavio," always partnering Raul because he couldn't, in good conscience, stick any of the others with the laziest guy on the farm.

"Cheer up." Amado let the electrical cable slip off the wooden spool as he walked over the uneven ground toward the next fence post. "We'll be finished and back before lunch," he said. "And this is better for the cows than barbed wire."

Raul gave a detailed suggestion of what Amado might like to do to the cows.

"Oh, I would," Amado said, "but I'm afraid I might hurt them, on account of being so large."

Raul roared with laughter. They reached the next post, and Amado clipped off the cable while Raul screwed an insulating plate into the wood and attached the conductor. Amado threaded the cable through, untwisted the wires, and fastened them around the conductors. Then he did the same thing in the opposite direction for the next length of cable.

Amado tied off the insulated black wire, and they picked up and moved down the line. This portion of the property was divided from the mountain by a swiftly churning stream that cut a hollow almost deep enough to call a gorge in places: an irresistible lure that would mean lost and trapped cows, in the best cases, and broken legs and drowned carcasses in the worst. Amado had no problem taking a little extra time and fencing it off nice and tight.

"Mark my words, they're going to have us back here next month, hauling in watering troughs and throwing hoses into that creek."

Amado, tugging the cable taut, grunted. "It splits, maybe a kilometer from here. One branch runs into the McGeochs' land. The cows can water from that."

Raul stared. "How do you know? We haven't worked this section before."

Amado knew because he had crossed this stream several times in the past weeks, headed up the mountain to meet with Isobel Christie in a high, sheltered meadow that straddled Christie and McGeoch land. Not that he was going to tell Raul that. "I followed the stream that runs past our bunkhouse one evening. I was curious."

Raul shaded his eyes against the strong rays of the morning sun as he followed the path of the water. "You're crazy. I wouldn't get off my bed if I weren't getting —" He took a step forward, then another.

"Hello there. Aren't you forgetting your buckets?"

"What's that?" Raul's voice sounded different. Amado holstered his wire cutters and walked over to where the other man stood, a scant foot away from the crumbling edge of the stream gully. Raul pointed. "There. You see that?"

Amado nodded. It was an odd shape, soft amid the sharp angles of rock and tree and spiky fern. Half hidden in a cluster of bushes and sucker vine. White and red against the brown and gray and green. He stooped, picked up a rock, and lobbed it as hard as he could toward the thing. A cloud of furious flies rose into the air. Something dead.

Raul's lips thinned. "A cow?"

"I don't think so." Amado stepped over the grassy edge, taking a moment to let his boot find a good firm hold in the gully's soil.

"What are you doing?"

"I'm going to take a look."

"Forget it! Whatever it is, it has nothing to do with us! Leave it alone!"

Amado ignored him, making his way down the steeply angled slope step by step, pausing when too much earth crumbled beneath his boots. He reached the water and walked downstream a few yards, until he reached a wide and shallow spot. He forded the stream the same way he descended into the wash, slowly and carefully.

Downstream and downwind, he could smell it. His nose wrinkled and he turned his head without meaning to, overwhelmed by the sour-sweet reek of corruption.

"You're crazy! You'll have the police out here! We'll have to hide in the woods again!"

Amado dipped his neckerchief in the water and held it close to his nostrils. It helped some. He hiked up to where the bushes were dug into the slope with knotted half-visible roots that looked like old men's fingers.

He saw the flat green leaves and the starburst clusters of tiny white flowers. He saw the pale birch saplings trembling in the mountain's exhalation. He saw the dead thing. He saw the bloat, and the burst skin, and the white bone and the gray brain. He saw the place where an animal had chewn off the cloth and started to —

He turned away. Closed his eyes and gritted his teeth against the acid rush of his stomach's contents. He retraced his steps downslope, recrossed the stream, and climbed the opposite side to the gully.

Raul just looked at him. He knew what it

was. He had known since he first spotted it. His eyes pleaded with Amado to ignore what they had found. "Let's just go," he whispered. "Finish the fence. We don't have to have seen anything."

Amado shook his head. The . . . thing caught in the underbrush may have had a family. Had a girl. Had friends. Somewhere, someone was praying. Waiting and hoping and dreading.

"Let's go get the truck," Amado said. "We have to go back."

IV

Clare attributed the sense that she was being watched to her general uneasiness. Standing in the McGeochs' barnyard, struggling to make light conversation with Russ Van Alstyne's sister, was not her idea of a fun way to spend a Friday morning. She kicked out her ankle-length skirt, surreptitiously checking to make sure she hadn't marked the black cotton with dust — or worse — from the barnyard. She had a Eucharist to celebrate at noon, and she didn't want to show up smelling like cow manure.

"So," Janet said. "I'm pleased Amado is working out for you. I mean, with his broken arm and all."

186

"Mmm." Where *was* the kid? Janet had called the bunkhouse's phone right after Clare arrived. That had been ten minutes ago. He knew they needed him at the church today. Or at least she thought he did. Giving him directions by reading out of a Spanish-English phrase book left room for misinterpretation.

"So . . . how's the lady who was driving them — him? The nun."

"Sister Lucia. She's in rehab in Glens Falls. Broken hip. She sounded mighty peeved about it when I called her. They're keeping a close eye on her. She was pretty banged up for a woman her age."

"Ah. Good." Janet shoved her hands in her jeans pockets. "Elizabeth's down in Albany for a conference?"

"Diaconate training." And what was with Janet? When they had met in the hospital, she had been to-the-point and self-assured. Very . . . Van Alstyne-like, Clare supposed. Now she was as jumpy as the proverbial long-tailed cat.

"It said in the paper you're having a choral concert tonight." Janet twisted around as she spoke, looking in the direction of the old bunkhouse, hidden from their view by the massive barn.

"Yeah. Last one of the season before the

choir disbands for the summer." Clare blinked. It wasn't her imagination. That shadow, the one between the side of the barn and the milk tank. It had moved. "Janet. Is that . . . Amado?"

The shadow detached itself from the barn and walked into the sunlight. No, not her employee. This clean-shaven man was a half-dozen years older, broader at the shoulders, with two whole muscular arms and the grimly determined expression of someone carrying out an unpleasant duty.

"My," Clare said. "You certainly got those legal replacement workers fast."

Janet's mouth opened. Clare could see her casting about for a denial. Then she shut her mouth. Her face collapsed into lines of guilt and anxiety. "You can't tell. I mean it, Clare, we could be seriously screwed if you told."

Clare sighed. "How long have they been here?"

"The first one got here the morning after the accident. The last one" — she flicked her fingers in the direction of the man crossing the barnyard toward them — "got in two days later."

"Did you check their papers?"

"Of course we did!" Janet ran her fingers through her blond hair. Clare could see where her roots were coming in, sandy brown and gray like her brother's. "They were all fakes. Just like the one Agent Hodgden showed us."

The man was almost to them. "Janet, have you and your husband thought this through? I mean, not just about the fines or what all you'll be liable for. What about Russ?"

"What about him?"

Clare put her hands on her hips. "Playing dumb doesn't suit you."

Janet exhaled. "He's not going to find out. We keep them out of sight if someone's here."

"Oh. You mean, like right now?"

"He's not supposed to come into the barnyard if he sees —" her voice switched abruptly from panic to control. *"Hola, Octavio. ¿Qué pasa?"*

"Señora McGeoch," he said. His dark eyes flickered toward Clare. She could see a resemblance to Amado, in his aristocratic cheekbones and his nose like an adze. She remembered what Paula Hodgden had said, about groups of men coming from the same village. If it was anything like Millers Kill, they were all related in some degree. "Señora Reverenda."

She nodded. *"Hola."*

"Raul y yo cercábamos el pasto lejano —"

189

He broke off. Looked at the expression of incomprehension on Janet's face, an expression Clare knew was mirrored on her own.

"I fix fence. *Encontré un hombre muerto.*" He spoke slowly and clearly. *"Hombre muerto."* He pointed past the barn, once, twice, three times. A long way that way.

Janet gaped. "A dead man?"

He nodded. "Dead." He held a finger like a gun next to the back of his head. "Man." He gestured toward himself, then expanded his arms, as if he were growing larger.

Bloating, Clare realized.

"Oh, my God." Janet's knees buckled. Clare and the man — Octavio — caught her by her arms. "Oh, my God," Janet repeated. "Oh, my God."

"Octavio," Clare said, *"El hombre es muerto con —"* she couldn't begin to guess the Spanish word for gun. She shifted, so she could support Janet with one hand, and made the same gesture he had, finger and thumb. *"¿Bang-bang?"*

His lips twitched, but he kept from smiling. *"Sí. Bang-bang. Allí hacia fuera lo están por un rato."* He pinched his nose and waved his hand in the air, as if dispelling a foul smell.

"No — uh, *¿Muerto naturale?*"

He shook his head. *"Bang-bang."* He

190

touched the back of his head again and, for a second, something moved behind his eyes. The photographic image of horror, that, Clare knew from personal experience, would never, ever leave him. She reached out and squeezed his forearm. He looked at her, surprised.

"Are you okay?" She hoped her quiet tone would convey everything she couldn't communicate with words.

His expression eased. "*Estoy bien. Gracias.* I am okay."

A nasty thought occurred to her. "Janet, are you sure every one of your missing workers showed up?"

Janet nodded. "Well, unless there was an extra man coming along they hadn't told us about."

"*El hombre. ¿Es anglo?* Or — um — *Latino? ¿Un amigo?*"

"*No Anglo. Latino. No amigo. Un extranjero.*"

"A stranger?" Clare said. The man — Octavio — looked at her steadily. Across the barrier of language, she suspected they were both thinking the same thing: *If it isn't one of the McGeochs' workers, who could it be?*

"Oh, my God," Janet said again. "Somebody's killed an illegal on our land. What am I going to do?"

Clare shook her. "First, you're going to

stand up." Janet took a deep breath and got her legs underneath her. "Then, you're going to call the police."

"I can't! What am I going to say? That my illegal employee whom I should have turned in to the ICE found a body on my property?"

Clare frowned, thinking. "It may not be important who found the body." She turned to Octavio. "Did you touch anything? Touch," she mimed poking, picking at, opening, *"el hombre?"*

He shook his head. Held up his hands. "No."

"Okay, then." She looked at Janet. "What was Octavio doing and where was he doing it?"

Janet took another deep breath. "He's our foreman. He and one of the other men were stringing electrical fencing. Out at the farthest pasture. About three miles from here, right up against the mountain."

"Is that a job you can do?"

"Of course." Janet's face cleared. "Of course! *I* was the one who found the body."

"Okay. Take Octavio with you to show you where, and as soon as he's done that, he can take off." There was a small voice in the back of her head suggesting that none of this was a good idea. She ignored it.

"I can stop by the bunkhouse on the way out and tell the hands to hide."

Clare raised her eyebrows. "They're in the bunkhouse?"

Janet looked down at her sneakers. "That's the drill if anyone pulls into the barnyard. Get out the back of the barn as quickly as possible and go to the bunkhouse."

Clare shook her head. "You have got to find some way of getting these guys papers. There's no way you can carry on like this for the entire summer." She rubbed at the back of her neck, where sweat was gathering beneath her dog collar. "I suppose Amado is hiding out there?"

The foreman looked at her.

"Yeah," Janet said.

"Well, tell him it's okay to come out. We've got to get the church cleaned for the Eucharist and then ready for the concert tonight."

Janet clutched Clare's arm. "You can't go!"

"Janet, you don't need me. Let Octavio show you where the body is, and then as soon as he's out of sight, call the MKPD."

"I need you to call them for me!"

"Me? Why?"

"Because I'm a terrible liar. You'll be able to do it so much more convincingly."

Boy, if that didn't win the prize for back-handed compliments. She thought of another summer, Russ, grinning at her from the driver's seat of his pickup. *You're pretty sneaky, for a priest.*

"Please, Clare. Please, please, please."

"Oh, good Lord." She tilted her head up toward the clear blue sky. "All right. I'll give you ten minutes to get there, and then I'll call. But I think it's muddying the waters unnecessarily."

"Thank you!" Janet hugged her, hard. "Cell phones can get tricky out here. Go ahead and use the phone in the tack room." She whirled and, beckoning to the foreman to follow her, vanished around the barn. A moment later, Clare heard an engine fire up.

It struck her that she was going to be on the fringes of a police investigation. Again. The bishop was not going to be happy with her. Her deacon was not going to be happy with her. Russ was most definitely not going to be happy with her.

That thought, at least, cheered her up. She headed into the barn to find the phone.

V

"Fifteen fifty-seven, this is Dispatch."

Russ slowed behind an eighteen-wheeler

signaling to turn into the Wal-Mart. He nodded to the officer riding beside him. "Go ahead. Pick it up."

Hadley Knox unclipped the mic and switched it on. "Fifteen fifty-seven, go ahead, Dispatch."

"What's your forty?"

"Uh . . . Morningside Drive, headed toward Fort Henry."

Outside the garden shop at the Wal-Mart, they had wading pools and riding mowers. He shook his head. Memorial Day was less than a week away. It had only been a little over four months, and they had already slid through two seasons. Was this how it was going to be for the rest of his life? Him, pinned to a snow-ravaged crossroads in January while the world reeled about him?

Harlene's voice slammed his book of remonstrance shut. "We have a report of human remains found on the property at Three-fifteen Lick Springs Road."

Knox stared at the mic. "Human remains? You mean, like a dead body?"

Russ should have corrected her response, but he was too busy trying to envision the farms along the Lick Springs Road. He had a bad feeling he wasn't going to like this. He gestured for the mic. "Harlene," he said, "isn't that my brother-in-law's new place?"

"You got it, Chief."

Christ on a bicycle. That spread had more trouble attached to it than the Dew Drop Inn on a Saturday night. "What do we know?"

"Possible gunshot victim. Latino. Not fresh. No identification as yet."

"Latino?" His stomach soured. Christ. None of the men who had fled the van wreck had been spotted since that night in April. What if one of them had been hurt bad? Not fresh. Yeah, a month-plus out in the open would definitely be not fresh.

"You call the ME?"

"Doc Scheeler from the Glens Falls Hospital is covering for Dr. Dvorak. He's on his way now, along with the bag boys."

"I want Lyle to run the Lost-and-Missing and have it ready for me when I get back."

"He's already on it."

"And get hold of that ICE agent who was supposed to follow up on the missing guest workers." Maybe whoever found the body had been mistaken. Nobody liked to look at a ripe one any longer than necessary — especially his brother-in-law, a guy who got upset when their barn cat killed a mouse. "Who called it in, Mike McGeoch?"

There was a pause. "I believe Mrs. McGeoch found the body."

196

He sighed. "We're on our way. Fifteen fifty-seven out." He switched on the light bar and stepped on the gas.

"She said gunshot victim. Does that mean it's a homicide?" He stole a glance at his newest officer. Unlike Kevin Flynn, who would be sparking like a live wire at the thought of responding to a violent crime, Knox just looked sick.

"It *may be* a gunshot victim. My sister — Mrs. McGeoch — isn't any expert. I'd rather go in there with an open mind and see what the scene and the ME can tell us. It could be an accident, suicide — lots of possibilities."

"Oh."

He glanced at her again. "You ever see a dead body before?"

"My grandmother. At the funeral home. I'm guessing this one won't be laid out on satin with an ugly arrangement of carnations draped over him."

Okay. If she could keep her sense of humor, she'd be fine. "Why don't you tell me what we need to do and what we'll be looking for once we get there."

She went through the list with minimal prodding from him, and by the time they emerged from the mountain road into the bright sunshine spilling across the valley he felt confident she could handle herself without a lot of babysitting on his part.

"Is that your sister's house?" Knox asked, pointing to the bungalow ahead.

"No, she and her husband live a few miles down the road. This farm's a new addition to —" He broke off. Janet's car was parked on a denuded piece of earth angled between the massive central barn and the silos, and right next to it was a bright red Subaru WRX. As he pulled in, he saw the old bumper stickers, THE EPISCOPAL CHURCH WELCOMES YOU and MY OTHER CAR IS AN OH-58 had been joined by JESUS IS COMING: LOOK BUSY. His throat felt thick with anticipation and dread.

"Isn't that Reverend Clare's car?" Knox asked. Her eyes went round. "Oh," she said. "Sorry."

He killed the engine. Turned to look at his juniormost officer, who had the same expression he'd expect to find if she'd lost the key to the evidence locker.

"Sorry? What for?"

She had one of those birthstone rings on her finger. She twisted it around in a circle, not meeting his eyes. "Um," she said. "Deputy Chief MacAuley told me not to mention the Reverend around you."

Sweet tap-dancing Jesus. "He did, huh?"

She nodded. "Or St. Alban's."

He opened the door and got out. Popped the locker and retrieved the backpack with their basic evidence kit and a fistful of bright purple non-latex gloves. She got out on her side, and he tossed her a pair. "You don't happen to know if that suggestion was just for you or for the whole department, do you?"

She shrugged, clearly wishing she had never brought the matter up.

Christ only knew what MacAuley had told the rest of the force. Either that he'd break down sobbing or go postal at any reminder of his . . . his former relationship.

Beloved, his inner voice corrected.

He shook it off. "Officer Knox. In the future, please feel free to talk about the reverend, or St. Alban's, or any other citizen or organization in town. Nobody is off limits to me."

Clare is.

The small side door of the central barn swung open, and she emerged. After picturing her in her BDUs for the past month, he was startled to see her sober clericals: black skirt, black blouse, white collar, silver cross. He became aware of Knox's nervous glance toward him at the same moment he realized he was staring.

"Reverend Fergusson," he said.

"Chief Van Alstyne." She looked at Knox and smiled. "Hi, Hadley. I thought you were teamed up with Officer Flynn."

Knox shook her head. "That was just the one time. Usually, I ride with one of the older officers."

"Mmm." She glanced at Russ, and her eyes lit with a well-worn private joke. "There're few older than Chief Van Alstyne."

"Don't start with me," he said, irrationally pleased that she was teasing him. He glanced over her shoulder, toward the gaping entrance to the barn. "Where's Janet?"

"I believe she's going to meet you halfway and show you the location of the body. It's at the far end of the property, where the new electrical fencing is going up."

"What are you doing here? Please don't tell me you were with her when she found it."

Clare shook her head. "I came to pick up Amado."

He looked at her blankly.

"The kid with the broken arm? Our interim sexton."

Oh, yeah. A fourteen-dollar name for the temporary janitor. "I remember."

"Janet asked me to call it in and wait

for . . . whoever showed up. She said cell phones rarely work out there."

"Did she give you a description of what she saw?"

Clare paused. When she spoke, she spoke as if dictating for an unseen recorder. "The body is a male Latino, bloated, with damage to the back of the skull that might be from a gunshot wound."

"Did she recognize him as one of the missing workers?"

She shook her head. "No. She was sure it wasn't one of them."

"How?"

She blanked. "Uh . . . pictures?"

"Anything else? Description? Clothing?"

"No. Janet was pretty upset." She looked into his eyes. "Go easy on her when you talk to her, okay?"

"As easy as I can."

She nodded. Turned and pointed to the other side of the barn. "There's a two-rut road running between the big barn and those outbuildings that leads toward the mountain. She took that."

A black GMC Scout slowed on the road and turned into the barnyard, doglegging tight to park on the other side of Janet's car. Russ didn't recognize the car, but he wasn't surprised to see the Glens Falls pathologist get out. By his jeans and WASH-INGTON COUNTY SOFTBALL LEAGUE T-shirt, Russ deducted they had interrupted Scheeler's Saturday morning game.

"Chief Van Alstyne." Scheeler crossed toward their small group. "Good to see you again." He shook Russ's hand. The clip-bearded pathologist radiated the kind of intellectual intensity Russ associated with revolutionaries and Jesuits. Now he trained that intensity on Russ. "I was so sorry to hear about your wife. It must have been a great loss."

"Yes. Thank you." Russ inhaled. "You haven't met our newest officer, Hadley Knox." Knox and the pathologist shook hands. "And this is the Reverend Clare Fergusson."

Scheeler's dark eyebrows went up as he shook Clare's hand. "Are you the one who found the decedent, Ms. Fergusson?"

Russ answered for her. "No. Unfortunately, that was my sister."

Scheeler's attention returned to him. "You do have a small town here, don't you? Is this going to be awkward?"

Only if she killed the guy. He pinched the bridge of his nose. Why had he come back to his hometown for this job? He knew there had been a reason, but damned if he could remember it.

"I arrested my mother a couple years ago," Russ said. "I figure I can handle questioning my sister. If I have to rough her up, I'll just ask Officer Knox to take over."

"Chief?" Knox's eyes went round again.

"He's joking, Hadley." Clare gave him a we-are-not-amused look. Scheeler's black eyes glinted. Russ gestured toward the Scout with his head.

"Does that thing have four-wheel drive?"

"It wouldn't do me much good in the winter if it didn't."

"Can we take it? We have to get across a few pastures to the site, and our squad car isn't built for off-roading."

"As long as I can bill the town for the car wash afterward."

"You got it," Russ said. "Throw in a wax, too."

"Do we need to wait for the State Crime Scene truck?"

"We haven't called them in yet. You're here to help us figure out if this *is* a crime scene."

Scheeler nodded. "Let's go see, then. Officer Knox?" The pathologist ushered the young officer toward the SUV.

Russ turned toward Clare. "I know asking you to stay away is a lost cause, but —"

She raised her hands. "My part in this is done. I'm collecting Amado and heading back to St. Alban's. I —"

"No, no, no!"

"What?"

"Your interim sexton is the only person I have who might be able to ID our body. I need him."

"Why? Because he's Latino? I told you, the dead man isn't one of the missing workers."

"How do you know?"

"I —" She poked at her hair, twisted into a knot at the back of her head. Her eyes slid past him to examine the silos. He frowned. She wasn't being straight with him.

"Clare . . . ?"

"I don't know," she blurted out. "But I really do need Amado. We have to get the church cleaned up after the noon Eucharist and ready for the choir concert tonight, and then put it back to rights after the concert." She glanced at her watch, a steel-edged Seiko hanging from a much-worse-for-wear khaki strap. "He should be done for the afternoon by three or four. Could you wait until then?"

He exhaled. "I'll send someone by St. Alban's to pick him up. *If* you promise me you won't discuss anything you know with him beforehand."

"I promise," she said, holding up two fingers like a Girl Scout. "Most of our communicating is done via the *Pocket Guide to Useful Spanish Phrases,* anyway."

"Yeah? How useful is it?"

"It would be great if I needed to tell him how long I wanted a hotel room or rental car. It's a little thin on 'Help me move this pew' and 'Can you vacuum here?' "

He snorted. "I bet. Look, what time do you need him back?"

"The concert's from seven to eight, so —" She frowned. "Wait a minute. It doesn't take four hours to identify a body."

"I may need to ask him a few questions."

"A few questions! The boy doesn't know a word of English."

"Entonces es una buena cosa que sé hablar español."

She looked at him, suspicion glittering green in her hazel eyes. "I want you to promise me you'll accord him the same rights and warnings you would any English-speaking citizen."

"What do you think I'd do?"

"I don't know. But I know you. You've got an unexplained dead man in your town, and that's going to ride you and ride you like a jockey with a whip until you can figure out

205

who and what and where and why. I don't want my poor sexton getting trampled because he's in the way."

He blinked. *I know you.* "Okay," he said.

"Okay?"

"I won't treat your guy any different than I would anyone else."

Her mouth quirked, one-sided. "I'm not sure that's a comfort."

"You know what I mean."

She nodded. "Yes. I do." Their words hung in the air like dust motes floating through the late-morning sun. He had that sense that he only ever got around Clare, that they were saying one thing and talking about something entirely different.

"So." She studied her watch. Glanced toward the barn. "I guess I'll see you around."

"Yeah." He took a step toward the waiting Scout. Turned back toward her. "How have you been?"

She looked surprised. "Good. I've been good. Keeping busy. Last Sunday was Pentecost, that's a big one, and this evening we've got the concert, and then the parish picnic is coming up next week, so . . . busy. Good." She looked at him, with her eyes that always seemed to say *You can tell me anything, and it'll be all right.* "You?"

"I'm doing okay. Still at my mom's for the time being."

She nodded. "I bet that helps. Both of you."

"Yeah. I —" *Miss you.* He cleared his throat.

"*¿Señora Reverenda?*" They both turned to see the young man they had been discussing lope across the barnyard, a small duffel bag clutched in his good hand.

"This way, Señor Esfuentes." Clare pointed toward her car, already moving, already leaving him. "Sorry," she called over her shoulder. "I can't be late for the noon Eucharist. Say hi to your mother for me." And then she was gone, slipping into her Subaru, starting up the engine before the kid had even shut his door. Eager to get away from him. Not that he could blame her.

The Scout honked. Knox powered down the window. "Are you coming, Chief?"

He nodded. Better this way. He climbed into the backseat. "Let's go," he said.

VI

She had worried about not knowing what to do. She had worried about not fouling the scene. She had worried about looking like a raw newbie with nothing but the fig leaf of eight weeks of classes to cover her.

What she should have worried about was her breakfast.

"You all right?" Chief Van Alstyne patted her back. In response, the rest of her stomach lurched up and out and spattered onto the ferns and grass at the creek's edge. Oh, God.

"Nothing to be embarrassed about," he said. "We've all done it."

From her doubled-over vantage point, Hadley saw jeans and sneakers approaching. "He throws up all the time," Mrs. McGeoch said. Now that Hadley had fallen apart, the chief's sister seemed a whole lot calmer. "Here. Water from the truck. It's clean." Hadley squirted a cupful into her mouth. It was hot and tasted of plastic. She bent over again and spat it into the creek.

"I do not," the chief said, over her back.

"You do, too. You throw up when you're stressed."

"If I threw up when I was stressed I wouldn't be able to leave the damn bathroom for more than ten minutes at a time."

Hadley straightened. "Sorry," she croaked.

"Don't worry about it," the chief said. She heard the snapping of footsteps through the brush and then Scheeler's voice.

"If we didn't vomit five or six times the

first year of medical school, the professors didn't think they were doing their job."

Hadley wiped her mouth with her sleeve and turned toward the pathologist, keeping her eyes on him so as not to glimpse the bloated, fly-blasted corpse.

"I remember this one old coot," he went on, "used to have us drink urine. We were supposed to be able to —"

The chief peered at her face. "I don't think that's the best topic of conversation right now."

"Oh. Right. All right, then, let's talk about John Doe, here. Or maybe we should call him Juan Doe."

"That *is* a gunshot wound, isn't it?" the chief said.

Scheeler nodded. "The occipital entry point has been enlarged by animal depredation" — Hadley's stomach lurched again when she translated the med-speak as *animals ate his brains* — "but there's no doubt. I suspect, from the lack of any anterior damage, I'll be digging out a small load. Maybe a twenty-two."

"Knox." The chief's voice, addressing her, caused her to snap to. "Tell me what you can infer from what Doctor Scheeler here has told us."

"Uh. . . ." She took a deep breath. The

surfaces of things seemed hallucinogenically bright; the sun bouncing off the chief's uniform buttons, the razor edges of the willow leaves drooping toward the ground. "A twenty-two. Not much stopping power. Whoever killed him would have had to have been pretty close."

"Do you think it could have been a hunting accident?"

"Do people hunt with twenty-twos?" Scheeler snorted.

"Yes," the chief said, his voice patient.

"Uh . . . no. A hunting accident would mean someone mistook him for an animal from a distance, or discharged their weapon up close by mistake. A shot in the back of the skull doesn't jibe with either of those."

"Good."

She was surprised to find she felt better.

"I very much doubt that the guy was a farmworker, not with two-hundred dollar sneakers and that trendy jacket. So what was he doing out here?"

"Flynn told me Mexicans sell most of the pot up here. Maybe he was a dealer?"

"The gangs dominate wholesale distribution. They have networks of locals who do the retailing."

"Maybe a carnie from Lake George?" the pathologist suggested.

"Maybe. I'm going to put in a call to the state CSI, see if we can get Morin or Haynes over here with the van. I want you to get up to the top of that rise in the woods —" the chief pointed to where the mountain first flanked up from the creek bed — "and start working downward. You're looking for anything: fiber, hair, impressions, cartridges."

She nodded.

"Do you think he was rolled from above?" Scheeler asked.

"Can you assure me he didn't drop where Janet found him?"

The pathologist shook his head. "It's been at least a month. His blood patterns are gone."

"It's a funny spot to be hanging around, waiting to get shot. But if he got tapped up there, he might easily roll until he lodged against that bush." He turned toward his sister, who was hanging back at the edge of the stream. "Janet, is that still your property?"

"Yeah. It goes back into the hills a ways, until you see some blaze markers. It's useless land."

The chief's mouth thinned. "Not entirely. It's a pretty good place to hide a murder."

VII

So far, Hadley hadn't found much in common between her old job guarding cons and her new job policing them, but working the crime scene was just like watching the cell block during open hour: a combination of detailed observation and mind-numbing boredom. Under Van Alstyne's direction, she squatted in the grass and scrub brush, parting saplings and peering under dock leaves for some bit of evidence. She worked her way up to where the chief stood, surmounting a heavily wooded rise. He did a 360, taking in the thick forest behind them and the fields spreading out below.

"Who the hell was this guy?" She didn't think he was speaking to her. "Damn, I want a look at the lost-and-missing file."

Across the stream, at the top of the bluff, the state CSI van had pulled in. A figure emerged from the driver's side. The chief pointed. "Knox, get over there and help Morin with his gear."

She thudded down the hill, picked her way across the stream, and climbed up to the van. Sergeant Morin of the NYSPD shook her hand, looked at her chest, stuttered a hello, and had her take one end of a footlocker-sized box. They staggered down to the stream, heels digging into the crumbling earth, the flesh at the back of Hadley's neck creeping and itching the closer they got to the body.

"Do you know if anybody moved him?" Morin asked.

Her eyes involuntarily went to the John Doe. "The chief thinks he might have rolled. . . ." Her voice trailed off.

Dr. Scheeler glanced up at her. "Uh-oh," he said.

"No." She shook her head. "It's not that. His hand." She could only see one. The other was rubber-banded inside a brown paper bag. "The tattoos. The symbols on his fingers. I saw two guys with the same tattoo. Last night."

VIII

The barn was on the edge of a pasture ringed with woods, the last things left, he guessed, from a long-ago homestead that hadn't worked out. From his side, a half-hidden trail led down the mountain, over the stream, and onto the McGeochs' land. On her side, a rutted sheep-churned path broad enough to admit a hay cart. Leading, he guessed, to her home.

The barn stood beside an oval fire pond levied up around a creek some long-ago summer. From inside the open doorway,

Amado watched the sluggish trickle, water in through one bank, out through the other.

The first time Isobel had brought him here had been a few hours before dawn, the night they met. She had left him there, to sleep away the morning, and when she'd returned that afternoon, they had found a fox skeleton against the cut-stone foundation. The skull, smooth and yellow-white, was their signal. Right now, it hung on a nail on the pasture-side door, letting her know, if she saw it, that he was here. Waiting for her.

It was a pole barn, straight up and down, designed for one thing: to store hay against the hard, long winter. The doorways, front and back, were set hay-wagon high, and he had to haul himself up to the edge and then climb a stack of square bales before getting to his feet. Then he could either climb again, to sit on one of the massive beams transversing the barn, or spread out the quilt she had left on the mound of loose hay in the corner. He usually chose the beam or sat cross-legged on the hard bales. The soft mow and the quilt were too casual, too . . . sexual. No need to chase temptation.

This had been her special place before she had ever shown it to him. She had a crate filled with books, CDs, a CD player, and water bottles. He knew she smoked here, too, though she never did so in front of him; there was a lingering smell of marijuana above the green and dusty scent of the new and old hay.

He balanced on the beam and peeked through the small off-center window that looked out over the pasture. His rib cage lifted, expanded, when he spotted her making her way across the field, stepping over sheep droppings and swishing at early daisies. It was stupid, he knew. Stupid and dangerous. At home, if she had been one of them, he could have courted her, met her brothers, taken her to his parents' home. Here, they couldn't even be seen together.

No, it was more than that. Here, he couldn't let himself think about her in that way. She was anglo, a North American, part of a family that owned, as near as he could tell from their halting conversations, an entire mountain and the rolling farmlands around it. And she was tangled in darkness and violence. If he hadn't gotten that message on the night they met, he would have figured it out today, when Raul had stumbled across a murdered man halfway between her property and the McGeochs'. No. She was out of bounds, for more reasons than he could count.

It wasn't as if she were a great beauty. She was too pale, the bones in her face too square. It was, he guessed, because she reminded him of girls he had admired at home. She was rounded, womanly, but tough. A hard worker. Quick to smile, but not cheap and available, like so many of the women up north. And she needed him, needed his strength, in some way he hadn't yet identified.

She vanished from his line of sight, to re-appear in a moment at the back door, swinging a paper sack up onto the hay before lifting herself over the edge of the doorway. "Amado?" She blinked in the dimmed light. "I have lunch. Um, *la comida.*"

He dropped down from the beam. "Oh!" She clapped her hand to her chest and said something in English too rapid for him to follow. He held his hand to his ear. "Eh?" he said.

"Eh?" She laughed.

"Lunch," he said. "I am hungry."

"*¿Yo hambre?*"

"*Tengo hambre,*" he corrected. He grabbed the quilt and snapped it open, letting it float down on the hay bales to make a picnic cloth. She opened the sack and removed

216

paper napkins and sandwiches and corn chips and apples. They sat on opposite sides. Not touching. The sandwich was delicious, real bread stuffed thick with meat and cheese. He wondered if she had made it for him or taken one that was meant for another of her family. He wondered if she felt the high, hard bars that kept them apart. He wondered what she thought of him when she was alone.

"*Por qué* . . . you . . . here now?" she said, around a handful of corn chips. "No work *por la día?*"

"Hide," he said. He swallowed the last of his sandwich. He didn't know if he was bringing trouble to her door, or if he was helping her avoid it, but he had to tell her about the dead man. It was too near to her land and too soon after her flight through the woods to be coincidental.

He spoke in Spanish, wanting to tell the whole story before trying to pick out the words and concepts he could convey to her in English. He told her about the smell, and the way it seemed to linger inside his nostrils all the way back to the barnyard. He told her about the surprise of seeing his brother Octavio's lady priest, and Mrs. Mc-Geoch's near collapse, and about rounding up the men — again — and having to deal with their whining about the heat and boredom of the ancient farmhouse they bunked in. He told her about hiding in the woods until the last possible moment, watching the black truck roll up and disgorge two *policía.*

All the while, she listened intently, though he doubted she understood one word in ten. And when he finished, she tilted her head to one side, looked at him as if she knew exactly what he'd been going through, and said, "I'm sorry. *Lo siento.*"

He took a deep breath. "I find a dead man," he said in English. "By the water."

Isobel went very still. No surprise. No horror. Instead, her eyes, usually as brown and deep as rich coffee, went flat. As if she was looking in, rather than out. "By the water," she said. "Where? *¿Dónde es?*"

He didn't know the English word, so he made rippling, winding motions. *"El arroyo."* He arched his hand up and over, representing the mountain, then traced the water's course along the imaginary edge of the property.

She drew her knees up and bent her head forward. Her face disappeared behind a curtain of hair. *"¿La policía?"* she asked, after a while.

"Yes." He felt sick at the thought she had

something to do with the bloated thing he had seen that morning, but he had to curl his hands into fists to keep from taking her by the shoulders and drawing her near. She looked up at him. Her eyes shone with tears. She said something low and rapid he couldn't make out, and he realized, at bottom, it didn't matter what she had done, he would still help her in any way he could.

"I help you," he said.

She shook her head.

"Please," he said.

She smiled, just a little, and the change in her expression broke the water in her eyes so that tears rolled down her cheeks. She said something else — he caught the word "man" and the word "good" — and then reached out and took one of his hands in hers.

He squeezed it. "I help you," he insisted.

She looked at him for a long moment. Finally, she nodded. "Okay." She rose, tugging him up with her. She released his hand, scooped up the empty paper sack, and walked across the bales to the open doorway. She jumped to the ground with an easy grace, and he followed her as she slipped around the corner. She stopped, dropped the sack on the grass, and traced the edges of the clapboards where they butted against the stone foundation.

Isobel tugged one of the peeling boards. "Help me," she said. He stood beside her, wedged his fingers into the narrow gap between one board and the next, and pulled. Once, twice, and a four-foot section of board came off, reeling him backward. She plunged her hands into the narrow slice of darkness. There was something odd about it, a space where there shouldn't have been any more than a few inches to the interior lathing, but before he could get close enough to study it, she hauled out the biggest, ugliest pistol he had ever seen and thrust its butt end toward him.

He dropped it. *"¡De qué joder!"*

She was still digging around inside the gap. He stared at the gun, horrified. She dragged something else from the interior and turned toward him. She had a hard-covered writing tablet in one hand and a cell phone in the other. She followed his gaze to the gun. Her eyes widened. Whatever she said was unintelligible to him, but he got the gist of it. He grabbed the thing awkwardly, trying not to touch the trigger, the barrel, or the grip. He wound up pinching it between two white-jointed, sweat-slick fingers, as if he were holding a dead rat that weighed eight pounds. He eased the gun into the sack. He had no idea if it was ready to fire or not. He didn't even know how to check to see if it was loaded.

She dropped the notebook on the grass. Considered the sleek, flat cell phone in the other. Finally, she shoved it into her jeans pocket. Reaching back inside the space, she emerged with a large padded envelope, the kind of thing used to post books or small presents. She pressed against the sides, popping the top open and tipped it upside down over the paper bag. With a mixture of fascination and repulsion, he watched as brick after brick of American cash thudded into the sack.

She bent down, retrieved the writing tablet, and stuffed it into the mailer. She put it back into her hiding space. Picked up the board and fitted it over the gap. Wedged it back into place.

The sack was still dangling, open, from his nerveless fingers. Isobel took it and rolled its edges down until it resembled an oversized lunch bag. She held it out to him. "Hide," she said.

God almighty above. He looked at the unremarkable brown paper sack in his hand. Looked at her face, full of desperation and fear and hope. "Isobel," he said. He cradled her cheek in one hand. How could he ask her what he wanted to know? *Did you kill that man? Is this your gun?*

"Amado." Only a whisper between them. Then she stepped toward him and not even that remained. Slowly, shyly, she wrapped her arms around him. He dropped the sack. Cupped her face in both hands.

He didn't know what made him tear his eyes away from her, toward the woods at the other end of the pasture. An instinct for self-preservation forged during two illegal crossings, maybe. Whatever it was, he looked — and saw a burly, blond Anglo framed in the footpath's opening. Even from that distance, he could tell the man was related to Isobel.

"Mierda," he whispered.

Isobel whirled. Inhaled. Turned to him. "Go," she said.

He shook his head. He wasn't about to leave her to face her family alone. "No. You come."

"Please! Go! Vamanose!" She glanced back over her shoulder. Said something fast and full of despair. She pushed at him. "Please, Amado, please. Go. No come back. I okay."

"No!"

She dragged him around the corner of the barn, out of sight of the approaching man, and pinned him in place with her body. "You no come back! I okay. He —" She struggled to find a word, then sliced her finger across her throat. Then she leaped over all those high bars and good reasons keeping them apart as easily as she jumped from the haymow and kissed him.

Time stopped in an endless moment of soft and wet and the taste of coffee and corn chips. His breath caught and his eyes fluttered shut, and then she pulled away and shoved him toward the woods. He tucked the sack under his arm and ran, his mind fogged, until the thrash of branches and the sawing of his own breath alerted him to the fact that a blind man could follow the noisy trail he was making. He stopped, chest heaving. Wait. He had to make sure she was all right.

He doubled back toward the barn, slipping between hemlocks and birch trees. He stayed low, sticking to shadows and scrub brush. He spotted a deadfall pine, moldering into the forest floor, and he dropped belly-down next to it.

He could hear them, faintly, the big man bellowing and Isobel yelling. He was demanding, she was defying — that Amado got from the pitch of their voices. Then — *oh, God* — there was the meaty sound of flesh hitting flesh. Isobel shrieked. He heard it again. He was up from his hiding place, up and moving, his hand flailing at the paper bag, reaching for the gun, when he heard her, over the sound of his thudding feet.

"Amado!" He skidded to a stop. She wasn't calling his name. She was . . . naming him. He moved closer, tree to tree to tree. He could hear her, sobbing. "Amado, okay?" she said. Then more — between the weeping and the English, he couldn't make it out — but he heard her say "McGeochs" clear enough.

His fingers curled around the butt of the gun. Through the leaves, he could make out the top half of the barn. He dropped the sack and fell to his stomach again, crawling through the underbrush until he could see.

Isobel was curled on the ground, trapped between the barn and the big man. She had both arms wrapped around her in futile protection. She shook with sobs. Her lip was bleeding. Amado brought the gun up and sighted it. The bastard's back was wide enough; even an inexperienced shot couldn't miss.

Then Isobel's attacker bent over and scooped her up. He cradled her tenderly, making soothing noises, stroking her back and hair. She clung to the monster, still weeping, and buried her face in his shoulder.

Amado lowered the gun. He turned away, fighting to keep his gorge down. He knew what that was. He had seen it before. There were a few women in his village whose husbands would beat them Saturday night and woo them Sunday morning. But he was sure Isobel was unmarried. A brother, then? Or an uncle? He stared at the gun in his hand, heavy and unfamiliar, and almost dropped it again. Sweet mother of Christ. Had the bearded giant been hitting Isobel because he had seen her with a dark-skinned man? Or because *this* was missing?

Hide, she had said. *Hide.* He bent, scooped up the sack he had dropped, and replaced the gun inside. Slowly, carefully, he threaded his way through the trees. Back toward the McGeochs' land. To do what she had asked him to do.

IX

The first person Kevin ran into as he snuck into the station that afternoon was the deputy chief. "What the hell are you doin' here?" MacAuley asked.

"Uh . . . I wanted to get in a little early for my shift."

"An hour early? Damn, boy, your hair's still wet."

"I showered at the gym. I was working out."

MacAuley's caterpillar eyebrows went up. "You. Were working out." He thwacked Kevin on the chest with a manila folder. "I thought you were more into pickup basketball games."

Kevin shrugged.

MacAuley shook his head and looked upward, to where acoustic tiles covered the hallway's original plaster ceiling. "God help us all," he said. He thumbed toward the briefing room. "May as well get back there. You can tell the chief about your stop last night."

"My what?"

MacAuley looked at him impatiently. "You stopped to pick up Knox, right? Ran plates on a Hummer driven by a guy with tattoos? A corpse cake turned up this morning in the woods off of Lick Springs Road. Matching marks on his hands. La-ti-no." He rolled his eyes. "Not PC to say *Mexican* anymore. Hunh. Maybe I'll start calling myself a Hibernian-American."

"I think you mean Caledonian-American, Dep. Hibernian-American would be Irish. Like me." By the look on MacAuley's face, that last "like me" might have been overdoing it.

"Get in there, before I go Irish on your ass."

Kevin hustled into the squad room, grinning to himself. To be rewarded by the sight of *her,* seated at the big table, studying a series of photos.

"Hey, Hadley," he said, his voice a pitch-perfect blend of friendly and casual. He had practiced in his Aztek on the way over.

"Hey, Flynn." She didn't take her eyes off the pictures.

"You can call me Kevin, you know."

That made her glance up. "I don't think so."

"What are you doing here so early?" The voice made him jump. Oh. Yeah. There was somebody else in the room. Kevin turned toward the bulletin board, where the chief was tacking up rap sheets. "Never mind," he continued, "Come here and tell me if you recognize any of these."

Kevin crossed to the board. The sheets had the familiar formatting of the NYS VCAP database. Eight young Latinos stared at him, captured by booking photographers in Brooklyn and Manhattan and the Bronx: defiant, stoned, sullen, smirking. Kevin tapped the smirking face. "That's the one I had to chase off. He doesn't have his piercings in this shot" — he touched his upper lip — "but that's him." He leaned closer to read the guy's short list. Fresh out of Plattsburgh, less than four months ago. Three possessions, carrying concealed, auto theft, assault, and assault with a deadly weapon. Possible associate of the Punta Diablos. No wonder he'd intimidated Hadley.

The chief grunted. "Knox ID'd him as well. Anybody else?"

Kevin closed his eyes for a moment. Tried to re-create the moment in his mind: his lights on Hadley's car, the men, two on either side as he drove up. One pair scuttling for the Hummer before he had gotten out of his cruiser. Leaving his rig twisted frontward some, so the big block of his Colt .44 could make an impression. The littler rat-faced guy squinting at his gun. Panicked.

He opened his eyes again. Pointed. "That one. He was with, uh —" he leaned forward to read the smirking guy's name — "Alejandro Santiago."

"You smell anything on 'em?"

"Nope."

Hadley looked at them, one eyebrow lifted.

"Pot," Kevin explained. "Like we talked about." He turned back to the chief. "Lyle says we've got a dead body?"

"Mmm." The chief's face was abstracted as he studied the two sheets.

"One of these guys?" Kevin gestured to the board.

"I don't think so. We don't have an ID yet, but he's been dead at least a month, maybe more, and we've got confirmation from the First District Anti-Gang Task Force that all these charmers were alive and well as of the beginning of this month, when they reported in to their parole officers. We're interested in the group in the car because Officer Knox said Santiago and one other guy had prison tats on their fingers that look very much like the ones on our John Doe."

"Just like," Hadley muttered.

The chief crossed to the table and picked up one of the photos. It was a close-up of a human hand, puffed up like a rubber-glove balloon, with what looked like gang tags between the knuckles and first joints. "Do these look familiar to you?"

Kevin shook his head. "No."

"I mean, do they look like the tattoos on Alejandro Santiago?"

Kevin glanced at Hadley. "I — uh, didn't see any tattoos, Chief. I may not have been close enough."

"I just want to make sure Officer Knox isn't accidentally conflating two different things. There's no mention of any hand or finger markings on either of these sheets."

"He had prison tats on his hands," Hadley said. "I worked in the California DOC for two years. Believe me, the ballpoint special is distinctive." She turned to Kevin. "I told you last night, remember? About how they were inked in?"

Oh, crap. "I — uh . . ."

The chief gave him a long look. "Kevin? Did Officer Knox describe any tattoos to you?"

"No," he said. *Shit.* "She didn't say anything about tattoos at the time." He grabbed at a straw. "But she was real shaken up by the whole thing. I wouldn't expect her to remember every little detail."

"Mmm." The chief turned toward Hadley, who was clench-jawed and rigid. "Kevin's got a point. You've been in two high-stress situations, back-to-back. It may be you're creating links where there aren't any. Not intentionally," he added, holding up his hands. "That's just the way people are. We all go looking for patterns."

"Like those trick abstract prints where the dots and dashes make you see a human face," Kevin said.

"Yes. Thank you, Kevin."

Too late, he realized that wasn't going to make Hadley feel any better. "I know what I saw," she said. "And I saw those markings" — she jammed a finger against the photo the chief was still holding — "on that man." Her arm swept toward the bulletin board, where Santiago's picture was displayed.

"We're still going to follow up on the guys in the car." The chief dropped the photo back into the file. "We have one dead Latino with gang markings, and two live Latinos with possible gang connections up from the Bronx. It's a pretty thin connection, but it's the only string we've got."

"I wanna know what the hell they were doing in Millers Kill." Lyle MacAuley strolled into the squad room. "Recruiting?"

The chief looked unsettled at the suggestion. "This isn't the Latin Kings or Los Traveosos. The AGTF classifies them as known associates, that's all. Besides, most gangs tend to be racially cohesive. Last I looked, Millers Kill and its surrounds didn't have much in the way of a Hispanic population."

"You're not looking hard enough. Every fourth farm in the county has Mexicans working for 'em nowadays." MacAuley handed the chief a mug of coffee. The chief took it and blew across the top. MacAuley cocked an eyebrow. "You don't think some of those farmhands up here for a crack at the good life wouldn't trade hard labor for a chance to walk tough and make big money? Sellin' drugs is a hell of a lot easier on a man than milkin' cows."

"Until you get gunned down." The chief took a sip, grimaced, then took another. "Did Harlene make this?"

"Just because I didn't put six teaspoons of sugar in it? Jesus." MacAuley gestured toward the hallway. "You get anything out of Pedro, there?"

"The kid's name is Amado. Amado Esfuentes. And no, I didn't get anything. It was a long shot, anyway."

"Amado?" Kevin asked. They both looked at him as if the filing cabinet had spoken.

"You should check 'im out, Kevin. He's the only guy I've ever seen has a worse beard than yours was." MacAuley stroked his chin.

"He's the guest worker who broke his arm in that accident back in April," the chief said. He took another drink from his mug, wincing. "I figured, since he *is* Latino and he's living out on my brother-in-law's farm — where the body was found — he might have some information."

"I thought he was shifty." Hadley's voice was still tight, but she sounded as if she was trying to let it go. "Like he was hiding something. He didn't like it when you asked him about anyone he might have seen around the McGeoch place."

The chief nodded. "I agree."

Kevin opened his mouth. *She got to sit in on an interrogation? I never get to do that!* He snapped his jaw shut. He wasn't going to move up from patrol by being a crybaby. A new and unpleasant thought occurred to him. Maybe he wasn't going to be the one stepping into departed officer Mark Durkee's shoes. Maybe he wasn't advancing from street work to investigations. Maybe they had hired Hadley Knox for that. That would explain why, despite her reluctance, the chief kept pushing her into the investigations. Maybe her DOC experience gave her an edge. Maybe they still thought he was too young. Maybe there was some sort of equal opportunity quota and they needed a woman.

The chief was still talking. "Don't forget he probably views any American in uniform as a threat. I suspect his uneasiness may have more to do with his legal status as an alien than with trying to conceal anything criminal. Still . . . let's keep that in mind."

"Maybe you should let Knox question him alone." MacAuley looked at Hadley speculatively over the rim of his coffee cup. "He might find her less threatening. Open up more."

Solo questioning! And she's not even out of Basic! God damn! Hadley, however, didn't seem to appreciate that she was in like Flynn — except this Flynn obviously wasn't. She got a panicked look on her face. "Uh . . ." she said.

The chief shook his head. "I want to talk with my sister and brother-in-law first. Kevin?"

"Chief?"

"I want you to drive Mr. Esfuentes back to St. Alban's." He paused. MacAuley turned his considering gaze on the chief. "Tell Reverend Fergusson we'll run him back out after he finishes work tonight," the chief continued. "We'll keep everything nice and informal and friendly-like."

"Uh . . . okay."

"Officer Knox, go with him to the interview room and let Mr. Esfuentes know what's going on." He glanced at the clock on the wall. "Then you may as well knock off for the day."

She stood. "Yes, sir."

In the hallway, out of earshot of the old

234

guys, Kevin said, "Look, I'm sorry about what went down back there. I mean, about not backing you up on the tattoos."

She gave him a jaundiced look. "I don't expect you to lie for me, Flynn." She inhaled. "It doesn't matter if they believe me or not. I shared like the chief told me to. What they do with it is their business." She turned and marched down the hall.

She was smack-dab in the middle of the corridor, so he had to bob and weave to keep up with her. "Is your car fixed?"

"No." She pressed on, past the dispatch room.

"Hi, Kevin!" Harlene yelled.

He paused. Waved. "Hi, Harlene!" He had to take two large steps to catch up with Hadley, which was something, considering his legs were a lot longer than hers. "Did you drive your grandfather's car?"

"No."

He stopped in front of the interview room. It differed from the interrogation room in that it had windows, and the table and chairs weren't bolted to the floor. "How are you getting home?"

"I'm walking."

"To Burgoyne Street?"

She finally looked up at him. "It's not the other side of the moon, Flynn. It'll take me thirty minutes, tops."

"Come with me. I'll drop you off after I run this guy to St. Alban's."

She shook her head. "No, thanks."

"You're angry with me. About what I said to the chief."

She set the edge of her jaw. "Forget what you said to the chief. It's just . . . Look. Last night was an emergency. I'm not letting you take me anywhere if I can get there on my own."

"Why not?" He meant it to be civil, inquiring; instead it steamed out, frustrated and perplexed. "It's not like I'm asking you out. I'm not trying to steal a march on your spectacular career in the department. I'm just trying to be friendly, for chrissakes. That's all. Why do you keep blowing me off?"

She looked at him as if he had donned a hockey mask and fired up his chain saw. "My spectacular career in the department?"

He erased the words in midair. "I didn't mean to say that. Forget it."

Her lush lips thinned, and two angry red blotches marred her perfect skin. "Are you making fun of me?" She didn't look so beautiful now, and it was a relief, because for the first time it felt like maybe they might belong to the same species. "Because

I haven't been studying to be a cop since I was in diapers? Which for you was, like, four weeks ago."

He could feel it, in that second, a fault line running through his head and heart as his blind adoration cracked and fell away. "I'm not making fun of you. I'm *trying* to be friends. I'm starting to guess you don't recognize the concept because you don't have any."

She held up her hands as if framing a camera shot. "Let me set you straight. I didn't come here to make friends. I came here to do a job, get paid, and go home."

"Where your life is so perfect, no doubt."

"Where my life belongs to me. And my children. And I don't have to explain, or justify, or meet anyone else's expectations. So, no, Flynn, I don't want to be your friend. If you thought otherwise because you caught me in a weak moment last night, I'm sorry, but that was your thought, not anything I said or did to encourage you."

She swung the door to the interview room open and stepped in, hanging off the doorknob. She rattled off a long sentence in loud Spanish, then swung back into the hall, pulling the door with her. Her eyes went round. "Sir," she said.

Kevin whirled around. The chief was a few

feet behind him, his expression a blend of irritation and weariness. "Kevin," he said, "are you bothering Officer Knox with unwelcome and unprofessional attention?"

"No! I mean, I didn't think I was. I didn't mean to."

The chief's eyes cut to Hadley. "Officer Knox?"

She jerked her chin up. "I was just setting down the ground rules for Officer Flynn, sir. No offense taken."

"Then let me set down the ground *rule.* Singular and simple. There will be no fraternization among members of this department. Failure to observe this rule will result in administrative notice, disciplinary action, and possible suspension. Do I make myself clear?"

"Yes, sir."

"Yes, Chief."

"Good. This is a police department, not a high school dance." The chief pinched the bridge of his nose beneath his glasses. "Appearances sometimes to the contrary."

X

"I don't know why he seemed nervous." Janet tucked the phone more firmly beneath her chin and lifted the lid on the pot. The water had come to a boil. "Maybe because he's a stranger in a strange land? Maybe because when you come over all cop you can be as intimidating as hell?" She ripped the top off a bag of egg noodles and dumped them into the water.

"I didn't try to browbeat the kid," her brother said. "For chrissakes, you sound like Clare — Reverend Fergusson."

Interesting. Should she pursue that line of —

"I just want to know if you've observed anything, anything at all, that might account for his twitchiness."

"Not here," she lied. "He spends most of his time working at St. Alban's. I suggest you ask Clare — Reverend Fergusson." She plunged a slotted spoon into the pot and stirred while listening to Russ breathe. He had this certain way of doing it when you pushed his buttons just right. She smiled to herself.

"I'm going to bring Amado back to your place — the new place — after he finishes up tonight. It'll give me a chance to check out the house he's living in. Just to get a feel for things."

Oh, shit. "Aren't you supposed to get a warrant before you search people's property?"

"Well, it sort of depends, Janet. Do I need

to get a warrant on you and Mike?"

She dropped the colander in the sink, letting the crash disguise her hiss of frustration. "Of course not," she said, when her voice was under control. "By all means, bring him home and check out the house. Maybe you'll find he's got a box of *Playboys* under his bed and he feels guilty about that."

His voice was dry. "If I do, I'll hand him over to Mom. Since she's already had experience with that sort of thing."

The doorbell dinged. "Emma!" There was no answering yell from her thirteen-year-old. The bell dinged again. "Hang on," she told Russ. "Somebody's at the door."

God. She was going to have to call over to the bunkhouse and have all the men clear out. Their stuff, too. Where was she going to put them, the barn?

She yanked the door open. A tall heavyset man in shit-kicker boots stood there. He wore a barn jacket and blond hair that had escaped from 1983. " 'Scuse me, ma'am," he said, "but I'm looking for Amado? He works for you?"

She shook her head. "He works at St. Alban's Church, in town. He just rooms out here." She'd seen this guy before, but she couldn't place where. The IGA or the Agway? "I'm sorry. Have we met before?"

He stuck out a grubby hand. "Dunno, but I've met your husband at the auctions. I'm Neil." He pumped her arm like he was trying to get water from a well. She resisted the urge to rub her shoulder when he finished.

"How on earth do you know Amado?"

"Hah. How I know Amado. Well. It's like this."

"Mom!" Oh, of course, *now* Emma was around. "Uncle Russ is on the phone and wants to know if you're going to be all night?"

"What are you doing picking up the phone?" She glanced at the guy. "Sorry."

"I wanted to know if you were using it! I'm waiting to get on line! If we had cable I wouldn't have to wait!"

"Oh, God," Janet muttered. Emma could go on in that vein for an hour.

"I can see you're busy, ma'am. If you could just let me know when he's getting home?"

Oh, sure. The last thing she needed was another stranger roaming around by the bunkhouse, ready to stumble over seven illegals. "He's at St. Alban's late tonight, cleaning up after their concert. Your best bet is to catch him there."

"Thanks, ma'am." He stepped off the porch and was vanishing into the dusk by the time she had the chance to close the door. She wondered again, for a second, how another local farmer had met up with their church-cleaning boarder. It teased at her, but then Emma started up again with her tirade against dial-up Internet access, and she remembered Russ was waiting, and she thought, *How am I going to hide my employees from my brother?* And the thought was gone.

XI

Peace be within thy walls,
And plenteousness within thy palaces!

The choir finished. The organ thundered to a close. There was a moment of silence, as the last triumphant notes of Parry's "I Was Glad When They Said Unto Me" reverberated. Then someone clapped, and in a second, St. Alban's stone walls echoed with deafening applause. Clare, whose official duties had been completed after welcoming everyone to the church and introducing the choir, whanged away with the rest of them, amazed, as she always was, that the same group of people she heard grumbling and going flat and repeating a single musical phrase over and over and *over* in their rehearsals could create a sound of such inexpressible beauty.

The choir bowed, and then the music director, Betsy Young, emerged from behind the organ, her cheeks brilliantly colored, bits of her hair sticking to the side of her face. One of the tenors brought her a hefty bouquet of roses, and she turned an even more spectacular shade of red.

Clare caught Doug Young's eye and slid out of her pew at the rear of the church. Betsy's husband had been pressed into service collecting the "suggested donations," and now it was time to see how well they had done. He scooped up the metal change box and Clare fished the sacristy key out of her skirt pocket. "They were wonderful," she said, as they threaded their way through the crowd to the front of the church.

"They were," he said. "And I am *so* glad it's over." He flashed her a grin.

Yes, well. Betsy had been a tad caught up in prepping for the concert.

Doug glanced around. "Your friend from New York's not here?"

"Hugh? No, he had to work. Some deal his bank is putting together. He had to fly to Las Vegas."

"Too bad. For you, I mean, not for him. Vegas isn't any hardship."

"It's okay. We're pretty casual. And he'll be up for the St. Alban's Festival next month."

"I hope he has some money left over from his trip."

Clare laughed.

"Reverend Fergusson," someone called. "Can I speak to you for a sec?"

She handed Doug the key and told him she'd be back as soon as she could. Which turned out to be forty-five minutes later. She fielded questions about the upcoming parish picnic, spoke to a woman who wanted to volunteer for their teen mother mentoring program, praised every choir member she clapped eyes on, and, gratifyingly, talked with no less than three different people who expressed interest in trying out next Sunday's Eucharist.

"I feel like we're getting them under false pretenses," she confessed to Betsy. The church had emptied out except for a few last choristers, gossiping in the center aisle. "They don't know the choir's about to break for the summer."

"We'll just have to rely on your preaching to snag them after Trinity Sunday, then, won't we?"

"Oh, yeah, they'll come for miles around for that." She let the music director precede her into the sacristy. "The only thing people want from a sermon in the summertime is that it be five minutes or less." She spotted Amado, peeping around the corner from the main office. His bright yellow cast glowed in the shadow. "It's okay, Señor Esfuentes. You can go ahead and start cleaning. Uh, *Limpiar la iglesia, por favor.*"

"I bet you can't wait for Glenn Hadley to come back to work," Doug said from his seat beside the lockbox.

"He is easier to communicate with," Clare admitted. "On the other hand, Señor Esfuentes doesn't feel compelled to call me Father."

"How'd we do?" Betsy asked. The choir was planning an August trip to a choral festival in England — *if* they could raise enough to cover some of their expenses. They had been fund-raising with concerts and bake sales since last fall.

"Four hundred fifty-two dollars and seventy-five cents." Doug grinned hugely.

"Yessss!" Betsy clenched her fists in triumph.

Clare and Doug signed off on the receipt slip and Doug zippered the deposit bag and dropped it into the lockbox.

"Are you two going out to celebrate your artistic and financial triumph?" Clare asked. She ushered them out of the sacristy and locked the door behind her.

Betsy shook her head vehemently. "I'm going to go home, have a large bourbon, and crawl into bed. And I'm not getting out until Sunday morning."

Clare laughed. "You let me know if you want to stay there. I'm sure I can enlist someone to play guitar for us."

"Not unless I'm dead. Guitars." The organist shuddered.

"Are you headed for the rectory?" Doug asked. "We'll walk you there."

Clare checked her old steel Seiko: 8:45 p.m. Kevin Flynn had said "they" would take Amado home. It probably meant he would return. Kevin. Not Russ. It probably wouldn't be Russ.

"Clare?"

"Sorry." She smiled at the Youngs. "No, I'll stay here until Señor Esfuentes's ride comes for him."

She made her farewells to the Youngs in the narthex. The choristers had gone, leaving only Amado, wrestling the large upright vacuum cleaner into position in the north aisle. He was getting adept at doing everything one-and-a-half-handed. She cruised the pews, looking for hymnals or prayer books out of place, picking up discarded concert programs.

She had reached the front of the church again when the inner doors opened. She looked up, but instead of Russ or Kevin she saw two big, burly country boys, one with a reddish ZZ Top beard, the other with an oh-so-fashionable mullet. She stepped into the center of the nave, blocking their path. "May I help you?" she said. The bearded guy looked familiar, but she couldn't place where she had seen him.

"Well, ma'am," the mullet began, and the bearded one said, "There he is," and they both turned toward Amado with the coordination of sharks spotting a tuna.

"C'mere, lover boy," the bearded man said. "We wanna have a talk with you."

Her sexton froze behind the vacuum cleaner. His caramel skin was pasty, throwing his scraggly beard and mustache into high relief. Clare doubted he understood anything they had said, but he didn't need to. The smell of violence clung to the intruders, filling the church. The kid shivered, toppled the vacuum into the aisle, and rabbited toward the hallway behind him.

"Hey!" ZZ Top roared. He and the mullet

accelerated down the center aisle. Clare, seeing five hundred pounds of good ol' boy bearing down on her, whirled and dashed for the same doorway Amado had disappeared through. Hide. Where? Everything still unlocked had to be locked by key. She'd never have —

Just short of the door, she lunged sideways, to where the processional cross and torches were cradled in their wooden brackets. She grabbed the processional cross and spun back toward the invaders. "Stop!" she shouted. Amazingly, they did so.

She held the heavy six-foot-long oak staff cross-braced in her hands, barring the way like Little John at the ford. The gleaming cross screwed atop it was a foot high, cast in solid bronze, weighty enough to break bones. "Get out of here," she said, her voice hard.

"What are you, a ninja? Get outta my way," the mullet said. He feinted toward the door she blocked. Clare rammed the butt of the staff into his chest and, as he folded with an explosion of hacking coughs, hit him over the head with a crack that sounded like a branch being snapped in two. He dropped.

"What the hell!" The bearded guy stared at the fallen man. "What did you do to my brother, you bitch?"

He lunged toward her. She tried the ramming trick again, but he dodged left, reaching for the staff. She let it drop out of one hand and swung it low with the other, slamming into his knees and calves, hard enough to hurt, not — *dammit all!* — hard enough to cripple him.

"You goddamn bitch!" He lurched forward, hands outstretched, deflecting her blows with forearms, left, right, left. She was backed against the wall beside the door, unable to get the leverage to make them count. He got his hands on the processional cross and shook, hard, Clare clinging on, jerking back and forth, knowing if she let go he'd use it to beat her unconscious. Bad breath and spittle and a stream of monotonously vile words spewed into her face. She brought her head back and then forward, fast, her forehead connecting to his nose with a crunch that left her eyes watering.

He howled. Rammed himself into her, oaken staff and all, splattering her with the blood running out his nose and driving the breath from her body. She stomped, stomped again, trying to get his instep, his foot, anything.

She heard a loud click.

"Step away from her or I blow your brains out," Russ said.

The bearded man let her go. Raised his hands. Stepped back. Clare sagged against the wall, clinging to the cross.

"On the floor," Russ said.

The bearded man looked at him sullenly. "She attacked me! I was just —"

Russ holstered his Glock, drew back his arm, and smashed his fist into the side of the man's head. Clare shrieked. The bearded man reeled, and Russ punched him, once, twice, his back and shoulders working, until the attacker fell to his knees. Russ reached for him, twisting his fists in the front of his sweatshirt, ready to haul him up and pound him again. Clare dropped the processional cross and grabbed Russ's arm, trying, without much success, to drag him away from the injured man.

"Stop!" she said, her voice a strangled whisper in her throat. "Stop!"

He looked at her with eyes she didn't recognize. "You're bleeding."

"It's not my blood. He was after Amado, not me. It's not my blood. I'm okay."

He shook himself. Looked at Clare's assailant, who was bleeding copiously into his beard. Released his sweatshirt. "Down on the floor," Russ said. The man slumped forward without protest this time, spread-eagled on the polished wood.

From outside, she heard the rising and falling of a siren. Russ yanked at the handcuffs on his belt. He got down on one knee and clicked them around the bearded man's beefy wrists. "You have the right to remain silent," he said.

She raised the cross off the floor with shaking hands.

"You have the right to an attorney."

The intricate bronze work was spotless.

"If you cannot afford an attorney, one will be provided for you."

She drew her sleeve across her mouth, wiping away the blood and spittle, and kissed it.

"Anything you say can and will be used against you in a court of law."

In thanksgiving. In apology.

The siren broke off, and a moment later the inner doors swung open. Kevin Flynn charged into the nave, his gun out, followed by Amado, who stayed well behind, clutching his cast.

"Call an ambulance, Kevin," Russ said, levering himself off his knee. The younger officer skidded to a stop, his eyes widening at the prone bodies and blood-spattered floor.

"What the — ?" He looked at Russ. "What happened?"

Russ glanced at the two on the floor. Then at her. "They were stupid enough to mess with Reverend Fergusson."

XII

Her kitchen light was on. He hadn't known if it would be. It had been at least two hours since he had stalked out of St. Alban's, his arms still spasming with unspent rage, his head pounding blackly behind his eyes. He had walked — across the street, into the park, around the circle — while Paul Urquhart arrived and Kevin took Clare's statement and the EMTs loaded the two Christies into the ambulance. He finally cooled off enough to be sure he wasn't going to break his hand hitting a wall, and went back to question the young sexton, who was both terrified and bewildered by the Christies' interest in him.

They hadn't gotten anything out of the Christies, of course — well, out of Donald, who was the only one able to talk. Neil was still unconscious. Russ hadn't been as neat and efficient as Clare. When she put a man down, he stayed down.

Christ, wasn't that the truth.

The Christies were in the Washington County Hospital, waiting for their lawyer and their medical releases before Urquhart transported them to the county jail. Their would-be victim, despite Russ's glowering and Kevin's offer to take him back to the old farmhouse on Lick Spring Road, was bunking at the rectory tonight, at the insistence of his employer and savior. When Russ had seen the hero worship in the kid's eyes, his warnings about Clare putting Amado up fell flat. After this evening, her latest charity case would cheerfully take a bullet for her.

Another poor sonofabitch down for the count.

Now he was sitting in the cab of his truck, pulled over across the street, looking at the rectory. It was dark, except for a single lamp deep inside the living room and the kitchen light shining out the side door.

He pulled into her drive, butting up snug against the rear of her Subaru. He got out, closing his door with a solid *thunk,* letting her know he was coming. He saw a shadow at the kitchen door, and as he trudged up the steps, he heard the sound of a bolt turning and a chain rattling as it was drawn away. She opened the door to him.

"You locked your door," he said, like an idiot.

"Yeah."

He stepped inside. The kitchen smelled of

chocolate and peppermint. "You never lock your door."

"You've been after me about it for three years now. Eventually, even I can learn something new." She looked up at him. "I'm not going to just let someone waltz in here and hurt me."

He stared at his boots until she walked back to the white enamel stove. Her feet were bare. She was wearing a blue and white seersucker robe loose over mint-green pajamas. "I didn't know if you'd still be up," he said.

"I couldn't fall asleep." She glanced at the ceiling, to where, presumably, her guest was dreaming of happier days south of the border. Although she kept her voice low, so maybe he wasn't asleep yet, either. "I got Amado settled in, but my mind was going a mile a minute, so I decided to come downstairs and make hot cocoa." She gestured to a mug on the white counter. HELICOPTER PILOTS DO IT WITH BOTH HANDS, it read. There was a bottle of peppermint schnapps and an open carton of eggs next to it. "I still have some in the pan, if you'd like a mug."

"No, thanks," he said.

"It's nonalcoholic. I put the schnapps in afterward." She took a long drink from her own mug.

"I'm not staying long," he said, even as he shucked his jacket and dropped it on the back of one of the chairs drawn haphazardly against the heavy pine table.

She shrugged. "More for me." She took another pull from her drink and turned toward the stove. He heard the *click-click-click* of the gas jet, and then the pilot caught and a blue flame shot up from the black iron burner. She turned it down and slid a cobalt-blue omelet pan over the heat.

"How're you doing?" he asked.

"Fine," she said. She reached for the egg carton. Cracked an egg into a grass-green ceramic bowl. "Grab the milk out of the fridge for me, will you?"

Her twenty-year-old refrigerator was almost buried beneath photos, clippings, comics, and brochures. He figured the whole appliance was held together by magnetic force at this point.

He set the carton on the counter next to where she was now whisking eggs furiously in the bowl. She took another drink of hot cocoa before slopping a measure of milk into the frothing eggs. He eyeballed the schnapps bottle. It was more empty than full.

She cracked pepper from a scarlet pepper-mill into the mixture and then beat it as if it might get up and walk away if not subdued. She crossed to the refrigerator, popped it open, and retrieved a lump of greasy white paper, which, unwrapped, proved to be a lump of greasy white something else. She hacked off a piece of it and dropped it into the omelet pan. It snapped and sizzled.

"What's that?" he asked.

"Pig fat," she said, taking another swig of hot cocoa. She bottomed out the mug and looked into it, frowning. "You can't make comfort food without pig fat." He noticed her Virginia accent was more pronounced. She took a spoon from the drainboard, stirred the pan at the back of the stove, and poured more hot cocoa into her mug. She unscrewed the schnapps and added a liberal splash.

"Don't you think you ought to ease up on that?"

She turned on him. Cocked her fist against one hip. "Maybe I should relax by beating somebody to a pulp instead?"

"Christ, Clare, you were the one who broke his nose!"

"I was defending myself. What's your excuse?"

He inhaled, took his glasses off, and rubbed them on his shirtfront. "I don't have any excuse." He tossed his glasses onto the pine tabletop and ran both hands through his hair, tugging at it, hard. "God knows, I already feel bad enough without you laying into me. If one of my officers had done that, I'da had him on suspension by now." He dragged a chair out and dropped into it. "I don't know what got into me. I just don't know." He stared at his hands. In the glow of the hanging lamp, he could see the nicks and scars from every accident he'd ever had. The knuckles of his right hand were reddened and puffy and aching.

"Do you want some ice for that?" she said, her voice quiet.

"No." He flexed his fingers into a fist and opened them again. "I want it to hurt."

She sighed. He heard the sizzling pan slide off its burner. He heard her bare feet as she crossed the floor. Then her hand settled over his, light and warm. "What did you come here for, Russ? Absolution?"

He shook his head. "I wanted to . . . make sure you were okay." He folded his hands on the table and stared at them. She hesitated for a moment, then touched his hair, her fingers stroking him like you'd pet a cat. "I'm sorry," he said. "I guess that was . . ."

She gave him time to finish, but he had no idea what he was saying. She sighed again. "I can't solve your problems, dear heart. I'm part of them."

He looked up at her, then. "No," he said. "Never that. It's me. I'm . . . stuck. I'm like an old truck up to its hubcaps in snow. I go forward, I go back, nothing ever changes or shakes loose, and the whole time I'm cold, inside and out. The only time I feel anything is when I'm angry. And that scares the crap out of me."

Her hand never stopped moving over his hair. "How do you feel now?"

He studied her face. Let himself feel for a moment. "Naked. Sometimes you scare the crap out of me, too."

She laughed a little. He pressed his palms against the table and pushed himself up. She stepped back. "I better head home," he said. "I think I've reached my maximum daily limit of honesty." He pushed the chair back into place. "If you hear or see anything, anything at all, that makes you nervous, call nine-one-one. And call me. We'd rather come out on a false alarm than see you get into trouble again."

She smiled, one-sided. "Thank you, Chief Van Alstyne."

He covered his eyes with one hand. "Christ, I'm pitiful, aren't I?"

He felt her arms go around him. She

hugged him, something she probably wouldn't have done without the encouragement of the schnapps. "No," she said. "You're human. And someday, when you can admit that to yourself, you'll stop feeling so bad that you can't save everyone."

He looked down at her, about to say that sounded like a pretty damn accurate description of her, but her eyes were X-raying through him, and her pointed half smile said *I know you.*

He didn't let himself think. He kissed her. As lightly and briefly as one of her blessings. A thanksgiving and an apology. Then he lifted his head and saw her face, tipped back like the survivor of a long winter on the first day of hot spring sunshine. "Clare," he said, his voice thick. She opened her eyes, full of heat, and just like that the desperate desire he thought he'd never feel again flamed to life like blue gas jetting out of cold iron.

He dug his fingers into her hair and pulled her to him, kissing her, deep, hungry kisses that tasted of chocolate and peppermint. She moaned in the back of her throat and wrestled her hands free from around his waist to twine them about his neck. He bumped against the kitchen table and bent her back, kissing her, kissing her, her mouth and her jaw and the pulse trip-hammering in her throat. He felt something huge and powerful racing through him, sparking every nerve end, blanking out everything in the world except Clare, the taste of her, the sound of her, panting and gasping, the feel of her, oh, God, better than anything he had ever fantasized, as he yanked open her pajama top and pushed it aside and touched her, touched her, touched her.

She cried out, and he shut her mouth with more kisses, wet and dark, remembering they had to keep quiet even though he couldn't remember why. She pushed at him, tugging at his shirt, and he reared back, taking her with him, the two of them standing hip to hip and toe to toe, frantic to remove his uniform blouse without letting any space or light or air between them. She undid the two top buttons and he yanked the shirt off over his head, tossing it on the table, and it was *Clare,* warm and alive and half naked in his arms. His eyes nearly rolled back in his head from the feel of her skin on his.

Bed. Bed. Bed. He herded her toward the kitchen's swinging door, the two of them stumbling around and between each other's legs, Russ dropping kisses on her hair, her ears, her temples while she pressed her face into his chest, her mouth and tongue making him mindless. They rocked through the door and staggered into the dimly lit living room, and when she bit him, he felt his knees buckling. The bed was too far away, he would never make it. He was going to burn alive before then. He hip-checked the sofa and dropped onto its squishy cushions. She let the pajama top and the robe fall to the floor, letting him look at her, look at her, and then she crawled on top of him. He gritted his teeth to keep from whimpering and begging and singing hallelujah. He seized her hips and pulled her to him, so she could feel how hard she made him, Christ, like he was seventeen again.

"Russ," she said, her voice unrecognizable. "Oh, God." She fit herself around him, and he could feel the weight and the strength of her, the long muscles of her thighs and her back beneath his hands. He heard a groan tearing out of his chest as he rolled her underneath him, his arms shaking, the breath hitching in his throat.

A light snapped on upstairs. "Señora Reverenda?" The voice sounded small and scared and about twelve years old. He stilled as best he could with his chest working like a bellows. Dropped his forehead to hers. Goddamn. It really was like being seventeen again. Next, Clare's parents would phone to see how the babysitting job was going.

Clare drew an unsteady breath. "It's —" She swallowed. Tried again. "It's all right, Señor Esfuentes. Everything's okay. Um. . . ." She looked at him helplessly.

He rolled off her, reaching out and snagging her robe off the floor. He handed it to her. *"Es yo, Amado.* Chief Van Alstyne. *Acabo de venir cerca comprobar en usted dos. Vaya de nuevo a cama."*

"Okay," Amado said. *"Buenos noches."*

"What did you say?" Clare whispered.

"I told him to go away, we were getting naked."

She whacked his shoulder, hard.

"Ow!"

She curled into a sitting position and put on the robe. He rolled onto his back, throwing his arm over his eyes, trying to calm the pounding of his heart. "You're going to toss me out, aren't you?"

There was a pause. "Yes."

"Christ, Clare. . . ."

She twisted to speak to him; then, as if she thought better of staying within arm's reach, she stood up and stepped back. Her cheeks and chest were stained with high color, her hair a wild tangle, her lips red and swollen. He had to shut his eyes before he broke something.

"We can't do this," she said.

He could smell her from where she stood. "Come back over here," he said, his voice heavy and full. "I'll show you how it works."

She sat in one of the overstuffed chairs that faced each other across the coffee table. Her hand, clutching the edges of her robe together, was trembling. "And what happens when we wake up tomorrow morning with your wife's dead body between us?"

"Jesus Christ!" He convulsed upward. His feet, still booted, thudded to the floor.

"It's too soon, Russ. Even if we didn't have this . . ." — she waved a hand in the air — "this mess between us, it would still be too soon. She's only been dead five months. There's a reason the old mourning period was a year. People who lived with death knew it took time."

"What is this about? You want to make me wait? For what? Payback? To see if I'll jump through some arbitrary hoop for you?"

She bent over, twining and twisting her hands together, letting them dangle between her knees. She finally looked at him. "I love you," she said. "And God knows, I want you." She laughed a little, without humor. "I think we just proved that. But I deserve to have your whole heart."

"I'm not going to stop loving her just

because she's dead." His voice was harsh.

"I know that. I don't expect you to. I meant you need to love me wholly, not half want me, half blame me for Linda's death."

"I don't —" he began.

"Oh, for God's sake!" She glanced toward the stairs and continued in a lower tone. "Can't we at least be honest about that? If you hadn't stopped to get me out of trouble, if you hadn't been with me, Linda would be alive right now."

He shook his head.

"It's true!" She jumped to her feet. "Admit it! Admit it!"

"All right, dammit! Yes! If I hadn't gone into that goddam barn, my wife would still be alive." He surged to his feet and grabbed her by the upper arm. "But don't you see? You would have been dead. *You* would have been the one to die. And that's what's killing me. I can't regret that. I can't be sorry. Christ, I can't imagine a world without you in it, Clare. But that means Linda was an acceptable loss. It means I chose you over her." He dropped her arm and ground his fists into his temples. "If you knew how many times I've replayed that afternoon over and over and *over* in my head, every decision I made, every word I said . . . and the hell of it is, I never, ever make the right decision. Because there is no right decision. I'll never be right on this. And if I just . . . come to you with open arms and a big smile on my face, it's like I'm spitting on her grave."

He turned away from her. Ran his good hand over his face. It came away wet. She touched his back, pressed her palm between his shoulder blades. Skin to skin.

"Don't," he said, not sure what he was forbidding her. *Don't love me? Don't comfort me? Don't touch me, because I don't know how many of your touches I can withstand before I break?*

"Dear heart," she said, "you have got to see a therapist."

It was so practical, so *Clare,* that he almost laughed. Instead he made a noise. "I don't need a goddam therapist. I just need some time to figure things out."

Her hand dropped away. "Because you're doing such a good job of it." Her voice was dry.

He looked at the reddened flesh on his knuckles. The bruises were starting to emerge. "I have to go," he said, his voice almost inaudible. He strode toward the kitchen, pulled his shirt back over his head, and put his glasses on. The kitchen sprang into focus, cheap white fittings and warm pine. Yanking on his jacket, he kept his eyes on the calendar by the door. A bunch of men in togas stared at each other, drop-mouthed at the flames sprouting from their heads. He wondered if the fiery hairdos were a blessing or a punishment. He took hold of the brass knob. Opened it to the cooling darkness beyond her door.

Behind him, he heard a *ca-chunk* as she walked into the kitchen. He inhaled. He was a jerk, but he wasn't enough of a jerk to walk out without facing her. He turned around.

She looked as miserable as he felt. Great. He had come here to make sure she was all right. Instead, he had screwed with her head and kicked her in the teeth. And still — still — he wanted her. If she opened her arms, he'd take her right here on the kitchen floor, no questions asked. God, he was pond scum.

"How do you stand me?" he asked her. "Most of the time, *I* can't even stand me."

Her eyes filled with tears. She opened her mouth. Shut it again. Shook her head.

His throat tightened so that he wasn't sure he could get anything out. "I'm sorry. I never meant to hurt you."

She nodded. Wiped her eyes with the heels of her hands. "I knew what I was getting into, remember?" She gave him a fractured smile. "I said we were going to break our hearts."

Trinity Sunday, The Last Day of Pentecost

MAY 26

I

She shouldn't have come to the parish picnic. She was behind on her reading for the criminology course. The house was an ungodly mess, and she had at least four loads of laundry to do. And to top it off, every time she turned around, there was another cheerful Episcopalian trying to get to know her. It made her miss the enormous Christian Community church she had taken the kids to in LA. It had been big enough to disappear into.

Hadley fished another Coke out of the ice-filled red-and-white cooler and rolled the dripping can over the back of her neck before popping the top. The things she did for her kids and granddad. At least the view was spectacular. The Muster Field stretched out a good quarter mile atop one of the rolling hills that characterized Cossayuharie. Across the two-lane county highway at its front and on either side, the land fell away in hillocked pastures studded with outcroppings of flinty bedrock and bouquets of nettles. Behind her, the forest that threatened to cover everything in this northern kingdom pressed against the uneven stone wall that outlined the field.

It was one of the few spots that she had seen in Washington County where the sky was huge: summer bluc, piled with mountain-high cumulus clouds as bleached-white as the linen shirts worn by the other group that had come out for the Memorial Day weekend, a company of Revolutionary-era reenactors. They were marching and kneeling, loading and reloading in front of their canvas tents, authentically decked out in mid-eighteenth-century breeches and coats. How they didn't keel over in those layers of wool was a mystery to Hadley.

"They look hot, don't they?" A middle-aged woman dug through the fast-melting ice to pull out a root beer.

"Mmm-hmm." The minimum response to be polite.

"One year, they had two men pass out from sunstroke. They had to get the ambulance up here, there was a big hullabaloo, and then as soon as they'd been carted away to the hospital? The rest of them started drilling again."

Hullabaloo? What next, twenty-three skid-doo?

"I'm Betsy Young," the woman said, reaching for Hadley's hand. "I'm the music director."

Hadley shook. They both had palms as cold and damp as fish from the chest-sized cooler. "Hadley Knox," she said.

"I know. We're all so thrilled you came out from California to take care of your grandfather."

Whoa. Was that what they were saying? "Actually, he invited me before he ever had his heart attack and surgery. He was the one helping me out, not the other way around."

"Really?" Betsy Young's bright expression invited Hadley to Tell Her All About It.

"Really."

"Ah. Well. I actually wanted to speak to you about your son."

"Hudson?" Hadley scanned the area around the grumbling granite stones at the shady rear of the Muster Field. The children, bored by the authentic firearms and tactics — Hudson complained they only fired their muskets once every half hour — had converted the three-century-old memorials into a combination obstacle course and battlefield. Their reenactment had far more explosions, automatic gunfire, and light sabers than that of the reconstituted Fifth Volunteer Highlanders.

"How old is he?"

"Nine. Why?"

Betsy took a drink of root beer before answering. "I've wanted, for a long time now, to have a children's choir here at St. Alban's. When Father Hames was rector, there just wasn't any opportunity. He was a wonderful man, very learned, but he did tend to appeal to an older crowd, God rest his soul. Since we've had Reverend Clare, things have perked up quite a bit."

Hadley wondered if the music director had heard about the assault at the church Friday night. Reverend Clare hadn't mentioned it at the service this morning; hadn't shown any sign of it — except, maybe, for a kind of emotionally bruised look in her eyes. Which Hadley might never have noticed if she hadn't heard about the Christies' arrest from Deputy Chief MacAuley.

"We've had quite a few families join in the past three years, and we finally have enough children in the right age range for me to give it a go. So what do you think?"

"Hmm? About what?"

"Do you think Hudson would be interested in singing in the youth choir?"

Hadley pictured her boy decked out in the sort of choir robes she saw in Christmas specials. She'd love it, but she knew she'd never get him into anything with a frilly neck. "What would he wear?"

Betsy looked surprised. "Um . . . a cassock, same as the adult choristers. With a surplice on special occasions."

Hadley thought for a moment. She wasn't keen on getting involved in any extracurricular activities herself, but she did want Hudson and Genny to take part, make friends, be comfortable in their new town. "What would the practice schedule be like? I don't want anything to interfere with his homework. We're still trying to come back from switching schools midyear."

"We wouldn't start until next fall," Betsy assured her. "Then it'd be an hour Wednesday afternoon or evening, depending on what works for most parents. And he'd have to be here at nine o'clock for the ten o'clock service."

That was doable. "Okay," she said. "He's in. But don't hold me responsible if he turns out to be tone-deaf."

"There's no such thing," Betsy said with confidence.

"Hey, you two." Hadley and Betsy turned to see Reverend Fergusson striding toward them, looking more like a well-toned soccer mom than a priest in her sleeveless blouse and shorts. "Have either of you seen Cody Burns?"

Betsy shook her head.

"Little guy with curly dark hair?" Hadley said. "Two, two and a half?"

"That's him." Reverend Clare's face relaxed.

"I saw him earlier with the kids playing around the tombstones, but I haven't noticed him recently."

The relaxation disappeared. The rector muttered something under her breath that Hadley and Betsy pretended they didn't hear. "C'mon," she said grimly. "We've got to find him."

Across the wide and grassy field, Hadley could see the word passing, people talking in little clumps and then separating to wander away from each other, scanning the horizon or peering at the ground. Picnickers flung open their coolers and looked inside. At the minutemen encampment, drilling halted, there was a confusion of wool coats and rectangular backpacks, and then the play soldiers began crawling through their canvas tents.

"Go check the cars!" someone yelled, and several men ran off to the front of the field, where the St. Alban's cars had pulled off the narrow highway to park in a ragged, overheated row.

Hadley followed Clare into the center of the maelstrom, where the trees from the forest stretching beyond the old gathering place cast their deep green shadows over lichen-blurred stones. She looked at the wall, the practical leavings from the harvest of rocks that came out of every field here. In places it had tumbled down to a few smooth pieces of granite. Nothing that would stop an adventurous two-and-a-half-year-old.

"I thought *you* had him!"

Hadley knew Geoffrey Burns by sight from church and by reputation at the station, where the male half of the law firm of Burns and Burns was known as "that officious little prick," and the other officers all wondered what the good-looking Mrs. Burns was doing with such a short, slight spouse. Hadley figured it out the first time she saw the man, radiating power, decked out in a five-hundred-dollar camel-hair coat.

"*Thought?* Why didn't you check with me instead of swanning off to drink beer?"

She had never seen Karen Burns looking anything less than rich, well-groomed, and perfect. She guessed, by the look on other spectators' faces, that they would have said the same. Evidently no one had ever caught a glimpse of this mottle-faced woman screaming at her husband.

"Because I assumed you're competent to look after our son!"

"And I assumed you had the decency to get your head out of your ass and notice what's going on around you!"

More and more congregants and reenactors drifted within earshot. Several started to look more interested in the Burnses' fight than in finding the boy.

"Break it up," Reverend Clare said, hooking Karen Burns's arm in hers and neatly turning her away from her clench-fisted husband. "We need to organize now." The rector raised her voice. "Parents, let's get a head count of the other kids. I want to make sure no one else wandered off with Cody."

Karen let out a terrible moan. Reverend Clare gave her a little shake. "We'll find him, Karen."

The remaining children were rounded up, some protesting, some demanding hot dogs and hamburgers. Genny wanted another soda, and after making sure she and Hudson were included in the count, Hadley sent them both off to the cooler, with orders to stay where they could see her. No one else was missing. None of the kids could remember seeing the preschooler leave.

"I want four volunteers to walk the road, one on each side, in both directions," Reverend Clare said to the assembled throng. Several hands shot up. The rector pointed. "Laurie and Phoebe, you go north. Judy and Terry, you head south." She turned to a couple Hadley knew as Sunday school teachers. "David and Beth, can you take charge of the other kids? Get some food into them and organize a game so they won't be underfoot?" They nodded. "Can anyone get a cell phone signal out here?"

Three quarters of the crowd began digging in their pockets for their phones, including, Hadley observed, several Revolutionary war soldiers. Most people glanced at their screens and shook their heads.

"Shit! The sat phone!" Geoffrey Burns smacked himself on the head and tore across the field toward the Burnses' Land Rover.

Karen, her face twisted, yelled, "Hurry, Geoff, hurry!" She turned to the rector. "Digital satellite phone. So we can reach clients or the office no matter where we are."

Reverend Clare raised her voice. "We're going to have to walk the woods. I want everyone to spread out at the rear of the field, in front of the stone wall. Leave several feet between yourself and the person to your right or left." She did not, Hadley noticed, specify "everyone who's helping search." Her assumption paid off when the crowd, St. Alban's people and reenactors alike, began to shuffle into a raggedy line.

Geoff Burns reappeared, panting and clutching a brick-shaped phone that looked like it had been left over from 1987. He thrust it toward the rector. She opened her mouth as if she were going to say something, then shut it. "Call nine-one-one," she said. "We're going to want the Search and Rescue team and their dog handler. I think she lives in Saratoga." She shook her head, as if dislodging irrelevancies. "Doesn't matter. They'll handle that." Something caught her eye. "Shoot," she said, under her breath. "Mr. Hadley."

Hadley followed her gaze and sure enough, there was Granddad, stumping off to join the search party, as if hiking through the woods in 84-degree heat wasn't any different from walking the treadmill at his therapist's.

"Mr. Hadley!" Reverend Clare called, at the same time Hadley yelled, "Granddad!" They jogged over and boxed him in, a woman on either side.

"Granddad, you can't do this," Hadley said. "Look at you, you're already all red and sweaty." She clapped a hand to his forehead. "You're overheated. You need to sit in the shade and drink something cold."

"I ain't one to sit on my fanny while a little kid's out there wandering through the woods," he said, sounding grumpy and short of breath.

Reverend Clare spoke up. "Mr. Hadley, we need someone responsible to stay here and meet the Search and Rescue volunteers. Could you be our coordinator? You'll have to tell them we're walking a simple straight-line pattern, and that we don't have any whistles or signaling devices."

He ran a palm over his bald head. Peered at both of them. "Well. Okay, Father. If that's where you need me."

Hadley shot the rector a look of gratitude. She got her grandfather into a chair by the ice chest, hollered at Hudson and Genny to behave themselves, and then trotted toward the human chain that now stretched to either end of the Muster Field.

Reverend Clare cupped her hands on either side of her mouth and paced down the line. "Walk slowly," she said, projecting her voice so that it echoed off the grave-stones. "Keep another searcher within sight on either side. That way, you'll be sure you're not missing anything. If you find the boy, pass the news down the line and return to the Muster Field. The search-and-rescue team is on its way, so if you hear three loud whistles, return to the Muster Field. Do not, under any circumstances, wander off alone! We don't want two people lost in the woods."

By the time she finished, she was at the other end of the field from Hadley. A ripple of words flowed through the line. The woman to Hadley's right said, "Let's go," Hadley passed it on to her left, and they all stepped over the low stone wall more or less in unison.

It was no-tech compared to the last search in the woods she had undertaken, but despite the lack of topo maps, flashlights, walkie-talkies, and whistles, it was fundamentally the same — walking in line, a flare of excitement when you saw a human-shaped bump on a log, disappointment and the dawning realization that one piece of forest looks pretty damn much like another. People yelled "Cody!" instead of *"No soy del I-C-E,"* and they had the benefit of sunshine turning the air beneath the trees green, but otherwise it was that night in April all over. Hadley hoped they would be more successful this time.

The line drew thin as men and women responding to the forest's size spread apart to cover the maximum amount of acreage. It wavered and drifted out of plumb as differing terrain — open, brushy, thickly forested — forced some to slow and let others pick up speed. Hadley stopped, and halted the woman to her right, when she noticed the man to her left had disappeared. She was about to bring the line to a standstill when he reappeared from behind a cluster of young pines, zipping his fly and looking abashed.

They walked past slim birch and alder, past immense maples and oaks. They parted the heavy black-green spill of hemlock boughs to look underneath, and they peered and poked at fallen and half-rotted eastern pines. The pine needles and humus beneath their feet, the *tock-tock-tock* of woodpeckers and the whine of mosquitoes, the shaded and broken light — they walked forward and forward and forward, but it never changed. Hadley began to lose her sense of time and distance. She found herself checking again and again to make sure her search partners were well in sight. She had never understood the whole "lost in the woods" thing; she always figured, just walk out the way you walked in. Now, though, if someone had challenged her to find her way back to the Muster Field on her own, she didn't know if she could have done it. How far north and east did this piece of the Adirondacks go? Two miles? Two hundred?

Another ripple of words, excited, flowed down the line from the right. The calls of "Cody! Where are you?" fell silent as searchers passed the message like a relay torch. Hadley was already feeling a sense of relief — God, she'd be half out of her mind if she was the kid's mom — when the woman to her right turned toward her and said, "They need Officer Knox at the other end of the line."

Hadley stopped in her tracks. Officer Knox?

The woman made a shooing gesture. "Pass it on."

"Uh." Hadley felt as much of a fraud as she ever did when she said it. "I'm Officer Knox."

The woman could tell she was a fake, because her eyes bugged out and she said, "*You're* a police officer?"

Hadley didn't bother responding. She called to the guy on her left to move into her place, and took off for the other end of the line. What the hell could they need her for? Her mind pulled a blank. The other searchers, reenactors and St. Alban's parishioners alike, stared at her as she hiked past them. Hadley Knox, imitation police officer. No one would have questioned Kevin Flynn if he had been here. Maybe she should start pumping iron. Except the last time she'd tried that, getting into shape between Hudson and Genny, she'd started to look way too much like Lara Croft, Tomb Raider. That wasn't going to buy her any cred, either.

The line strung out almost to the breaking point. Past the last remaining searcher, she could see four or five people clustered together. Reverend Clare was among them, head up, looking toward Hadley, but the others were all focused on the ground. Her stomach churned. *Oh, my God, please don't let anything have happened to the baby.* The fear sizzled up her spine as she recognized Anne Vining-Ellis, an emergency-room doctor, among the grim-faced group. Hadley forced her sneakered feet into a jog. She didn't want to know, but she couldn't stand the waiting to find out any longer.

"What is it?" she asked, before she could see. "What is it?"

They all looked up. Stared at her. Moved aside. Expecting to see a toddler sprawled on the ground, Hadley at first couldn't make sense of the jumble of dirt and dead leaves and ivory and . . . and . . .

The ivory was bone.

"We've found a body," Reverend Fergusson said.

II

"Another one, huh? Somebody got tired of planting corn?" Doc Scheeler grinned at his own wit, his teeth flashing whitely in his black beard.

Russ pinched the bridge of his nose. "Christ only knows." He glanced around at the Muster Field, which looked like a cross between a municipal parking lot and a circus: ambulance and morgue wagon, three squad cars and a state K-9 cruiser, canvas tents and portable grills, SUVs and trucks and station wagons and sedans, people dressed for hard work in the woods, for a picnic, for a revolution. At 4 p.m., the late-spring sun was only just starting to slide into the western sky, and it was still hot enough to make Russ wish it were possible to project authority in shorts.

Scheeler hefted his kit over his shoulder. He was one of those dressed for the woods, in ripstop cargo pants and a hunter-orange vest over his shirt. Russ was thankful Emil

Dvorak, their usual pathologist, was passing on most of the criminal cases these days. He couldn't have handled the trip into the forest with his bum leg. "Let's go," Scheeler said.

"I'm going to let Officer Knox take you over," Russ said. "I'll meet you there. I need to get updated on the search for the missing boy."

"I'll want to talk with whoever found the body. As, I'm sure, will you."

Russ waved his hand. "Dr. Anne Vining-Ellis is one of them, but I have no idea where she is right now. Probably treating poison ivy and picking deer ticks off people."

Scheeler nodded.

"Reverend Fergusson is another. She's —" He scanned the crowd of humans and vehicles, zeroing in on her head, her hair like raw honey falling out of its twist. She was talking with Lyle MacAuley, the Burnses pressed in close, listening, for a change. "There." He pointed.

"Sharp eyes," Scheeler said.

Russ grunted. It wasn't his eyes that made him uncomfortably aware of Clare's location. His head was still screwed up around his wife's death, but the rest of his body was quite sure he was a free man again.

"Wait a minute. Reverend Fergusson. Isn't she the same minister who called in the last John Doe?" Scheeler sounded incredulous.

"I know, I know. If trouble were a winning lottery ticket, she'd be a multimillionaire by now." Russ was saved from going into Clare's turbulent history by the arrival of his newest officer. The pathologist wasn't the sort to do a double-take, but his eyes widened at the sight of Hadley Knox filling out a T-shirt and cutoffs. The reflective MKPD vest she wore didn't do much to lessen the impact.

"Officer Knox." Scheeler took her hand. For a second, Russ thought he was going to kiss it. "Millers Kill's finest."

"Doc Scheeler." Russ was beginning to recognize that quashing tone in her voice. "Drink any urine lately?"

"I'll leave you two to it," Russ said, keeping his amusement to himself, "and catch up as soon as possible." He strode off to join MacAuley. And Clare. And, God help him, the Burnses. He was still a good bow shot away when he picked up Geoff Burns's voice, ragging on Lyle. He thought the listening part was too good to last.

"— put out now!" Burns sounded like he was going to pop an aorta. "He could be halfway to Canada already!"

"Mr. Burns —" Lyle began, then spotted Russ. Whatever he was going to say became, "Here comes the chief now."

The Burnses turned to face him. Even under these circumstances, Geoff Burns's bantam-cock rage set him on edge, but the sight of Karen Burns, red-eyed and puffy-faced, reined him in. Whatever he thought of them personally, these two were going through a parent's worst nightmare. "Geoff," he said. "Karen."

"Your deputy says there's no use calling in an Amber alert for our son," Burns snarled.

"I explained that an Amber alert is for suspected abductions." Russ could tell Lyle was trying to remain patient. "Not for a child lost in the woods."

"Who's to say he didn't wander out by the side of the road and get picked up? Who's to say there's not some goddamned pedophile lurking in the woods behind the Muster Field? Everybody knows this place is a picnic ground!"

Russ held up a hand. "Lyle," he said, "radio our Amber alert contact. Give 'em all the information." Lyle looked at him skeptically. "It can't hurt. And it's not like they can say we've overtaxed the system. This'll be the first one we've called." He looked at the Burnses. "It would help if we had a picture, but I suppose that'll have to wait until we've gotten to a fax machine."

"Wait!" Karen Burns clutched at Lyle's sleeve. "I have pictures saved on my cell phone. If we drive down to where I can get a signal, I can send them."

Russ nodded. "Go." She didn't need more encouragement than that. Russ turned back toward her husband. "There are two dogs out there right now, and another on the way. John Huggins called me while I was on my way over; he's already alerted the Plattsburgh and Johnstown search-and-rescue teams. They're standing by. We'll find your son for you, Geoff. There's a limit to how far even the most active two-year-old can hike."

If he hadn't fallen into a crevasse or found a mountain creek. Russ wasn't going to mention any of those possibilities to a father who appeared to be one word away from a complete meltdown. Instead, he nodded to the woman who had been standing behind the Burnses. "Reverend Fergusson." Through sheer willpower, he managed to not picture her naked.

"Chief Van Alstyne." Her greeting was directed to a point two inches below his chin.

"Oh, for God's sake, just call each other by your first names," Burns exploded. "It's not like everybody doesn't know about you two already."

"Geoff," Clare said, "it looks like another group is ready to head out." She gestured with her chin to where a gaggle of volunteers had been teamed with one of Huggins's men. "Maybe you should join them. You'll feel better if you're doing something."

Amazingly, Burns took her suggestion. He stomped away like a pint-sized Godzilla looking for Tokyo.

"Sorry about that," she said, still talking to Russ's Adam's apple. "He's very emotional right now."

"Mmm." Apparently, they weren't going to discuss if what Burns said was true or not. He was happy to take a pass. "I'd like you to take me to the body."

That earned him an actual look in the eye. "I should help with one of the search teams."

"It won't take long. I'd like to hear your impressions. Please?"

She looked down at her Keds for a moment. "Okay." She wheeled and headed for the stone wall separating the field from the forest.

"I do a pretty good Scarlett O'Hara," she said.

"Not that kind of impression." He stepped over the wall. "Did you find him?"

"What makes you think it's a him?"

"Just a habit of speech. Saying it always sounds — I dunno, disrespectful." The temperature decreased beneath the forest cover, an advantage balanced by the increase in mosquitoes.

"One of my parishioners, Tim Garrettson, was near the right — I mean, near the northeastern end of the line. He stumbled over him." She swatted a mosquito on her arm. "Literally."

"Damn."

"He backpedaled right quick, as you can imagine. Fortunately, Dr. Anne was close by. She and I came over, and as soon as I saw what it was" — she shot him a glance — "saw him, I sent for Hadley Knox. We kept everyone else away."

"Good girl."

She smiled one-sidedly.

His uniform blouse — the same short-sleeved one he had worn to the rectory two nights ago — had already started sticking to the middle of his back. He found his eyes drifting up to the branches of the trees. Looking for snipers. He shook his head and forced himself to keep his gaze close to the ground. "Tell me what you noticed," he said.

"I think he had been buried."

He stepped over a moldering log. "Buried? Why?"

"He was just upslope of a big old pine that had toppled over. You know how they do sometimes, roots and all?"

He nodded.

"It looked like when the roots went, a portion of the topsoil slid into the hole. That's why Tim had gone around to take a look at it; he thought Cody might have gotten in there. Instead, what he got was a partially uncovered body — well, what was left of it."

"The description I got was 'partially skeletonized.' "

"That was Dr. Anne. She said she's no expert, but she thought it must have been in the ground since maybe last fall." She *hmm*ed in consideration. "Hunting season."

He found himself scanning the high cover for a Dragonov SVD-63. *There aren't any snipers in these woods. Snap out of it.* He focused on what Clare was saying. "Somebody got mad at their brother-in-law and took the opportunity to settle his hash during deer season? Maybe."

"You don't sound very convinced."

He held a pair of birch saplings aside and let her past. "We don't have any outstanding missing persons that might support that theory. Lyle got records back from the whole county. There's nothing but the usual assortment of troubled teens and deadbeat dads skipping out on child support."

"There are people who can disappear without setting off any alarms. A homeless old or mentally ill person. Someone who's easy pickings for a predator."

"Don't go there."

"Go where?" She stepped wrong and skidded in the loose, dry pine needles. He caught her arm and steadied her.

"We do *not* have a predatory killer in Washington County. Don't even start thinking it."

"Well, it would certainly explain —"

"No. It wouldn't." He heard a noise. Faint. Far away. Shouting? "Did you hear that?"

She stopped beside a barrel-trunked oak. Cocked her head. When the radio at his belt squawked, it startled them both. He unhooked the mic.

"Van Alstyne here," he said. "Go ahead."

"Huggins here," the voice said. "We found him."

"Oh, thank God," Clare said. "Thank God."

Russ found the heat and humidity and unwelcome memories were suddenly much less oppressive. "That's good news," he said. "Where was he?"

"Looks like he tried to climb a maple and got stuck in the crotch. He was sittin' in there suckin' his thumb when the dog caught his scent. We're taking him back to the Muster Field now."

"Thank your dog handler for us. She's just made a lot of people real happy."

"Roger that. Over."

Russ grinned at Clare. "Damn, I like a happy ending for a change."

"Me, too."

He rehooked the mic. "Okay, now let's go deal with the unhappy ending."

"We're not far," she said. "Once you're in sight, do you mind if I head back to the field?"

His reply was cut off when his radio squawked again. He unhooked the mic a second time. "Van Alstyne here. Go ahead."

"Chief? This is Trooper McLaren." The state police K-9 officer who had joined the search. "We've got a body here. Over."

"Thanks, McLaren, I know. Isn't one of my officers already there? With the pathologist?" Belatedly, he added, "Over."

"No, Chief. We were briefed about the body the initial searchers found. This is something my dog's just dug out of the ground. It's a second dead guy. Over."

THE SEASON AFTER PENTECOST — ORDINARY TIME

MAY AND JUNE

I

Monday. Memorial Day. Everybody in the United States was going to be hanging out and having a good time — except the sworn officers of the Millers Kill Police Department. *Maybe this is why my social life sucks,* Kevin thought, taking his seat for the morning briefing. At least it wasn't sucking alone. Everybody was on today, all shifts: the part-time guys and the volunteer fire traffic wardens, too. Memorial Day, Fourth of July, Labor Day — they were always big.

But they didn't always arrive with three unidentified homicide victims.

"The two discovered yesterday were both killed in the same way as John Doe number one." The chief, sitting in his usual spot atop the table, was grubby and crumpled around the edges. He, MacAuley, Hadley Knox, and Eric McCrea had been up half the night, working the scenes with the state CSI techs.

"Single tap at the back of the head with a small-caliber weapon, probably a full jacket. Classic execution style."

"Scheeler's report noted there wasn't any signs the first John Doe'd been restrained," MacAuley pointed out. "If he'd been taken out to the woods for an execution, you'd think whoever did it woulda trussed him up beforehand." He was standing at the whiteboard, summarizing the briefing.

The chief paused. "Taken by surprise, then. Wham, bam, thank-you-ma'am."

"So what are we looking at?" Paul Urquhart said from the back of the room. "Gangland slaying? Organized crime? If we had something like that moving into our area, we'da noticed it before this."

The chief held up his hands. "Let's go through what we know step-by-step." He slid off the table and turned to the bulletin board, almost covered with photos of John Does one, two, and three, environmental placing shots, and the downstate rap sheets Kevin had looked at Friday night. "John Doe one."

"Juan Doe," Urquhart muttered.

"Male Hispanic aged between twenty-one and twenty-eight. Killed sometime mid-April. John Doe two. Male, possibly Caribbean or African-American, based on hair fragments —"

"DeWan Doe." Urquhart sniggered.

The chief stopped. "You got something you want to share, Paul?" Urquhart shook his head. The chief gave him a long look before continuing. "Age between twenty-one and twenty-eight. Killed sometime last year in the late fall or early winter. John Doe three: male, age between twenty-one and twenty-eight. Killed more than a year ago."

"The ME any more specific than that?" MacAuley asked.

"He had some fillings. Doc Scheeler's going to get a dentist to try to date the amalgam. We probably won't have anything until tomorrow at the earliest."

The chief crossed to the laminated township map that covered half the other wall. "Location of the bodies," he said. "John Does three and two were found roughly a mile north-northwest of the old Muster Field off Route seventeen in Cossayuharie." He marked a three and a two with a dry-erase marker. "They were slightly less than three-quarters of a mile away from each other" — he drew a broken line that slanted drunkenly northwest from the pale green rectangle representing the Muster Field — "buried along a natural flint formation that runs along this line and then drops off steeply into the valley below."

"Somebody walked in."

Kevin hadn't realized he said it aloud until the chief nodded. "Somebody walked in."

"And went as far as he could go along fairly level terrain," MacAuley added.

"Who owns that land?" Eric McCrea asked.

The chief looked at Noble Entwhistle. Noble was no Sherlock Holmes, but he gave you better results than Google if you needed a name or date for something that happened in Millers Kill. "The town," he said. "It used to belong to Shep Ogilvie, but they took it for unpaid taxes back in 'eighty-seven, when his dairy went under."

"Easy access from the highway," McCrea said. "If there's no snow, you can drive a car almost all the way back to the tree line on that field."

"That's one big difference between John Does two and three and the first guy we found," the chief said. "It's a coupla kidney-cleaning miles from the nearest public road to where John Doe one was dumped." He put a *1* on the McGeochs' farm.

"But it is in the same general area where you were out chasing those runaway illegals," MacAuley pointed out.

"I think we can safely say that's a dead

end." The chief went back to his table and picked up his coffee mug. "The men running around in those woods were in Mexico last year when the last two John Does were killed."

"The Christies and their kin weren't."

The chief let his hand fall open. "Put them on the board."

"Chief." Kevin tried to control his face from pinking up as everyone turned toward him. "How do we know they were in Mexico a year ago? I mean, if they were illegals, there wouldn't be any trail, because that's kind of the point. I know they weren't employed by your sister and her husband, but maybe they were in the area working for somebody else." He paused. The chief made a "go on" gesture. "Maybe we should canvass area farms and see who might've had migrant workers last year and over winter."

"Maybe." The chief leaned against the table. "My problem with that is I don't see the connection between dairy hands and professional executions."

Kevin figured everyone was thinking the same thing. So he said it. "What if it's not professional?"

"What do you mean, Kevin? A sport killing? Somebody doing it for kicks? No." The chief pinched the bridge of his nose. "I refuse to believe we're dealing with some sort of serial killer here."

"You need to at least put it on the table, Russ." MacAuley wrote the words "Thrill killer" at one corner of the board.

"Serial killers go after vulnerable populations. Kids. Prostitutes."

"What about Jeffrey Dahmer?"

"Bob Berdella?"

"Randy Steven Kraft?"

MacAuley gave them a look that said *shut up.* He turned to the chief. "The vics already fall into a class," he said. "Young men in their early twenties." He ticked a point off one finger.

"Watch out, Kevin," Urquhart said.

"Non-Caucasians." The deputy ticked off another finger.

"We can't say that about three." The chief crossed his arms over his chest.

"Killed during tourist season." MacAuley ticked off his third finger.

"April? Nobody comes to Millers Kill in April."

"Bodies left in remote locations in Cossayuharie." MacAuley ticked off a fourth finger. "And finally, all three of them killed in the same fashion with the same-caliber weapon." He held his hand up and waggled his fingers. "We can't rule out a serial killer. Not with three bodies agreeing on five points."

"Why —" Hadley started to say, then shut her mouth.

"Go, on, Knox," the chief said.

She swallowed. "Why was the first guy — I mean, John Doe one — why was he dumped? The others were buried. Not deep, but they were buried. He was just laying out there in the open."

The chief slid up onto the table and braced his boots on a chair. "What do you think?"

Her face fell into the cool expressionless mask that had completely unnerved Kevin when she'd directed it toward him. *She's panicked,* he realized. *She's afraid of coming across like an idiot.* The chief looked at her patiently. MacAuley looked at her like a guy who was running late for his proctologist's appointment. Kevin twitched in his seat. Urquhart was smirking.

The search. He tried to beam the thought into her head. It must have worked, because her eyes slid toward him. He put his hand up to his mouth. "Huggins," he coughed.

"The search for the men who ran away after the accident interrupted the killer," she said instantly. "There was no chance to

300

bury the victim because the area was crawling with searchers."

"Which means," the chief said, "somebody who was there that night may have seen something. We need a list of everyone on the SAR team who participated, and the various Christie relatives who turned out. That'll be your job, Eric."

McCrea slid low in his chair and groaned. Several "baas" erupted from the back of the room.

"The other possibility," the chief said, "is that the body found in the back of the McGeochs' property is unrelated to the two found past the Muster Field." The dep snorted loudly but didn't say anything. "We've sent the pictures and the ME's preliminary report down to the Bronx, where they're trying to find the two men Knox and Flynn stopped last week." He stared at the whiteboard, which had a lot of theories and very few solutions. "Kevin, you go ahead and follow up on the local migrant worker population."

Kevin clenched his fist in triumph. *In like Flynn.*

"Knox, you're with McCrea. Noble, you take the SAR volunteers. Lyle, since you like the serial killer angle so much, you get to work on the VCAP database and see if you can find anything that sounds familiar."

"Any evidence that John Doe one was sexually assaulted?"

The chief's eyebrows went up. "I didn't see anything in Scheeler's report. Although, since he did his prelim before we found the other two, maybe he wasn't looking in that — uh — direction." Urquhart snickered. The chief ignored him. "You thinking someone preying on young gay men?"

The dep shrugged. "Two guys alone in the woods with no signs of coercion? It's not like we haven't seen it before."

The chief pinched the bridge of his nose again. "Yeah."

Hadley leaned toward Kevin. "What are they talking about?" she hissed.

"Three summers ago," he whispered, "two gay guys were beaten up and another one killed."

She flinched. "That's awful." Then her expression changed. Became thoughtful. "Why are we assuming it's a guy?"

"Knox? Kevin?" The chief was frowning.

"If you two brought candy, you better have enough for the other kids," the dep said.

"Why are we assuming it's a guy?" Hadley said, loud enough for everyone to hear. She looked up at the chief. "Maybe the killer is

302

a woman." Hadley looked around the room, measuring the others' reactions. "She could have lured them into the woods." She turned to MacAuley. "You don't need to restrain someone if he's busy taking his pants off."

"If it was poison, or there was money involved — those are the sort of situations where women've appeared as serial killers." The dep sounded like he was trying to be diplomatic. "Naked guys tapped in the woods — there just aren't many recorded instances of women doing that."

"Maybe that's because they're better at covering it up than men," Hadley said.

II

Clare hoped she would miss Janet when she took Amado back out to the McGeochs' to get the rest of his stuff. It was Memorial Day Monday, after all, and most reasonable people were taking the day off.

No such luck. Russ's sister came running out of the barn as soon as Clare's Subaru pulled in the dusty yard. Clare and Amado hadn't gotten out of the car before the apologies started.

"Oh, my God, Clare, I'm so, so sorry! I had *no* idea when that man showed up that he was — well, I thought it was odd that he

knew Amado, but I was so distracted —
when Russ told me, I nearly *died,* I was
so . . ." Apparently, there wasn't a word big
enough, so Janet threw her arms around
Clare and hugged her. "Thank God, thank
God you weren't hurt. I thought Russ was
just being — well, cranky, when he said
you're as tough as an army boot, but he was
right!" She hugged her again. "Oh, there's
Amado!"

Clare listened while Janet repeated her
whole apology to the young man, who
looked at her with alarmed incomprehension, protecting his cast with his good hand.
Smart kid, Clare thought. *If she hugs any
tighter she'll rebreak that bone.*

"I thought, all things considered, that
Amado should stay at the rectory after all,"
Clare said, loudly enough to catch Janet's
attention. "The Christies will probably
make bail as soon as court opens tomorrow." She made a *go on* gesture to Amado,
who needed no encouragement to escape.
He took off around the barn at a trot.

"Are you sure that's safe?" Janet, having
disgorged the apologies she must have been
holding in for two days, visibly settled. "I
mean, what if they come back?"

"It's a lot less likely in the middle of town
than out here in a trailer."

Janet ran her hand through her Medium Golden Blond No. 5 hair. "Is it true you broke Donald Christie's nose?"

Clare rubbed her own nose. "I didn't mean to."

Janet whistled. "You go, girl."

Clare held up her hands. "Violence is not the answer, to paraphrase . . . a whole bunch of people. Including your mother."

"Mmm. So, have you seen Russ since that night?"

Oh, God. What did he tell her? But no. He wouldn't have spoken about the two of them. Or about the bodies they found at the Muster Field. Janet didn't know her John Doe had been reclassified as the first of a series of murders.

She was saved from coming up with a truth that told nothing by the thrum of tires along Lick Springs Road. Janet craned her neck and shaded her eyes. "Shit," she said under her breath.

Clare twisted around to see the squad car speeding down the long sweep of hill toward the McGeochs' barnyard.

"I gotta call the men," Janet said. She raced toward the barn, leaving Clare alone at the end of a train of dust puffs rising and falling in the air.

Her heart rose in her chest to sink again

305

when she glimpsed the red head through the driver's window. *Not fair.* She wasn't going to hold it against the rest of the MKPD just because they weren't Russ.

"Hey! Reverend Fergusson!" Kevin waved jauntily as he unfolded from his cruiser. "What're you doing out here?"

She gestured toward the barn and, by implication, the bunkhouse that lay somewhere beyond it. "I brought Amado out to get the rest of his things. I'm moving him into the rectory."

Kevin considered that. "Does the chief know?"

She resisted the first comment that came to mind. "I think he's got a little more on his mind than my interim sexton's living arrangements, don't you?"

He hooked his thumbs over his gun belt in a perfect copy of Russ. "Those Christies will be making bail tomorrow, you know."

"That's why I'm out here today. How about you?"

His face lit up. "I suggested we ought to find out what migrant workers might have been in the area last year, when the other two were killed, and the chief agreed with me." His pleased expression wavered. "Well, honestly? He didn't exactly agree. But he's letting me follow up on it." He looked around, taking in the white-paint barn, the harrow and hay wagon and truck corralled between outbuildings, the cows grazing just far enough away to be scenic rather than smelly. "This is my first stop."

At Russ's sister's. Who allegedly didn't have any migrant employees.

"Are you hoping to track down who the two men from yesterday are?"

"Nope. We're trying to track down their murderer." There was a certain relish in the way Kevin said "murderer."

"A migrant worker? You must be kidding. Those men do backbreaking labor six or seven days a week for wages most of us would turn our noses up at. Why on earth would one of them get involved in something like this?"

Despite the absence of anyone else in the barnyard, Kevin leaned in close. "We're thinking . . . serial killer."

"Oh, please. In Millers Kill? Pull the other one."

He shrugged. "There are three men dead, all of 'em killed in the same way, by a similar weapon, in the space of a year or so. All of 'em left within seven miles of each other. If that happened along the Green River instead of in Millers Kill, what would you think?"

Good Lord. Kevin Flynn is growing up into a real cop. A civilian Humvee drove past the barnyard, its woofer rattling their car windows. *This has gotten way too deep. Janet has got to come clean with them.*

As if he could read her mind, he said, "Are the McGeochs around?"

"In the barn," she said.

"Thanks." He strode toward the barn while she told herself it wasn't her business and she wasn't going to get involved. This didn't have anything to do with her, or her people, or her church. Except . . . Sister Lucia had asked her to take care of these men. And so far the only thing she had done to uphold the sister's charge was to keep her mouth shut about their location.

"Wait for me," she called. Kevin paused in the wide doorway and watched as she jogged across the dusty yard. Inside, it was cool and lofty. They alarmed a pair of barn swallows, who fluttered through the mote-hung air before arrowing out the door. The sound of wings echoed in the almost-empty haymows.

"Mr. McGeoch?" Kevin shouted. "Mrs. McGeoch?"

"In here!" The faint answer came from the small doorway set opposite the tractor-wide entrance to the barn. Clare dogged

Kevin as he ducked through and they emerged into a long, low cow byre. Clare stumbled, and the young officer caught her by her arm. She looked up and down the center aisle. Cement. Drain holes. The steel-basketed lights hung, one each, at the stall entrances. Her skin went clammy. She swallowed.

"Are you okay?" Kevin let her arm go.

"Yeah," she said. "This just . . . looks a lot like the MacEntyres' barn." She breathed in. Manure and urine and hay, earthy and sharp and green. No copper-sweet smell of blood.

"Don't worry," Kevin said, "You're safe here." He meant to be reassuring, but all Clare heard was the perfect assurance of someone who had never had anything horrific happen to him.

"Clare?" Janet emerged from one of the stalls, pitchfork in hand. "Officer Flynn?" That last sounded genuinely surprised. She jammed her pitchfork into the manure cart squatting in the middle of the aisle. "What's up?"

"Hi, Mrs. McGeoch. Sorry to interrupt, but when I went to your house, your daughter said you were over here, and I wanted to talk to you first, because the chief said you'd talked to some local farmers about migrant workers before you hired that service to, you know, help you get your own, so I was hoping you or Mr. McGeoch could fix me up with some contacts so I can find out a little more about who's hiring migrants and if they've had workers stay year-round."

"What?"

Clare shook off the shadow of the angel of death. "Officer Flynn needs a list of farmers in the area who employ migrant workers."

Kevin looked a bit affronted. "That's what I said."

"Maybe," Clare said, "if Mike's around, he could help Officer Flynn?"

"He's cleaning the equipment. I can —"

"Because I want to talk to you — um, about Amado possibly returning to work here." She was speaking so broadly, she might as well be winking and nudging.

"O-kay." Janet walked toward the center of the byre. "You see those doors there?"

Kevin nodded.

"That's the equipment room. Go ahead and tell Mike what you want. He's better with names and numbers than I am."

"Thanks," Kevin said. He started down the central aisle. Stopped. Turned. "Big place you got here. How on earth do you two manage it by yourselves?"

"Oh, we've got help." Janet's voice was as

light as air. "But it *is* Memorial Day, you know."

"Don't I just." He resumed walking toward the equipment room.

Clare gestured toward the narrow walkway leading to the larger barn. "Can we talk out there?"

"He won't be able to hear us. With the steam cleaning equipment on, he'll hardly be able to hear Mike."

"It's not that. This place is way too much like the MacEntyres' for my comfort. I keep expecting to see someone with a gun coming out of the abattoir at any moment."

Janet looked, frowning. "Sure." She led the way, the top of her head almost brushing against the low ceiling of the passage. Clare took a deep breath once they were in the sun-shafted expanse of the hay barn. "So," Janet said. "Let me ask you something. Do you think my brother would react in the same way? If he were in the byre?"

Clare thought about how, thirty-odd years after the need, Russ still couldn't walk through heat and green leaves without watching for the glint of a gun barrel. About the way his face would still and his words dry up when conversation wandered onto certain old cases. "Yes," she said. "I'm pretty sure he would."

Janet shoved her hands in her jeans and looked around the three-story cross-beamed space. "Okay," she said. "That helps explain some stuff. Thanks." She focused on Clare. "What did you need to speak to me about?"

"You've got to come clean about the workers you have here."

"What? Why?"

"I didn't tell you something — earlier." Clare caught a strand of free-falling hair and shoved it into her twist. "There were two more bodies discovered yesterday. Killed the same way as your John Doe. Buried in shallow graves a mile past the Muster Field. It'll probably be all over the local news tonight or tomorrow." She looked into Janet's eyes. "Kevin's asking for names of migrant workers because they're thinking this may be the work of a serial killer."

"What, a guy who comes up here from Mexico and whacks people on his day off? That's ridiculous."

"I'm not saying one of your men is responsible. I'm not saying the migrant-did-it theory even makes much sense. Russ gave the job to Kevin, so you know it's not their top priority." She opened her hands. "What I'm saying is that something terrible has happened. And your brother needs every piece of information he can get to find the person responsible."

Janet was shaking her head. "I can't. I just can't. We haven't started the application process for new workers, and we can't get these guys permits retroactively. They have to leave the country and stay out for sixty days before they can apply again. If the police show up here to question them, what do you think's going to happen? They'll scatter to the four winds. *He* won't get any information from them and *we'll* be up the creek without a paddle."

"Janet, how are you going to feel if someone else shows up dead and you didn't do anything to help stop it? For what? To save a few bucks on payroll?"

"You don't understand what a razor-thin margin we're working on. Almost everything we pay out is a fixed cost: gas, feed, vet bills, insurance. We sure as hell can't charge more for the milk. The only place where we have some flexibility is our labor. Hiring locals would cost twice what we pay the Mexicans, plus Social Security and unemployment insurance. That "few bucks" on the payroll would be thousands more. Thousands."

"You're not paying Social Security and unemployment?"

Janet had the good grace to look embarrassed. "We would have, if the original plan had held up and we had workers with permits. But now . . . the seven guys we have aren't supposed to be here, so how would we explain having a payroll?" She rubbed her hands on the front of her jeans. "We're doing the whole thing under the table at this point."

"Oh, good Lord." Nervous energy sent Clare pacing in a circle. "That's just dumb. Just plain dumb. Now you're going to be in trouble with ICE *and* the IRS."

Janet crossed her arms. "I'm not telling my brother about them. I can't." She twisted, following Clare. "You can't tell him either."

Clare stopped. "How can I not?" She waved her arms in the air, wanting to snatch her hair out in frustration. "Christ on a bicycle," she said.

Janet stared at her. Then laughed.

"What?" Clare said. "What?"

Janet sobered. "You can't tell," she said. "You promised me."

"Promised you what?" Kevin straightened as he came out of the narrow passageway from the byre. Mike McGeoch followed him, looking as calm and contented as one of his cows, as if he lived in a world where murder and illegal aliens and tax fraud never intruded. Maybe for him they never did.

"It's personal," Janet said. She glanced at Clare, then at Kevin. "About my brother."

Clare saw the lights go on in Kevin's upstairs. His face pinked. "Oh. Sure. Personal." He was shaking hands with Mike when he looked toward the barn's entrance. "Who's that?"

Clare turned. Amado and the McGeoch's foreman were silhouetted in the wide doorway; an identical height, one gangly and broken-armed, one broad and muscular. The foreman hugged the younger man, held the back of his head, murmured something too low for them to make out. He handed the kid a backpack, adding to the small duffel and bulging shopping bag he was already toting.

"My interim sexton," Clare said. "Amado." The kid and the foreman both looked up. The foreman spotted Kevin's uniform, slapped the younger man on the back, and strolled out of sight, not fast, not slow.

"No, the other guy. I thought you didn't have any Latino workers here."

"Oh, that's one of our neighbor's men." Janet's voice was thin and high. "Works for us on his off days." She laughed, a brittle, unconvincing sound. "We're lucky to get him."

Kevin frowned. "He seemed pretty tight with Amado for someone who's just dropping in once in a while."

Janet looked at Clare, who kept her mouth shut. She wasn't telling any more lies for Russ's sister.

"I think a lot of the guest workers around here come from the same area in Mexico." Janet shrugged. "They may even be related." She raised her voice. "Do you know Octavio from home, Amado?" The young man stared at her. "Octavio? *¿Un amigo?*" He tightened his grip on the backpack and continued to stare at them like a spooked horse.

"It's okay, Amado. Go ahead, get in the car." Clare turned. "I need to get him back to the church. Janet, please consider what we talked about." She gripped the other woman's arm, trusting it would look like a friendly squeeze to Kevin. "Officer Flynn. Good luck on the — um, investigation. It's a big responsibility."

"It is, isn't it?" His face brightened. "See you later, Reverend. Enjoy the rest of the holiday weekend."

Friday night she'd been attacked in her church. Sunday, they had found two bodies

316

at the annual picnic. She opened her mouth to point these facts out, then shut it at the sight of the young officer's cheerful expression. "Thanks, Kevin. I'll try."

III

She went into the church to pray that evening. She hadn't anticipated how dislocated she would feel with a houseguest, a disturbance made worse by Amado's shy formality and their lack of a common language. Her unsettled feeling wasn't helped by the fact that every time she passed her sofa or sat at the kitchen table, she experienced erotic flashbacks hot enough to make her wonder if she were going into premature menopause. When had she last had sex? She couldn't pin down the exact year, but it was at least two presidential elections ago. She had been celibate a long time. A looong time.

So she fled to St. Alban's. She loved coming here alone at night, lighting only the candles and reading Compline at the old high altar. She would trace the carving along the edge of the marble — PRAY FOR THE SOUL OF THE REVEREND DR. MATHIAS ARCHIBALD DUNN, RECTOR OF THIS CHURCH — and pray she would, though she suspected the late Dr. Dunn rolled over in his grave every time an ordained woman broke bread at his altar. Tonight, she spent a long time in the quiet and the candlelight, praying to be opened, to discern God's way, to know what to do.

Go see Lucia Pirone.

The thought was there, fully formed in her mind. Her hands fell open and her head came up. Of course. She should visit Sister Lucia. In person.

You should have paid a call weeks ago.

That was the voice of Grandmother Fergusson, not the Almighty. Tomorrow, she'd head over to the rehab center and spill her guts to the missioner nun. If she baked a homemade treat, she thought, absently rubbing Dr. Dunn's name, she'd satisfy both God and her grandmother.

IV

"Clare. How wonderful to see you." Sister Lucia's eyes were as keen as ever, but her hand shook as she took Clare's. "And what's this? For me?" She leaned forward, coughing, to accept the box Clare held.

"Let me help," Clare said. She untied the string and pulled the top off.

"Good heavens. These look delicious. Are these pecan tassies? And" — Sister Lucia took out a round cookie and put it in her mouth — "bourbon balls?" She chewed and swallowed, closing her eyes. "I haven't had one of these since the last time I was in Texas. Wherever did you find them up here?"

"I made them this morning." She grinned. "Since they don't let you bring in a bottle of bourbon itself."

"There's enough there to feed the entire floor! You didn't have to do that."

"It's by way of penance. I should have come to visit long before this. How are you doing?"

"Well, the pneumonia has cleared up, and they tell me that's good. But it put me behind on my therapy for this darned hip." She made a face. "A broken hip. If that doesn't tell me I'm an old woman, I don't know what does. Ah, well." She looked at Clare sharply. "I'm guessing you didn't come all the way over here from Millers Kill to learn about my exercises."

Clare shook her head. "I'm afraid not." She told the nun about Janet and Mike McGeoch, the bodies, the investigation, her own part in concealing the truth of the situation from the police. By the time she finished, Sister Lucia had put away several more bourbon balls and was nodding.

"Oh, what a tangled web we weave," she said, when Clare ran out of steam.

"What should I do?"

"Who'd you say was the lead detective on this?"

"Our police chief, Russ Van Alstyne. He was there the night of the crash — I don't know if you saw him."

"Surely not the redhead. He didn't look old enough."

"No, no. That's Officer Flynn. He's a sweetheart. No, the chief was the older man with the" — she couldn't help it, she gestured with her hands, shaping Russ's broad shoulders — "tall. Very tall. Blue eyes."

"The really attractive one?"

"Oh. Yes."

The nun's lips twitched upward. "I didn't see him."

Clare felt her cheeks go red.

"Evidently, you know him." Sister Lucia's glint of amusement mellowed. "Do you trust him? To do the right thing, if you tell him about the men working at the Mc-Geochs?"

"Our definition of 'the right thing' is sometimes very different." She thought for a moment. "If he feels it's his duty to turn them in, he'll do it. He may not like it, but he'll do it."

"Even if it hurts his own sister?" The nun sniffed. "Sounds inflexible to me."

"Not inflexible. Honor-bound." She couldn't help smile. "Admittedly, it does make him a pain in the ass at times."

Sister Lucia laughed, which set off another bout of coughing. One of the nurses came in just at the moment Clare began to be concerned.

"Sister?" She helped the nun lean forward until the coughing fit stopped.

"Sorry," Sister Lucia gasped.

Clare stood. "No, no, I'm sorry. I've overtaxed you."

The nurse nodded. "It may be time for another treatment."

Sister Lucia grasped Clare's arm. "Tell him," she said, her voice a rattle in her throat, "justice is important. Rights and jobs and working conditions are important. But the bottom line is, without life, none of those matter." She looked up at Clare, her face fierce in its weakness, like a martyr's. "If there's some connection, anything . . ." She left the implication unsaid. "Tell him."

V

Clare was on her way home from the rehab center when her phone rang. She turned down her Jason Mraz CD and glanced at the number: Russ. For a second, she considered letting her voice mail pick it up. She had to talk to him, she was clear on that, but in fairness's sake she felt she had to let Janet know what she was going to do first.

She flipped it open. "Hey," she said.

"Hey. It's me. Where are you?"

Huh. That was to the point. "On my way back from the Rehabilitation Center at the Glens Falls Hospital. I was visiting Lucia Pirone. You remember her."

"The nun from the crash, yeah. Look, can you meet me at the county courthouse? You know where that is?"

"Certainly. Why? What's going on?"

He made a disapproving noise. "Amy Nguyen of the DA's office wants to talk to us."

"Us? Together?"

"The Christie brothers are up for bail, and apparently their lawyer wants to start the horse trading right now. Can you get over there?"

"Yeah. Where?"

"Just ask for Amy when you check in. Thanks. 'Bye."

He hung up before she had a chance to say anything else. Maybe he was in a tearing hurry. Maybe they were back to not talking. That's what she missed the most: talking. Serious, silly, bone-deep, flippant, all their words and thoughts like gifts to each other, the only gifts they, with their hobbled hearts, could give. She turned the CD player back up. *Another day to sing about the magic that was you and me.* Oh, yeah. Always time for that.

The Washington County Courthouse was in a low, modern brick building that could have passed for a bank center or a modest corporate headquarters. Its lines were softened by ornamental crab apples in full flower and row upon row of daffodils and paperwhites. She paused a moment on the walkway from the parking lot, breathing in the scent of apple and thick May grass rising over the tinny smell of cars baking in the sunshine. She wondered if the small slices of spring soothed or taunted the prisoners who went in and out of here.

At the security station, she asked for Amy Nguyen and was pointed toward a meeting room that was, when Clare opened the door to a "Come in!", scarcely bigger than a broom closet. A petite Asian woman about Clare's age stood behind a table stacked with manila folders and Redweld document cases.

"Amy Nguyen?"

The woman looked up from the open file

she had been reading. On someone less harried-looking, her expression would have been a smile. "You must be the Reverend Fergusson." She held out a hand. Only the faintest trace of an accent indicated English had not been her first language.

"No one else seems to want the job," Clare agreed, shaking Nguyen's hand. That earned her an actual grin.

"Same here. Take a seat."

Clare pulled out one of the molded plastic chairs shoved beneath the table. "What's up? Chief Van Alstyne said you wanted to talk to me about the Christies."

"Let's wait until Russ gets here so we can all —" Amy broke off as the door opened, almost banging into Clare, and Russ sidled into the room, taking up any remaining free space.

"Sorry if I'm late," he said. He glanced at Clare. "Reverend Fergusson." Looked at Nguyen. "Amy. It's been awhile."

She reached over the table to shake his hand. "It has been. I was so, so sorry to hear about your wife. I can't imagine what a terrible loss it must be for you."

"Thank you," he said stiffly. "It's been — yes. Thank you." At Nguyen's gesture, he attempted to wedge himself into one of the chairs. He did not look at Clare.

"Okay, here's the situation." Nguyen laid her hand on the file she had been reading. "The Christies' attorney is holding up the bail application because she wants us to drop all charges against her clients."

"What?" Russ sounded outraged. "The hell she does! If I hadn't gotten there when I did —"

Nguyen held up one hand. "In exchange," she stressed, "they will drop their suit against you and the Millers Kill Police Department for assault and battery."

Russ rocked back, threatening to tip the flimsy chair.

"Yes," Clare said. "I'm willing to drop all charges. Go ahead."

"No!" Russ turned toward her. "That bastard could have killed you!" He scowled at the ADA. "Neil and Donald Christie broke into her church and tried to beat the crap out of her. Look at her! Either one of 'em is twice as big as she is."

Nguyen picked up a piece of paper. "According to the Christies, they went into an open unlocked church seeking an acquaintance. When they tried to find him, Reverend Fergusson" — she looked over the top of the paper at Clare — "assaulted them with a large wooden staff."

"The processional cross," Clare said, realizing the moment she said it that only the worst sort of pedant would correct someone accusing her of attacking them.

"They claim Ms. Fergusson struck Donald unconscious, broke Donald's nose, and battered both of them with the — ah, cross." She picked up five or six papers clipped together. "Their attorney helpfully included the records from their admission at Washington County Hospital, which backs up this account of their injuries." She almost smiled at Clare. "If I'm ever in a dark alley someplace, I hope you're with me, Reverend." She turned to Russ. "Donald Christie then goes on to attest that before he had a chance to comply with your demand that he assume a prone position pursuant to arrest, you punched him several times in the face." She rattled the hospital records. "Also borne out by the medical evidence."

"Look," Russ began.

Nguyen shook her head. "I don't want to hear it. If their attorney files this, our office will have a responsibility to investigate. Don't tell me anything." She dropped the papers and braced her arms on the table. "I read your report. And the Reverend Fergusson's statement. Believe me, I get the picture of what really went down. But this is going to be a bear to prosecute, Russ.

The trespassing will never stick, they have good traction with the self-defense, and if we go ahead with resisting arrest, their lawyer's going to make damn sure the jury knows about their pending lawsuit against you. Which, I will point out, is going to cost the town a hell of a lot of money, even if you successfully defend yourself against judgment. Maybe — *maybe* — I can get a win on threatening, for a whopping five-hundred-dollar fine."

He stared at his knees, shaking his head like a bull that had been gored one too many times.

"I'll drop the charges," Clare said again. "I'm fine, and Amado's fine, and that's the only thing that matters."

"That's not the only goddam thing that matters," he said, his voice low.

Clare risked laying her hand on his arm. "Maybe not," she said. "But I'm not willing to —"

Buy my happiness with your marriage. She could see it in his eyes, the echo of the words she had said to him so many months before. Before his wife died. Before they had both been broken.

She inhaled. "To see you endanger your job and the reputation of the police department." She looked at the ADA. "I don't need state-sanctioned punishment. As long as they stay away from Amado and me, I'm willing to drop the whole matter."

Nguyen nodded. "We can absolutely make that part of the deal."

Russ snorted. "Like a restraining order is going to stop those guys? Please."

Nguyen steepled her fingers. "I leave the enforcement up to you."

He still looked deeply unhappy.

"If it makes you feel any better," she went on, "it appears they truly weren't after Ms. Fergusson. They indicated in their statements that your handyman" — she gestured toward Clare — "had been seeing their sister, and they wanted to speak to him. They didn't even know your name."

The mechanics of dropping the complaint were simpler than Clare had feared. The assistant DA had already prepared the order of restraint, and all Clare had to do was sign it in front of one of the frazzled court clerks, who then stamped her notary seal on the paper and sent them out to wait. After half an hour, they were ushered into Judge Ryswick's chambers — the ADA had pointedly suggested Russ go out for a sandwich, and he had just as pointedly ignored her — and Clare got to repeat her account of the events of Friday night. Ryswick made a few disapproving *tch*s, jotted a couple of lines on the papers Nguyen had given him, and, after a long look at Clare that made her feel as if she must be guilty of something, approved the order.

She was back outside in the parking lot an hour after she had arrived, clutching a sheet of paper that was supposed to stand between her and the Christies. "That was fast," she said to Russ, who was scowling at the sunshine as if it were a personal affront. "Who said, *The wheels of justice grind slowly*?"

"That wasn't justice," he said. "That was convenience."

"I told you, as long as they leave me and Amado alone, I'm happy." She glanced up at him, shading her eyes. "Do you think they told the truth? About Amado dating their sister?"

He rubbed the back of his neck. "Maybe. That would certainly clear up how they knew him. I haven't been able to figure out any other explanation. It's not like the kid's been out partying at the Dew Drop Inn."

"So how did he meet the sister?"

"I dunno. You've spent more time with him than anyone else. Is he a Latin lothario?"

"Hardly. He strikes me more like Kevin

Flynn, if Kevin had been born in a poor village in northern Mexico. Sweet, helpful, and can't say boo to a woman."

"Huh. Not anymore. Friday afternoon I caught Kevin propositioning our new officer. Had to read them both the riot act."

"Kevin Flynn? Propositioned Hadley Knox? I don't believe it."

"Well." Russ hitched at his gun belt. "It was more along the line of asking to carry her books home from school. Which for Kevin is the equivalent of inviting her to meet him up against the wall in the alley. I laid down a blanket no-fraternizing rule." He glanced back as the courthouse doors swung open, discharging a group of men and women suited in every hue from black to charcoal. "I suppose I'll have to get the town's attorney to draw something up for us and make it all legal."

She was facing away from the sun, toward the parking lot, while he was talking, which is why she saw trouble coming first. "Uh-oh," she said.

He turned. "What?"

She gestured with her chin to the man ambling across the asphalt toward them. Sleeves rolled up, no jacket, tie loosely knotted — as he drew closer, she could see it had a picture of Snoopy on it — in this bas-

tion of lawyers and defendants and witnesses, no one would mistake him for
anything other than a reporter.

"Oh, crap on toast," Russ said. "Ben
Beagle."

VI

"Be nice." Clare sounded like his mother.

"Nice? He printed a story in the *Post-Star*
implying we spent the night together before
I killed my wife! Do you know the circulation of the *Post-Star*? Twenty-five thousand!
I looked it up."

"Ssh." She got the same look on her face
he had seen on the times he'd been to her
church: bright, open, welcoming. It wasn't
fake, but it was certainly whitewashed.

"Hey! Chief Van Alstyne. Just the man I
was hoping to see. You've saved me a trip to
the MKPD." Beagle pulled a small notepad
from his pocket and clicked his pen, smiling
as if Russ was an old army buddy who owed
him a drink. "What can you tell me about
the two bodies found this past Sunday in
Cossayuharie?"

"How do you know about that?"

Clare cleared her throat. "Uh, Russ —"

"There were close to two hundred people
there," Beagle said cheerfully. "You know
what they say. Two hundred can keep a

331

secret if one hundred are dead. Or something like that." He waggled his fingers at Clare. "Reverend Fergusson. Nice to see you again. I understand it was a little boy from your congregation who started the whole hullabaloo."

"Uh, yes," she said.

"For chrissakes, Clare, you don't have to talk to him." She frowned at him. Him! "I'm just trying to save you trouble," he said under his breath. "Every time you land in the newspaper your bishop has a fit."

"Really?" Beagle's eyes lit up. "Why is that?"

Her frown became a glare before she turned to Beagle. "Oh, you know Chief Van Alstyne," she said, going all southern. "He will have his little joke." Russ was pleased to see Beagle looked dubious. He didn't have a reputation for little jokes, and he didn't want one, either.

"A two-and-a-half-year-old wandered away from the St. Alban's parish picnic," Clare went on. Her voice took on that precise tone people get when speaking for attribution. "He was lost in the nearby woods for — oh, almost three hours before the Millers Kill Search and Rescue team located him, with the help of a wonderful dog handler from Saratoga. I can't recall her name, but John Huggins will have it. We're all very grateful to have him back, safe and sound. That's St. Alban's, Five Church Street, Millers Kill: Holy Eucharist Sundays at seven-thirty and nine in the summer, child care provided." She crossed her arms and smiled sweetly while Beagle scribbled on his pad. Russ couldn't decide if he wanted to kiss her or drop her on her head.

"Thanks," Beagle said. "Now, Chief. About those bodies —"

"No comment," Russ said.

"Can you confirm that they're contemporary and not historical?" Every few years, someone in the county plowed up a forgotten burial site from the eighteenth century.

"No comment," Russ said.

"Can you confirm that the medical examiner's office has possession of them pending a homicide investigation?"

"No comment."

The unending string of rebuffs was making Russ's jaw tight, but Beagle absorbed them without losing his serenity.

"Can you comment on the connection between the two unidentified bodies found on Sunday and the one found the Friday before?"

He managed to stop himself from demanding to know where the hell Beagle had gotten that information. It must have shown on his face, though, because the reporter's expression sharpened. "I understand the — ah, Joe Friday was Hispanic. Kind of unusual for this part of the state. Are you considering it a possible race-related hate crime?"

Clare's brows pulled down in worry. "You mean, somebody targeting Latinos?"

"Or migrant workers." Beagle clicked his pen as if emphasizing the possibility. "It wouldn't be the first time. In the teens and twenties of the last century, this area was a KKK hotbed. Lots of anti-Irish, anti-Catholic, anti-immigrant violence."

"You're kidding!" She looked appalled. "Russ?"

"No. Comment."

She drew in a breath, ready to rip into him, but stopped herself. She glanced at Ben Beagle, then at Russ. Her eyes narrowed: *Later for you.* He wasn't sure if it was a promise or a threat. "I need to be going," she said. "It was nice to see you again, Mr. Beagle."

"Please." The reporter took her hand. "Call me Ben. We should get together for lunch sometime, talk about maybe doing a day-in-the-life story on your church."

Clare smiled warily. "I don't think we have much at St. Alban's to interest an investigative reporter."

Beagle was still holding her hand. "It'd be a human-interest piece. Heartwarming. Heartwarming sells papers." He grinned at her. "Not as much as crime and car crashes, but — this being Washington County — sometimes we run short on those."

Clare looked amused. It struck Russ that the reporter was a lot closer to her age than he himself was, and that Beagle might even have some appeal — to *some* women. Like a scruffy teddy bear won at a carnival, maybe.

"Weren't you going?" he asked. It came out harsher than he intended.

She stiffened. Then smiled brilliantly at Beagle. "I'd like that, Ben. Give me a call." She withdrew her hand and, never once glancing at Russ, stalked away to her car.

"Good-*bye,*" he yelled. She sketched a wave without turning.

"Quite a woman," Beagle said.

Russ grunted.

Ben clicked his pen again and turned to Russ. "So, Chief. Are you going to be able to give me any information on this serial killer haunting the Millers Kill area?"

VII

POLICE DENY SERIAL KILLER, the headline read. Hadley picked the paper up from
the kitchen table, where Hudson had
dropped it — his morning chore was bringing the *Post-Star* in for Granddad — before
dashing back upstairs to get his backpack.

Millers Kill chief of police Russell Van
Alstyne refused to comment on the possibility that a serial killer is responsible for
three murder victims found in Cossayuharie over the past week, despite strong
similarities in each slaying.

Hadley shook her head. The chief would
have a heart attack when he saw this.

Speaking of which . . . she took Granddad's medicines from the cupboard, untwisted the complicated seals, and shook his
daily dose into a cup next to the coffee-
maker. He hadn't been taking them regu-
larly, despite her nagging, so she was trying
to make them unavoidable.

"Hudson! Geneva! Hurry up or you'll
miss breakfast!" She grabbed three boxes of
cereal from the shelf and hefted the gallon
jug of milk out of the fridge. Half gone. She
jotted MILK on the back of the National
Grid envelope she was using for her grocery

list and stuffed it into her tote bag.

A clatter on the stairs, and Genny trotted into the kitchen, holding a pair of dress boots Hadley had picked up on sale at Wal-Mart a week after they arrived in the North Country. "Mom, will you help me zip up my boots?"

Hadley pulled out a kitchen chair and deposited her daughter in it. "Lovey, it's June. We don't wear boots in June."

"But these are Hello Kitty boots. And I have a Hello Kitty shirt on."

She couldn't argue with that. "What about the sandals Grampy got you?"

Geneva gave her a look like Joan Rivers dissecting a badly dressed actress on Oscar night. "Those are Strawberry Shortcake sandals. Strawberry Shortcake is for pre-school. I'm in first grade." She wriggled the boots on and stuck her legs out.

Hadley weighed the teacher's reaction to the unseasonable footwear versus the time lost convincing Geneva to change her mind, and decided she could live with Mrs. Flaherty thinking she was a neglectful mother. She zipped the boots. "You get your cereal and I'll help you with the milk," she said. She strode through the family room to the foot of the stairs and yelled, "Hudson!"

He emerged from his room, an overfull

backpack swinging from one shoulder, clutching a fistful of papers. "I need signatures," he said, handing them to her. "And two checks." Behind him, she could hear Granddad thumping down the hall.

Hadley examined the papers as she followed her son into the kitchen. Permission slip for a field trip to Saratoga Performing Arts Center. Cost, ten bucks. Permission slip for a field trip to the Mohawk Canal museum. Cost, five bucks. So much for getting her hair cut this week. A notice of upcoming field days — please make sure your child is adequately sun-screened. She dropped the forms on the table and poured milk into Genny's bowl, holding it away from herself to avoid splashing her uniform. "I don't know why they bother to have school into June," she said to Hudson. "You're not spending any time there."

She grabbed her checkbook from the tote and started filling out the forms. "You should have given these to me last night," she told her son, who was steam-shoveling spoonfuls of cereal into his mouth. He nodded.

"Hey, Honey," Granddad called from the family room. "Come on in here and check this out."

"I can't," she said.

"Your police department's on the channel six news."

Hudson and Genny both looked up, eyes wide. "Finish your breakfast," Hadley ordered, even as they slipped from their chairs and ran into the next room. "I am not driving you to school," Hadley warned, following them. "You're out the door at five to eight whether you've finished breakfast or —"

She broke off. A streaked blonde in a pink jacket was breathlessly talking into a microphone in front of the MKPD. Before Hadley had a chance to hear what she said, the picture changed to dawn breaking over the Muster Field. "This was the site where the second and third bodies were found." The blonde, wearing a trench coat in this shot, turned to an "area resident who witnessed the recovery of the victims." She thrust the mic toward a heavyset man who seemed excited about his moment of fame, despite the early hour. He launched into a description of the events of Sunday afternoon.

"Mom, we didn't see any bodies," Hudson complained.

"That's 'cause we went home like sensible people once they found the Burns boy," Granddad said.

The screen switched back to the MKPD.

"Mom, look!" Hudson said. "Maybe you'll be on TV, too!"

God forbid.

"Could this be the work of a serial killer?" the reporter asked the camera. "So far, the Millers Kill police refuse to confirm or deny the possibility. But meanwhile, the residents of this far-flung rural township watch. And wait. And wonder. This is Sheena Bevins, WREB News." The screen switched to the anchor.

"Mom, what's a serial killer?" Genny asked.

"Someone who puts poison in cereal." Hudson leered menacingly. "You may have already eaten it. Do you feel sick?"

Genny shrieked.

"Stop it," Hadley said. "Both of you, into the kitchen and finish your breakfast."

Granddad shook his head. "What's this world comin' to?" He heaved himself up out of his recliner. "You any closer to solving this?"

"We've got nothing." Hadley flopped her checkbook open against the top of the television and began to write out the field trip payments. "We don't even have an identity for the first guy." She ripped the checks out and folded them in the permission slips as she crossed the kitchen. "Upstairs and brush your teeth, you two," she said, zipping the papers into Hudson's backpack. She scooped up the bowls — still half full of milk and cereal, in Genny's case — and dumped them in the sink.

"I'll take care of those," Granddad said. "You better get going. They're going to need you at the station."

Granddad was convinced she was one rung below the deputy chief at the department. He seemed to think her twice-weekly trips to Albany were some sort of high-level investigator's training, instead of Police Basic. Albany. Tonight. Shit. That meant she had to fill up her gas tank.

She ran up the stairs to her room, pausing just long enough to stick her head into the bathroom and say, "Brush!" without checking to see what the kids were actually doing. She had five bucks and change in a mug on her dresser. She emptied it into her pocket and then took her gun safe down from the closet shelf. She didn't like to put on her belt before the kids left for school, but it couldn't be helped when they were running late. She unlocked the safe box, checked the gun just like her instructor had told her, and snapped it into its holster. She wondered if she would ever feel at ease with the thing. She made sure everything else was secure — baton, cuffs, radio mount, ammo pouch — then buckled it on. She twitched the rig around a few times to try to get more comfortable, then banged on the wall adjoining the bathroom. "Finish up!" she yelled. "It's bus time!"

Geneva bolted past her as she left the bedroom, with Hudson following. He eyed her rig. "Ooh, Mom," he said. "Could I —"

She held up one finger. "No. I don't even want you to ask. If you ask again, you're getting a consequence."

He gave her a Look and slumped downstairs, muttering just quietly enough for her to ignore it. In the kitchen, the kids shouldered their backpacks and kissed their grampy, who had abandoned the morning news long enough to make coffee. The pills lay untouched in the cup. "Take your medicine," Hadley said. "And no smoking!"

"I'm not smokin' no more," he said, with the same expression Hudson got when he was lying.

"I'll try to get home at lunchtime and return the cans and bottles." She kissed Granddad. The deposit money and what she had in her pocket should get her to Albany and back. She hoped. She shooed the kids out the door before her and tossed her tote into the back of the car. The bus rumbled to a stop and Hudson and Genny climbed aboard without a backward glance — which, she supposed, was a good thing.

She spent the five-minute drive to the station worrying about what she was going to do for child care over the summer. Granddad was going back to work sooner rather than later, and even in a small town she didn't want to leave Genny and Hudson home several hours a day. The Millers Kill recreation department had a seven-week day camp that sounded perfect, except that it was four hundred per kid. The sight of the TV vans parked in front of the station put an end to her pity party. There were three reporter/cameraman pairs on the front steps that she could see, bringing traffic to a near standstill as drivers on their way to work slowed down to rubberneck.

She pulled into the lot that ran beside and behind the station and killed her engine. She sat, hands still wrapped around the steering wheel, wondering how in hell she was going to get by those people without getting caught on camera.

VIII

A flash of copper near the asphalt caught Hadley's eye. Kevin Flynn's disembodied head rose from the edge of the parking lot.

What the hell? He beckoned to her. She slid out of her car, snagging her tote bag, and hiked toward him. He was, she saw as she got closer, standing in a stairwell. Rotting leaves drifted over half the cement steps. At the bottom, a door stood ajar.

"In here," he said.

She didn't need to be told twice. She descended carefully so as not to slip on the leaves and ducked inside, Kevin treading on her heels. She was, she found, next to the evidence locker.

"They used to have cells on this floor in the olden days," Flynn explained, tugging the heavy door back into place. "This was the way they took prisoners out."

In the enclosed area, Flynn towered over her. She moved forward, well away from his body space, out of reach. She had decided she was going to approach him with a kind of big-sister courtesy unless and until he hit on her again. Cold and standoffish was a turn-on for some guys, and while she didn't think Flynn was like that, she wasn't taking any chances. She figured if she treated him like everyone else on the force did — as if he were sixteen years old — he'd get over his crush fast.

"Thanks for sneaking me in," she said. She threaded her way past file boxes stacked

344

three deep against the wall and headed for the stairs. "When did the reporters show up?"

"They were here when I got in," he said, his voice echoing along the subterranean hallway. "The chief's not a happy guy right now."

At the foot of the stairs, she paused. Almost made him go up first. Then she pictured the two of them maneuvering around each other, changing positions. The hell with it. She mounted the stairs. If he wanted to get an eyeful of her brown poly-clad ass, so be it.

She could hear voices coming from Harlene's dispatch when she got to the top. "—gotta make a statement," MacAuley was saying.

"I know, I know." That was the chief.

She walked in and was surprised to see the deputy chief spiffed up in the brown wool uniform jacket none of them ever wore, his cap tucked beneath his arm.

"Morning," she said.

Harlene rolled her chair away from the board and stood up. "Looks like I better make more coffee."

"Don't bother on my account!" Hadley called after her, but it was too late.

The chief frowned at her. "Did you say

anything to the reporters coming in?"

She shifted her tote bag to her other arm. "No, sir." She could feel a solid mass in the doorway behind her, and knew, without turning, it was Kevin Flynn. "Flynn let me in through a downstairs door. By the evidence locker."

MacAuley raised his brushy eyebrows. "How'd you know to let her in?" He directed the question well over her head.

"Um." Flynn's boots scraped the floor. "I was watching. From the interview room."

MacAuley and the chief looked at each other. The chief opened his mouth.

"I really appreciated it." Hadley leaped in before the chief could say anything. She spoke in a just-us-grown-ups tone, as if she were talking to Hudson's teacher with him standing there. "He's a thoughtful kid."

"Mmm." The chief gave Flynn one more considering look before turning back to MacAuley. "You sure you know everything you're going to give them?"

MacAuley flicked an invisible piece of lint from his hat. "You want to talk to them? Go right ahead."

"Hell, no," the chief said. "I've seen myself on camera. I always look like I'm about to grab the mike and start threatening people with it."

"Then trust me. I'm good at this." MacAuley buffed the bill of his already shining cap on his sleeve and settled it square on his head. He stood up straight, tugging his jacket into place, and was transformed from his usual sly, slouching self to a gray-haired diplomat for law enforcement. He immediately spoiled the effect by winking at them. "Once more into the breach, dear friends."

"C'mon," the chief said, as MacAuley sauntered down the hall toward the station entrance. "Let's get into the briefing room and catch everybody up."

"Everybody" consisted of Eric McCrea, leafing through the Glens Falls Area phone book and jotting down addresses and numbers in his notebook. "Lyle and I have already gone over things this morning," the chief said, tossing his folders on the table. "We got the report from Doc Scheeler on John Doe three's fillings. The amalgam's contemporary, no more'n five years old. Which jibes with Scheeler's estimate of his age as between twenty-one and twenty-five. We have DNA samples from both bodies taken from behind the Muster Field, and the state lab'll be happy to run a comparison for us within two to three years."

Flynn groaned.

"What about dental records?" Hadley asked. It was a lot easier to risk sounding dumb when most of the force was someplace else.

"Dental records are great when you're comparing an unknown victim to a known missing person. They're useless in tracking down an identity. We'd have to go through every dental office in New York State — assuming this guy was from New York. Where we are, he could just as easily be from Canada or northern New England."

"Anything on John Doe one?" Flynn didn't sound hopeful.

"No." The chief sat on the table and planted his boots against a chair seat. "It's making me nuts. We got prints. We got those damn tattoos. Even if there's no —" he cut himself off. Hadley was pretty sure the rest of the sentence would have been *connection with the guys Knox saw*. No one believed she had seen the same tattoos on Stud Boy: Santiago. She didn't know why that bothered her. It shouldn't matter. She got paid whether they caught whoever did this or not.

"John Doe one did time," the chief went on. "I'm sure of it. So why don't we have an ID for him yet?"

It was a rhetorical question. Hadley and Flynn looked at each other. "Eric." The chief pitched his voice to include McCrea. "You got anything to add?"

"Hadley and I interviewed the members of the volunteer search-and-rescue team yesterday. No one noticed anything unusual."

Hadley didn't realize she was making a face until the chief asked her, "What is it?"

She glanced toward McCrea. He grinned. "John Huggins wanted to know what a sweet little thing like Officer Knox was doing on the force."

The chief pinched the bridge of his nose. "Huggins has some . . . difficulties with women that don't fit his — ah, traditional ideas." He looked at Hadley. "He's harmless, though. And our departments often work closely together, so let's try to keep things civil."

Hadley frowned. "So I shouldn't have told him to eat shit and die?" The expression on the chief's face was priceless. She held up her hands. "Just kidding. I was very civil."

He gave her a withering look. "Kevin?"

"Between Mr. McGeoch and Agent Hodgden, I got a list of area farms that employ immigrant workers year round, and the names of laborers with legal permits and sponsors."

The chief's eyebrows went up. "Paula

Hodgden just passed on that info?"

Flynn looked as if he couldn't decide to be embarrassed or proud of himself. "I — um, may have given her the impression that I was going to be rounding up anybody I found who wasn't on her list."

"I see."

"I didn't promise anything."

"Uh — huh."

"Anyway, I'm ready to get out and interview people, but I have a problem. I don't speak Spanish." Flynn's forehead creased, as if he were afraid his language skills were letting the department down. "I do speak some German. I took three years in high school."

"That's great, Kevin," the chief said. "The next time we find a John Doe wearing lederhosen, you're on it. In the meantime, however —"

"Hadley can go with Kevin instead of me," McCrea said. "I'm going to be tackling the Christie relatives today, and it might be better if I don't have someone inexperienced around."

Well. That stung. But at least McCrea was up front with her.

The chief crossed his arms over his chest and stared into the middle distance. She was beginning to recognize it as his thinking stance. Finally he said, "Okay. But if I'm going to send the two of you out there, I want to maximize the possibility of getting useful information. I want you two in civvies."

"What?" Hadley said.

"We've already noticed that the sight of a cop car and a uniform doesn't exactly inspire confidence in these guys. Change into something you can wear with a shoulder or a pancake holster and go in one of your own cars."

"I don't have a pancake or a shoulder holster," Hadley started to say, but her objection was drowned by Kevin's excited, "You want us to go undercover?"

"No, Kevin. I want you in plainclothes. There's a difference." He looked at Hadley. "You can draw a holster from the gun locker."

"Plainclothes," Flynn breathed, in the way someone might have said, "The Holy Grail."

"I haven't practiced with a pancake or shoulder holster!"

A disapproving sound rumbled out of the back of the chief's throat. He stood up. "Look. Maybe this is going too far too fast for you two —"

A clamor of noise from the front of the station cut him off. There was a flap-flap of footsteps, and a squeaky-pleased "Hel-lo!" from Harlene, and then MacAuley was ushering in Reverend Clare, whose neat black clerical garb looked at odds with her flushed face and falling-down twist.

"The Reverend here arrived near the end of the press conference," MacAuley said. "Some of the reporters got a little overexcited."

"Thank you so much, Lyle." She laid a hand on MacAuley's arm. "I wasn't expecting to be keelhauled by the Fourth Estate."

MacAuley's eyes half closed, and he smiled a wide, wicked smile. "Shucks, ma'am. 'Tain't nothing."

"Don't you have a case to clear?" the chief snapped. "What are you doing here?" he asked Reverend Clare. "Is it the Christies?"

"The Christies? No. I, uh" — she glanced around, taking in Hadley, Flynn, and Mc-Crea — "need to speak to you."

The chief gestured impatiently.

"Privately."

He exhaled. "My office." He motioned for her to go through the doorway ahead of him, perhaps not noticing Reverend Clare's narrowed eyes and set jaw. They stalked away through the dispatch room. This time, Harlene didn't say anything.

MacAuley pursed his lips. When they

heard the chief's door slam shut, he asked, "Did he have that stick up his ass before Reverend Fergusson got here?"

Hadley looked at Flynn to see if he was going to say anything. No way she was going to answer that one.

"Nope," McCrea said.

"Interesting."

Flynn shook his head, as if dismissing the chief, his moods, and the minister from his mind. "I've got a change of clothing in my car. Do you have something here, or do we need to hit your house before we go?"

"Wait a minute," Hadley said. "I think he was about to tell us not to go."

He looked at her like she'd grown a second head. "That's why we have to move now. Do you wanna take your car? Or my Aztek?"

She thought about her less-than-half tank of gas. "Your Aztek," she said, then realized she was committing herself. "Wait!"

"I'll get you a pancake holster. Trust me, it'll feel just as natural as the one you're wearing now."

Oh, there was a great recommendation.

"Do you want me to drive you to your house or meet you over there?"

"Meet me," she said without thinking. Flynn nodded and headed out the door.

"Wait!" she said.

A bellow from the chief's office stopped her short, but Flynn kept right on going. The baritone yell was followed by a loud and impassioned alto voice, which was drowned out by more deep and angry words, which were topped by an even more strident female response. Hadley couldn't make out what they were fighting about, but it sounded like a doozy.

"Interesting," MacAuley repeated.

McCrea pushed back from his desk and gathered his notepad and phone book. "I'm getting out of the kill zone," he said.

MacAuley nodded. "You might want to think about that as well," he told Hadley.

She groaned and shouldered her tote. Looked like will-she, nil-she, she was going to be driving around the North Country acting as Kevin Flynn's translator. As she ducked down the stairs, the sound of her minister and her boss going at it hammer and tongs, she was already trying to come up with a civilian outfit as ugly and unflattering as her uniform. It wouldn't do to give Flynn any ideas.

IX

Kevin Flynn was having the best day of his life. He had the window rolled down and his arm hanging out, the late-May sun warming his skin, dry sweet air blowing through the Aztek. No heater like in March, no manure smell like in April, no blackflies like in — well, they were a plague all summer long, but they weren't getting in at forty-five miles an hour. He was in plainclothes, his polo shirt hanging loose over his Colt .44, managing — managing! — the investigation, deciding where they would go and who they would question next.

The best-looking woman in Millers Kill sat beside him, listening to his Promise Ring CD, and if she wasn't saying much, she also wasn't tearing his head off. When they had stopped for lunch, she had even let him buy her a sub, after he told her it'd be her turn next time.

She had on a T-shirt and those baggy shin-high pants only girls wear, with a vest to cover up her Glock 9mm, and she looked so damn cute it was all he could do to keep from grinning at her. It was a relief, he decided, getting smacked down by the chief. Embarrassing as hell at the time, but after he'd cooled down, the no-fraternization rule started to seem like a sturdy fence along an observation post at, say, Niagara Falls. Something that let him look all he wanted at the magnificent work of nature without getting swept away and killed.

For real, it didn't get any better than this.

"Flynn," she said. She leaned forward and turned down the music. "I don't think this is getting us anywhere."

For a minute, he panicked. Was she talking about . . . could she be talking about . . . then he realized she meant the interviews.

"All we're getting is a bunch of negatives. 'No, I didn't see anything. No, I don't know anything. No, I don't recognize the man in the picture.' " They'd been showing the best head shot they had of John Doe one — although even cleaned up and in tight focus he didn't look anything other than good and dead.

"That's what you hear in most interviews. Unless, you know, you're breaking up a fight or something. Where everybody in the crowd saw what happened. *No* just means you're closing off one more dead end."

"I get that, but what are we going to learn? I mean, what if the guy we want is working on one of these dairies? What's he going to do? Give it up to us?"

"Sometimes. Yeah." Kevin glanced at her. She was worrying her birthstone ring. "The chief or MacAuley gets a guy into the interrogation room, they ask him a few questions, and *boom!* next thing you know, we're calling the DA's office because the guy's spilled his guts. Never underestimate a perp's need to get it off his chest." That last bit of wisdom came from the deputy chief, but he figured he didn't need to quote chapter and verse.

She looked at him skeptically. "We're not the chief and MacAuley."

"Hey, everybody's got to start some-where." He pointed his elbow toward their folder. "Who's next on the list?"

The three farms after that were repeats of the morning interviews. It was slow work, trailing after workers scattered between the barn and the field and the machine shed, assuring them and their employers that no, they weren't from ICE and no, they didn't have any interest in seeing visas or work permits or Social Security cards. After their first stop that morning, when Hadley told him to stop scaring the workers by towering over them like the damn Statue of Liberty, Kevin found everybody relaxed more when he got as low profile as possible. He'd taken to squatting on his haunches as if he were powwowing at scout camp. Hadley, who'd acted like she was giving an oral examina-tion the first few times, had smoothed out her patter, even — based on the occasional laugh she got — tossing in a joke now and again.

Kevin thought they were creating about as good a rapport with the migrants as they could, but they still didn't shake anything loose until Jock Montgomery's place. It was after four when they pulled into the dooryard, scattering a horde of small boys who turned out to be Montgomery sons and their friends. There was a bit of confusion as to why Hadley was there, since her oldest kid was in the same class as the middle Montgomery boy. Then the babysitter, Christy McAlister, recognized Kevin from when he wrote up her boyfriend's accident last winter, and she had to catch him up on everything going on with both the boyfriend — deployed overseas — and the car — totaled and replaced.

The good news was that it was coming up milking time. Montgomery's three full-time year-round farmhands were all in what the dairyman called the milking parlor, which, despite its old-fashioned name, had the same stainless steel and sterilized hoses as the other farms. Back at the Hoffmans', Hadley had commented, "It's all rubber and restraints. I bet there's some serious fetish activity going on after hours in a few of these places." He'd turned the same color as the red Ayshires in the field, but now he couldn't stop thinking about it.

They had gathered the men in the tack room, and, since the concrete floor was stained with unidentifiable brown blotches, Kevin forsook the squatting for sitting atop a plastic five-gallon bucket of antibiotic feed additive. Hadley perched on another bucket and showed them the photo, asking — he assumed — if any of them had seen John Doe one.

The three men — short broad-faced Mayans with arms large enough to wrestle calves out of their mother's bodies and skinny, bowed legs — shook their heads. Lined up in Astroturf-green lawn chairs, they looked like teak garden ornaments that had been stored in the barn for a season.

Hadley asked them another question, smiling, her voice inviting confidence.

The men glanced at one other. Kevin, examining the straw and manure glued to the edge of his sneakers, sat up straight. This was the first time they hadn't gotten an almost-instant denial. "Hadley," he said, his voice quiet, unthreatening. "Remind 'em we're just here for information."

She rattled off something in Spanish, still trying to sound upbeat. One guy said something to another. The third nodded, adding what might have been an encouragement or an order. The one in the middle was still, like he was weighing what the other two had told him. Finally, he said something to Hadley. A short sentence.

"*¿Qué?*" She was obviously surprised.

"What is it?" Kevin asked.

She didn't turn to answer him. "He says he was shot at."

He kept his mouth shut while she asked the guy another question. Got an answer. Asked something else. Got a longer, more detailed reply, with the other two nodding along. Kevin made himself wait, not wanting to bust up the flow of the interview. After ten minutes of back-and-forth, Hadley said *"Gracias,"* and everybody except Kevin stood up.

The three men left. Kevin exploded off his bucket once the last one vanished into the milking parlor. "What?" he said. "What?"

Hadley rubbed her lips, her eyes still on the lawn chairs. "We need to take a look at Mr. Montgomery's van. The guy in the middle, Feliz, says he was driving it to the Agway to pick up a load of feed and somebody shot at him. Put a hole through the back panel."

"When?"

"April."

Yes! In like Flynn. He was out the door in two strides. "Mr. Montgomery!" he called. "Mr. Montgomery?"

Jock Montgomery emerged from the cold room, wiping his hands on a cloth. He was a Caucasian version of his workers, bandy-legged, powerful shoulders, with an up-country Cossayuharie accent you could use to stir paint. "They tell you what you needed to know?"

"Did your van get shot this past April?"

"Ayeah."

"Why didn't you report it?"

"Aw." Montgomery shoved the cloth into his overalls pocket. "There's no need to kick up a fuss. Just somebody jacking deer. I figured if he needed the meat so bad, I wun't gonna put trouble his way."

"Do you know who did it?"

Montgomery rubbed the back of his neck.

"We're not asking 'cause we're looking for game violations. We're investigating multiple murders."

Hadley piped up for the first time. "Someone may be targeting Latino migrant workers."

Kevin winced. He didn't think the chief wanted that theory floating around Millers Kill.

"Huh. So you think . . . maybe he wun't huntin' after all?"

"Maybe not for deer," Hadley said.

"I don't know who did it." Montgomery sighed. "But it happened when Feliz was on the Cossayuharie Road, passing though the Christies' woods. I figgured — well, they're hard up enough to do it. Huntin' out of season, I mean."

Hadley caught his sleeve and tugged him away from the farmer. "The twenty-two?" she said quietly.

"That'd be hard to punch through a moving vehicle. But maybe." Kevin turned back to Montgomery. "May we see the van, please?"

"Right out here next to the feed room." They followed Montgomery, keeping a few paces behind so they could talk.

"The Christies," Hadley whispered.

"That'd put a different spin on them going after that Mexican guy working at St. Alban's."

They stepped over a chewed-up wooden lintel and out into the late-afternoon sun. "There 'tis," Montgomery said. "You can see why I took it for a hunter."

Kevin could. The ragged-edged hole was the work of a large-caliber weapon. But it wasn't the size of the shot that interested

362

him. It was the van itself. The big, white, paneled Chevy Astro was identical to the one Sister Lucia Pirone had been driving.

X

He hadn't called before hauling over to his sister's farm, so it was his own damn fault his mother was there to see the blowup. He heeled his squad car into her driveway — the old one, not the new one — and was pounding up the steps before the engine stilled. He hammered on the front door. "Janet! Goddammit, open up!"

The door opened. He saw empty air where he expected Janet's face and looked down. His mother frowned up at him. "What on earth are you fussing about now, Russell? Swearing at the top of your lungs right out in front of God and everybody. What if the girls had been home?"

One-handed, he swung the door all the way open and pushed past her rotund form. "This is official business, Mom." He strode into the McGeochs' living room, nearly knocking over his niece Kathleen's music stand. Empty plastic laundry baskets and piles of folded clothing covered the sofa. Sneakers in assorted sizes and shades of pink were piled like a canvas landslide against the TV console. "Janet!"

Janet appeared from the kitchen, a full laundry basket in her arms. Her lips thinned. "Clare told you."

"Clare told me," he said. "And I don't know who I'm madder at, her for keeping it a secret or you for laying it on her. This is a goddam murder investigation, Janet. Don't you get it? We got three dead men to account for. That's a little more important than you saving a few bucks on your taxes."

"I told you everything you needed to know about the body! It doesn't matter who found it!"

"That's not your call to make!"

"Would somebody tell me what in Sam Hill's goin' on?" their mother asked.

"Janet and Mike have a whole crew of illegal workers at the new farm. It was one of them found the body on their property, not Janet. She lied about it, and she got Clare to back up the lie, and she's kept on lying despite the fact that we're up to three bodies now and there may very well be some connection between the migrant workers and the murders." He shoved his hands in his pockets and tried to breathe deep. The drive over hadn't cooled him off any.

Their mother pinned Janet in place with narrowed eyes. "This true?"

"We hired those workers in good faith. It

wasn't our fault we got screwed over by the employment agency!"

"Is it true?" Margy's voice was relentless.

Janet glared at the wall. "Yes."

Their mother closed her eyes for a moment. When she opened them, she had an expression both Russ and Janet knew well. Knew and dreaded. "Janet Agnes," she said, "I am ashamed of you."

Russ could see Janet fighting not to drop her head. "I'm sorry you feel that way, Mom." Her voice was unsteady. "But when it comes to the farm's future, to my family's future, I have to do what I think best."

"I'm tryin' to think of a way hidin' the facts in a murder investigation could be *best*," Margy said.

"We need those workers to survive. I was afraid that if he knew about them, Russ would have to turn them in to Immigration and Customs, and Mike and I'd be left trying to run two hundred head between the two of us. Native-born hands would cost us twice as much, *if* we could find anyone to take on the job."

Russ shook his head. "You should have just asked me. I checked with the town attorney back in April, when your men first went missing. Unless someone's been arrested for a crime, I don't have any obligation to ask about their status, legal, illegal, whatever." He felt his anger leaching away. "Why didn't you just ask me?"

His sister looked at him, disbelieving. "Because if the answer had been different, you would've called ICE. You might've been sorry, but that wouldn't have stopped you."

"Then you should have told me." Margy's voice was sharp. "It's my farm too, you know. I don't expect to be treated like some old fool with an open purse and a closed mind."

"I'm sorry, Mom. Really." Janet turned to Russ. "And . . . I apologize to you, too. For the . . . for not asking. And for coming between you and Clare."

He did not want to go there. "Forget it. Lemme interview your men. See if anyone saw anything. Then we'll call it quits."

The Feast of St. Alban

June 23

I

The Feast of St. Alban was traditionally celebrated, in Millers Kill, with a bake and white-elephant sale, the sort of fund-raiser designed to maximize the work required of parish volunteers and minimize the return. In the three years Clare had been rector, she'd been inching the senior festival committee members — a blue-rinse bunch who had controlled the event for close to two decades — toward a more active and profitable fund-raiser.

The arrival of Elizabeth de Groot in January, followed by the unfortunate slip-and-fall of the committee chair later that month, opened the door for a change. With half the committee in Florida for the winter months, the new deacon and the equally ruthless-in-a-good-cause Karen Burns engineered a bloodless coup, inserting themselves as "temporary chairs." They shot down the white elephant, source of so much of Clare's office furniture, and took the bake sale off the table.

In its place, on Sunday night they were having an all-you-can-eat dinner (one ticket), a silent and live auction (another), and, as an inducement to hang around till the end of the bidding, a public dance in the park across the street from the church with Curtis Maurand and his Little Big Band (free, but contributions accepted).

Thanks to Elizabeth's ability to wheedle donations — she got such extraordinary results Clare wondered if threats of force were involved — they were having a blowout that, with luck, would fund half their yearly outreach program.

Elizabeth and Karen agreed that well-lubricated bidders were free-spending bidders, so the auctions were accompanied with cheese, hors d'oeuvres, and a never-ending stream of donated bottles — one of which was clutched in the hands of Clare's date.

"Vicar! Mrs. Burns!" Hugh Parteger waved plastic glasses toward an auction table, where Clare and Karen were counting their chickens before they hatched. "Merlot? Or Cabernet?" Several female committee members behind the silent auction tables stared at Hugh. With his British accent, double-pleated trousers, and two-hundred-dollar haircut, the New York resident was an exotic specimen for Millers Kill.

"Merlot," Karen said.

"For me, too." Clare glanced at the bid sheet for a weekend of sailing and catered meals at Robert Corlew's summer home on Lake George. Her eyes bugged out. "I knew we had some reasonably affluent folks here, but I didn't expect this." She kept her voice low.

"They're not all ours. Elizabeth has a ton of contacts in Saratoga, and she got the word out." Karen also spoke under her breath. An older gentleman Clare had seen at the dinner approached the table, and Clare and Karen drifted out of his way. "I was afraid with this serial killer scare on, people would be reluctant to come out at night," Karen went on. "Thank heavens it's not holding anyone back."

"Maybe folks feel there's safety in numbers," Clare said.

Hugh appeared again, brimming plastic cups in hand. "Maybe they feel there's safety in being white. I read the murders may be race-related." He handed one cup to Clare

"Read?" Karen accepted a glass. "Where?"

"Oh, there were several news sources with stories. I get Google alerts for anything containing the phrase 'Millers Kill,' did I tell you? That, and 'hot-n-sexy Episcopal priests.' "

Karen coughed out half a mouthful of wine.

"Ignore him," Clare said. "He's only a few Internet sites away from complete deviancy."

"You can leave your collar on," Hugh sang.

"Remind me to take you to the church's next General Convention. There are a number of my sister priests I'd love to introduce you to."

He sighed. "You see what I have to fight against?" he asked Karen. "I travel up here from New York, I wine her and dine her, and she's still trying to foist other women on me. I may as well wander out into the night and let myself fall victim to the Cossayuharie Killer."

"You travel to Saratoga from New York," Clare pointed out. "I'm just conveniently located. And you might have trouble locating the alleged serial killer, since the town's promised us a police presence at the dance."

"Oh, goody." She could have dehumidified the undercroft with that tone.

Karen, no slouch when it came to managing awkward social moments, smiled brightly and handed Hugh her plastic cup.

He stared at it for a half second before his usual good manners reasserted themselves. "May I freshen you up?" he asked.

"And get some for yourself," she encouraged.

"Alas, I'm not indulging. I have to drive to the Stuyvesant Inn, and" — his mouth twisted — "I have no wish to attract the attention of local law enforcement."

There was a moment of silence as Clare examined the nearby air molecules and Karen did not look at Clare.

"Of course," Hugh said, "if I could stay at the vicarage . . ." It was almost, but not quite, a joke. Karen, thank God, looked more amused than scandalized.

"Hugh."

He raised his hands. "Sorry, sorry." He assumed a pained expression. "She is an unassailable tower of virtue," he told Karen.

"I've been assailed once or twice in the past," Clare said.

"Yet you never sail with me."

"You're a venture capitalist. Go venture," Clare said. "Talk up the auction. Run up the bids. Loosen some purse strings."

"Sadly, the only strings I'll be loosening tonight." He took Karen's hand and squeezed it before pointing a finger at Clare. "Don't forget, I have the first dance, Vicar."

They watched him cross the floor, working the crowd.

"He's awfully nice," Karen said.

"Yes, he is," Clare said. They had met at a party three summers ago and had managed a weekend together every couple of months since then.

"He seems pretty fond of you."

"Yes, he is." He'd been pushing to move their relationship up a notch since the past fall. Nothing obnoxious, nothing that backed her into a corner. Reasonable, considering the dinners in Saratoga, the phone calls, the trips she had made to New York.

"It's so pleasant being around someone happy and uncomplicated, isn't it?"

Clare's mouth quirked. "You mean like Geoff?"

Karen sighed. "I know. I could never fall for the easy guys either." She looked at Clare. "It's always the difficult ones that get under your skin, isn't it?"

"Yes, it is." The two women looked at each other in perfect understanding.

Clare didn't know if it was Hugh's influence or not, but they topped out the silent auction almost 20 percent above projections, according to financial officer Terry McKellan's calculations. The live auction following went faster than Clare had expected, much faster, and an hour after it had started, St. Alban's was close to four thousand dollars richer and Terry and his volunteers were shooing her out of the sanctuary. "Go," Terry said. "Dance."

"I should help with the checks," Clare said, almost convincingly.

The finance officer grinned, his luxurious mustache spreading like two glossy brown wings. "Think of it as an act of mercy, then. Logging in these checks is going to be the highlight of my week. Dancing? Not so much."

She decided not to push her luck by arguing further. She slipped into her office, locked the door, and shucked off her clericals in favor of a poppy-red dress whose skinny-strapped top was balanced by yards and yards of skirt that made her look like Ginger Rogers whenever she twirled.

There was already a modest crowd across the street, diners who had skipped the auctions and dancers drawn by the free music. The sky over the mountains glowed with sunset's red and orange and pink, but the fairy lights twining the gazebo and hanging over the park were lit, twinkling like a thousand lightning bugs against the green leaves and the violet shadows. Clare stopped on the church steps, listening to the laughter and the chatter and the squeals and squonks of Curtis Maurand and his Little Big Band tuning up.

Impossible, for a moment, to believe anything bad could ever happen here.

Then a flash of tan beneath one of the cast-iron street lamps caught her eye. Their police presence. Officer Flynn, pressed and shined and looking ready to help little old ladies across the street. And the chief himself, solid, steady, every line of his body a reassurance that they were safe. Protected. Because bad things could happen here. She smiled a little. But not if Russ Van Alstyne had anything to say about it.

He turned. Saw her watching him. Her thread of wistful amusement tightened into a prickly awareness. She hadn't seen him since she'd kicked her way out of his office more than three weeks ago, swallowing bile and several bad words. For which, yes, she needed to apologize. She moved down the steps and across the walkway, conscious in every step of her skirt sliding around her legs, the warm, humid air stroking her bare shoulders, the smell of St. Alban's roses, and the heat from the street's asphalt beneath her flat-soled shoes.

He walked away from the streetlamp to meet her. A couple sat on the bench facing the church, the woman rifling through her purse. The Campbells, crossing from the parking lot, passed her. "Great auction!" Sabrina said. Clare waved an acknowledgment.

"Reverend Fergusson," Russ said.

"Chief Van Alstyne." She wrapped her arms around herself and inhaled.

Before she could launch into her apology, he settled into parade-rest posture and cleared his throat. "I shouldn't have gone off on you like that, when you told me about the men at Mike and Janet's. I realize . . . she put you in an impossible situation. It wasn't your fault."

She paused, knocked off-kilter by his preemptive apology. Although, she noticed, he never used the words *I'm sorry*. She decided to supply them. "I'm sorry, too. I should never have agreed to go along with a lie in the first place. And I'm sorry I lost my temper. It was very . . ." — undignified? unprofessional? — ". . . childish of me."

They stood there, face-to-face, not quite looking at each other. At the center of the park, the band swung into "String of Pearls."

"Reverend Fergusson!" The voice was lilting and Swedish. Clare turned to see Lena Erlander and her husband, Jim Cameron, approaching. Clare pasted on a bright smile. Lena's husband was the mayor and had signed off on the use of the park, the street closing, and the police protection. Over, she had heard, the objections of some of the aldermen. "How good to see you again," Lena said, shaking Clare's hand. "And how wonderfully clever of you to put on this dance."

Jim Cameron grinned at Russ and Clare and beamed at his wife. His expression said, *Isn't she the perfect politician's partner?* They'd been married two or three years, and the honeymoon was evidently still on. Maybe it was true, what they said about Swedes.

"Thank Elizabeth de Groot and Karen Burns, not me," Clare said. "They put the whole thing together."

"Perfect timing, either way," the mayor said. "Proof positive there's nothing to fear in Millers Kill, no matter what trash the reporters like to throw up."

"I saw your handsome friend from New York over by the refreshments table," Lena said. "He was looking for you." She smiled at Clare as if the two of them shared a secret. "I think you were smart to have the old-fashioned band. Dancing close, it gives a man romantic ideas, right, *alsking?*" She wrapped her arm around her husband's.

Mayor Cameron's smile glazed over. He looked from Russ, to Clare, then back at Russ. "I think it's smart to attract the right sort of people. Older couples who want to spend money and then go home at a reasonable hour. Not like the god-awful crowds we get at the Riverside Park on the Fourth of July, eh, Russ?"

Russ looked over the mayor's head at the well-heeled dancers swinging to Glenn Miller. "I don't think we'll have any broken beer bottles or fistfights with this group, no."

Lena tugged on her husband's arm. "Come on, I want to dance. Oh, and tell Chief Van Alstyne he can't just stand like a stuffed bear. There are never enough men to go around. He must dance once or twice." She smiled up at Russ. "You must dance with some of the single ladies." She winked at Clare. "Since I don't think you'll be loaning out your date for the cause."

Mayor Cameron dragged her away in what was either a passion to dance or a fervor of embarrassment.

"String of Pearls" ended. The crowd clapped. "So," Russ said. "Hugh's here."

"Thank you very much!" Curtis Maurand

said. "This next one's for all you guys and gals who were in the armed services. It's called 'American Patrol.' " The band blew out a full-fledged jitterbug.

"He's staying at the Stuyvesant Inn," she said, then mentally kicked herself. She didn't have to explain anything to Russ.

He made a rumbling noise in his chest. It sounded to her like disapproval.

Pricked, she said, "Of course, if it gets too late, I could always put him up at the rectory. I'm sure I have a spare toothbrush somewhere."

Russ slanted a look at her. "Why not? He could room with Amado."

She couldn't help it. The thought of Hugh's face, confronted with the temporary sexton and the guest room, made her laugh. "Poor Hugh," she said. "That certainly would not be what he was expecting."

"No one expects the Spanish Inquisition," Russ quoted, which made her snort, which was how Hugh found them.

"Vicar," he said, taking her hand and kissing it. "You look like the proverbial long cool woman in a red dress." He glanced at Russ. "Chief Van Alstyne. Imagine my surprise at seeing you here."

"Mr. Parteger."

"Isn't all that unrelieved polyester hot on

a night like this?"

"You sure notice a lot about clothes. I bet you're real good at home decorating, too."

"What's that supposed to mean?"

Russ's face was bland. The jitterbug ended, and the band segued into "Steppin' Out with My Baby."

"Gosh," Clare said pointedly. "I love this song."

Hugh redrew his expression into something more pleasant. "Of course, Vicar. By all means, let's dance." He paused, as if a thought had just occurred to him. "Unless," he said to Russ, "*you'd* like to escort Clare onto the dance floor." He swept one arm toward the low wooden platforms that had been bolted together over the largest wedge of the park that afternoon. "After all, you're free to ask her now, aren't you?"

Clare would have killed Hugh, except that she was caught, stomach clenched, wondering what Russ would say. Loathing herself for hoping like a girl at a middle-school dance.

He stood very still. Finally he said, "I'm on duty." He nodded to her. "Enjoy yourself." Then he walked away, leaving Hugh looking triumphant and Clare wishing she were a lesbian. Maybe then she'd never have to deal with male idiocy again.

That damn skimpy red dress drew his eye all night long. He patrolled the edges of the park, exchanging hellos and commenting on the weather and answering the few folks brave enough to ask questions about the so-called Cossayuharie Killer. And all the time, he kept spotting her, like a flame in the dark. He saw Parteger begging and begging hard after that stunt he pulled, following her around like a dog while she flitted from parishioner to parishioner. The Brit eventually hit on the right apology or wore her down, because she let him dance with her.

She wasn't a great dancer, not like some of the older women on the floor who had learned to swing and foxtrot back in the white-glove days, but damn, she looked like she was having fun with it. Between dances with Parteger, she partnered Norm Madsen and Robert Corlew and even Geoff Burns, who managed to look semihuman, twirling Clare past the gazebo.

She started smiling — really smiling, not just being polite — and then she started to laugh, and he swore he could hear her laugh over the music and the talk and the dull rumble of the traffic, rerouted through streets a block away.

Linda would have liked this. She would have

laughed like that and danced like that and pushed her hair off the nape of her neck like that — such a tender, intimate gesture in a public place, and then he realized he was thinking about Linda *and* about Clare, holding them both in his mind at the same time, and he waited for the bitter black weight to come over him and it didn't. He felt a lingering sadness, like the clarinet line, but he also felt the excitement of the brass, and he caught a glimpse of a realization, that something of Linda, in some way, survived in Clare, but he couldn't get a handle on the wisp of a thought and his concentration was busted by the growl and crunch of one of his patrol cars, slipping up the street and pulling in next to the park's fire hydrant.

His deputy chief stepped out of the cruiser. "Hey," he said.

"What are you doing here?"

"What am I doing here? What're you still doing here? You were scheduled to go off duty an hour ago. I figured you forgot to call in."

"Huh. Guess I lost track of the time."

Lyle shoved his hands in his pockets as he joined Russ. "Bucking for overtime won't do you any good, y'know. You're on salary. That's why you wouldn't catch me taking your job."

"You wouldn't take my job because you might actually have to show up for work during hunting season."

"Yeah, well, there is that." Lyle looked between the trees to where the dancers were going around to "Begin the Beguine." "How're things goin'?"

"Nobody dragged off to a shallow grave yet. Although the night's still young. What's happening out there?" He gestured with his chin toward the rest of the town and beyond.

"Quietest damn Sunday night I've ever seen. I think the Cossayuharie Killer's keeping everybody home. Or headed down to Saratoga. Paul called in, said he's given out a few tickets on the Schuylerville Road."

"Jim Cameron's not going to like that."

"What, tickets? Sure he will. Paul's scoping out the cars from away. No skin off his voters' noses."

"I meant, people taking their money out of Millers Kill."

"On a Sunday night?" Lyle blew a raspberry. "The only things to spend money on in this town are those idiot arcade games at Alltechtronik and a couple ounces of grass. You have to go to Glens Falls to bet on bingo."

"I dunno about that. I think Geraldine

Bain's running a floating canasta game around here. Penny a point."

Lyle laughed. Russ grinned. They stood side by side, watching the dancers, and for a moment it was like it used to be. The music slid smoothly into a new song, the bandleader's voice sweet and melancholy. *I can see, no matter how near you'll be, you'll never belong to me —*

"Who's the fellow with Reverend Fergusson?"

Russ blinked. "Hugh Parteger. Forty. Unmarried. He's an investment banker from the city. Resident alien. One DUI, got it bargained down to DTE. No other record."

Lyle looked at him sideways. "It was more in the line of a social question."

He felt his cheeks heat up and hoped the light from the streetlamps wasn't enough to give him away. "Guy comes dropping into my town for no good reason every couple of months, why shouldn't I run him? Forewarned is forearmed, or however the saying goes."

"Mmm." Lyle turned back to the dancing. Anne Vining-Ellis and her husband blocked Clare from view, but as the Ellises twirled out of the way, Russ could see her, locked up tight in Hugh's arms, the overdressed bastard sliding one hand all up and down her half-bare back.

"Looks to me like he's got a perfectly good reason for coming to town."

But I can dream, can't I?

"Whyn't you go over there and ask her to dance?"

He rounded on Lyle. "Why don't you mind your own business?" He turned back toward Clare and her date, determined to poke the knife in himself a little deeper. "You're the last person who oughta be handing out advice."

Lyle was still a moment. "You're right," he finally said. "I've managed to ball up every relationship I ever had. Includin' our friendship. But you know what? That means I can recognize when someone's making a dumb-ass mistake." He waited, as if inviting Russ to chime in. Russ kept his mouth shut. "Whatever." Lyle sighed. "I'm gonna take a turn around the park and check in with Kevin. See ya around." He strolled off beneath the trees.

The song ended to a clamor of applause. Russ turned on his heel and strode across Church Street without looking, headed for his truck, parked in the lot across from St. Alban's. He unlocked it and stripped off his gear belt, dropping the whole thing into his lockbox along with his pump-action shotgun and .40-.40. There. Officially off-duty.

He climbed behind the wheel and fired up the truck. Wondered if his mother was still out at Cousin Nane's. Probably not. He wished he had someplace to go where he could be alone.

How about your own house?

He shook his head. He had been back to the house on Peekskill Road several times since Linda's death, but he was never, he realized, going to spend the night there again.

What was he going to do? Sell it? Then what? Buying another house seemed pointless. Keep living with his mother? He had a sudden vision of himself, a decade on, sixty years old, coming back to his eighty-five-year-old mother's house — the women on her side of the family lived a long time, he had no doubt she'd still be alive and kicking — eating the same low-carb dinner, watching the Yankees kick the hell out of the Red Sox, nothing changing, everything exactly the same as it was now. As it had been since Linda died. That's what he had wanted, wasn't it? To stop time? To never let go of her?

God Almighty. What was he doing to himself?

He swiped his hand over his face. Rolled down the window. In the park across the street, the band was playing "In the Mood," and somewhere in the crowd Hugh Parteger had his hands all over Clare Fergusson.

Jesus Christ. What the hell was he doing sitting in this damn truck?

He twisted the key out of the ignition, popped open the door, and thumped to the asphalt. He recrossed the street. The dancing had been going on long enough that people had wandered out to the edges of the park, women fanning themselves, men tugging at their ties and unbuttoning their cuffs. He passed a "Chief Van Alstyne!" and a "Hey, Russ," but kept his course single-mindedly toward the bandstand.

The music stopped, and applause burst like champagne bubbles in the air around him. He looked around, but for the first time that evening he couldn't spot the red dress. His stomach tightened. *I could always put him up at the rectory.* What if she decided . . . What if they had —

"Why, hello, Chief Van Alstyne." He looked down to see Mrs. Henry Marshall, one of Clare's vestry, smiling up at him. She was in bright pink tonight, with matching lipstick that was almost fluorescent compared to her white hair. Her hand was looped through the arm of her — "gentleman friend" was the right term, he guessed.

"Evening," Norm Madsen said.

"Hi," Russ said. "Have either of you seen Clare?"

The elderly lawyer frowned. "Not more trouble, I hope?"

Mrs. Marshall gave her escort a look of loving contempt. "I don't think that's why he's asking, dear." She cocked her head at Russ like a sharp-eyed sparrow. "Is it?"

He shook his head.

"She said she was going to get something to drink. But I'm sure she'd be happy to dance. . . ."

He didn't stay to hear the rest of her comment. He tossed a "Thanks!" over his shoulder as he elbowed his way through the crowd.

He found her as promised, near the refreshment table, sitting on one of the folding chairs strewn haphazardly beneath the chestnut trees, drinking from a paper cup. Parteger, standing behind her, was trapped in conversation with Robert Corlew. Clare looked up. "Russ." She sounded surprised. "Is something wrong?"

Her eyes were large and dark in the halflight filtering through the leaves. She was faintly flushed, a little damp, as if she had just toweled off after a shower. She looked . . . edible.

"I'm off duty," he said.

She dropped her gaze to his hip. "Oh," she said.

"Dance with me," he said.

She jerked her head back up to meet his eyes.

"Please," he added.

She glanced around. Unfolded herself from the chair. "There are a lot of people we know here," she said, keeping her voice low.

"Yeah," he agreed.

"Are you sure you want to dance?"

"Yeah."

"With me?"

He grinned. "Oh, yeah."

She drained whatever she had been drinking. "Why, then, thank you, Chief Van Alstyne. I'd like that." She turned and handed the empty paper cup to Parteger. "Hugh, will you excuse me?"

He took her hand — and didn't that feel weird, holding her hand in public — and led her to the dance floor. He didn't recognize the opening bars until the bandleader began to sing *There may be trouble ahead,* and Clare laughed and he swung her into his arms.

"Did you request this?" she asked.

"Just coincidence."

"You don't believe in coincidences."

"No, but I'm working on believing in fate." He put a little cha-cha into it and she followed perfectly. The tiny white lights overhead made her skin glow.

And while we still have the chance . . .

"There are people looking at us," she said.

"Yeah?"

"This is going to be all over town by lunchtime tomorrow," she said.

He didn't answer, concentrating on moving them toward the less crowded edge of the floor. Her red skirt twirled around the front of his legs. He decided if she let Parteger do it — and slid his hand up her back. No bra. Lots of bare skin.

Let's face the music and dance.

"Stop looking at me like that."

"Like what?"

"Like you want to eat me or something."

He smiled slowly. "I do."

She stumbled. He caught her and steadied her until she regained the rhythm.

"You make me think of those great glazed doughnuts they have over at the Kreemie Kakes diner," he went on.

"I make you think of a doughnut?"

He shrugged. "I *am* a cop." The music segued into "Old Devil Moon" without missing a beat. "Anyway, you know when they have them straight out of the fryer? They're all hot and the icing is just running off them?"

Her cheeks and chest were flushing.

"I love 'em like that. I like to lick the icing off, bit by bit, until it's all over me" — She made a barely audible sound — "and then I wolf it down in great big bites." He pulled her closer and she went, unresisting, until she was pressed against his chest, their thighs moving together in the steps of the dance. She turned her face up to him, her eyes dilated almost to black.

Finally she said, "Mrs. Robinson, I think you're trying to seduce me."

He laughed quietly. They swayed together. He ran his thumb along her jaw, where a piece of her hair clung. "Actually," he said, "I'm doing all this talking because I'm scared that if I don't, I'm going to start kissing you. First here" — he brushed his fingers over her lips — "then here" — he trailed down her neck, making her shiver — "then here" — he rubbed his hand over her collarbone and shoulder before sliding it down her back — "and from there, God only knows."

She swallowed. Inhaled. "Would you like

to walk me back to the rectory?"

Now it was his turn to breathe in. "I don't think that'd be such a good idea. In fact, it's probably not a good idea for me to be manhandling you on the dance floor like this." It was like bench pressing his own body weight, but he managed to push her a few inches away and resume a stance that suggested dancing more than making love.

"That's very thoughtful and responsible of you," she said. "Dammit all."

"I'm trying."

She looked at him, heavy-lidded, and brushed close to him. He could feel the heat rising off her body. "Is it hard for you?"

He groaned and closed his eyes. "Okay, I deserved that."

"I could walk home by myself."

He shook his head. "No."

"All right. Mr. Madsen and Mrs. Marshall could escort me. He's parked in the small lot behind the church." Which was separated from the rectory's driveway by a tall hedge of boxwood.

"I'll accept that."

"Where's your truck?"

"The lot on the corner of Elm."

"Why, that's just two houses down from where I live. But conveniently out of sight of the neighbors."

"Uh-huh. Although somebody might notice if it's still there at six o'clock in the morning."

She raised one eyebrow. "My, aren't you the confident one. Are you forgetting my live-in duenna?"

"I thought we could play three-hand pinochle."

She laughed. "Nobody really knows how to play pinochle."

"Okay, Scrabble."

The music ended and they broke apart to clap. She leaned toward him to be heard over the noise. "Double score for dirty words."

He smiled at her, helplessly. "God, I love you."

She opened her mouth, then closed it. "I better go tell poor Hugh good night."

He lassoed Mr. Madsen. "Clare's leaving," he explained, "and I don't want her walking up to the rectory by herself. Could you and Mrs. Marshall go with her?"

Mr. Madsen squinted toward where Clare and Parteger were talking. The Englishman didn't look too happy. "I thought that young man was her escort."

Mrs. Marshall had to crane her neck to see. Parteger was gesturing toward Clare, toward the dance floor, toward heaven.

Clare folded her arms and shook her head. Mrs. Marshall tsked. "Not anymore, I think. Come on, Norm, let's rescue her."

Russ made a point of staying as far away from Clare as possible while still keeping himself in the public eye. He chatted with this person and that, listening to news about grandkids and vacations as if he were running for town office. In the background, he could hear a chorus of "Good night, Clare!" and "Thanks, Reverend!" Minutes later, he watched Parteger stride off toward the parking lot, head down, hands jammed in pockets. His BMW peeled out of the lot much faster than necessary. Russ hoped he would cool down before he hit Paul Urquhart's speed trap on the Old Schuylerville Road.

When the band leader announced the last song of the night, Russ slipped away. He walked straight to his truck and kept on going, to the back of the lot, where a tornado fence and straggly sumacs marked off the first house on the south end of Elm Street. The only streetlight was on the corner, at the front of the lot, so he disappeared into velvet dark, untraceable except for his footsteps, slapping on the pavement.

He focused on that noise, and the thudding of his heart, and the warm dry air on his skin, and the smell of grass clippings and night jasmine. He didn't want to think, because he was afraid he'd shoot himself in the foot if he did. He hadn't done so well with thinking, these past months.

Then he saw Clare's house, just as it had been a month ago, one dim light in the living room and a glow coming from the kitchen door, and thinking became academic as all the blood rushed from his head into other places.

He crossed the street, mounted the kitchen steps, smiled as she pulled the door open for him. Then he saw her face, pale and strained. "What is it?" he said. He looked past her. The place was a mess. The cabinet doors hung open and all the drawers were yanked out.

"Amado's gone," she said, "and somebody's torn apart my house."

III

Nobody ever told you how messy fingerprint powder was. After the state police technician had photographed Clare's closets gaping open and her clothing strewn across the floor, after she had unlocked the church for Lyle MacAuley and Kevin Flynn to search, after she had listened to Russ's phone calls rousting Eric McCrea and Hadley Knox out of their beds and over to the McGeochs' workers' bunkhouse, after she had said good-bye to Russ — a stiff, grim farewell at the foot of her driveway, surrounded by officers strapping on their tac vests and checking weapons, already planning for the reception they would find when they knocked on the Christie brothers' door — after all that, she shut her door against the world and tackled the fingerprint powder.

A sudsy bucket and a couple of old T-shirt rags. The dust was everywhere because the mess was everywhere: kitchen, living room, bedroom, bath. First she had to stop to sweep up the various bits of broken glass, and then she had to keep trekking back to the sink to rinse the rags — no use streaking wet powder and grime over the picture frames, the banister, her jewelry box. Once she had the powder up, she could tackle the clothes and the books and the papers. Replace the recyclables in the bin. Restock the pantry shelves.

She was wiping down her dresser top when she realized she had to strip her bed and wash her sheets; she had to do it right away, right now. She tugged and pulled and wrestled the linens off, and the blankets, too, and the quilt and the mattress pad as well, then lugged them downstairs to the alcove off the kitchen, stuffing them into the machine, stuffing and stuffing, unable to find the water temperature control because she couldn't see the dials, stabbing at the button until she broke one of her already-short fingernails off at the quick, and then she couldn't see anything because her eyes were full of tears.

She crumpled to the floor, leaning against the cool white metal of the washing machine, crying and crying for Amado, who had trusted her to keep him safe. Crying for Russ, wearing his hard face and body armor. Crying for herself, foolish and pitiful because a few things were missing or broken. Like her heart. Like her life. And she didn't know how to begin to clean up the mess.

Someone was knocking at the door, a steady *rat-tat-tat* that sounded as if it must have been going on for a while. She lurched to her feet, grabbed a washcloth from the clean laundry teetering atop the dryer, and scrubbed her face with it.

She went to the kitchen door and looked out. Elizabeth de Groot. Oh, God. Just what she needed. She unlocked the door.

"I came over as soon as I heard," Elizabeth said, barging through the door. She looked around the kitchen, wide-eyed. "Good heavens. This is awful. You poor thing." She turned toward Clare. "You're all right, aren't you?" She swept Clare with an appraising glance, taking in her crumpled dress, which now seemed indecently bare, given the hour and the events. "I mean, he wasn't still here when you got in, was he? He didn't. . . ." Elizabeth let her voice trail off, suggesting A Fate Worse Than Death.

"I'm fine," Clare said. "Whoever did this was gone before I arrived."

Elizabeth stripped off her windbreaker and hung it over a chair back. "What do you mean, 'Whoever did this'? There were two police cars over at the old Peterson place looking for Amado Esfuentes. That's how I found out what happened." She shook her head, then began picking cans up off the floor. "Where do these go?"

"Elizabeth." She had to take control of the situation right now or God knows what rumors would be whipping around town. "The police are looking for Amado because he could be a victim. They think he may have been taken by the — by whoever killed those other men."

Elizabeth stacked the cans on the counter and bent to retrieve two more. "That's what that nice officer I spoke with said. But he also said Amado might be the murderer." She straightened and glanced around the kitchen. "Seeing this mess, I can believe it. Was anything stolen?"

"Fifty bucks. The MP-Three player I use when I run. A few pieces of jewelry. Nothing of much value."

"Ah." Elizabeth put the cans on the counter. "Easy to drop in his pocket and walk away with. I wouldn't be surprised if he wrecked this place because he was angry you didn't have any more. Thank God he didn't go for the communion silver." She looked at Clare. "He didn't, did he?"

Clare shook her head. "I was over there earlier with Deputy Chief MacAuley. Nothing's missing. And I reprogrammed the alarm system," she said, cutting off the question forming in the deacon's eyes. "I left a sticky note on the front and back doors, so, hopefully, no one will try to get in tomorrow before me." She resisted the urge to sit at the kitchen table and bury her face in her hands. "I'll have to think of some way to let everyone know."

"Don't you worry about that. I made a few phone calls while I was driving over. To the vestry and the wardens. I asked them to let others know. Sort of an informal phone tree."

"You did what?" This time, she didn't resist. She needed a chair to support her.

"Good God, Elizabeth. Next thing you'll tell me you've already informed the bishop." There was no answer from the deacon. Clare raised her head and glared at the other woman. "Elizabeth? Tell me you haven't spoken to the bishop."

"Don't be silly. It's ten thirty at night. I wouldn't pester the bishop at this hour."

"Good, because —"

"I left a message with his chancellor. And with Deacon Aberforth, of course. You ought to call him, by the way. He was very concerned about your well-being."

Clare wanted to knock her head against the wall. No, she wanted to knock *Elizabeth's* head against the wall. "There was absolutely no need —" she began, but Elizabeth cut her off.

"The bishop isn't just our superior, Clare, he's our pastor as well. Wouldn't you want to know if one of your flock had been assaulted and vandalized?"

"I wasn't assaulted!"

"You were a month ago. That Amado Esfuentes was neck deep in it then, and instead of letting the police handle it, you brought him into the rectory. Lord knows, I'd never say 'I told you so' —"

Oh, yeah?

"— but these things do *happen* to you,

Clare, and it's because you simply don't *think* before you act."

Clare opened her mouth to argue, then thought of the dance. Russ, and the music, and the warm night air, and the words. *Walk me back to the rectory.* She hadn't exactly been thinking then, had she?

"Clare." Elizabeth sat down opposite her. "I'm not here to *be* right. I'm here to help you get it right." She patted Clare's hand. "Don't look so glum. I know you're trying to keep your promise to the bishop. He's not going to blame you for this bit of nastiness." She stood up and faced the kitchen, hands on hips. "Now, let's tackle this —"

The door swung open. "Clare?" Anne Vining-Ellis tumbled in. "Oh, thank God, you're okay. Mrs. Marshall just called me and told me what happened." Clare stood to greet her and was almost knocked down by a bear hug. "Elizabeth, are you taking her home?"

The deacon looked surprised. "Well . . . no. I'm here to help put the rectory to rights."

"What, tonight? To hell with cleaning up. Clare, go get your pj's and a change of clothing. You're coming to my place." Dr. Anne sounded every inch the emergency room physician, snapping out orders and making split-second decisions.

Clare hadn't thought of leaving, hadn't been thinking of anything except putting the pieces of her life back together, but the idea, the freedom of simply walking away for a while, stunned her. "Really?" Then she remembered. "I can't. After morning Eucharist tomorrow, I've got to go down to Fort Dix for National Guard training. I won't be back until Tuesday evening, and I can't stand the idea of coming back to this disaster."

"You won't. Karen Burns is already organizing a crew to take care of everything tomorrow. Tonight, you're going to come home to where my large and thuggish sons can protect you, put your feet up, and have a good stiff drink. I'm sure Elizabeth will take tomorrow morning's service for you."

"Well." Elizabeth looked doubtful. "It'd have to be Morning Prayer instead of Morning Eucharist —"

"Perfect. It's settled, then. Elizabeth" — Dr. Anne slung her arm over the deacon's shoulders — "however in the world did we get along before you came to St. Alban's?"

It took Clare five minutes to throw her things into a duffel and get back downstairs. In that time, Dr. Anne had gotten Elizabeth de Groot back into her windbreaker and was easing her out the door, slathering the deacon with comfort and praise and appreciation like it was so much melted butter. "Night-night, Elizabeth," Dr. Anne called out the kitchen door. "See you tomorrow!" She shut the door. Turned toward Clare.

"Thank you," Clare said. "Thank you, thank you, thank you!"

"Lacey Marshall told me she was headed for your house. I figured I'd better get over as fast as I could to prevent the murder-suicide."

Clare laughed shakily.

"C'mon. I meant it about the drink." She opened the door again. "I heard Russ Van Alstyne was practically necking with you at the dance tonight, and I want all the juicy details."

IV

Kevin started to worry when he heard the dogs.

It had been exciting, getting the call from the deputy chief, everybody pulled back on duty, digging the tac vests out of the trunk of his squad car. He was sorry Reverend Fergusson had been upset and that her place was trashed, of course he was, but — tac vests! The chief had commandeered both his cruiser and the second vest, and, with Kevin riding shotgun and MacAuley and Noble right behind, headed out to the Christie farm in Cossayuharie.

In daylight, they could see the place from Seven Mile Road, but to reach it they had to go across a narrow side road and then up a rutted dirt lane. A gate barred the way, a metal pole-crosspole fastened to a sturdy-looking fence that ran off into the darkness in either direction.

"What's that for?" the chief asked.

"They raise sheep," Kevin reminded him.

"And they roam all the way down here? Huh. Open that thing for me, Kevin."

He sprang out of the car. And that's when things started to go to hell. He had taken one step toward the gate when two pole-mounted motion-sensor lights blazed on, flooding the lane and its surroundings, spotlighting him like a Friday-night quarterback.

Then he heard the dogs; a full-throated baying, as if a pack of hellhounds had been set loose up by the house.

And they were headed for him.

"Kevin," the chief shouted, but he didn't wait to be ordered back into the car. He pounded toward the latch, popped it free, and pushed the top rail as hard as he could.

It fetched up against something, jarring his arms, making him stumble back.

The chief was yelling something over the din of the approaching dogs. ". . . rolls to the right!" Kevin made out. "It rolls!"

He pulled the heavy gate open just far enough to wedge himself between the fence and the crossbar, and pushed. The gate rolled. He ran with it, pushing, the dogs getting closer and closer, visible now at the edge of the light, black and tan and white pointed teeth, and the chief gunned the cruiser and jerked it forward and the passenger door bounced closed and then it was open again, the chief stretched across the seats, screaming, "Get in! Get in!"

Kevin made a flying leap past the seething whipcord bodies and snarling jaws and landed inside the car. He and the chief scrambled for the handle, yanking it shut as one, two, three German shepherds thudded against the metal and glass, howling and barking and snapping their teeth. He let out the breath he'd been holding. *In like Flynn.*

"Jesus, Kevin." The chief sounded like he had been the one running out there. "Don't do that to me again. I thought you were puppy chow." He unhooked the mic and tuned the radio for car-to-car. "Lyle?"

"Here."

"No chance of sneaking up on 'em. May as well go in with lights." Behind them, MacAuley's cruiser blinked into whirling red and white.

"Awful lot of security for humble sheep farmers." MacAuley's voice over the radio was laconic.

The chief triggered the mic. "The Christies are sheep farmers the way trucking agents in New Jersey are legitimate businessmen. When we reach the dooryard, go as far around the side of the barn as you can. I don't want anybody slipping away through the back forty."

"Will do. Over."

The chief threw the car into gear and rolled forward. The German shepherds paced them, too smart to charge a moving vehicle, too focused to let them pull away.

As they reached the dooryard, another two motion sensor lights came on, one over the front porch, the other up on the barn. The two buildings were set kitty-corner to each other, with the dirt lane looping past each and rejoining itself. The house, from what Kevin could see, looked as if every generation of Christies had made one addition or another, until the most recent: a trailer on blocks at the far side of the yard, electrical wires running between it and the main

405

house. The trailer was dark, but a handful of windows in the house were lit.

The chief cracked his door open. Instantly, the dogs surged forward, growling and baring their teeth. He slammed it shut again, swearing. He grabbed the mic and switched the speakers to outside broadcast. "This is the Millers Kill Police." The chief's words, amplified, echoed back from the house and barn. "We need to ask you a few questions. Call back your dogs and restrain them." The echo caused a feedback, and the chief's speech ended with an electronic squeal. He dropped the mic.

"Hate that thing," he said.

They waited. Nothing happened. No lights came on or off, which Kevin supposed was good, but no one stepped onto the porch to whistle in the German shepherds. "What do you think's happening in there?" he asked.

The chief held up one finger. "They're just now figuring out what they heard wasn't part of the ten o'clock news." He held up a second finger. "Or they're running around the house like rats, collecting bags of pot and meth and Oxys and flushing them down the toilet as fast as they can pull the chain." He held up a third finger. "Or they're arming themselves, because you can't get rid of a body in five minutes. That's the one that worries me." He unsnapped his holster and drew his Glock .40. "Hope for the best, plan for the worst," he said. He opened the magazine and checked it.

Kevin unholstered his Colt .44 and did the same.

The chief flicked the speaker system on again. "Donald and Neil Christie. If you're not out here in three minutes restraining these dogs, my men and I will have to shoot them." This time, he turned the mic off before it could catch the bounceback.

"We're not really going to shoot the dogs, are we?" Kevin knew he sounded unprofessional, but shit. Dogs? He didn't know if he could do it.

"I sure as hell don't want to," the chief said. "On the other hand, if Amado Esfuentes is in there, I'm not going to sit on my ass out here while they do what they want with him."

"But . . . the dogs? It's not their fault they're behaving like this. Somebody trained them to do it."

The chief shifted in his seat a little to where he could see Kevin straight on. "Sometimes you're going to be in a situation where there aren't any good choices, Kevin. You just have to pick the better of

407

two bad ones, and learn to live with the outcome." The chief got a funny look on his face. Kevin thought he might say more, but then a light flashed from the house and they straightened to see the two beefy brothers step out onto the porch. Tweedle Dum and Tweedle Dumber, Eric had called them. They looked pissed off, but they appeared to be unarmed. Then a shorter, more slender man joined them.

"Interesting." The chief rubbed his thumb over his lip. "I wonder why Bruce Christie's making a late visit to the old homestead." After the Christies called up the German shepherds and shut them in the house, the chief and Kevin got out. The chief secured his weapon again, but left the holster unsnapped. Ready to go. Kevin did the same. He heard the heavy thunks of the other cruiser's doors closing from somewhere beside the barn. MacAuley and Noble, making sure no one was stealing away out back.

"You got a lotta nerve —" Donald Christie began.

Bruce thumped him in his chest. "How can we help you, Chief?"

"You can start by telling me where you all were tonight."

"Right here. At home."

"You living here now, Bruce?"

Bruce Christie grinned. "Just until your boys catch the sumbitch who trashed my trailer." He gestured toward them. "You guys look like one a them SWAT teams, all armored up like that. What's goin' on?"

"Someone broke into Reverend Fergusson's house in town." Donald Christie's hand flew to his nose. Kevin pressed his lips together to keep from showing his amusement. "They tore it up pretty bad. The church's janitor, who was living there, is missing." The chief looked at Neil Christie. "You remember him, right, Neil? I mean, before Reverend Fergusson knocked you unconscious."

The big man grunted.

"Sounds like it might be the same crew as broke into my place," Bruce said. "You sure the Mexican isn't workin' with 'em?"

"I'll tell you what I'm sure of. I'm sure your brothers went to St. Alban's in May looking for Amado Esfuentes. I'm sure they would've beat the crap out of him if they could have. And I'm sure interested in taking a look around here to see if maybe you all brought him home tonight for a little talking-to."

Bruce Christie kept on smiling. "You got a warrant, Chief?"

Without taking his eyes off Bruce, the

chief pulled his phone from his pocket. He tossed it to Kevin, who tried to look matter-of-fact about catching it. "Officer Flynn," the chief said, "Assistant District Attorney Amy Nguyen is number eight on my speed dial. I want you to ask her to take the Christies' case file to Judge Ryswick with a search warrant request." His voice took on a confidential tone, clearly directed at Bruce. "Your brothers' case was filed, not dismissed. Which means it can be reopened at any time." He glanced at his watch. "I expect we'll be here about two hours, waiting for the warrant to arrive." He looked back up to the porch, where Bruce Christie's pleasant veneer was cracking. "I figure by then, in order to justify our overtime, we'll have to go over your place with a fine-tooth comb." He glanced at Kevin. "Officer Flynn, where's the nearest K-Nine unit?"

Kevin stepped up to the plate. "The Capital Area Drug Enforcement Association has a trained narcotics-sniffing dog available in Kingston, Chief. His handler could be here in under an hour." He held up the phone. "You want me to call him?"

"I don't know, Officer Flynn." The chief looked at the Christies. "What do you think, Bruce?"

"The Mexican's not here. He got the message to stay away from our sister. We don't have no other business with him."

"Izzy ain't seeing him no more," Neil said. "He didn't understand when she told him to clear off, 'cause he don't speak no English."

Kevin thought Neil wasn't doing so hot in that department himself.

The chief spread his hands. "All we're looking for is Amado. I'm not interested in anything else. Yet."

The Christies looked at one another. Donald spoke up. "I don't want you scaring nobody. We got kids here, some a my fiancée's and some a mine while their mom is outta town."

"I suspect the best way not to scare them is if we all cooperate."

The Christies looked at one another again. Bruce nodded to his brothers. Turned toward the chief. "All right," he said.

The chief motioned toward the barn. "Two of my men will search the barn. It'd go faster and easier if one of you went with them."

Bruce Christie cut a sharp glance at his brothers. "I'll go." He clattered down the stairs and headed for the three-story structure. Kevin tagged the barn as the most likely spot for whatever illegal substances the Christies were hiding.

The chief reached inside the cruiser and snatched the mic. "Lyle?" he said.

The speaker cracked on. "Here."

"Bruce Christie is headed your way to show you around his barn. Make sure you get a look at any outbuildings as well."

"Roger that."

The chief rehitched the mic and held out a hand toward Kevin. It took him a beat, but he figured out what the chief wanted. He dropped the phone in his hand and bent close enough not to be overheard by the two remaining Christies. "Won't Bruce just get in their way? Try to keep them from seeing what he doesn't want them to see?"

"I want to split them up," the chief said, in the same low tone. "If we stumble onto something, we'll only have one to deal with." He stepped toward the porch stairs and raised his voice. "Do you have a kennel or a run for the dogs?"

"Ayeah," Donald said.

"Good. I'd like one of you to put them away. None of us wants an unfortunate accident because a dog got overexcited."

"I'll do it," Neil said to his brother. "You better stay with Kathy so's she don't freak out."

The chief waited next to Donald while

Neil went inside. He returned in a moment, leading four German shepherds straining at their leashes. The shepherds looked like they'd been crossbred with ponies. Mean-tempered ponies. Kevin's exhilaration at escaping the dogs at the gate turned to a queasy awareness of what they could have done if they had caught him.

"Officer Flynn?" The chief's voice snapped him out of it. He thudded up the stairs and followed Donald Christie and the chief into the house.

They were in what must have once been a fine front hall: plaster moldings and mahogany woodwork and an elegant twelve-over-twelve window. Now it was dusty and bare, except for a coatrack and a pile of boots. Broad carpeted stairs curved to the second floor. A door ahead of them listed open to what looked like a dining room. Through the closed double door to the left he could hear the sounds of an overloud television and the babble of high-pitched conversation. Donald Christie thumbed in that direction. "Kathy and mosta the kids are watching a movie. I better go tell her what's goin' on. She gets some touchy at times."

"Why don't I come with you," the chief said, smooth and easy, like he was Donald

Christie's best bud. "I know how women can get." He tapped Kevin and, without looking, pointed at the open door.

Kevin got moving. The next room was indeed a dining room — dark, depressing, anchored with a table large enough to perform surgery. He heard a woman's voice say, "What?" and turned back toward the front hall. There was another closed door behind him. He could hear Christie, sounding apologetic, and the low rumble of the chief's voice.

He reversed himself slowly, looking for anything that might be a lead. On the other wall, a coffin-sized sideboard surmounted by a depressing painting of dead animals separated two more doorways. One appeared to contain a closet-sized hall. The other opened onto linoleum. He picked the lino.

The kitchen was a mix of old wooden cabinets, knocked-together shelving, and 1970s appliances. There were two more doors, one ahead of him and one to the left. He shook his head. Old houses. Three doors to every room but no closets. He crossed the kitchen to the far door, wedged between shelving and a skinny laminate cupboard. It led to a narrow roofed porch; washer and dryer on one end, clothesline looping off a wheel into the darkness in front of him. He frowned at the steps leading down to the backyard. He backed into the kitchen and headed for the other door, between the sink and a harvest-gold chest freezer. From the other side of the house, he could hear a woman complaining at top volume. Must be Kathy, getting touchy. Kevin was grinning to himself as he opened the next door.

A woman looked up from where she was reading on a fluffed-up marshmallow of a bed.

"Oh! Geez." Kevin could feel the blush starting. "I'm sorry! I didn't know anyone was in here. I would've knocked."

The woman shut a skinny paperback and slid off the bed. "It's okay," she said. "I heard the first part of tonight's show. You guys didn't kill the dogs, did you?"

"No!"

"Too bad." She didn't sound sarcastic, just sad.

"I, um. . . ." He glanced around the room. It was decked out like a French boudoir for a six-year-old, although the woman standing in front of him had to be his age or a few years older. Blond, brown-eyed, built like a former Dairy Princess. "Are you the sister?"

"That's me," she said. If Bruce Christie

got the brains in the family, this one got the looks.

"I have to, um . . . do you mind if I look around?"

She swept her arm wide. "Help yourself. What are you after?"

"Um." What if the brother was wrong, and she wasn't over her Latino boyfriend? He didn't want to deal with another Kathy, who was now so high-pitched, he could hear her from where he stood. "The janitor from the Episcopal church is missing."

She looked at him as if he were cracked. "And you're looking for him here?" Then her mouth opened. "Oh. Is this the guy my brothers went after?" Her mouth quirked in an odd sort of smile. "The Mexican guy at the church?"

"Yeah. Have you seen him recently?"

She shook her head. "I never saw him." She put air quotes around the word "saw." "They just . . . Neil gets . . ." She smiled that smile again. "They got nothing to worry about."

"Did you tell them that? That he wasn't your boyfriend?"

She snorted. "No. Why? They'd just go after —" She jammed her hands into the pockets of her jeans. "It's done with. I don't wanna bring it up again." The angle of her arm slid her short sleeve back, and Kevin could see the edge of a purple and green bruise that must have gone to her shoulder.

"Um," he said. "But your brothers. If they're still under the impression you had a relationship, maybe *they* wanted to bring it up again."

She frowned. "No, they wouldn't. . . ." She trailed off. "I don't think they would." She was talking to herself now. "Would they?"

"You mind if I go ahead?"

She waved him on. He made short work of the place — no closet, one bed, no trap door leading to the cellar. It'd be hard to hide a guy in here, since, he noted, there were nothing but screw holes in the door-jamb where locks or a hook-and-eye would have gone. There was another door at the far end of the room, but when he tried it, he was on the washer and dryer end of the porch. Convenient. He had a feeling the male Christies didn't do much housework.

He fished in his breast pocket and took out a card. "Here," he said. She took it. Read it. Her face closed. She handed it back.

"I don't need this," she said.

"Then pass it on to another woman who might," he said. "It's a toll-free line, twenty-four hours a day, no questions asked. They can keep you safe."

She snorted. "You don't know much, do you?"

Nothing he could say to that. He apologized again and left her, still standing, still frowning. At least she kept the card. He met up with the chief at the entrance to the narrow hall in the dining room.

The chief looked like a man who'd been verbally blowtorched. "Next time," he said, "we bring a trank gun."

"For the dogs?"

"For the fiancée." He raked a hand through his hair, skewing it in odd directions. "There's a baby and two little ones asleep upstairs. Two more kids and Donald's teenager live here, as well as the teen's baby daddy, sometimes, and the Christies. Bruce is out in the fifth-wheel trailer. We're looking for anything anomalous."

"Geez, Chief," Kevin said. "I didn't know you knew the phrase *baby daddy.*"

The chief gave him a look. "I used to say *bounder* and *cad,* but I updated."

The upstairs was a bust, as was the trailer. No sign of Amado, no sign that any of the Christies had been vandalizing the rectory.

"Now what?" he asked the chief. They had closed the rickety trailer door and were

418

walking across the grass.

"Now we send out an APB and hope somebody spots the guy." The chief blinked as another motion-detector light came on from the side of the house. "Unless Eric and Knox turn up something at the workers' bunkhouse, we've just blown through our only lead."

"I spoke to the sister," Kevin said.

"Yeah?" The chief paused. "What'd she have to say?"

"That she never went out with the guy. Said her brothers misunderstood the situation."

"Huh. Lot of misunderstandings around that relationship." The chief crossed to their cruiser. "You believe her?"

"Dunno. She seemed more concerned that her brothers might have gotten themselves into trouble again than she did about the church janitor." He paused. "I think somebody's been beating up on her."

The chief frowned. "Did she say anything?"

He shook his head. The chief sighed. "Doesn't mean she's not protecting her brothers, if one of them's doing it."

"I know." The crunch of wheels caught Kevin's attention. MacAuley's squad car reversed onto the looping drive from its parking spot beyond the barn. He backed up until he was parallel to them in the classic driver-to-driver position. His window powered down.

The chief leaned forward, his hands on the door. "Anything?" He jerked back. "Whee-ooh! What the hell've you been in?"

"Sheep," MacAuley said. He didn't sound happy. Kevin could understand why. He was several feet away from the open window, and even he could smell it. "We found diddly-squat," the deputy chief went on. "Although I'd by damn like to go back there with a good dog. I'm betting whatever they sell is there, in the byre. That stink could cover up a multitude of sins."

"Later," the chief said. "We need more." A dog's yelp made Kevin jerk around. Bruce and Neil Christie sauntered across the drive, Neil holding back two of the devil dogs. Kevin felt a clammy dampness along his spine.

"Everything okay, Chief?" Bruce grinned at them.

The chief jerked his chin down in a nod. "Thank you for your cooperation," he said.

"I hope you're putting the same effort into finding the guys who shanked my place," Bruce said.

"We treat all reported crimes seriously."

The chief's good-citizen voice was starting to slip. He jerked his head toward Kevin. "Time to go, Officer Flynn. We've disturbed these folks enough for one night."

"You bet your ass you have," Neil Christie said.

Bruce shot his brother a look. "We'll keep the dogs back until you're past the gate." He grinned at them again. "Please don't forget to fasten it. We don't want the livestock getting out."

Kevin slid into the passenger seat. The chief got in, and fired up the engine. They followed MacAuley and Noble slowly along the rutted drive. Kevin glanced at the chief. He seemed lost in thought.

"Chief?" Kevin kept his voice low. "Whatcha thinking?"

The chief pinched the bridge of his nose. Made a noise deep in his chest. "I'm thinking this isn't the way I wanted to spend tonight."

ORDINARY TIME

JUNE AND JULY

I

Clare walked over to the church early Wednesday morning for the seven-thirty Eucharist. The night before, exhausted from the drive from Fort Dix and tense over the state of her home, she headed straight for the rectory, which had turned out to be so much neater and cleaner than it had been before the burglary, she was a little embarrassed.

Anne Vining-Ellis and her youngest son, Colin, were waiting at the great double doors. Her skirt and blouse said she was headed for the Glens Falls Hospital. Colin, in pipe-cleaner jeans and pointed shoes, looked like he was auditioning for an eighties revival band. "I'm delivering your acolyte du jour," Dr. Anne said.

The boy pushed his overgrown bangs away from his face. "Under protest. Organized religion is a tool of the capitalist machine."

"He's taking a summer AP course in Marxism-Leninism," Dr. Anne said. "God help us all."

Clare handed the teen her overloaded key ring and Thermos of coffee. "Would you open up for me, Colin? And drop this in my office?"

He took the jangle of keys. "Why not? I'm only a member of the proletariat, crushed by the oppressive boot heels of history. Want me to light the candles, too?"

"Thanks." Clare turned to his mother. "Remind me to give him some books on liberation theology."

"Don't bother. The second half of the unit is Adam Smith and John Maynard Keynes. He'll probably be selling the church silver on the free market." Dr. Anne watched Colin disappear into the narthex. "How are you doing? I almost came over last night, but I figured you'd be wiped after the drive from New Jersey."

"Thanks, yeah. I'm okay. I'd be better if I heard Señor Esfuentes has been found safe and sound."

Dr. Anne shook her head. "Nothing yet that I know of."

Clare sighed. "That's what I thought. I figured Russ — someone would call if anything turned up." She looked past

Church Street's steady stream of commuter traffic, headed for Glens Falls or the Northway. The park appeared much less magical in the strong morning sun. "I keep going over Sunday night in my head, wondering what I could have done to prevent it. Should I have dragged him over to the party? Gone home early? Left someone to watch over him?" She reached for the back of her head, ready to repin falling pieces of hair, but this early in the day her twist was still inviolate.

"At the risk of sounding like a broken record, it's just as likely he trashed the place and went off."

Clare shook her head. "No."

Dr. Anne started down the sidewalk. "Sometimes I think you carry this look-for-the-good-in-all-people thing too far," she said over her shoulder.

"I know," Clare said. "It's an occupational hazard."

It was a typical Wednesday morning, ten communicants, if she counted herself and Colin. No one, thank God, wanted to linger and chat about last Sunday's events, and she was disrobing in the sacristy five minutes after she had dismissed her flock.

In the office, Lois greeted her with a hymn. "Onward, Christian soldiers, marching as to war," the secretary sang, "with the hel-i-cop-ters, flying on before."

Clare peeked into the tiny hole-in-the-wall that was the deacon's office. No one was there yet. "It's no wonder Elizabeth thinks we're both deranged."

Lois rolled her eyes. "I think the National Guard ought to pay *me* for putting up with that woman while you're gone."

"What happened?"

"She wanted to know what I thought of you taking up with Chief Van Alstyne again."

"Taking up with — ?"

"I told her I don't gossip and I don't care to listen to those who do. Then, of course, she was sweet as cream, saying she was just worried about people thinking it a scandal. I told her the only scandal would be if you let the best man in Millers Kill get away." She leaned on one elbow and pointed the letter opener at Clare. "Which is not to say I don't give a thumbs-up to Hugh Parteger. He has lovely manners, and he makes five or six times what the chief of police does."

"Maybe you should ask him out, then. I don't think he's going to be calling me anymore. Not after this past weekend."

Lois pulled a stack of pink phone messages free from a spiked note keeper. She selected one and held it up. "I don't know about that. He phoned three times. Wants to talk with you soonest."

Clare groaned. "Please tell me there are a lot of work-related messages I have to return first."

"The bishop wants you to call. Her Holiness was complaining to him about your having a dangerous criminal in the rectory, that sort of thing. And he wants to know why you're in the paper. Again."

"I'm in the paper?"

"There was a story about the break-in and poor Señor Esfuentes's disappearance in the *Post-Star*. It doesn't mention *him* by name — I suppose they have to find his next of kin and all, poor souls — but *you're* featured front and center. That reporter called for a statement."

"Ben Beagle?"

"Mmm-hmm. I told him you were away, preparing to defend the freedom of the press with your life."

"You didn't."

"Well, no, not in those words. I did tell him it was National Guard duty." She plucked a pink message slip off the spike and rattled it between her long fingers. "I swear, that rag's getting no better than one of the tabloids. Made it sound as if none of us are safe in our beds. Well, none of us who might be Hispanic."

Clare held out her hand for the rest of the pink message slips. "I suppose I should count my blessings. At least Elizabeth isn't holding a press conference about my scandalous carryings-on. Yet."

"I heard poor Mr. Parteger was left kicking his heels on the sideline while you and Chief Van Alstyne danced all night."

"I thought you never listened to gossip?"

"I never repeat it. I can't help it if people like to confide in me. It's the job. Sooner or later, the church secretary hears everything."

Clare squared her shoulders. "The chief and I danced for two songs. If we were on the floor for more than eight minutes I'd be surprised."

Lois smiled widely. "You're blushing."

"I am not." Clare resisted covering her cheeks. "Would you please call the IGA with the usual order of lunch things for the vestry meeting?"

"Yes, I will."

Clare fled the office with Lois still smiling like the owner of a dumb dog who has just learned a new trick.

At her own desk, Clare poured a mug of her home-brewed coffee and dug right in to answering the messages that had accumulated in her absence. After she had returned most of the calls, she applied herself to the proposals for fall projects the vestry would be discussing at today's lunchtime meeting. The pink message notes from the bishop and Ben Beagle and Hugh glowered at her whenever she glanced away from her paperwork. For once, it was a relief to have Lois buzz her about the vestry meeting.

"It's time," the secretary said. "The deacon is already in there with copies of the agenda and the proposals."

The babble of voices from the meeting room died away when she came through the door. With linen-fold paneling and diamond-paned windows, high-backed chairs and a threadbare Aubusson rug, it had been the best Tudor copy that 1860s technology could buy. Perhaps the builders of St. Alban's had wanted to salute Henry VIII, the founder of the church.

"Hello, everyone." They had left a place for her at the head of the black oak table. Without any formal plan or discussion, the vestry always seemed to arrange themselves in the same way. Robert Corlew, the senior warden, sat at Clare's left, with Terrance McKellan supporting him, in much the same way that Terry's bank supported Corlew's developments. On her right, junior warden Geoffrey Burns held his position opposite Corlew; lawyer versus contractor, forty versus sixty, thinning hair versus toupee.

At least she *thought* that pelt on Corlew's head was a rug.

Mrs. Henry Marshall, bright-eyed and brilliantly lipsticked, sat between Burns and Norm Madsen. Mrs. Marshall was Clare's most faithful ally on the vestry, tart-voiced and decisive, while Mr. Madsen was the one who always saw every side to an issue. *Faith, here's an equivocator, that could swear in both scales against either.*

Clare snagged a Coke off the sideboard and dropped into her chair.

Sterling Sumner, retired architect and sometime lecturer at Skidmore College, sat across the long expanse of the table from Clare, about as far from Corlew as possible. He was sliding the usual platter of sandwiches and chips to Elizabeth de Groot, who was at his right hand. They had discovered they shared similar tastes in buildings (historic), liturgy (formal), and literature (nothing written after 1890). Clare wasn't sure if Elizabeth knew she and Sumner also shared similar tastes in men.

The platter reached Terry McKellan, who glanced up and down the seats before taking two sandwiches and chips each. His wife had him on a diet, which had turned the finance officer into a stealth eater. Clare thought he looked like a guilty English sheepdog stealing food off the counter.

Robert Corlew took a sandwich and slid the platter toward Clare. She dropped what she hoped was chicken salad on whole wheat on a napkin. "Since this is the last meeting before we pick up again in September, let's get right to it." She spread her hands, inviting them to prayer. "Lord God," she said, "help us to discern your will, and discerning, to serve your people, to the glory and honor of your name. Amen." Short but serviceable. "Okay, Looking at the first item, a proposal to turn volunteer education director Gail Jones's job into a part-time paid position —"

"I'd like to find out more about what happened at the rectory Sunday night," Corlew said.

"Hear, hear," Sterling said.

Clare sighed. Laid her pen atop her stack of papers. Reminded herself to relax her shoulders.

"Amado Esfuentes, our temporary sexton, robbed Clare and then took off," Elizabeth said.

Clare felt her shoulders bunch right up again. "We have no proof of that, Elizabeth."

"I already heard that." Corlew waved the

deacon's words away with an irritated expression. "I mean, was there any damage to the rectory? Do we have any insurance exposure?" He turned to Clare. "After all, you did invite the little weasel to come in and make himself at home."

"Now, Robert." Mrs. Marshall gave Clare a small smile. "I think Clare realizes that was not, perhaps, the best idea. No need to belabor the point."

"The point is that it's far too dangerous for any member of St. Alban's to be driving these wetbacks around to the welfare office or Roman Masses or what have you." Sterling Sumner jerked his silk aviator's scarf for emphasis. "We never should have gotten involved with that nun's ministry. Let the papists take care of their own, I say."

Clare was caught between open-mouthed outrage at the range of Sterling's bigotry and amazement that someone could use the word 'papist' in a sentence in this century.

"I don't agree with Sterling's sentiments," Geoff Burns said, "but I have to concur that we need to suspend the migrant worker outreach immediately." He turned toward Clare. "I'm the last person to say guilty until proven innocent, but I already have two Hispanic clients awaiting trial for drug charges. There are some bad people out there, Clare."

"And you can tell they're bad by the color of their skin?" Clare's voice rose. She swallowed and tried again. "St. Alban's volunteers are reaching dozens of men each week, providing them with cell phone service, transportation, and access to the free clinic." She nodded toward Mrs. Marshall, whose mother had founded the health center. "It's one of our most successful outreach programs, and it doesn't cost the church a dime."

"We have reimbursed for gas," Terry said. Clare gave him an exasperated look. "Just being accurate," he said.

"Oh, sure." Corlew glowered at Clare. "It's all wine and roses until one of our congregation gets mugged, just like you would have been if you'd been home Sunday night instead of playing kissy-face with Russ Van Alstyne."

"I was *not* —"

Mrs. Marshall giggled. It was such an unexpected sound — like hearing the Queen of England snicker — they all stared.

Clare recovered first. "Señor Esfuentes may well have been a victim of crime, instead of a perpetrator. There's no conclusive evidence either way."

"In which case," Sterling said, "he may

432

have fallen prey to this serial killer who seems to be haunting our area. Which brings me straight back to the central thesis: We cannot condone our people hanging about with men who may be targeted for violence at any moment."

"So you're saying we should dictate to our volunteers? Tell them we've decided it's too risky for them to be driving around the mean streets of Cossayuharie? Shouldn't they be able to make that call on their own?" She turned to Corlew. "Robert, you're a Republican, for heaven's sake. Don't you believe in individual responsibility?"

"Not," he said, "when we're in a position to get sued."

II

The meeting devolved into a wrangling session. Clare got the board to agree that volunteers who signed a statement that any further migrant outreach on their part was entirely a personal decision could continue. After all, how could the vestry stop them? But there would be no more central communication and coordination by St. Alban's. They never did get back to the question of the education director. By the time the Civil War–era grandfather clock chimed the hour,

Clare was seething. From the way the vestry members tossed their good-byes and hurried out the door, she knew she was doing a lousy job of hiding her feelings.

Elizabeth de Groot fluttered up to her after everyone else had left. "Clare," she said, in her cultivated voice, "I know this is a disappointment to you, but I'm sure that in time you'll see —"

"Elizabeth," Clare said, "don't you have something to do?"

The deacon looked at her hesitantly. "Uh, yes. Hospital visits."

"Then I suggest you go forth, spreading the good news of Jesus Christ." *And leave me the hell alone.*

Clare was sitting on the priceless antique table, wrapped in a blue devil, when Lois stuck her head in the door. "Want me to put away the leftovers?" she asked, waving toward the remaining sandwiches and chips.

"Thanks, Lois. Go ahead and take your lunch break. I'll carry this downstairs and put it in the fridge. I can deliver the sandwiches to the shelter later."

She found a plastic grocery bag in her office and tossed the chips in. Hanging it over her arm, she collected the sandwich platter and tottered downstairs to the church kitchen. The lights in the hall were already on. Good Lord, had she forgotten to turn them off after she and Lyle MacAuley went through the place Sunday night?

Wonderful. Another collection plate for the National Grid Power Company.

Then she heard a step behind her.

She whirled, saw the shape of a man emerge from the sexton's closet, and screamed. She was raising the tray in self-defense, hitting herself in the chest with the bag of chips, when the man said, "Father? It's just me."

She lowered the food. The sandwiches slid toward her, mashing into her stomach, mayonnaise and tuna smearing over the black cotton. "Mr. Hadley," she said. She cleared her throat to steady her voice. "You startled a year's growth out of me."

"Grampa? What was that?" At the other end of the hall, Hadley Knox's little girl popped out of the nursery. "Are you okay?"

Her big brother stepped into the hallway beside her. "Should I call Mom?"

"No! G'back inside, you two. I just startled the Father some." He ran one hand over his bald scalp. "Din't mean to scare you. We got here when you was meeting with the vestry. Din't want to interrupt."

"No, no." She looked down at the mess on her clerical blouse. "I was going to put

435

this in the fridge." She looked at the sexton. He was in his usual work clothes: baggy, stained twill pants and a plaid shirt. He had a backpack in one hand, and even from several feet away she could smell cigarette smoke. "What are you doing here?"

"Honey told me 'bout the Mexican boy disappearing. I figgured it was time for me to get back on the job."

"With the kids in tow?" Another thought occurred to her. "Has your doctor —" the bag of chips was beginning to cut into her wrist. "Let me get rid of this, hmm?" He followed her down the hall into the semisub-terranean kitchen. She laid the sandwich platter and the chips on the wide center island. "There are some sodas left in the meeting room. Would the kids like lunch?"

"Don't want to be no bother." He waved his hand in the vague direction of her upper body. "Better take care of that stuff on your shirt, there. 'Fore it stains."

She grabbed a dishcloth and turned on the cold water. "Has your doctor given you the okay to go back to work?"

He grunted. "Somebody's got to. This place ain't gonna clean itself, y'know."

She looked up from scrubbing the mayo off her blouse. "Does your granddaughter know you're here?"

Mr. Hadley shifted from foot to foot. "Long as I'm watching the kids and they ain't parked in front of the TV like she axed, I don't see as it makes no never mind where we are."

"Mr. Hadley —"

He lifted the backpack and placed it next to the sink. "I found this in my closet. Figgured it belonged to the Mexican."

She recognized it now. Amado had been carrying that bag when she had come to pick him up at the McGeochs' farm. Before the choir concert. Before the Christies invaded her church. Before Russ —

She dropped the dishcloth in the sink. The mayo was gone, but now she had an enormous oily wet spot on her midsection. "I suppose the police will want to see it."

"I s'pose they will." Mr. Hadley unzipped the bag and held it toward her, opened wide.

"Holy —" She inhaled. Inside, a monstrous .357 nestled between wrapped stacks of currency.

"Oh, dear lord." She thought of the young Latino's nervous eyes. The way he'd scrub at his half-grown mustache when she spoke to him. "What did you get yourself into?"

III

He wished he had kept the gun. It would have felt good, riding heavy against the waistband of his jeans, raising a bruise as he toiled up and down the forested hills, making his way to the Christie farm. It was a form of communication those *hijos de putas* could understand.

Amado paused and wiped the sweat out of his eyes. The air was sticky with the scent of pine. Only an hour past dawn and already hot beneath the forest cover. Raul thought he was a liar, with his stories of cool mountain mornings and evenings where you needed to wear a jacket. Those were past years. This year was different.

He wished he had never come back to this place.

He wasn't sure how he was going to get them to admit what they had done with Octavio. He wasn't even sure they were there. The policewoman who had come last night, asking questions while her partner searched the bunkhouse and the barn and the outbuildings, had said other police were talking with the Christies at the same time. She had said they should call if Amado showed up. Everyone looked straight ahead and pretended they didn't know the real Amado had swapped names and papers with his

438

brother. She had said they should watch out for anyone suspicious and should stick together in pairs. She didn't know much about dairy work.

He had two utility knives in his pockets. A farmer's tool. Sharp enough to slash through tangled leather straps, sturdy enough to pry a stone out of a hoof. He was a farmer, not a fighter, but he knew he could hurt the Christies badly enough to make them talk. If they didn't kill him first.

He hiked up the last rise — the same stretch of woods he had stumbled through a month ago, fleeing with gun and money and Isobel's kiss and the sounds of her beating in his ears. He wondered, for the hundredth time, if he should have stopped her brother and taken her away. To save her. To save Octavio from this stupid mix-up he had created. One lie, to keep Octavio from deportation. And now it might be the boy's death warrant.

Did they come after him because they thought he was the brown-skinned man kissing their sister? Or had Isobel crumbled and told them a man named Amado had the gun and the money, sending them after Octavio in a stupid, deadly mistake? Either way, he was to blame. For losing his mind and pretending he could be with an Anglo woman. For agreeing to keep her secrets, even when he wasn't sure what they were. For handing a bag full of death over to Octavio. He had counted the money. It was more than enough for someone to kill for. And he had given it to the boy with no more warning than to keep it private. What could be safer than a church?

What had he been thinking?

He heard something ahead of him. He froze. A *ting-ting* sound, like sweet small bells. The *skritch-skritch* of squirrels running up a tree. Bleating. He relaxed until he remembered Isobel's family raised sheep. If they were grazing in the old wood-ringed pasture, would one of the brothers be there? He reached inside his pocket and gripped the handle of the utility knife. One man, he could take on and hope to succeed. Unless there was a dog, too.

He slunk to the edge of the pasture like a wolf. There were perhaps fifteen or twenty sheep mowing the grass, their coats half-grown from a spring shearing, belled to make them easier to track. No shepherd. No dog that he could see, although that didn't mean there wasn't one napping in the shade of the pole barn.

A fox skull hung beside the hayloft door. Facing him. He almost turned and retraced his steps, but he was a man, and a man didn't run from a woman. He emerged from the underbrush and headed for the barn. Maybe she had news of Octavio. Maybe she wanted the gun and the money back. Maybe she needed his help again. Maybe she found herself thinking of him in the quiet moments of the day, pausing at the sight of hay in the cow barn, drifting away when the men discussed their women back home. . . .

He jerked himself into the moment. The knife handle was slippery in his hand. He ought to stab himself in the thigh. Perhaps that would keep him focused. He reached the door. Hauled himself up over the lip. Heard her whisper, "Amado?"

For a split second, he worried about a trap, but then she bounded across the bales toward him, arms outstretched, hair streaming behind her like a pennant. She flung herself at him, arms wide, and all he could do was embrace her, teetering, and then he lost his balance and the two of them toppled backward onto the hay.

She was speaking, a torrent of English like choppy water pouring over him, and he could hear relief and fear and apology in her voice. He rolled to one side, letting her slip off him, and the motion seemed to make her aware of where they were, chest to chest, arm by arm, legs entangled. She said something, fast and low, and scrambled out of range. When she turned again, her cheeks were pale pink.

He sat up. Marshaled his thoughts. He couldn't afford to let sentiment mess up his judgment. "Your brothers," he said, "take Octavio." He rose to his feet. He wasn't any taller than she, but he was strong. Very strong. "Where?" he demanded.

She shrank back. He felt like a slug, but he continued to glare at her. "Where?"

"Octavio?" Another flood of English, this time questions.

He held up one hand. He didn't want her to know the relationship between Octavio and himself. Anything she knew, her brother might beat out of her. "Octavio work at" — he sketched a cross in the air — *"la iglesia."*

"The church?"

"The church, yes. Your brothers take him."

"Mi familia," she said, "no take him. No." She spread her hands open. "I ask. They no take him. *Yo promesa.*"

"You promise? You promise?" He spat on the hay next to his work boot. "Your brothers lie."

"No." She should have been offended or angry, but instead her face softened. She stepped toward him, tentatively, as if he might snap and slap her like her abusive brute of a brother.

Mother of God. What sort of man was he, frightening a woman who had learned to expect the side of a hand? He reached out to her. "Isobel," he said. She came to him, no reluctance now, and he held her as he would hold a child, his anger and misery leaching away as he murmured, *"Lo siento.* I am sorry. *Lo siento."*

After a few moments, she pushed away from him. He released her instantly. She faced him, her lips pressed firm, her eyebrows knitted, the face of someone trying to put something complex into simple, understandable words. *"La policia* ask for . . ." — she frowned — "Octavio?"

"Octavio."

"La policia ask my brothers." She mimed a burly man, arms akimbo, holding out one arm in a sign to stop. "No here," she said in a gruff voice. "No Octavio." She reverted to her own voice. "I ask my brothers. They —" She held her belly and faked a deep laugh. "Ha-ha-ha!"

"Risa."

"¿Risa? Laugh?" She nodded. "My brothers" — she enacted the big man again, complete with deep voice — *"¿El hombre de la iglesia? Pffft."* She made an elaborate show

of *who cares?* She shifted back to herself. "I ask, me *promesa?* My brothers" — she dropped her voice again — "Okay. *Promesa.*"

She came to a standstill. "*Lo siento,* Amado." He could hear the truth in her words. A cautious voice inside him whispered, *She may be a brilliant liar,* but one thing he had learned, traveling through a strange land, is that sometimes you have to trust. And believe. He wanted to believe in Isobel. He wanted that very much.

He reached for her hand. The price of belief was losing his only hope of recovering Octavio. Because if the Christies didn't have him, who did? How could he ever find him?

He let her draw him to where the old quilt had been spread over loose hay. He sat, then flopped backward, tired of dread and rage and suspicion. Tired of the *patron* relying on him and the men looking to him and the weight, the immovable, unchangeable weight of responsibility, to his brother in this country and to their family at home.

Isobel perched beside him, as if uncertain where she was allowed to be. He opened his arms, and after a moment she lay down snug against him. She rested her hand on his chest. He drew his fingers through the ends of her hair. He found himself talking about his parents. About his family's home. About his fears that he was the cause of Octavio's disappearance. He opened up his mouth and let every sad, mad, bad thing in his head out, named them all, and let them fly up into the shadows like the swallows nesting above. Finally, he looked at her, into her grave, patient eyes, and confessed his own foolish heart.

She lay beside him, her hand smoothing across the front of his shirt, until he ran out of words.

"Amado." Her lips were a little chapped. He wondered how they would feel. *"Te amo."*

He raised his eyes back to hers. "Isobel?" He hadn't taught her that. *Do you know what that means?*

She sat up. Began unbuttoning her shirt. Her fingers were shaking, but she never took her eyes from his. He lay still, afraid that if he moved he would frighten her off. Make her think he didn't want her.

Her shirt fell away. She unhooked her bra. In the rich shadows of the haymow, her skin glowed. She took his hand. Placed it on her breast.

Now he was shaking. It was insane. He didn't know this woman. If she brought him home, her brothers would murder him. If he brought her home, his mother would cry.

They didn't even speak the same language. How could he love someone who wouldn't understand him when he proposed?

"Te amo," she repeated, sounding scared and determined. *"¿Tu?"*

He could have resisted her bare skin, but her naked faith broke him. He surrendered, gathering her to him, rolling her onto the quilt, stroking her hair away from her face as he whispered, *"Querida, mi Isobel, mi corazón.* Yes. I love you too."

IV

"Ten thousand dollars," the chief said. He thrust the last brick into a clear plastic evidence Baggie and sealed it. He braced the edge of the bag against the church's kitchen counter and signed and dated it.

"Looks like he was gettin' a damn sight more'n me for operating the carpet cleaner," Granddad said.

Hadley shot the old man a warning look. When Reverend Clare had called in the latest development in the Esfuentes case, Hadley had been riding along with the chief. She had been plenty surprised to find out her grandfather had reported for duty at St. Alban's. With her kids. She glanced at the other end of the island, where Genny and

Hudson, parked on tall stools, were plowing through sandwiches as if they hadn't eaten since yesterday. Had Granddad forgotten to feed them breakfast? She watched him as he headed to the refrigerator. If his memory started to go, if he wasn't safe with the kids, she was well and truly screwed.

The chief looked across the kitchen island to where Reverend Clare was braced against the sink. "You know what this means, don't you?" She dropped her gaze to the countertop. Nodded. "He never would have left on his own without this."

"I know." She plucked at her black shirt, which had somehow gotten wet and greasy. "Do you think whoever . . . took him . . . was looking for this?" She finally lifted her head and met his eyes.

"If they were, he hasn't told them where it is. None of St. Alban's alarms have been triggered since you reset them Sunday night."

"Then maybe he's still alive."

"Maybe." His attempt at sounding hopeful fell flat. Hadley couldn't see why, regardless of Esfuentes's fate, his kidnapper hadn't come after the cash. If the bad guy had been after the money, he would have been pressing the boy from the start. And if he was what the chief didn't want to consider — a

serial killer preying on young Hispanics —
why wouldn't Esfuentes have told him
about the money in hopes of distracting
him? "Don't hurt me, I can give you ten
thousand dollars" would have been the first
thing out of her mouth.

Over the sound of her children eating —
she couldn't help herself, she reached over
and wiped Genny's mouth with a napkin —
she registered Van Alstyne's silence. She
glanced back at him. He and the reverend
were watching each other across an expanse
of granite and stainless steel. She'd heard
they'd been plastered together at the fund-
raiser. You couldn't tell by looking at them
now, all buttoned up in black and tan. Hadley didn't get repression — if they had the
hots for each other, why not just jump in
the sack and work it out? — but right now
she was grateful for it. If Van Alstyne's mind
was on the rector, maybe he wouldn't stop
to wonder how good a job Hadley could do
as an officer when she hadn't even known
where her own kids were.

Reverend Clare wrapped her arms around
herself. The chief's hands convulsed. He
shifted and blinked, as if he had just remembered Hadley was there. "Officer Knox. Did
you find anything else?"

"Granddad says everything left there is

his." She raised her voice. "Including two cartons of cigarettes."

Granddad slammed the refrigerator door shut and brought two cans of soda to where Genny and Hudson were sitting. "Can't just throw 'em away. You got any idea what a carton costs these days?"

The chief's mouth twitched up. "Was there anything out of place in the — uh, sexton's closet, Mr. Hadley? Maybe moved around, so as to hide something?"

The janitor shook his head. "No, sir. And that bag there wa'n't hid. Just hangin' on the hooks where I keep my coat and mackintosh."

The chief cocked his head toward Reverend Clare. She shrugged. "I have no idea," she said, answering a question he hadn't asked out loud. "I never saw him do anything or go anywhere that might explain ten thousand dollars. He worked here, and he went to the Spanish language Mass at Sacred Heart in Lake George a couple of Sundays with one of our volunteers. That's it. Elizabeth drove him to your sister's place a few times so he could hang out with the men there, but she always brought him right back to the church or the rectory."

"You said he brought the bag with him from Janet's farm the morning you were attacked."

"The bag, yeah. What he had in it, I couldn't say." She frowned at the backpack.

"This much money, I'm thinking drugs." He leaned on the counter, where bricks of cash lay piled like a bank withdrawal from hell. "But I'd've laid good money Esfuentes wasn't involved with the trade. So the question is, whose money is this?"

The rector paled. "Oh, God, you don't think it might be somebody here at the church, do you?"

He shook his head. "No. I mean, anything's possible, but given that Mexicans dominate distribution upstate and that Esfuentes came up from Mexico just three or four months ago, I've gotta go with that."

"What if the money doesn't have anything to do with selling pot?" Hadley eased down the island, away from her kids. "What if it came from . . . from —" The only other industry she knew that generated large amounts of untraceable cash was porn. She wasn't going to throw that on the table. "Something else?"

"Like what?"

"Maybe it's money all the men who came north with Amado saved," Reverend Clare said. "Maybe they gave it to him to store here because they thought it would be safer.

Sister Lucia told me many migrant workers don't put their earnings into banks."

"Nice idea, but that hardly explains the gun."

Her face fell. "Oh. Yeah."

"Speaking of which, we need to get it back to the station and start the forensics workup on it." He picked up the plastic evidence bags and thrust them into the backpack. He glanced toward the end of the island, where Genny and Hudson were now shoveling birthday cake into their mouths. "Officer Knox, do you need some time to take your kids home?"

She could feel her face heat up. "No, sir. My granddad is supposed to be taking care of them."

The chief glanced toward Reverend Clare. "At the church?"

"It's fine if they're here, Hadley." Clare laid her hand on Hadley's arm. "It's just a shame —" She glanced at the backpack and bit her lower lip.

They saw the gun and the drug money?

"A shame they have to be inside on such a beautiful day."

Nice save.

"You probably don't know this, being new to town, but Gail Jones, our education director, runs a wonderful day camp for the

Millers Kill rec department. Seven weeks in July and August. It's very affordable."

Eight hundred dollars for two kids. The reverend had a different idea of affordable than she did.

"Told her all about it," Granddad said. "She just waved me off. Maybe she'll listen to you, Father."

Reverend Clare's eyes lit with comprehension. She stepped closer to Hadley, turning her back toward the chief, shutting out the two men. "Hadley, have you ever heard of the priest's purse?" She spoke quietly, but Hadley could see Van Alstyne prick up his ears. "That's discretionary money, left out of the budget, that I can use as necessary. No questions asked. We have enough to pay for a couple of summer camp memberships."

"Thank you," Hadley said, her voice tight, "but we'll be fine." That was it. She was never going to be able to show her face in this church again. She tore herself away from the priest's sympathetic, understanding, unendurable gaze. "I'm ready to go if you are," she said to the chief.

Van Alstyne, thank God, just nodded. "Okay." He shouldered the backpack before glancing back. "Clare," he said.

The rector nodded.

"Keep the doors locked and the alarms up. Here and at your house. I'm going to put you and the church on the patrol sweep for the next few days, so expect to see squad cars a lot more frequently."

She lifted her chin. "Can I expect you to check in as well?"

Hadley, hugging Genny and Hudson good-bye, couldn't see the chief's face, but his tone made her think he was talking about something more than police business.

"Oh, yeah," he said. "You can expect that."

V

Another thing about police work Hadley was discovering: it was nothing like the television shows. For one thing, the uniform didn't look half as good on her as it did on actresses. She suspected hand tailoring, and maybe a higher quality fabric than poly/rayon Wear-ev-r. For another thing, scoring a bag of money and a gun didn't immediately open up new avenues for the investigation. Instead, they waited and waited and waited to get a report back from the state ballistics lab.

In the meantime, she went on patrols with the chief or Eric McCrea, and drove her beater down to Albany for Basic, and worked all day on the Fourth of July. She shopped and trimmed Genny's hair and kept a worried eye on Granddad, who was smoking again when he didn't think she'd know and skipping his medication unless she poured it out and handed it to him. "I feel fine," he'd grumble, all the while looking pale and sweaty. He wouldn't hear of her mowing the lawn instead of him, and only by sending him to church with the kids Sunday and staying home was she able to sneak the job in. Even then, she lied and told him one of the neighbor's kids did it to earn a few bucks. In some ways, living with Granddad was as exhausting as living with her ex had been, although with Granddad she didn't have to worry about drugs or STDs.

On Monday, assembling for the morning briefing, her head was still half at home, worrying about what the kids would be doing and how Granddad was holding up. If Flynn hadn't nudged her, she would have forgotten her notebook.

"Here's the bad news," the chief said, hiking himself onto the table. "This is today's *Post-Star.*" He held up the front page. CONCERN MOUNTS AS STRING OF MURDERS REMAINS UNSOLVED, the headline read. Squinting, Hadley could make out the subhead: AREA BUSINESSES FEAR TOUR-

ISTS WILL STAY AWAY.

Paul Urquhart snorted. "I say we can do with a few less straphangers. They just grab all the parking spaces and make it so it takes ten minutes to drive up Main Street."

"Because they're shopping at our stores and pumping money into our economy." The chief folded the paper in half and laid it on the table. "There were a lot fewer people around on the Fourth this year. The local businesses have a right to be concerned."

"Does this mean the board of aldermen's gonna be on your tail, Chief?" Noble Entwistle asked.

"You let me worry about them. The rest of you need to be prepared to field even more questions about the investigation. Here's the company line: it's proceeding well, leads are developing, and there's no reason to be afraid."

"That'd be more convincing if we knew whether Amado Esfuentes was snatched or not," Eric McCrea pointed out.

"Which brings me to the good news. We've got ballistics on the gun found in Esfuentes' backpack."

"You're kidding," Lyle MacAuley said, from his position propping up the whiteboard. "Less'n two weeks? How much extra did you grease 'em?"

The chief grinned. "As Noble guessed, the mayor and the board of aldermen were screaming at me. I suggested they'd be of more use screaming to our assemblyman and representative. I understand several phone calls were made."

"Hah! Finally. Our tax dollars at work."

The chief pulled a stack of papers from a folder and handed them to Flynn, who took two, for himself and Hadley, then passed them back. "Here are your copies. The gun was a Taurus three-fifty-seven Magnum, not used in any of our unsub killings. We already knew that, because it wasn't a twenty-two. However, the CAF lab says there's a good chance it was a three-fifty-seven Magnum that fired on Sister Lucia's van back in April." He nodded toward Hadley and Flynn. "First District Anti-Gang Task Force says Taurus three-fifty-sevens are a hot item with various gangs in New York."

"Mexicans?" MacAuley asked.

"Yeah," the chief said. He flipped to the second page. "Fingerprints matched those taken from Reverend Fergusson's house and identified as Amado Esfuentes's. There are several good prints from a second — unknown — handler, and a third set on the cartridges. Those prints are nowhere else on the gun, and the second set don't appear on the cartridges."

MacAuley jotted down the info on the whiteboard. "Guy number one was the last to load, he hands it to guy number two, who gives it to our missing boy."

"That's my thought," the chief said.

Hadley looked around. No one was sitting poised at the edge of his chair, waiting to ask the question percolating in her mind. She sighed. "Chief, why wasn't the gun wiped down? If it's connected to the money, and we think the money comes from the drug trade, we're talking about professionals, right? Why wouldn't they take a basic precaution like getting rid of their fingerprints?"

"They're stupid. Or cocky," Eric McCrea said.

"Or," MacAuley said, "they're amateurs." He set the marker down and reoriented himself to face the chief. "You've never liked the serial killer angle."

"Damn right, I haven't."

"What if what we're seeing here is the fallout from a turf war? What if we've got a group of guys up from Mexico on work passes who've figured out that selling pot is a lot more profitable than milking cows? Maybe they've got connections back home, relatives already in the trade in Central America or something?"

"Or raising it here," Flynn said. "There're always farmers growing plants between rows of corn or guys up in the mountains with microplots."

The chief shook his head. "Homegrown is a little cash on the side up here. The weather's too harsh for any kind of major cultivation, unless you've got a greenhouse, and that's a hell of a job to conceal." He twisted to face the deputy chief. "What about distribution? If somebody's going head to head with the big boys, they've got to have distributors up here. Those guys sell wholesale, not retail. CADEA thinks the various gangs that control the trade have been building up their networks for years. You're not going to replace that overnight, no matter how many relatives you've got growing the stuff down in Guadalajara."

MacAuley flipped his hand open, as if throwing a card into play. "The guys on the street will go with whoever has the product. You replace the wholesaler, the rest of the organization falls into line."

"If you know who and where the dealers are. This isn't Brooklyn or Manhattan. This is the North Country." He pointed, and they all stared at the big map, three counties and a state park the size of Massachusetts splashed out in pastels against the stucco wall. "How the hell do you find the dealers in a territory this size? Not even counting the difficulties of being a Spanish-speaking alien in one of the least ethnically diverse parts of America."

There was a long pause as they all stared at the map. Hadley thought about how she, moving into a town she had only known as a visitor, found a hairdresser, a second-hand clothing store, the day-old bakery outlet. She had to ask around. It didn't seem a likely technique for would-be drug lords.

"Maybe someone's switched sides?" The chief and MacAuley turned their attention to Flynn, who looked surprised that he had spoken out loud. "I mean, say you have the established distributor," he went on. "It works a lot like any other company, right? A couple CEOs at the top make a lot of money, a few middle managers make decent money, and the rest of them are living from hand to mouth. Then some competition shows up. Maybe one of the little guys decides there's a lot more potential for advancement if he takes what he knows and starts working for his bosses' rivals."

MacAuley shook his head. "The little guys know whoever shows up and gets the stuff out of the back of the truck. They don't have the big picture."

"Kevin's got the right idea, though." The chief reached for the coffee mug on the table beside him. "A turncoat makes the scenario more feasible." He took a long pull, then sat cradling the mug in his hands. "The part that doesn't fit is the timing of the murders. One in March, one roughly a year ago, and one older than that. If it's intergang rivalry, it's the slowest conflict in history."

MacAuley rubbed his lips with two fingers and nodded.

"Okay, send everything we've got to the First District Anti-Gang Task Force. See if something rings a bell with them."

"You got it," MacAuley said.

"Eric, you're continuing with background checks. See if you can get anything out of the CADEA."

"Yep."

"Everybody else is on patrol. I've called in Duane and Tim to handle the radar guns, so I want the rest of you very visible in town and in Cossayuharie. I want the community to know we're on the job, looking out for them."

"What about the migrant workers?" Urquhart asked.

The chief raised his eyebrows. "What

about them?"

"Well, if we think some of 'em might be moving pot, shouldn't we round 'em up and fingerprint 'em? Send the info back to Mexico and see if anything pops up? They got some sort of Mexican FBI, don't they?"

Hadley could see the chief trying not to roll his eyes. "Yeah, they do. It's the Agencia Federal de Investigación. However, we can't just go rounding up migrants because we've been tossing around theories in the bullpen."

"Don't see why in th' hell not." Urquhart crossed his arms.

"Because nonresident aliens in the United States are protected by the same constitutional criminal protections as the rest of us," Hadley said. "Oberlinski v. United States." *Jerk.*

The chief cracked a sideways smile. "Glad to see you're paying attention at the Academy, Officer Knox."

She felt her face heat up.

"On a happier note, I was checking the funds for the police basketball association, and there's still money left for this year." The chief looked somewhere over Hadley's head, his face bland. "Since the PBA was meant to give kids something constructive to do —"

"You mean, keep 'em from knocking over convenience stores," MacAuley said.

"— I've decided to use the remaining money to fund some campers at the rec department's summer camp. I've already given the director enrollment info for two kids; if any of you know a family that could benefit from this, have 'em call Gail Jones at her office at the town hall." He picked up his folders and his coffee cup and slid off the table. "That's all, folks."

Hadley sat, frozen, while chairs scraped and shoes slapped and belts jingled. Something bumped against her, and she looked up to see Eric McCrea. "You feeling okay?" He squinted at her. "You look kind of feverish."

She nodded. "Yeah," she said. "I mean, no." She stood up, forcing Eric to scramble out of her way. "Excuse me."

She caught up with the chief right before he entered his office. "Chief," she said. "About the summer camp thing —"

"Oh, yeah. That's right." He glanced at the clock. "The drop-off is at the middle school. If you hurry, you can get your kids there and be back in about forty-five minutes. You can work through lunch to make it up."

"Sir." Her voice sounded strangled. "I

can't accept —"

He looked down at her. "Officer Knox. This department is spending a good chunk of change on your training. I count a few hundred bucks to safeguard that investment as money well spent."

"I'm handling my home situation fine. I don't need charity." Now she sounded like a bitch. It was his fault. She didn't ask to be put in this situation.

He stepped into his office. Beckoned her in. Nudged the door half shut. He dropped his voice. "Look, Knox — Hadley. When Noble's mother started to wander away from her house at odd hours, we wired her doors with a security alarm and checked in on her four times a day. When Harlene's husband, Harold, got sick and had to go down to the Albany medical center twice a week, we drove him. This isn't an insurance office or a restaurant. We have to trust each other with our lives. And that means we take care of our own."

There was a knock, and the deputy chief stuck his head in the door. "Hey," he said. "You got a minute?"

The chief looked at MacAuley a long moment, an expression on his face Hadley couldn't make out. Then he nodded. "Sure." He turned back to Hadley. "Go ahead.

When you get back, you'll patrol with me."

Hell. She'd look like an antisocial loner if she continued to protest. She tried to say thank you, but she couldn't get the words out. She settled for jerking her head up and down before fleeing the office. Out in the hall, she heard MacAuley ask, "What was that all about?"

"Oh, just touching base," the chief said. "What was it you wanted?"

She took off before she could start to feel grateful.

VI

Driving back to the station, Russ thought he had never been so busy doing so little in his entire career. He had dropped into enough stores, galleries, roadside stands, and mom-and-pops to write a shoppers' guidebook. He checked in with anxious proprietors, listened to their worries, and assured them they and their customers would be safe and protected. In between, he and Knox responded to at least a dozen reports of possible intruders and suspicious persons, every one of which was either non-existent or a befuddled innocent.

The last call of the day — surprise, surprise — was Mrs. Bain. He groaned when Harlene gave him the report. "She says she's

464

heard thumping and clattering noises out back of her barn, and she says there was a carload of real suspicious-looking Hispanic men driving slowly past her house, checking it out."

He keyed the mic. "Hispanic men. That's a new one. What about the prowler?"

"Ayeah, the prowler's back."

"Okay, copy the last report, change the date, and add in the Hispanics. Oh, and call one of the Bains and see if someone can come over, will you?"

"You got it. Dispatch out."

Knox was looking at him with a doubtful expression. "Shirley Bain," he explained, heeling the car around toward Cossayuharie. "Her only son lives down in Westchester. He likes to forget he grew up with manure on his boots, which I could forgive, except he also forgets to spend any time with his mother. So every three–four months she sees a prowler. We come out, look the place over, and write up a report, which we send to the son. He comes home for a weekend to make her feel safe, and then a few months later we do it all over again."

Mrs. Bain was sweet and apologetic and even more worried than usual as they walked around the barn, past clumps of day lilies and rhubarb gone to flower. Russ pointed out where some of her wood stack, drying in the late afternoon sun, had fallen.

"Oh," she said. "I'm sorry, Russell. I guess I'm just a silly old woman. But with all these terrible things happening to the Mexicans, I've been so frightened. I have half a mind to buy myself a gun."

Russ spent the walk back to her house convincing her that would be a bad, bad idea. Mrs. Bain had, as always, baked before they arrived, and in the kitchen she bustled about serving chocolate chip cookies and iced tea. Russ silently drew Knox's attention to the stack of recent *Post-Star*s in the recycling basket and the pile of true crime books waiting to go back to the library.

When the elderly woman found out Knox had children, she was in ecstasy. She insisted on emptying the owl-in-spectacles cookie jar and giving the entire paper-bagged contents to the junior officer to take home.

Russ was beginning to worry they weren't going to escape before dinner, but then there was a knock at the door and Geraldine Bain yodeled, "Shirley? Let me in."

Mrs. Bain unlocked the door for her sister-in-law. At seventy, Geraldine was well past retirement age but kept her position in the Millers Kill Post Office through sheer determination not to miss a word of gossip

466

circulating through the town.

"Hello, Russell," she said. "And who's this? Is this Glenn Hadley's granddaughter I've heard so much tell about?" She hugged her sister-in-law while keeping an avid eye on Knox. "Don't you worry, dear," she said. "I've come to spend the night." Russ spotted the small suitcase on the doorstep and sprang to pick it up. He toted it to the second-floor bedroom, abandoning Officer Knox to Geraldine's interrogation.

She had gotten to who-was-Hudson-and-Geneva's-father-and-why-wasn't-he-here-with-them by the time Russ got back downstairs. He snagged the bag of cookies from the table and thrust it at the shell-shocked Knox. "Time for us to go, ladies. Mrs. Bain, you call us if anything else makes you nervous, okay?"

"Rushing off to St. Alban's?" Geraldine gave him a roguish wink. "Word is you've got yourself a sweetheart over there."

"Geraldine," Mrs. Bain said in a repressive tone.

"What? He can't wear the willow forever, a good-looking man like that." Geraldine looked him up and down. "If I weren't old enough to be your mother, I'd give that Reverend Fergusson a run for her money."

Beside him, Hadley Knox made a gurgling

noise. He leaned in toward the Bain women. "I don't know as you should let that stop you, Geraldine. You know what they say about older women." Then he winked. She hooted with laughter.

Mrs. Bain frowned at her sister-in-law. "Oh, you and your foolishness!" She turned and looked up at him. "Russell, you will let Warren know what happened, won't you? He does worry so about me."

"Of course." He opened the door.

"Be good!" Geraldine's voice trailed after him. "Don't do anything I wouldn't do! And if you do, don't get found out!"

On the ride back down Route 17, Knox peeked at him several times, as if trying to work up the nerve to ask something. He figured it was about him and Clare, so he was surprised when she said, "Don't you find it kind of frustrating? Spending the whole day holding hands and soothing nerves?" He glanced over at her. "I mean," she went on, "it's more like babysitting than police work."

"Weren't you the one who said being a cop was like being a mother?"

"Oh, crap." She covered her face with her hands. "I did, didn't I? I can't believe I said that in a job interview."

"Don't be. It's one of the reasons I hired

you." Ahead of them, the light at the intersection turned red. He took his foot off the gas. "Sometimes it gets a little frustrating, yeah. Mostly because I want to see some development on this case, and nothing's happening. But I try to remember that for most of the folks here, this is police work. Making sure Mom's not trapped in her house with a broken hip. Stopping cars from speeding around the schools and the park. Asking the neighbors to turn it down so everybody can keep it friendly."

"Do you ever wish it was more . . . I don't know, exciting?"

"I was an MP for over twenty years. Believe me, I saw plenty of exciting. No, I knew what I was getting when I came back to my hometown." The light turned green again, and he rolled onto Main Street. "Did you?"

She looked startled. Then thoughtful. "I don't know. I knew what I wanted, though."

He expected *fresh air* or *a safe place to raise my kids* or *a new start.*

She pursed her lips. "Anonymity."

"Huh." He bumped the cruiser over the walk and into the station parking lot. "I suppose, to the rest of the world, Millers Kill is pretty anonymous." He twisted the key in the ignition and the engine died. "Of course, *within* the town, you can't ask someone for a dance without everybody weighing in on it."

Getting out of the car, the heat that had been soft and drowsy in Mrs. Bain's grassy yard pressed down on them like a tar-smeared steamroller. All he wanted to do was check in, sign out, and get to his mother's house, where he could strip down to his shorts and try to catch a breeze in the backyard.

Clare's house would be cool. She believed air-conditioning was a constitutional right. He had helped her install a window unit last summer. She would have iced tea — sweet, like they made it down south — and cold beer. A glass for him and a bottle for her. He could stretch out in one of her oversized chairs and they could talk.

Yeah. Talk.

He knew, as soon as he stepped onto the marble floor of the entryway, that something had happened. He could hear the churn of conversation all the way down the hall. Eric emerged from the squad room, grinning. He sketched them a jaunty wave. "I'm outta here. My son's got a game."

"What's up?" Russ asked.

Eric's grin widened. "Go take a look."

Russ strode in, Knox on his heels. Lyle

and Kevin were bent over a desk, heads bumping together, examining what looked like circ sheets. "What's up?" Russ asked.

Lyle looked up, grinning. "We've ID'd John Doe one. He's Rosario de las Cruces, late of Prendiepe, Mexico. The Agencia Federal de Investigación faxed a whole buttload of stuff on him." He waved Kevin back and handed the papers to Russ. "He's associated with the Punta Diablos gang, which has members on both sides of the border: pot coming north and guns going south. He spent a nickel in prison, *Federales de* somethin'-or-other; you can read it for yourself" — he jammed a finger at the appropriate spot — "but he's got no record of ever being in this country, which is why his prints didn't turn up with our usual search." He grabbed the papers back out of Russ's hands and yanked one sheet to the top. "Here's the Anti-Gang Task Force report on the Punta Diablos; they think de las Cruces was fairly high-level management but not at the top. Didn't get near the product — he was put away for unlicensed possession of a gun, criminal threatening, and currency violations."

"Currency violations?"

"Money laundering."

Russ felt a flare of excitement as the facts

finally began to line up. "Our midlevel manager?"

"Could be. Although, seeing as he's dead, he's not telling anybody the names and addresses of his distributors."

"Unless he recorded the info somewhere." He and Lyle smiled at each other in wolflike satisfaction. "CD?" he asked. "Or one of those little whatchamacallits that you stick in the side of a computer?"

"Flash drive," Kevin Flynn said.

"Thank you, Kevin."

Lyle shook his head. "Too easy to duplicate. Plus, it's hard to really erase one of those things. They'd want something they could destroy completely if the Feds came knocking."

"Good old paper and pen?"

"A notebook," Lyle said. "Or a diary, or a journal."

"When they tossed Clare's place" — some of the good feeling fizzled away — "that's what they were looking for. Whoever 'they' are."

Lyle rocked back on his heels and rubbed two fingers over his lips. "They didn't find it that night. And it wasn't bagged with the money and the .357 Taurus. So either Esfuentes never had it, or he kept it someplace else entirely."

"Or it's still hidden at the church," Knox said.

They both turned to face her. She shifted from foot to foot, looking like she wished she hadn't spoken up. "There are books and notebooks all over the place. In the main office. In Reverend Clare's office. Hell, in the Sunday School room. Amado went everywhere, cleaning. He could have slipped it between a couple of other items and no one would have noticed."

Lyle was nodding. "Makes sense." He looked at Russ. "You said he led a pretty prescribed life, right? The Catholic church in Lake George, visits to the house out at your sister's farm, and St. Alban's."

"Right."

"He's not gonna leave it at the Catholic church. What if he can't get back? Same deal for stashing it in one of the volunteers' cars."

"It's possible he left it at the migrants' bunkhouse." Which meant the same crew who tossed Clare's house might be coming over to the McGeochs. He'd have to warn Janet not to let the girls anywhere near the new farm.

"Possible," Lyle said. "But he didn't leave the gun and the money there. The place has been on the patrol list ever since we twigged to the Hispanic connection, and so far it's been quieter'n a — well, quieter than the church, that's for sure."

Russ glanced toward Knox, the only other one of them to speak Spanish. "It's not urgent, then. Knox, you and Kevin can head over there tomorrow to do a search. I'll call ahead and let my sister and her husband know."

She nodded. He remembered her kids. Made a point of looking at the clock on the wall. "Okay, you're off duty. Stop bucking for overtime and go home."

She nodded, her relief plain. She turned.

"Hadley," Lyle said. "One more thing about de las Cruces." She turned back, her face half curious, half wary. "Those tats he had on his fingers? They were gang markings. Which means that the guy you saw in the Hummer —"

"Alejandro Santiago."

"That's him. He and his crew have maybe hooked up with the Punta Diablos. The AGTF didn't know that." The grin on his face widened. "We actually got a thank-you for passing on that piece of information."

Knox stared.

"Good work," Russ added, to clarify.

She nodded, then vanished through the squad room door. They listened to her footsteps clatter down the hall.

"I don't know about that girl," Lyle said.

"Woman." Russ picked up the sheets and shuffled back to the first one. "She'll do fine. She's coming along."

"I got two kids older'n she is. That makes her a girl in my book."

"Yeah? Your hunting rifle is older than Kevin. Doesn't make him a Remington."

Kevin quivered to attention. "Anything else, Chief? You want me to check out St. Alban's for you?"

"No, thank you, Kevin. I'll handle that myself." He ignored Lyle's huff of amusement. "See you tomorrow."

Kevin left with a great deal more reluctance than Hadley Knox had shown. When it was down to just the two of them, Russ let his feet wander to the big worktable. He hitched himself up onto its top. "Sister Lucia's van —" he stopped. Shook his head. "A van with a load of Hispanic men gets shot in April."

Lyle crossed to the whiteboard and wrote it down.

"Also, sometime in March or April, Rosario de las Cruces is killed in Cossayuharie."

"Or dumped there."

Russ nodded acknowledgment. "In May, Hadley and Kevin run across a carload of

Punta Diablo gang members."

Lyle jotted on the board.

"End of June, Amado Esfuentes is kidnapped and his residence is searched."

"If that kid was a gangbanger, I'll eat my shorts."

"We agree on that." Russ tapped the circ sheets and arrest papers against his chin. "Maybe we're looking at this from the wrong end. What if it's not a power struggle?"

Lyle shrugged. "I dunno. I like that idea. It fits."

"It fits de las Cruces. It doesn't fit Esfuentes. Or the van shooting. What if what we're dealing with is the fallout from an intergang rivalry? Something happened. Maybe involving the older, unidentified bodies. And now what we're seeing is a hunt for witnesses."

Lyle squinted at the ceiling for a moment. "Possible." He glanced at the whiteboard. "A witness who has physical evidence. Money, the .357 Magnum, and this could-be list of distributors."

"You think I'm barking up the wrong tree with that? They were just looking for money when they tossed Clare's place?"

"Nope. Ten thousand's a lot to you and me, but if we're talking guys who import junk wholesale, it's penny ante. Job money, for the driver."

"Shut-up money?"

"Maybe. What's the definition of an honest politician?"

Russ smiled a bit. "One who stays bought. I take your point." He slid off the table. "I'm going over to St. Alban's. Maybe I'll find this mystery list and you and I can stop chasing our tails."

Russ expected his deputy's usual lazy assent and was surprised when Lyle stopped him with a hand to his arm. "We should call Ben Beagle tomorrow. Catch him up on some of this and tell him that we've searched the church and the rectory and come up empty-handed."

"What? Why?"

"Because." Lyle looked dead serious. "When the Punta Diablo boys figure out Esfuentes might have hidden something at St. Alban's, they'll be over there themselves."

VII

"What are we looking for?" Clare asked.

"I don't know." Russ frowned at the bookcase taking up one wall of her office. "Something that doesn't have anything to

477

do with Jesus or the Episcopal church, I guess."

She pulled one of her Lindsay Davis mysteries off the shelf and handed it to him.

"Or Roman history," he said. "Smart-ass." He looked at her with a mixture of amusement and exasperation. He had been in what she'd have described as a fey mood since he arrived; restless, upbeat, talkative.

"It could be a journal or a diary or a notebook. I suppose it could even be a few papers stapled together."

"We ought to start in the office, then. There are a lot more bits and pieces there." She led him into the main office. He groaned when he saw the bookcase built into the wall. It ran from the doorway to the corner, ceiling to floor, filled with ledgers and books and file boxes and three-ring binders.

"It's a church. What the heck do you do that generates so much paperwork?"

She almost laughed. "Let's split the job. Do you want here or my office?"

"I'll tackle this."

She retreated back to her own bookcase, grateful for the space between them and resenting it at the same time. He shouted out questions now and then: "What's a proposed canonical amendment? . . . Did you know you have minutes to meetings from 1932?" — while she worked her way across her shelves.

She had removed and replaced everything on her bookcase and was considering the feasibility of checking the coloring books and picture Bibles in the nursery when Russ charged up the hall with a spiral-bound notebook in his hand. He flipped it open to show her the printed entries: names, dates, numbers.

"Sorry," she said, taking it from him. "This is the overflow baptismal registry." She walked back to the main office and eased an oversized leather-bound volume from its place on the middle shelf. BAP-TISMS was impressed in gold leaf deep into its cover. "We need to buy another one of these, but they're ridiculously expensive." She opened it. "See? Name of the baptized, godparents or sponsors, date, age at baptism. Celebrant's initials." R.H.D.D., in the entry she was pointing to. "Robert Hames, Doctor of Divinity," she said.

He glanced at the notebook. It was arranged identically, although, without the example of the bound baptism record, the entries looked like strings of names. "C.F.M.D." she said. "Clare Fergusson, Master of Divinity."

"How come you don't just put down your name? Or 'The Rev. C.F.'?"

"I don't know. It was the first time I've ever been in charge of a baptismal registry. I just copied what the last guy did."

He snorted. "That's probably the origin of half the traditions you Episcopalians are so gung-ho about. Just copying what the last guy did."

"Mm-hmm. Which doesn't sound like much until you try to do something differently. How many Episcopalians does it take to change a lightbulb?"

"Uh. I don't know. How many?"

"*What? Change* the lightbulb?"

He laughed, which she appreciated, since it was a very old joke. "I didn't find anything," she went on. "We've got some odds and ends in the nursery. Do you want me to look there?"

"I guess." He replaced the heavy old leather-bound book and then the fifty-cent spiral-bound version. He took the same care with each one.

"You guess?"

He made a noise in the back of his throat. "I don't want to rule anything out. But let's face it, sticking a list of dealers where any three-year-old might turn it into an art project isn't likely." He stepped back to size

up the office bookcase again, almost knocking into her. He turned and grabbed her
shoulders, steadying her. "Our best bet was
right here. More loose bits and pieces. It
woulda been easy for him to slide something
in. If you or your secretary accidentally
pulled it from its hiding place, you would
have just put it back again as soon as you
saw it wasn't what you were looking for."

He was right. She could picture Amado,
vacuuming in here, maybe wiping the
shelves and the woodwork with a dusting
cloth. Reaching into his pocket and slipping
something between the papers. Hidden in
plain sight. She poked her hair into place.
Tried to get her mouth around the unpalat-
able truth. "It's not looking good for
Amado, is it? I mean, if he was hiding
something important from whoever
snatched him."

He looked at her. "No. It isn't."

She rubbed her arm. Once in a while, she
wished Russ would sugar-coat things for
her. "Why wouldn't he just come to the
police, if he had seen something illegal? Or
come to me? I would have helped him." She
looked at her hands. Folded them up tight.
"I could have helped him."

Russ smiled a little. "You did everything
you could, darlin'. You gave him a job and a

place to live and you beat the crap out of the Christies when they tried to attack him."

"I defended myself," she said. She brought her fists up, shoulder width, knuckles up and knuckles down, as if she carried an unseen oaken shaft. "I wish I had been there when whoever it was came to my house." She looked up at Russ. "If I had only gone home an hour earlier — half an hour."

She was shocked when he took one of her hands, folding his fingers over hers.

"Thank God you weren't there. Because I know you, and I know you wouldn't have let him go without a fight. And whoever has him, Clare, they're bad people. I don't know if you could've run them off with a cross and a candlestick." He lowered her hand without releasing it. Tugged her closer. "Though if anyone could . . ."

"What are you doing?" She sounded like a high school girl behind the bleachers, breathless and naïve.

He caught her other hand. Forced her arms behind her back so easily it seemed as if it were her idea, as if she were stretching invisible wings, readying herself to fly. She bumped into his chest.

"What do you think I'm doing?" He bent his head toward her.

"We" — she swallowed — "we haven't

decided anything yet. We haven't come to any sort of understanding."

He laughed, a low sound that she had only heard once or twice before. "Clare. We decided everything about three days after we met."

She could smell him, salt and sun and something unique to him. She felt dizzy. *You know when you're captured?* Hardball Wright asked. *When you give up control in your head.* "Russ," she got out, "I don't think —"

"Good. Keep on not thinking." He kissed her, kissed her right down to her foundations, kissed her until she was a cathedral burning: lead melting, saints shattering, not a stone left on stone. He lifted his hands, hers, pressed her against the bookcase, interlocking their fingers and *palm to palm is holy palmers' kiss* and the edge of the shelves bit into the back of her hands, hanging there with his sweet weight against her, nailed to the wood by her own reckless desire.

Then his hands were on her face, her jaw, sliding through her hair, plucking out the pins keeping it in place, tracing the edge of her collar. "How does this come off?" he asked, his voice like dusk against her ear.

"Uhn." Thinking was like sweeping

through cobwebs. "It buttons. In the back."

The rub of his knuckle, a tug, and her collar came free.

"So it does," he said. His lips slid over her neck and for a moment she couldn't breathe, literally couldn't breathe at the feel of his teeth and tongue. She let her head roll back, exposing her throat, while what passed for her brain wondered if they could make it to the loveseat in her office. The lumpy loveseat. In her office. In her church.

In her church.

She shoved him away. "Stop it," she said. She could barely speak. "We're not doing an Abelard and Héloïse."

"What?" He sounded like her, dazed and winded.

"We're not doing this here." She inhaled. Eyed him where he stood, braced against the desk. Hair askew — had she done that? — eyes hot, his chest heaving as if he had been running the Independence Day 5K.

"Okay," he said. "Your house." He moved toward her again.

"No! Stop!"

"What?" His face creased with frustration, but he stopped all the same. "Not in the church. I got it. It's sacrilegious. But don't tell me there's a problem with your house because it's the rectory."

"The problem's not my house." She rubbed her face. Wished she had some cold water she could splash on. Or dunk her head in. "The problem's you. And me."

"Oh, for — not that again. Look, let me point something out to you, okay? For two and a half, three years now, I never touched you. I didn't kiss you, I didn't" — his hands flexed as if he were grabbing hold of her — "I didn't do anything. And let me tell you, it wasn't for lack of thinking about it! Jesus, I used to go for weeks where I swear the only thing I could think about was having you. But I didn't do anything about it." He stepped closer. "I exercised self-control." He enunciated every word. "Because I was married."

He jammed one hand through his hair, making it stick up even farther.

"Now I can't keep my hands off you. Doesn't that tell you I've" — he cast around for the right word — "I would've never let myself while Linda was alive. Never."

"I know that."

"Then why the hell can't we work with what we have? I love you. I want you. Why can't you trust that to be enough?"

"Because it wasn't enough before!"

He looked dumbfounded. "What are you talking about?"

"I'm talking about last winter. I broke it off with you for the sake of your marriage. Do you have any idea what that felt like? To just give up everything and walk away?"

"Of course I do. You think it was any easier for me?"

"Yes! I do! You had someone you loved to console you. I had nothing! Then, when you found out Linda had been murdered, you came crawling right back —"

"Wait a minute —"

"— looking for help and understanding and sympathy and what all, using me like an emotional life-support system, to hell with whether it was peeling me raw or not —"

"*Using* you?"

"I gave, and I gave, and I gave, and what did I get in return? When that bitch of a state police investigator accused me of murder, you believed her!"

"I did not!"

"You did so! I was there! I saw you!"

"Christ, Clare, I thought about the possibility for thirty seconds. You're going to hang me up to dry for thirty seconds? I'm sorry I'm not so perfect and all-giving as you are."

"You see? It's all about you. Again. When does it get to be about me, Russ? When does it get to be about what *I* need?" Her eyes teared up, but the words kept coming, as if she had tapped some vat of acid and now it had to gush out until it ran dry. "I killed for you. I killed a man to save you. And then I had to turn around and let you go *again,* and you know what? I know your wife died. I know it was the worst moment of your life. But I was having the worst moment of *my* life, too, and you just turned your back on me. You rejected me, everything I had to give and everything I needed. We always said we were holding on, and *you let go.* You . . . let . . . me . . . fall." She was crying freely now, wiping away the tears with the back of her hand. She opened her mouth and found herself saying, "I *hate* you for that."

She had reached the bottom of it. Her head felt emptied out, except for the echo of Deacon Aberforth's words, *Are you angry with your police chief?*

And her reply. *Of course not.*

Russ was pale beneath his tan. He opened his mouth. Shut it. Scrubbed his hand over his eyes. He turned away from her, then jerked and spun back around, and she knew with a sick certainty that the words *you turned your back on me* had been driven into his ear like a spike.

He shook his head. "I'm sorry," he said.

487

His voice was hoarse.

His phone rang. He slapped his pocket, stricken. She waved one hand. "Go ahead," she said. He checked the number. Flipped the phone open.

"Van Alstyne" — he coughed — "Van Alstyne here." She watched him as he listened. Who said getting everything out into the open was a good idea? She didn't feel better, or healthier, or more honest. She just felt dirty. And empty.

"Aw, shit," he said. He closed his eyes for a moment. "Where?" He nodded. "I'll be right there." He listened again. "Yeah. That's fine." He glanced at her. "No, I'll tell her."

Fear stirred in her gut.

"Yeah," Russ said again. " 'Bye." He snapped the phone shut. Looked at her. "That was Lyle. Some kids were in the Cossayuharie Muster Field. They found Amado's body."

VIII

She followed in her own car. He could see her headlights behind him, bright against the tree-shrouded twilight of the mountain road. While he had been in St. Alban's, getting his intestines handed to him on a steaming platter, the sun had set. That

488

seemed appropriate. On the stereo, Bill Deasy sang *Is it my curse, to always make the good things worse?* He had bought the CD as a present for himself last Christmas, because the songs made him think of Clare.

When had he started listening to music again?

He didn't know. He didn't know much of anything, it seemed. How the hell had he wound up gutting the only two women he'd ever loved? He ought to go home and tell his mom he hated her. Make it a perfect trifecta.

From the high ground of the Muster Field, headlights, roof lights, portable lamps, and road flares blazed against the pale violet sky, as visible as the solstice fires or mountaintop beacons of ancient Scotland. He hoped the modern-day descendents of those Scots would ignore the call, or else his people would be dealing with an unholy mess of spectators and speculation.

He parked his truck at the end of a line of vehicles crowding Route 137's nonexistent shoulder. He spotted at least two SUVs with FIRE AND RESCUE tags. Lyle must have called for help in dealing with the traffic. They would need it. There were already more cars around than official personnel could account for.

He stepped out as Clare pulled in ahead of him. He waited until she emerged from her Subaru. She had reattached her collar. She didn't look at him. "Find whoever's handing out those flares and put one in front of your car," he said. She nodded. Walked past him, up the shadowy road. He reached for her as she went by, then dropped his hand. What the hell was he going to say to her, here and now? He shook his head.

As soon as he stepped onto the field, he heard Lyle bellowing his name. Russ couldn't see anything in the glare of light bars and headlights, but he headed for the sound. Past the rescue vehicle and the squad cars, the rear of the field spread in darkness, the black bulk of the two-hundred-year-old trees picked out against the star-glimmering sky. Heat lightning flickered over the western mountains. A pair of Maglites barely dented the gloom.

"Over here!" Russ followed Lyle's voice, to find the deputy chief struggling to set up one of the halogen site lamps while Kevin Flynn trained two flashlights on the contrary apparatus.

"Kevin, what are you doing here? You're not on tonight." Russ reached for the lamppost and held it aloft so Lyle could unfold the base. "Where's Noble?"

"Lyle called me," Kevin said. He sounded subdued, for a kid whose usual response to a major crime was "Whoopee!"

"I sent Noble back to talk with the kids who found Esfuentes." Lyle grunted as he wrestled the sectional flaps into position.

"Instead of setting up the lights?" Russ crouched down and seized the battery pack. "You're not working to your strengths, here, Lyle."

"I don't want him near the body." Lyle pressed one hand over Russ's and, with the other, jammed the plug into the battery. The darkness exploded into white light, and all three men shielded their eyes.

"He's here?" Instinctively, Russ looked down to see if he was fouling evidence.

Lyle gestured with his thumb. "By the stone wall." He waved at Kevin. "Go get the next light." The junior officer nodded and trotted back toward the squad car.

Russ watched him go. A group of what looked to be civilians were rubbernecking near the road. He didn't like it. "So. Not taken into the forest like the other two."

"No. This is different from the others."

"I'm not going to second-guess you," Russ said, "but I've never had any problems with Noble mucking up the scene." He dropped his voice. "Kevin's working on overtime right now."

Lyle looked him in the eye. "It's bad. Kevin can handle that. Noble can't."

Russ's mouth dried up. "Bad?"

Lyle nodded.

"Shit." He took a step toward where Lyle had indicated, then stopped. "Let's get the rest of the lights up. I don't want to screw things up by stomping around in the dark."

A gust of cool wind rustled through the trees. "I hope to hell tonight's not the night we finally get rain," Lyle said. "We could use another officer. Tim and Duane both lit out after the Fourth."

"Call in Hadley Knox. She needs the O.T."

"Okay."

"Can you and Kevin manage the next lamp? I want to talk to whoever found him."

Lyle tilted his head. Next to the ambulance, five or six people had gathered around Noble's broad-shouldered form. "It was a carload of kids. Two couples. They'd had a few, and somebody got the bright idea to come up to the Muster Field and hunt for another body. Watched too many damn horror movies, if you ask me." He glanced behind him, into the gloom. "They found what they came looking for."

"Not unless they got laid first." Russ

strode off toward the group. He saw a flash of black and white. Clare, talking to one of the young men. Another breeze lifted her hair, and he thought, *It's loose?* and then he remembered pulling the pins out of her twist. The feel of her hair sliding through his fingers. A jolt of desire hit him, heavy and low, about as welcome as a kick in the head under the circumstances. He shook it off. Kept walking.

Clare lifted her head, as if she had sensed him coming, and said something to the boy at her side. Anyone who didn't know her would see a calm, caring, collected priest. He saw the taut line of her jaw and the strained expression in her eyes. There was another adult there as well, a fleshy soccer-dad type with his arm around a girl. At least one of the kids had had sense enough to call a parent.

"Officer Entwhistle," he said.

Noble turned toward him. "Chief." His relief was evident. The two girls' faces were wet from crying, and one of the boys looked ready to toss his cookies any second. The father ping-ponged between consoling his daughter and glaring at the other young man, standing beside Clare. Russ guessed he was the daughter's date. Fox-featured, he looked like he normally might enjoy mischief but was smart enough not to get too far in. Right now, he was just holding it together. Didn't want to lose it in front of his girl. Well, Russ could identify with that.

"Hi. Russ Van Alstyne." Russ bypassed the dad and shook with Clare's kid first. "I'm the chief of police."

The boy took his hand. "Hi. I'm — um, Colin Ellis."

Russ glanced at Clare for a second. "Any relation to Anne Vining-Ellis?"

The boy nodded. "She's my mom."

"She and Chris are on the way," Clare said.

Russ turned to Noble. "Officer Entwhistle, will you clear the rest of the onlookers from the area? And tell the traffic guys there'll be some parents arriving."

"Will do, Chief."

The father stepped forward. "Can you take the kids' statements and release them, please? I want to get my daughter out of here. She's had one hell of a shock."

"And you are . . . ?"

"Clifford Sturdevant. This is my daughter Lauren."

Lauren snuffled something that might have been a greeting.

"This is Kearney" — Clare indicated the queasy-looking boy — "and Meghan."

Meghan wiped her eyes, smearing blue mascara across her cheeks.

"Why don't you kids tell me what happened," Russ said.

"They were supposed to be at the —"

Russ held up one hand. "I'd like to hear it in their own words, Mr. Sturdevant."

The story was pretty much what he expected from Lyle's brief description. The two couples had been going to the Glen Drive-In, got to talking about the "Cossayuharie Killer," and whipped each other up with dares until they had no choice but to go to the Muster Field at twilight. They had stumbled around — Russ got the impression they were looking for soft ground at this point — and through sheer dumb luck had run across the body. They fled back to Lauren's car, where, after a short argument about driving away or not, they called 9-1-1, Sturdevant, and the Ellises. They hadn't seen anyone else coming or going from the field.

It was the Ellis boy who screwed up the courage to ask what they all must have been wondering. "Are we in trouble?"

Russ eyed him. "Were you drinking?"

The kid swallowed. "Yeah. Yes, sir. But not much. We had a six-pack."

"If I catch you drinking again, you will be

in trouble. But I think this time I'll let your parents deal with it." Kearney looked relieved, Colin horrified.

A flash of arriving headlights and another gust of wind caught Russ's attention. He squinted in the glare. Clare glanced over, then at him. Questioning him without words. "The medical examiner," he said.

IX

"Any objection to me taking Lauren and Meghan home now?" Sturdevant's tone implied any objection would be overruled. The boys looked at each other. Russ figured they would eat their own tongues before admitting they wanted an adult to stay with them.

"I'll keep the boys company until the Ellises get here," Clare said.

He shot her a grateful look. "You're free to go," he told the girls. "Thanks for your cooperation. And thanks for keeping your heads and calling us right away."

Sturdevant was already dragging them off. Russ excused himself and bolted for the new headlights. It was indeed Dr. Scheeler, stepping out of his Scout in a suit that must have cost as much as a month's rent in Cossayuharie.

"I was having a romantic dinner at the

Sagamore with a woman I had to beg for a date," Scheeler said under his breath. "I hope to hell this is worth it."

A lean, tan brunette in a pink suit got out of the passenger side of the car. She wasn't wearing anything under the jacket. No wonder Scheeler was pissed off. She crossed to the driver's side. The pathologist handed her the keys. "I'm so sorry about this, Barb." He glared at Russ.

The woman smiled. Not happy, but good-natured. "Oh, Chief Van Alstyne and I are practically old friends. I'll cut him some slack." She was, Russ realized, the manager of the Algonquin Waters Resort. One of the last people to ever see Linda alive. "How are you?" she said, in a different tone. "I was so sorry to hear about your wife. It must have been terrible for you."

"Thank you. Yeah. It was," he said for the seven hundredth time.

Scheeler pulled his bag out of the back. Hot date or no, he was prepared. He helped the woman up into the driver's seat and took his time retrieving his hand. "So. I'll see you later, Barb?"

She flashed him a killer grin. "If you want your SUV back." Then she gunned the engine and was gone.

"Day-um," Scheeler said. He rubbed the

back of his neck, then glowered at Russ again. "You better have found Amelia Earhart."

Russ started walking toward the back of the field. "Since when do doctors have trouble getting women?"

"Pathology is not always the big turn-on some people assume it is," Scheeler said, falling in beside him. "Plus, the pay sucks. Dermatology, that's where the bucks are. A certificate in plastic surgery is like a license to print money. Hang on."

He climbed into the back of the MKPD ambulance and emerged a minute later, zipping himself into a pale blue jumpsuit. He glanced around the edge of the ambulance as they passed, then did a double-take. He turned to Russ. "It's that minister again!" He looked again to where Clare was talking with the boys. "Have you checked her out? It's not unheard of for perpetrators to come back to the scene of the crime, you know."

Russ pinched the bridge of his nose beneath his glasses. "She's here because the victim worked for her church."

"Have you investigated her thoroughly?" Scheeler asked.

"Uh . . ." *Not as thoroughly as I want to.*

"Because a clerical collar can hide a lot."

Clare's neck bared, her eyes closed, the

hot pulse in her throat — *Christ*. He adjusted his pants under the guise of redistributing the weight of his rig. He was as bad as one of those seventeen-year-old boys, creeping around the old stones, hoping to score. Worse. He knew better.

The area was lit up like a used-car lot with the additional lamps Lyle and Kevin had set up. "Doc Scheeler," Lyle said. Kevin was stringing police-line tape around trees and stones. Lyle stepped over the tape and held it down for the medical examiner. "Hadley's on her way. And the state tech team, although they say it may be another hour."

"Let's see what we can ascertain before they get here." Scheeler snapped his gloves on. They walked one after the other, in Lyle's footsteps. Russ kept his eyes moving as he pulled on his purple gloves, hoping against hope to see a hair, a fiber, a track, anything that might —

They stopped. Russ stepped around the pathologist for a better view. Scheeler sucked in his cheeks. "Holy Mother of God," he said. Russ lifted his eyes and met Lyle's. The older man looked as grim as Russ had ever seen him.

"All right," Scheeler said. "All right. Let's see what he can tell us." He opened his case and knelt, laying it next to the body. He began removing instruments and evidence bags.

"The VFW was up here on the third," Lyle said, "putting in flags. We may be able to place someone on the scene later than that, but that's a positive."

"Dumped," Russ said. "Already dead."

"Probably," Scheeler said from where he knelt. "The ground's so dry, it would have soaked up a lot, but active bleeding would have stained all these dead pine needles." He slid one long, rust-colored needle from beneath the body and held it up. "Dry," he said. "And unstained. When did he go missing?"

"June twenty-third," Lyle said.

"So. Two weeks."

"How long has he been dead?" Russ asked.

"Very preliminary estimate, twenty-four to thirty-six hours." The ME's assured voice thinned out. "Whoever did this kept him alive for a long time."

A silence followed that observation. After a while, Lyle said, "Different gun than the other three."

"I can tell," Russ said. Whatever had finally put Esfuentes out of his misery was a lot bigger than a .22.

"They're not just getting rid of witnesses.

They wanted information," Lyle said.

"Jesus. You think?"

Lyle turned, his expression stung. Russ waved a hand in apology. "Sorry. I'm just . . . yeah. Information. If he had been meant as a warning, he would've turned up someplace a lot more public than this."

"Whatever they wanted to know, this poor bastard couldn't tell them," Scheeler said. He gently lifted one hand with a slender steel rod. "This was done while he was alive. After the third finger, he would have told them anything." The medical examiner slipped an evidence bag over the hand, concealing it from sight. "Who in God's name was this kid?"

Russ's throat tightened. "Nobody. Just a hardworking farm boy who came north for a decent job. He thought we were keeping him safe."

"We did everything we could at the time." MacAuley's voice was rough. "Don't start second-guessing yourself."

It was good advice. Russ had passed it on to more than one young officer in his day. It didn't make him feel any better.

"Russ?"

He snapped around at the sound of Clare's voice. He could just see her outline in the unlit dimness behind the police tape, silhouetted against the whirl of white, red, and blue lights in the distance. He strode toward her.

"I'm sorry," she said, "I don't want to interrupt. It's just that the boys have left, and I didn't know" — he was close enough to make out her face, now — "nobody told me. I wanted to find out." He stopped in front of her. The shivering police tape drew a line between them. "Is it definitely Amado?"

He balled up his hands to keep from putting his arms around her. "Yeah. It is."

"Oh, God." She looked up at him. "Are you sure?" Before he could say anything, she answered herself. "Of course you're sure." She looked away. Wiped her eyes with both hands. "Can I see him? I won't touch anything or get in the way. I just want to —"

"No," he said.

"I've seen dead bodies before, Russ." She straightened her spine. "I won't break down."

"No. Listen," this time he didn't stop himself. He gathered her against him, holding her tightly, hating to be the one to tell her. "Clare, he was tortured. Before he was killed. It wasn't —" He shook his head. "I don't want you to see — Christ, nobody should have to see something like this."

He felt her inhale. Then stillness. Finally, she said, "Are you all right?" Her voice was unsteady.

"Yeah. Or I will be." He took her shoulders and pushed her to arm's length. "I'm sorry."

"For what?"

"For last winter. For letting go. For treating you the way I did. I've been an asshole, Clare, but I love you, and I swear to God, I'd rather die myself than see you hurt." Lyle's words about letting the press know there was nothing to be found at St. Alban's took on a new and terrible urgency. "Whatever the hell piece of information we're missing, these guys looking for it want it bad. And they're junkyard-dog vicious. I don't want you alone until we've found them. Go to the Ellises' house, get your deacon to move in with you, whatever you have to so you're not by yourself."

"I can't promise that." He couldn't tell if it was anger or anguish in her voice.

"Russ!" Lyle called.

"Please, Clare. I don't expect you to do anything because I ask you to." She flinched at that. "But do it for Amado. His death at least gives us a warning. Don't waste it."

"Russ!" Lyle was impatient.

He left her with one glance over his

shoulder. Walked back into the circle of cold light, inching his fingers into his glove once more. All around, the oak and maple leaves whispered and hissed in the wind.

"Take a look at this," Lyle said. He and Kevin — pale, stiff-faced, but functioning — had rolled the body to one side. Doc Scheeler, kneeling, was tweezing some sort of short hairs or fibers from where they had crusted on the blood-soaked shirt. There were a lot of them, black and pale golden and tan where they weren't stained with blood.

"What are they?" Russ asked.

Scheeler held a small tuft up before slipping it into an evidence bag. "I can't be certain until I inspect this under the microscope, but I'm pretty sure it's hair. He brought it with him; it isn't on the pine needles beneath the body. I'm just finding them in one area, here, where the body rested on the ground, but that may not signify much. They could have appeared elsewhere and then blown off while he was exposed up here."

"Maybe he was laid someplace where there was a lot of hair," Lyle said.

"Or wrapped in a rug or blanket," Russ said. "That would jibe with his being transported here. If somebody didn't want to get blood all over the trunk of his car."

"A dog blanket," Kevin said. He looked at Russ. "You know. You put an old blanket on the sofa or on the backseat of a car? So the dog won't shed on the good stuff underneath."

Russ examined the hairs again. Sharp-tipped, two or three inches long. Black and tan. He remembered their last visit to the Christies: Kevin hurtling into the cruiser, half an inch away from being savaged. He looked at the young officer. Saw him nod.

"German shepherds," Russ said.

X

This time, they went at dawn, warrant in hand. They had the animal control officer with them, a rawhide woman whose sleepy expression concealed an ability to think fast and move faster. P.J. loved animals, but Russ had no doubt she could put down the German shepherds if needed. He had dated one of her older sisters in high school. All the Adams girls had a ruthless streak a mile wide.

P.J. had said the dogs were likely to be asleep by morning, and she was right. Kevin opened the gate slowly and quietly this time, watching the drive every second, but no ravening beasts showed up to try and take a chunk out of him. The sky arched overhead, rose and pearl, and grasshoppers whirred out of the grass as they drove up the lane.

Russ parked in the same spot he had two weeks before. This time he could see how badly the house and barn needed painting. The Christies had inherited a lot — he glanced at the century-old maples shading the house and the fields and woods falling away in every direction — but they were lousy stewards.

Getting out of the car, he could hear the sheep bleating. Another car door *cachunk*ed, and Lyle walked up to stand at his side. "If anybody's hiding in the sheep pen, you're going in this time," he said.

"Are you kidding? That's what we brought Kevin for." Russ turned away from the house. Kevin and Eric were in backup positions and P.J. was readying a trank gun, muzzles and restraint straps dangling off her belt. "Ready?"

"Yep."

They mounted the porch steps. Russ rang the doorbell. Nothing happened. He rang it again. The door jerked open, revealing a twenty-something blonde in a baggy T-shirt and pajama bottoms. Her face was creased from sleep. "What is it?" she asked.

Russ dredged the sister's name out of his

memory. "Isabel?" he said. "We'd like to speak to your brothers."

She blinked several times and rubbed her face. "Why?"

MacAuley pushed against the door, opening it farther. She stepped back. "We want to ask them about Amado Esfuentes."

She came awake. "Amado? Why?"

"He's been killed," Russ said. "We believe your brothers may have some knowledge of the murder."

She clapped a hand over her mouth. Her eyes went wide and white-edged. *Oh, hell. Looks like Kevin was wrong about their relationship — or lack thereof.*

"Are you sure?" she whispered. "Are you sure it was Amado Esfuentes? Not one of the others?"

"We've positively ID'd him," Russ said. "I'm sorry."

"He was tortured." MacAuley had dropped his usual easygoing persona. "For information he may have possessed. Over many days. He must have thanked whoever put a bullet in his head."

Isabel Christie made a sound like an animal in a trap. She backed away even farther. Russ stepped into the house.

"You knew him, didn't you?" He kept his voice sympathetic.

She nodded.

"I met him a couple of times, too. He was a good-hearted, hardworking young man, with his whole life ahead of him. He didn't deserve to die like that." He bent down so he was speaking to her face-to-face. "Will you help us?"

She nodded.

"Where are your brothers?"

She took a deep breath. "Bruce . . ." Her voice wavered. She stopped. When she started again, it was steady. "Bruce is in the fifth wheel next door." From the corner of his eye, Russ could see Lyle turn and point Kevin and Eric to the trailer. "Neil's upstairs. Donald and Kathy were fighting last night, and he took off after she locked him out of their bedroom. He's prob'ly at his ex's house. Desiree Dwyer."

"I thought she was out of town."

She pointed in the direction of the dining room. "Different ex." Russ and Lyle followed, skirting the long table and heavy Victorian chairs, into the minuscule back hallway. A narrow staircase rose steeply to a windowed alcove.

"Isabel," Russ said. "Could you call your brother downstairs?"

She looked at him. There were purple shadows beneath her eyes that hadn't been there when they arrived. "You think they did it?" she whispered.

"Evidence with the body points toward your brothers, yeah."

She took another deep breath. Her face smoothed, became a mask of normalcy. She faced the second floor. "Neil!" she yelled.

"Wha'?" A single snarling male voice, muffled by a door.

"Giddown here!"

"What the hell for? Jesus Christ, you know what time it is?"

She took a few steps up until she was level with the second-floor landing. "The ram's busted the gate again. He's at the ewes."

They heard feet thudding on the floor, accompanied by steady cursing. "Donald!" The unseen voice — Neil — bellowed. "Git your lazy ass out of bed. The ram's out!"

A door thudded open against a wall. "Shut up!" a woman yelled.

Russ winced. "The fiancée," he told Lyle.

"He ain't in here," she went on. "He's coolin' off downstairs."

"No, he's not," Isabel said loudly. "He went to Desiree's."

"Uh-oh," Russ said.

What? The shriek rose like a siren. "That no-good, belly-crawling, rat bastard son of a bitch —"

Isabel ducked out of the stairwell. Russ and Lyle backpedaled as someone large and heavy crashed down the steps. Neil Christie emerged, pulling a T-shirt over his head. He stopped when he saw them. "What the hell?"

"Neil, we want you to come with us," Russ said. "We want to ask you some questions about Amado Esfuentes."

The big man's jaw unhinged, then clamped shut. He narrowed his eyes. "You arrestin' me?"

"Not yet," Lyle said.

Neil swung his head, left, right, like a bull readying for a charge. Russ hoped he wasn't going to try to take them. Then his gaze fell on Isabel, pressed against the dining room wall. "You," her brother said. "You let 'em in. You — the ram ain't out, is he? You lying bitch!" He raised one meaty hand in a fist. Isabel cringed.

"Touch her and we'll have you up on assault," Lyle said.

"C'mon, Neil." Russ dropped his voice some. Confidential. Persuasive. "You don't want any trouble, and neither do we. You come on down with us and answer a few questions. You'll be back in time for lunch."

He could see the wheels and pulleys clanking slowly in Christie's brain. But he

510

was surprised when Neil turned on Isabel again. "Is Don really at Desiree's? Or is that you lyin' again? Do they already have him?"

"No! It's the truth!"

"We'll pick up your brother from his girlfriend's house," Russ said.

At the same moment, Neil said, "So it's just me? God damn!" and swung at the girl.

Lyle, who was closer, lunged forward, wrapping both arms around Christie's midsection and heaving backward. Isabel ducked. Russ was unsnapping his cuffs from his belt, yelling, "Get his arm," when a shrieking harpy flew from the stairwell and landed square on Lyle, screeching, "Leave him alone, you rat bastard son of a bitch!" Lyle staggered and released Neil, struggling to shake off the woman clawing and punching him.

Isabel ran. Neil pivoted after her. Russ slammed into him with a shoulder block, but his angle was wrong to put Christie down. Instead, he jolted sideways against the table, which scraped over the wooden floor.

The fiancée was screaming nonstop, and over the din Russ could hear the rumble of many footsteps overhead. Oh, no, not the kids, too. In this house, they were as likely to join in as to be traumatized.

"Lyle, can't you —" Russ began. Neil reeled around and nailed him in the breast-bone with a ham-sized fist, knocking him into the sideboard. Every last molecule of air exploded out of his body as the clash and clank of dishes added to the noise. Russ managed to roll out of the way as Christie leaped like a TV wrestler coming into the ring. The big man landed with a bone-rattling thump on the floor. Russ heaved up to his hands and knees and threw himself on Christie's back. Still gasping for air, he dropped all his weight onto the man's arm.

Lyle howled. "Jesus hell! She bit me!" Russ heard the crack of bone on bone and the high-pitched swearing broke off. The fi-ancée thudded to the floor next to Neil.

Russ wrestled a first cuff onto Neil's wrist and yanked the man's arm back, not much caring what damage he did. As Neil hol-lered and flailed, Russ snapped the second cuff on. He sat up, still on Christie's back, still trying to catch his breath.

Lyle was cuffing the unconscious Kathy. "Damn," he said. "I hate to hit a woman."

"Why the hell'd she go after you?"

Isabel peeped around the door, ready to bolt again if Neil managed to shake off Russ's 220 pounds and tear loose of the restraints. "She was sleeping with Neil, too.

512

Donald doesn't know."

Neil bucked beneath Russ. "You goddamn trouble-making bitch!" His yell was muffled by the carpet. "I shoulda let you go with that Mexican! You ain't worth it! What we done for you? You ain't worth it!"

XI

"How does that feel?" Lyle gestured toward Russ's chest with his mug of coffee. In the dispatch room behind them, Kevin was filling Harlene in on his thrilling capture. Since Bruce Christie had nodded, called his lawyer, and gotten in the cruiser without fuss or mess for Eric and Kevin, it was going to be a short story.

Russ touched his sternum. It was tender, with an ache that went right through him. How did it feel? *Like letting go.* "Sore," he said.

"You ought to have it looked at. Make sure you didn't crack anything."

Russ pointed to the bandage swathing Lyle's hand. "Pot, meet kettle."

"Hell, I'm going in for a tetanus shot soon as we're done here. I want P.J. to impound that woman for ten days to make sure she doesn't have rabies."

"And we were worried about the dogs."

Hadley Knox came in from the squad

room. She looked at them like a mom checking out two kids who've fallen suspiciously silent. "Children and Family Services are sending a caseworker to the Christie farm."

"Good," Russ said.

"Ms. Adams called in. The German shepherds are in the shelter for the time being." She raised her voice for the benefit of Kevin, who had drifted in to see what was up. "She says they're really sweet dogs."

Lyle snickered. "Maybe it's just you, Kevin."

Russ swigged his coffee, wishing there were some way to add a couple shots of espresso and double the caffeine content. He had gotten four hours of sleep on one of the old cell cots downstairs, waiting for the warrant to come through. He had sent Lyle home from the Muster Field, but there was no way he had gotten more than five. By comparison, Knox and Kevin glowed with vim and vigor. He had been that age once. A long time ago.

"I want Noble to take the guns to the ballistics lab." They had seized four sidearms that might match the caliber that had killed Amado.

Lyle nodded. "Didja see the twenty-twos?"

"Yep." The Christies had an arsenal worthy of a militia.

"I wish to hell we could get those to ballistics."

"Take it up with Judge Ryswick." The judge had a horror of general warrants. When he wrote large caliber, he meant it, and the fact they had three unsolved killings by .22s didn't impress him.

Eric came in and took in the crowd. "What? We finally got good coffee?"

"Not a chance," Lyle said.

"Eric," Russ said, "You've been working the Christies all along. I want you to question Bruce and Donald."

Eric nodded. "What about Neil and the girlfriend?"

"They can go on the back burner while they're getting booked and waiting for a bond hearing. I'm going to my mom's for a shower and a change." He checked his watch. "I'll be back before noon." He caught Eric's sleeve before he left. "Find a wedge. Maybe the cheating fiancée thing, maybe imply one of 'em's cutting a deal to roll on the others. The Christies are tight; if you can split 'em apart, you'll have 'em."

Eric nodded, then left for the interrogation room. Russ took another drink of coffee. "Lyle, go to the hospital and get that bite looked at. Then head home and get some sleep." Lyle opened his mouth to protest. "Just go," Russ said. "I'm getting some, too."

Lyle shrugged. Slouched toward the squad-room door. "That's not what I heard."

Russ ignored the remark. "Knox, I want you to head over to the Christies'. Check in with the social worker and see if you can get anything useful from the sister or the kids. Kevin —" His youngest officer straightened, his expression bright and eager. Good God, it was no wonder the Christies' dogs went after him. The boy was a human Irish setter. "You're on patrol."

Kevin's face dimmed. Knox frowned.

Russ sighed. "What?"

"No offense, Chief, but are you sending me to talk with the kids because I'm a woman?"

"I'm sending you because I think you're the best officer for the job. Just like I'm putting Kevin on patrol because Lyle and I are beat up and sleep-deprived and not much good to anyone right now. Look." He gathered them both in with his voice, focusing their attention. "This case has been one horror after another. It's been long hours and frustration and leads going nowhere. And you two have performed admirably through it all. I'm proud of you both. I'm proud to serve with you. And I know whatever I need you to do, you're going to do it. Competently and professionally." He drained his mug and set it down. "Now let's go do what we gotta do."

XII

The gate to the Christies' farm had been left open. Hadley jounced her cruiser up the rutted dirt drive. On one side, golden hayfields rolled away to the distant forest's edge. On the other, past an ancient stone wall, sheep drifted over the green grass like dusty clouds. It looked like a picture out of Genny's children's Bible. All that was missing was the Good Shepherd.

She parked on the grass at the other side of the house, beneath a spreading maple that also shaded a junky little trailer. She should stay on the drive, but she knew if she left the cruiser in the sun it would be an oven by the time she got back in, and the AC didn't work so well in this unit.

She got out. The heat pressed against her, dry and windless. She plucked her blouse away from her body. If it felt like this at mid-morning, it was going to be a breathlessly hot day.

She crossed the drive and mounted the porch steps. The windows were closed against the heat. She rang the bell. She heard a murmur of voices. She squinted, trying to see through the shirred curtains in the door. She knocked. "Hello!" she said, loud enough to be heard inside. "Millers Kill Police."

The door cracked open. A young woman peeked out. She had strawberry-blond hair pulled back into a ponytail and ghost-ridden eyes.

"Hi," Hadley said. "I'm Officer Knox of the Millers Kill Police. Can I —"

"It's not a good time," the woman said. "I have guests."

"I know about the caseworker from Children and Family. I'm the — uh, liaison with the department." Hadley smiled reassuringly. "Are you —"

The door shut in her face. She thought of Hudson's favorite Elmer Fudd line: *How wude!* She banged on the door, insistent this time. "Ma'am," she said.

The door jerked open. A short, broad, weasel-faced man stood in front of her. His protruding eyes made him look like Peter Lorre, updated with jailhouse chic clothing and tattoos, visible on his fingers, which were braced against the jamb to bar her way.

"Look," he said, in a barely accented voice. "She doesn't want to talk to you right now —"

She saw it, the moment when he recognized her, and realized she recognized him. She hurtled off the porch as he was yelling something in Spanish. She half landed in the straggly bush below, fought her way free, and sprinted toward her unit. She heard glass shatter, glanced over her shoulder, and saw the barrel of an enormous revolver tracking her from the upper half of one of the windows. She dove behind her squad car as the thing went off. A bullet smacked into the maple, showering her with wet splinters. She wrenched the door open and clawed at the mic. "Dispatch!" she yelled. "Harlene? This bastard's shooting at me!"

XIII

Russ had just pulled into his mother's drive when his cell phone rang. *Hell.* He checked the number. The ant-sized hope that Clare might be calling was squashed when he saw it was the station. He flipped the phone open. "Van Alstyne here."

"Chief." The usually unflappable Harlene sounded stressed. "We have an officer under fire."

His heart stopped. "Who?" Images of

Kevin, a robbery, Paul, a traffic stop gone south.

"Hadley Knox."

Oh, Christ, no. The rawest person on the force. He threw the truck in reverse and rolled down the window. "Where?"

"The Christie place."

What? He pushed the crowd of questions away. Reached up and clamped the light to the top of the truck. "Give me a sitrep."

"Gunfire from a three-fifty-seven Magnum. Other weapons unknown. There may be another man inside, she couldn't say for sure."

He rolled the window back up. Flicked on the light and siren. Tromped on the gas. "Unknown number of women and children inside as hostages." Harlene raised her voice to be heard over the siren's whoop. "Kevin and Lyle are on their way. Eric's coming from the jail, SWAT team's scrambling."

"I'll be there soonest." He thought of Hadley Knox, with her threadbare tote filled with criminal law texts. Her panicky voice: *I haven't practiced with a shoulder holster!* "Harlene," he said. "Send an ambulance."

XIV

He didn't know you could get speeds like that out of a Ford 250. He went airborne on the Christies' drive, bounced, ground against the dirt and gravel, and there was the house, and there was Knox's unit, and there was Knox, sprinting across the side yard — no vest on, for chrissakes — and there, in the broken and whole glass, an outline, and a hand, and a gun.

He slewed the truck to a stop and tumbled out the door, his gun already in hand, and fired at the porch roof. It was a wild shot, unaimed, but the guy inside ducked out of sight and Knox rolled safely to a stop against the house's foundation. He took a better stance behind the hood, figuring his engine block would stop even a .357.

"Millers Kill Police," he said loudly. "Put your weapon down and walk out with your hands on top of your head." This suggestion was greeted with a torrent of obscenities. From the corner of his eye, he could see Knox flopping around. "You okay, Knox?"

"Yeah. I mean, yes, sir."

"Stay right there. Don't move." He could see something behind the window. It was hard to make out in the shadow of the porch. Then he saw an eye, the side of a face, the gunman scoping things out. Russ dropped an inch lower, sighting him.

"You shoot one more time and I swear I'll cap one of 'em here," the man screamed. "I'll blow one of these bitches' heads off!"

O-kay. He did his best work talking, anyway. He waved his empty hand in the air and ostentatiously laid his sidearm on the hood. He heard the rumble and whine of an engine, and Kevin's unit popped over the horizon, coming in too fast, screeching to a stop in a cloud of dust next to the truck. Lyle shoved Kevin out the driver's side and crawled over him. They were both, thank God, in their tac vests.

Lyle scanned the barn, the house, the side yard, the trailer. "Just in the house?"

"Looks like," Russ said.

Lyle glanced at his empty hands. "Forget your piece?"

"He's threatened to shoot hostages if we fire."

"What's going on?" the gunman yelled.

"Sounds Latino," Lyle said.

He hummed in agreement. Then spoke loudly. "My deputy here says the state SWAT team is on the way. They're not interested in talking to you. But I am."

"Screw you!"

"C'mon, man, talk to me." He started his patter. The first thing was to get him talking. A guy who's talking isn't shooting. The second was to be his friend. I'm on your side. We're in this together. "C'mon," he said. "You put your gun down, I put my gun down, we'll call it drunk and disorderly." He tried to remember how many kids were there. Donald had five or six by a string of girlfriends, bouncing back and forth between homes. His oldest had a kid of her own, though, and she lived with him. Plus the foul-mouthed fiancée's bunch.

The gunman had moved away from the window. He — or was it another voice? — was yelling at someone in the interior of the house. He needed more info. He caught Knox's eye, signaled her to check out the back. She nodded and rolled to the ground, belly-crawling away from them like a marine in an obstacle course.

"Why doesn't she just duck down and walk?" Lyle said. "They can't see her if she sticks close to the house."

"Probably taught her that at Basic."

Lyle huffed. "We'll be another year un-learnin' her after she's through there."

If she survived the afternoon. "Any way to get her a tac vest?"

"Two in the trunk of her cruiser."

They both looked at her squad car, maybe ten yards from where they were parked and another fifteen from the house. Open ground. No cover.

"Get Kevin to the tail of your unit. If I can distract this guy, he can sprint to her car, grab the vest, and meet her at the side of the house."

"And what about you?"

He twitched the question away. The shooter reappeared in the window. "Hey!" Russ said. The third thing was to get him to say *yes*. Didn't matter to what. One *yes* leads to another. "It's hotter'n hell today, isn't it?" The shadowy figure stared at him. "Hard to keep things cool when it's ninety degrees."

"You think this is hot? This ain't nothin'."

"For you, maybe. Me, I'm dying out here." Out of the corner of his eye he saw Kevin taking up position at the back of his unit. "I could use something cold and wet. What about you? You want a cold beer? I can bring a six-pack up to the porch, and we can talk."

The guy laughed. "You think I'm an idiot? Whadda you take me for?"

Russ spread his hands. "Okay. You know what we want. We want everybody here to walk away unharmed. We want a win-win solution. You tell me what you want."

The shooter ducked away from the window for a moment. Russ glanced at Lyle. Lyle held up two fingers. Two guys. At least.

"You know what I want? I want our property back. These rednecks stole something from us, and I want it back."

Russ got that sensation in his head, like bottle rockets popping off, one after the other. "The directory of dealer names," he said, tossing out another wild guess.

The man — the Punta Diablos foot soldier — hissed in surprise. *A hit, a palpable hit.* "What you say?" the shooter asked after a moment. He'd be a lousy poker player.

"We arrested the Christie brothers this morning. You know how it goes. Any valuable information goes on the bargaining table."

"Son of a bitch monkey-balled mother—" Russ let the guy rave on. He'd be a good match for Donald's latest fiancée. He almost smiled, until the last bottle rocket went off, and he realized it was the Punta Diablos, and not the large and thugly Christies, who had done those horrible things to Amado Esfuentes. *These guys are junkyard-dog vicious,* he'd told Clare. And now they had an unknown number of women and children at their mercy.

The shooter was going on about how you couldn't trust anyone. Russ wasn't sure if the rant was directed at him or at the unknown accomplices inside, but he was getting worried. These guys were trapped. That's when dangerous animals attacked. Where the hell was Knox? Had something happened to her?

Then she appeared from the back of the house. He kept his face forward, fixed intently on the Punta Diablo point man, who was working himself up in a major way. He slipped one hand off the hood of his truck and signaled to Kevin. Nothing. He signaled again. No long tall streak of red loping toward Knox's squad car.

Then Kevin's voice was behind him, in his ear. "There's a dead woman out back," he said quietly. "Shot in the chest."

Russ thought about hapless, knocked-around Isabel Christie, with her strawberry-blond hair and her sad eyes. What a goddamn waste. He suddenly felt twenty years older.

"Chief?" Kevin kept his voice low.

"Have Harlene patch you to the SWAT team. Brief 'em. Then get ready to run for that vest."

"Roger that." Kevin sprinted for his cruiser, bent double. He flung open the door and lay on the seat, reaching for the mic.

"What's going on?" the Punta Diablo guy asked. "What's he doing on the radio?"

"I just told him to ask the state troopers to stay back a ways," Russ said. "I want you and me to have the time we need to talk our way out of this thing." He kept his face forward and rattled on, good faith, blah-blah-blah, listening as Kevin briefed the state assault team sergeant he'd been connected to. It was informative, detailed, and short. The kid was finally learning to get to the point.

"You tell those bastards to stay away from us," the shooter yelled. "Anybody tries to mess with us, they gotta go through one of these kids to do it!"

Kevin hung up the mic. "Fifteen — twenty minutes."

Shit. Might as well be tomorrow, for all the good they were going to do.

The guy disappeared from the window. Inside the house, a woman screamed. "Knox!" He grabbed his gun off the hood. "What's he doing in there?"

She jumped up like a jackrabbit and looked in the window. Ran to the next one. He flapped at Kevin. "The vest! Go! Go!"

"He's holding a kid," Knox yelled. "He's — oh, shit, no!"

This was going straight down the crapper.

"Are there other shooters?"

"I can't tell!" she screamed. "Maybe in the front —"

The window above Knox exploded. She dropped, and for one sickening moment he thought she'd been hit, but then he saw she was crouched, her hands over the back of her neck. Kevin had popped the trunk and was yanking a vest out. "Go through the back," Russ yelled. "Go through the back!"

Kevin waved acknowledgment and tore through the side yard. Knox rose and ran after him. They disappeared around the corner.

"Don't move," Lyle said. "I'm getting you the other one." He raced toward Knox's unit.

Up on the porch, the door flew open. A teenaged girl with a baby under her arm made a dash for it. The shooter lunged forward, long rope-muscled arm extended, and snagged her by her collar. She rebounded, gagged, and almost dropped the baby. Her captor dragged her backward by the neck.

Russ broke cover and ran for the house. Lyle was shouting something at him, but he couldn't hear it over the thudding of his feet, the rasp of his breath, the crying and yelling inside.

He took the porch steps in two strides and slammed through the door with the side of his body, leaving him face-to-face with the open double doors and the wild-eyed shooter, tattooed fingers, just like Knox had said, backing away with a squirming, squalling teen and her baby as a shield.

"Police! Drop your weapon," Russ roared: habit, not hope.

"Drop *your* weapon!" The Punta Diablo guy had a monster .357 Taurus pointed at the girl. Russ kept his Glock lined and sighted for a head shot. The gangbanger started to look scared. It was damn hard to keep your gun pointed *away* from a man when you could see his bore drilling you between the eyes.

Then the girl lunged to the side, yanking her captor off balance. His instinct took over; he swung his .357 toward Russ, arms wide, chest unguarded. Russ dropped his Glock three inches and squeezed twice. He dove right as the Magnum went off, but the young man was already crumpling, the gun falling from his tattooed fingers.

The girl and her baby ran screaming into the dining room. Russ hit a brown corduroy chair, the weight of his body skidding it across the floor. He stumbled upright, swung toward where the shooter's body had fallen, saw Isabel Christie sagging, unconscious, against the couch. And then a baseball bat smashed into his chest.

Russ turned, not understanding, and another bat struck his upper thigh, white-hot pain streaking along his hip, and he slipped, his leg useless, and saw him in the doorway to the front hall, the second man. Russ saw the gun pointed at him, tried to raise his Glock, too slow, too slow. Russ squeezed off a round but the next shot punched him in the chest and blew him over.

He heard more shots, three, four, like a movie playing in a different room. His awareness burrowed inward, as if all the universe were six feet three inches long and contained within his skin. Labored breathing. Sluggish heart. Burning hip. Throbbing chest.

Lyle's face dropped into view for a moment. He didn't bother Russ with a lot of talking, just turned and started ripping his uniform blouse open. Lyle. His friend. Why hadn't he forgiven him? Instead of carrying his grudge around like an old set of keys. He closed his eyes.

"Call nine-one-one," Lyle said to someone. Russ's skin was clammy. He shivered convulsively. The wooden floor beneath him was winter-cold.

"Get me something I can use for compresses," Lyle said.

He tried to breathe in, but there was a bubble blocking his throat, like swallowing inside out. He gurgled and hacked.

"Hurry, Knox!" Lyle's hands were cradling his skull, turning his head so he could spit. Liquid gushed out of his mouth. He could breathe again. Lyle's hands went away.

"Oh, Jesus," Knox said. She didn't sound so good.

"Shut up," Lyle said. "Get these civilians out of here."

There were noises, children, but they seemed increasingly far away. The pain was everything. The only thing. He didn't want that. He didn't want that to be the last thing. He opened his eyes. Lyle was on his knees, stripping his belt out of his pants.

"Didn't know . . . you felt that way," Russ managed.

Lyle's hands stuttered for a second. "You should be so lucky," he said. He finished pulling his belt free. "I'm gonna tourniquet your thigh, slow down this bleeding. It's gonna hurt like a ring-tailed bitch." He bent over, out of Russ's line of sight, and then a five-thousand-volt electrical shock went through his leg.

"Je . . . fu . . . Chr. . . ." Russ gasped. The pain curled him forward, as if he could rise and escape it. He caught sight of his own chest.

"Lay back," Lyle said. He did. Lyle laid something over his chest. "I'm gonna compress you until the EMTs arrive. Won't be long."

He lifted his hand, stopping Lyle with a strengthless motion. "Lyle." He could feel another bubble rising in his throat. He wanted to say this before it choked him off. "I'm sorry." He opened his hand. "Friend."

Lyle took his hand and squeezed too hard. His face pinched. "I don't wanna hear any goddamn last words or deathbed apologies from you, you hear?"

He tried to say something, but the rushing liquid filled his throat, his mouth, his nose. He turned his head and retched, coughed, spluttered.

As soon as his mouth was clear, Lyle leaned on him, crushing him, hurting him. Russ tried to bat him away but he didn't have anything left. It was heavy, so heavy, like cold concrete burying him. He heaved for air. Lyle was going to suffocate him trying to save him. "Can't . . . breathe . . ." he got out.

"I think you've punctured a lung," Lyle said. "The EMTs will set you to rights. Listen." He heard his breath, his heart, his blood taking its last few trips around the system. "They're almost here."

It wasn't Lyle. It was him. He was dying. He thought of Clare. *Oh, love. I wish we had had more time.* He was going to die, and she would be left with hateful, angry words as their last good-bye. *Already forgotten,* he wanted to say. *I always knew what was in your heart.* Now, right now, the slate was wiped clean.

"Lyle . . . tell Clare. . . ." He struggled to get enough air to push out the words. "Tell her . . ."

"You can tell her yourself when you see her," Lyle said.

He inhaled again, but it wasn't enough. His lungs burned. His head buzzed. She would know. She would have to know.

"Russ?" Lyle's voice receded into the distance, with the children and the gunshots. "Don't you die on me, Russ!"

So, how do you pray? he'd asked her once. She'd thought about it a long moment. She always listened, always took his questions seriously. *Say what you believe,* she said. *Say what you're thankful for. Say what you love.*

He'd never been one for prayer. But there was a last time for everything. "Clare," he said. Then everything stopped.

XV

No official church involvement, that was the dictat. Volunteers, on their own, could work with the migrant farmhands. That's what they had agreed on. Well, it was her day off. She could do what she wanted on her day off. And if she wanted to drive to the Rehabilitation Center and pick up Lucia Pirone for a sedate drive around the countryside, that was her own business. If they happened to stop in at a few farms and check in with the Spanish-speaking workers, that was her own damn business, too.

"You're sure this isn't going to get you in trouble with your bishop?" Sister Lucia shifted in the passenger seat. The pin in her hip was healed enough for the center to release her for the afternoon, but it was plain it hadn't healed enough to be comfortable.

"Absolutely sure," Clare said. "If he doesn't find out."

Sister Lucia laughed. "I like the way you think."

"We're going to have to find a better solution, though. Sooner rather than later. I'm away one weekend out of four as it is. Smuggling you out of the center three days a month doesn't cut it."

"You know Christophe St. Laurent? From Sacred Heart? He's willing to drum up volunteers, but he'd like to talk to you at some point and see if any of your people would consider continuing on, even if the outreach isn't sponsored by your church."

In the rearview mirror, a whirl of red and white bloomed. She glanced at the speedometer; caught up in conversation, she had eased off the gas. She was now going the legal speed. She steered for the shoulder.

The first car blew past her at a speed that rattled her windows. A second car, and then an SUV, flew in its wake. State police. No sirens. Responding to a call.

Her chest squeezed, as if someone had wrapped an unfriendly hand around her heart.

Then she heard the *whoop-whoop-whoop* of an emergency vehicle. She stomped on the brake, grinding her front wheels into the dirt at the shoulder. "What on earth?" Sister Lucia threw out a hand to brace herself on the dashboard.

Clare turned around in time to see the ambulance crest the rise behind her, blue lights beating in time with the pulse of her blood. From the corner of her eye, she could see Sister Lucia cross herself.

The vehicle blazed past, almost too fast to read MILLERS KILL EMERGENCY on its side.

"Do you think —" Sister Lucia started. She read the papers like everyone else. "Could they have found another body?"

Clare shook her head. "Those weren't Millers Kill police cruisers. They don't normally get the state police involved, unless they need one of their special units, like crime scene or a dive team or" — the penny fell as she said the words — "tactical response."

"Which is?"

"The men who show up if there's a hostage situation or officers under fire." Clare released the brake and tromped on the gas, jumping her Subaru back onto the road, sparing a glance for oncoming traffic only after it would've been too late to avoid it.

She accelerated down the country highway. Sister Lucia kept one hand wedged against the dash and grabbed her armrest with the other. "Perhaps," she shouted — the open windows that had let in a pleasant breeze at forty miles an hour were shrieking wind tunnels at sixty-five — "they've found the killer!"

That's what Clare was afraid of. *Oh, God, please be with them. Please let the ambulance just be a precaution. Please let nobody be hurt.*

She reached an intersection. "Which way?" she asked. "Where'd they go?"

Sister Lucia's hand, soft and powder-dry, settled over her arm. "Wait," she said. "If they came along this road, chances are good they'll return this way as well."

"But it might be too late!"

The nun looked at her, a twist of a smile drying her face. "My dear, what do you think you're going to do?"

"Not sit here and wait to see what happens." Clare spun the wheel, and the Subaru squealed onto Seven Mile Road. Sister Lucia whooped and grabbed for the door handle.

"What if this is the wrong way?" the nun shouted.

"Fly or die," Clare yelled.

Sister Lucia rolled her window up, shutting off half the rush of air. "Remember what I said about fearlessness?"

"Sure do."

"I take it back."

A wail from somewhere, rising, falling. Clare glanced in her rearview mirror. A whirl of blue and white. Another ambulance.

She took her foot off the gas and let the Subaru roll, half on, half off, the narrow dirt shoulder. The Corinth ambulance screamed past them, followed by a Millers Kill squad car. Clare caught the driver's blocky outline, but it could have been almost any of them. She kicked the car back up to speed and then some, racing after the emergency vehicles, bombing over the low hills, bouncing into the hollows, slanting way over the lines as she powered through curves.

The ambulance and the cruiser had turned up a skinflint country road and she followed too fast; she skidded, lost her grip on the road, the whole car sliding toward the ditch. She cursed and gave the wheel some slack and trod on the gas, and the tires caught, spinning a shower of shredded Indian paintbrush and buttercups as she surged back onto the asphalt.

She took the turn onto the dirt road a little slower. Roared through a wide-open gate, up and up until she crested and saw the carnival from Hell, ambulances and cop cars and uniforms and guns. Children and trees and peeling clapboards and broken glass. Dust hanging in the air, loud voices, weeping, and the electric-burr sound of radios demanding information.

She hit the brakes and skidded, heeling her car onto the grass at the side of the drive. She leaped out, spun in place, and pointed to Sister Lucia. "Stay here!"

State SWAT team members, ominous in black and armor, stalked across the dooryard and around the house and barn in patterns that made sense only to them. She slowed down, uncertain what was going on, where the center was, the thought dawning that maybe the ambulances were just a precaution, like she had hoped, and she was going to look pretty silly when — then she spotted Kevin Flynn. Standing alone at the bottom of the porch steps. Crying.

Her feet moved her forward even though her head was howling, *Run! Run!* She had been here before, at this moment. No going back to before. There would only be after. After the diagnosis. After the accident. After hearing whatever terrible thing Kevin was going to tell her.

Hadley Knox ran onto the porch, followed by Eric McCrea. "Flynn!" she yelled, then stared, open-mouthed, at Clare. Movement, voices, behind the officers. McCrea shoved Knox out of the way, and the paramedics emerged, carrying their burden with controlled speed. One of them was rapid-firing unintelligible information into her radio.

One of them held a trembling IV bag aloft, and the third balanced a portable heart monitor against the side of the cart, its *beep-beep-beep* counting out the seconds.

The rest of it she saw as fragments: his sandy hair, the oxygen mask, one boot lolling off the stretcher. Khaki sleeve, blue surgical bandages, red blood. So much blood.

Kevin was sobbing beside her, but she couldn't make a sound. It felt as if her chest was bound and locked.

"Careful, now." Karl, one of the Millers Kill EMTs. "Careful!" They descended the porch stairs, quick and smooth, and as they passed her, she saw his hand, tan, limp, still wearing his wedding ring. Her voice tore free in a wrenching, animal cry.

She lunged after the pallet and Lyle was in the way, more blood, soaked in blood, reeking of it — and he caught her and held her, saying, "Stop it! Stop it," wrapping her and smearing her and marking her with Russ's blood while she howled like a dog.

The steady *beep-beep-beep* turned into a single warbling alarm. The breath caught in Clare's throat. One of the EMTs swore. They dropped the pallet. Annie ripped a syringe off a Velcro pack and tore it open. Karl threw himself to his knees and began chest compressions, sharp fast pumps that looked like they would snap Russ's already-wounded body in two. The third paramedic moved in, blocking Clare's view, leaving her with only the high, piercing alarm to tell her that Russ was dead.

Yea, though I walk through the valley of the shadow of death, I will fear no evil.

Dead. How long? Death was a process, not an on-off switch. She knew that.

For thou art with me, thy rod and thy staff, they comfort me.

The EMTs communicated in short harsh bursts, microwave information. Annie broke open another syringe.

Thou spreadest a table before me in the presence of mine enemies.

Kevin's sobs fell to gasps. Silence spread around them like ripples from a pond.

Thou anointest my head with oil, my cup overfloweth.

Was it a minute? Two? The alarm began to sound like an inconsolable cry. A wailing for the dead that will not return.

"Surely" — her voice cracked — "thy goodness and mercy will follow me all the days of my life?"

The alarm blipped. Blipped, beeped, paused, beeped, and settled into a steady rhythm. Clare sagged against Lyle, whose fingers she finally felt cutting into her arms.

"Go, go!" the third man said. They heaved the pallet up and surged toward the open ambulance doors.

And I will dwell in the house of the Lord forever.

"Christ Jesus Almighty," Lyle said, his voice shaking.

"Amen," she said into his shoulder.

He released her. "You fit to drive to the hospital?"

She nodded. "Where are they taking him? Glens Falls?"

"Washington County. One of their ER docs used to work in New Orleans. He's seen more gunshot cases than anyone else in the area."

The ambulance doors slammed shut. The lights and siren started up.

"Go on," he said. "I need a word with the rest of 'em, then I'll be along."

She took a step toward her car. Turned. "Lyle," she said, "what happened?"

"I had a vest for him. Right in my hand." He stared at the gore running down his fingers. "It was right in my hand. But he had to be a goddam hero." He wiped his face into his upper arm. "If he lives, I swear to God I'm going to kick his ass from here to Fort Ticonderoga."

XVI

They were at the scene all day: him and Hadley, Eric and Noble, and four state CSI technicians. Two mortuary vans arrived for the dead gang members and the body of the Children and Family Services caseworker. An assistant DA and a plainclothes investigator from the NYSPD were checking out whether the chief and MacAuley had fired their guns lawfully at the gangbangers. They made Hadley talk to the suit; the rest of the MKPD had bad feelings about state investigators. Emergency counselors from CFS were teary-eyed over the death of their colleague. Relatives came to claim the kids. By phone, an agent from the First District Anti-Gang Task Force and the mayor reminded them they were all eligible for free mental health services after traumatic events. They made Hadley talk to the mayor, too; she had lived in California for fifteen years, and Californians believed in that sort of stuff.

The deputy chief kept them updated with calls to Kevin's cell phone. "He's gone into surgery." That was good. "His heart stopped again." That was bad. "He survived surgery." Hadley and Noble thought that was good. Eric thought it was pretty thin gruel. "Survived?" Eric said. "What's that, the minimal?

Like batting .100?"

Kevin didn't say much. Thinking about the chief dying made him feel sick to his stomach. His head was stuffed with death: the sprawled and bloody bodies of the Punta Diablo gang members, the slack-mouthed corpse of the CFS woman, and the mutilated remains of Amado Esfuentes. He couldn't seem to stop tears from rolling down his cheeks at odd moments. One of the staties made a crack, but Eric McCrea dragged him aside and said something to shut him up.

Eventually, they finished. One after another, the counselors and investigators and technicians and morticians rolled away down the drive, until it was only the MKPD and it was time to go.

"Get in the car," Hadley called from behind the wheel of her cruiser.

He was standing in the spot where his squad car had been. "MacAuley took your unit," she went on. "For God's sake, let's get out of here and get something to eat. I'm starving."

He got in. He wasn't sure he could eat anything. He looked out the window while she drove, the green fields, purpled with loosestrife and thistles, the indigo mountains standing against the long western rays of the sun. It didn't seem right, that everything went on, beautiful and oblivious, while people who had been alive this morning lay on cold slabs this evening.

"What was the last word from the dep?" Hadley's voice was quiet.

"He's on a ventilator. He hasn't regained consciousness."

Hadley worried her lower lip. On another occasion, he would've thought it was hot. "Sometimes, that's good," she said. "You know. Like a healing sleep."

"Yeah."

They both watched the countryside unfold as they rolled up and down the Cossayuharie hills. Suddenly, she said, "You got anything to eat at your place, Flynn?"

"Uh . . . yeah. Frozen meals. Leftover pizza."

"Good. Give me directions." She looked over at him. His confusion must have been plain. "I just . . . I can't face my kids and my granddad yet. And I sure as hell don't want to hang out someplace where anybody can gawk at my uniform." She was right. The word had probably already gotten out. Whoever didn't know about the shooting already would get the news tomorrow, when the *Post-Star* hit the doorstep. "So let's go eat at your place." She glanced at him again.

"You don't live with your parents, do you?"

He wheezed a laugh. "No."

He told her how to reach his duplex in Fort Henry. He had the top half of a Depression-era workingman's house, plain as crockery, but the street was quiet and shady and he had garage space for his Aztek.

"Nice." Hadley parked in front of his space and dropped her rig in her cruiser's lockbox. Upstairs, he showed her the kitchen and excused himself to secure his own gun. "Get changed," she said. "Believe me, if I could get out of this damn outfit, I would."

He locked up his .44 and traded his uniform for baggy shorts and a T-shirt. It felt weird, stripping with her right down the hall in the kitchen. By the time he got back, she'd turned on the oven, found his stash of Miller's amber ale, and unwrapped four packages of frozen stuffed potatoes. "You know," she said, "these aren't that hard to make from scratch. Takes six minutes to nuke a potato."

He held out a T-shirt and a pair of gym shorts. "You want to borrow these? I mean, they'll be big, but the shorts have a drawstring." She stared at the clothes. He felt his face heat up. It had seemed like a good idea in the bedroom.

"Yeah," she said, finally. "I do."

He showed her the bathroom. Got the potatoes in the oven. Tried very hard not to imagine her undressing. Opened a beer. At least he wasn't feeling so stone-cold miserable anymore. It was hard to be depressed and awkward at the same time.

He heard the toilet flush. She was laughing. *Oh, shit.* The bathroom door opened. "Flynn," she said, "you've got the rules of admissible evidence taped to the inside lid of your toilet seat." She laughed some more. "That's about the geekiest thing I've ever seen."

"It was from a long time ago," he protested. "I was studying. I forgot to take it down."

She picked up her beer. His T-shirt hung off her like a beach cover-up. "I bet you put a new topic there every week." She grinned at him. "Maybe I ought to try that with Hudson. He's been having trouble with his fractions." She wandered out the other end of the kitchen, where a table and four chairs divided his small living room from the enclosed porch. "Wow. You have a ton of books. Maybe I should just send Hudson over here. Let you tutor him."

"Sure," he said. "I like kids." He rolled

open the glass door to the porch.

She rested her bottle on one of his bookcases. "That's because you are one."

He picked up her beer. "Come out to the porch. It's cooler."

She sat on the rattan couch that used to be his parents' and he stretched out in an Adirondack chair that had been his oldest brother's shop project. They propped their feet up on the rattan coffee table. The early evening breeze sighed through the screens. They sat in silence, drinking their beers. Hadley studied the beads of condensation rolling down the amber glass.

"I'm going to quit the force," she said.

He stared at her. "What?"

"It hit me, today." She looked at him. "What the chief told me. This isn't like working at an insurance office or a restaurant. This is like signing up for the army. People get killed."

"No officer on the MKPD has died on the job since 1979."

"Thank you, Kevin," she singsonged. Her voice hardened. "That statistic's about to change."

He pushed himself out of his chair. He couldn't sit still and talk about this at the same time. "The chief will be fine."

"We don't know that! Even if he lives, he

548

could be disabled, or have brain damage from his heart stopping so many times, or —"

"Don't. Please, don't." He crossed to one screened-in window, then another.

"I'm sorry." She got up herself, now, and blocked his pacing. "I'm sorry." She looked up at him. "It's different for you. To you, it's still like a kid's game of shoot-'em-up."

"No," he said. "It's not."

She dropped her eyes. "No," she said. "It's not. I'm sorry."

He took a step closer to her. "And for once and for all, I'm not a kid."

"No." She looked up at him again. "You're not."

Then — he had no idea how — she was in his arms and he was hoisting her up, crushing her against him, and they were devouring each other, kissing, biting, sucking all the oxygen out of the room.

"I don't want to be alone tonight," Hadley gasped. "I don't want to be alone."

"No. No."

She hugged her arms and legs around him so tightly she nearly cut off his circulation. "Take me into your bedroom. Now."

"Yes. Oh. Yeah." He staggered down the hallway, and then they were in his room, then they were throwing off their clothes, then they were in his bed, and — oh my God — she was hotter, softer, wetter, sweeter than anything he could have imagined. He almost lost it, trying to touch her everywhere at the same time, but she slowed him down, said, "Here" and "Like this," and, "Oh, yes, that's just right." *Let her show you what she likes,* he had read, so he did. He was good at following directions, damn good, maybe, because she shook and then she clutched at him and then she arched off his bed, her voice strangling in her throat, and he felt amazed and powerful and tender all at the same time. Then she drew him over her and wrapped her legs around him and he *pushed* and everything in the moment must have been written all over his face because she laughed low in his ear and whispered, "In like Flynn."

XVII

There was no place to kneel and pray in the Critical Care Unit. A funny oversight, Clare thought. They had every other type of lifesaving equipment stuffed into the windowless space. They only had one chair, which she and Margy and Janet had rotated between them until Janet had to go home to her kids and her cows and Margy fell asleep on a wide sofa in the CCU waiting room. Clare dragged the chair's footstool to the foot of Russ's high-tech bed and knelt there. A little idolatrous, perhaps, as if she were praying to the long, broken body lying still and pale beneath the blanket.

She knew she ought to pray for God's will, not her own. She knew that bad things were not tests or punishments. She knew God was not a celestial gumball machine, and there was no combination of words or rituals that could force God's awful hand.

But desperation stripped away her knowledge, leaving her praying like a small child. *Please, God, please, please, don't let him die. I'll do anything. Please don't let him die.*

She had stopped in at the church and gotten her traveling kit after returning Sister Lucia to the Rehabilitation Center. The old woman had framed Clare's face between her hands and said, "I will pray without ceasing. For him and for you."

Now, at three in the morning, she anointed Russ with oil. "I lay my hands upon you in the Name of the Father, and of the Son, and of the Holy Spirit," she said, "beseeching our Lord Jesus Christ to sustain you —" It was meant to be an outward and visible sign, but in her slippery fingers it was a talisman, a seal, a dare to God to take him

551

now she had protected him. She would have drenched the room in holy water, hung crosses on his ventilator and saint's medals over his heart monitor if she had thought she could get away with it. Magic. Faith. Her will. God's will.

Please, God, please, please, please. Let him live. . . .

She woke with a start when the day nurse entered. She was sagging off the end of the bed, her arms completely numb, her thighs cramping. She fell off the footstool when she tried to get up.

"Good heavens, Reverend. Fell asleep, did we?" The nurse hauled her to her feet and sent her lurching toward the waiting room. "We need to clear the room for a few," the nurse said. "Why don't we get something to eat and some fresh air in the meantime?"

"Why don't we?" Clare mumbled. She collapsed on a sofa opposite the sleeping Margy and tried to ignore the shooting pain of the circulation coming back into her limbs. She was lined up with the opening to the corridor, and so had a perfect view of Lyle MacAuley getting off the elevator. He had changed into a fresh uniform — she hoped he had burned the other one — but he was red-eyed and haggard from lack of sleep.

"You look terrible," Clare said.

"Not compared to you, I don't." He halted in front of her, like an out-of-gas car rolling to a stop where the road comes level.

"Sit down." She slapped the cushion next to her once, the best she could manage. "The CCU nurse is in there. No visitors right now."

MacAuley collapsed with a groan. He sat, simply sat, for a moment. "Any change?" he finally asked.

"No."

"Hell damn."

"Yeah."

They were silent for a while. She wondered if he was afraid to talk about it, like she was. Afraid that one wrong word, two, and she'd find herself saying *I don't think he's going to make it.*

"What's going on with the case?"

The lines in his face fell into something resembling a smile. "Well, that answers that."

"What?"

"I always did wonder if you were playing with police work because of Russ, or because you're terminally nosy."

"Both," she said. "Plus, it's a lot more interesting than the Mary and Martha's Guild meetings."

"Too damn interesting, these days."

She nodded. It seemed as if she could hear the slow *whoosh . . . whoosh* of the ventilator, breathing for Russ.

"We're pretty sure the Punta Diablos — that's a gang running pot out of New York — are the ones who did Amado. Looks like they left him up on the Muster Field so's we'd run into him sooner and head straight over to the Christies'." His face worked, as if he was chewing on something bitter. "They used us to clear out the dogs and the Christie men, and then went to the farm to get their property."

"The distribution list?"

"Told you about that theory, did he?"

"Yeah."

"Well, we still don't know for sure if that's what they were after. Neither of them can tell us." There was a grim satisfaction in his voice. "Have to sweat it out of the Christies."

"But why Amado? He had no connection to the Christies."

"They came after him, didn't they? And two of 'em got booked for it. Woulda been all over the county jail. You never heard gossip till you heard jailbirds."

"But why would they think a man the Christies hated would know anything?"

"Dunno."

"How did the Christies get hold of the list?"

"Dunno. Yet."

"What's the connection to the bodies behind the Muster Field?"

"Dunno."

"There's a lot you don't know, Deputy Chief."

He sank back farther into the couch. "You got that right, Reverend."

They sat silent again. Across the way, Margy Van Alstyne snored gently. She'd been up until two o'clock or so. Clare hoped she'd sleep on. Asleep, she wasn't eaten up with fear for her only son.

"You might want to go visit Isabel Christie while you're here."

"The sister?" she said.

"Ayeah. When Russ told her about Amado yesterday morning, she was pretty broke up about it."

"Oh, God." Clare exhaled. "So there was something there." She looked down at her clerical blouse. There was dried blood crusted on it. "I don't know if I'm in a fit state to help her."

He rolled his head to one side and looked at her. "Can't think of anyone better."

She gave him a wavering smile. Thought about losing someone you loved. Someone you weren't supposed to love.

"Lyle?"

He grunted.

She took a breath. "Was it true? About you and Linda Van Alstyne?"

He paused for so long she thought he wasn't going to answer. Finally he said, "Yeah."

"Have you talked to Russ about it?"

"Apologized. He wouldn't take it. We've been limpin' along since last January." He swallowed. "After he was shot, he —" He held up one hand and closed it around empty air. "He apologized to me. Called me —" His voice cracked. He snapped his mouth shut, muscles jumping in his jaw. "Friend." His voice was so husky she could barely hear him.

She took his hand and held it tightly, tears filling her eyes. "I know he forgives you. He loves you."

Lyle made a noise. "Jesum." He cleared his throat. "Don't be saying that in public. I'll never live it down." He looked at their hands. "He was thinking of you," he said. "The last thing. He said your name."

She closed her eyes. Hot tears spilled over her cheeks. "We were fighting," she whispered. "Before he got the call about Amado's body. I told him I hated him. Oh, Lyle —"

He reached around and pulled her against his shoulder. "Shh," he said. "Shh. Just what you said to me. He forgave you. He loves you."

"I told him we had to wait," she said between sobs. "I told him it was for him, but it was really for me. I was a coward. I was too afraid of getting hurt again to take the chance, and now — oh, God, that was the only time we had together, and I wasted it! Why? Why did I do that?"

"Shh." Lyle rubbed her back in comforting circles, just like her father would have. "Shh. I don't know why, Reverend. We don't have near enough time on this earth, and what we do have, we fritter away acting like damn fools."

XVIII

She took Lyle's advice and went to see Isabel Christie that afternoon. She found her propped up in bed, her face half hidden by a bandage, the parts that weren't covered up puffy and purpling. Clare introduced herself.

"I never saw a lady priest," Isabel said. Her voice was stuffy, as if she had a head cold.

"I'm not much of a lady," Clare said. *And sometimes not much of a priest, either.*

Isabel eyed her warily, as if Clare might spring onto the bed and forcibly convert her. "Pastor Bob at the Free Will Fellowship used to say that priests were an abomination in the sight of the Lord." Even in her clogged voice, there was a note suggesting Pastor Bob hadn't been her favorite person.

"I bet ol' Pastor Bob said women should submit to men, right?"

"Yeah."

"And that parents that loved their children should chastise them?"

"Uh-huh."

"And that everybody who didn't worship at the Free Will Fellowship was going to roast marshmallows in hell?"

"Especially Catholics." Above her bandage-swathed nose, Isabel's forehead creased with worry. Amado had been a Catholic.

"Well, if Pastor Bob was right, then I probably am an abomination and all that. I say that male and female are equal in the sight of God, that Jesus would never have smacked a little kid, and that God's grace means we're going to be very surprised by who-all gets into heaven."

Isabel stared at the opposite wall, where a

muted television showed the channel 9 news. "I never liked Pastor Bob. After I started developin', he used to hug me." She looked at Clare. "You know?"

"I know."

"There's my house," Isabel said.

Clare looked at the television. It was a distant shot of the Christies' farm from yesterday afternoon, with cops and SWAT team members still walking around. It was replaced by a photo of a smiling middle-aged woman standing on a mountaintop somewhere in the High Peaks. "That's the lady from Children and Families," Isabel said. "She tried to get away." She picked up the remote and switched the volume on as the screen switched back to the farm.

"Millers Kill Chief of Police Russell Van Alstyne is still in critical condition at Washington County Hospital following the high-stakes hostage-taking —"

"My niece Porsche said he saved her life. And her baby's. Scared the heck out of her, though."

"I know." Clare looked away from the TV, where Lyle MacAuley was asking viewers to be on the alert for other members of the Punta Diablo gang. "He's a friend of mine. The police chief."

"Is he gonna be okay?"

"They don't know yet. It's been twenty-four hours since he got out of surgery, and he's still on a ventilator." Doctors clumped around his bedside. Frowns and pursed lips. The discussion falling off when they spotted Margy's pale face.

"I'm sorry," Isabel said. "It's my brothers' fault."

"No." She gestured toward the TV. "You saw the report. They were gangbangers from New York City." Clare paused. Hoped she wasn't about to reopen a wound. "I don't know if this helps, but Deputy Chief MacAuley told me they were also responsible for Amado Esfuentes's death. They were after something, just like at your house, and they thought Amado knew where it was."

Isabel's already inexpressive face became a mask. Her eyes were dry and hollowed out. "One of the cops said he'd been . . ."

"Yes." Isabel deserved the truth. "We who survive like to comfort ourselves by saying 'It was quick' or 'At least he didn't suffer.' It's a hard thing, when we can't believe that."

"Yeah."

"But we do know that whatever happened, whatever he went through, it's over now. And nothing can ever hurt him again." She smiled a little. "I bet Pastor Bob used to preach Revelations."

"Oh, yeah. A lot."

"They shall hunger no more, neither thirst any more; the sun shall not strike them, nor any scorching heat. For the Lamb in the midst of the throne will be their shepherd, and he will guide them to springs of living water; and God will wipe away every tear from their eyes."

Isabel was very still for a moment. "Even Amado's?"

Clare thought of the shy young man, vacuuming one-handedly, polishing the choir stalls, humming to himself when he thought no one could hear. "Especially Amado's," she said.

Isabel leaned back into her pillows. Framed in white, the violet and green on her face stood out in high relief, until she seemed to be made of bruises and tired, flat eyes. "It's our fault. Mine and my brothers'. No, I know" — she held up a hand to stop Clare's objection — "we weren't the ones actually tortured him to death. But we're to blame. All of us." She looked out the window. "Christies stick together," she said. "That's what we had drummed into our heads by our dad. Stick together. Watch out for one another. You wouldn't think something that sounds so good could twist around and hurt so many people."

"Isabel," Clare said, "what we talk about privately stays private. I can't — I won't — repeat anything you say to me. But if you know why those men came to your house and what they were after, please, *please* tell Deputy Chief MacAuley."

Isabel rolled her head toward the window. "I'm tired, now."

Clare stood up. The girl's flat affect worried her. A lot. She dredged one of her cards out of her pocket. "Isabel, I'm leaving you my numbers. If there's anything I can do for you, if you want to talk to me about anything, call me. At any time. Would you do that?"

Isabel made a sound that was something like a laugh. "You think I might kill myself?"

Clare thudded back into the chair. "Are you thinking about it?"

"Suicide's a sin. Don't you know that?" She closed her eyes. "Please go."

Clare got up.

"Wait," Isabel said. "Would you do me a favor?"

"Uh . . . if I can."

"My jeans are in the closet over there. Could you get them for me?"

Clare crossed to the closet. Wondered if a

word to Isabel's nurses would be enough, or if she ought to go straight to the social services caseworker. She handed the jeans to Isabel, who removed a very expensive-looking little cell phone from the front pocket.

"I been carrying this around every day for months," she said. "But I never turned it on. I wonder if there's any battery left."

"Um," Clare said. "Maybe. You may not be able to get a signal in here, though."

"I don't want to use it to call. I just want the address book."

"The address book." The caseworker, she decided. Isabel's voice was too light, too disconnected.

"I have to make arrangements," Isabel said. "For when my brothers get out of jail."

XIX

Hadley left Flynn's duplex before dawn so she could slip into her own bed without the kids — or Granddad — noticing she hadn't been there all night. She kissed him and whispered, "Thank you." He reached for her sleepily, one long bare arm, but she laughed quietly and said, "No. One more time and neither of us will be able to walk."

She wasn't sure she could manage it, even without an extra toss. No wonder the matrons in LA went for younger trade. Eventually, you'd croak from sheer exhaustion, but oh, my God, what a way to go.

She drove the cruiser home, to discover MacAuley had left her a voice mail. She had a mandatory day off, courtesy of her ever-increasing overtime. She supposed it was the best excuse he could come up with. She wondered if Flynn got the same message.

She got an hour's sleep in before Geneva woke her up. She tried to interest the kids in the novelty of a stay-at-home day with Mommy, but Rec Camp was going to Aquaboggin — "With ice cream cones afterward, Mom!" — so she settled for a special breakfast of scrambled eggs before taking them to the middle school. On Barkley Avenue, a glint of red hair made her whip her head around, but it was just the director of the Free Clinic, unlocking the door.

She got back home, dodged Granddad's none-too-subtle remarks about late nights, tossed a load into the washer, and crawled back into bed as soon as he left for St. Alban's. She dreamed; intense, erotic dreams about Flynn's lean body and his hands all over her, and woke up reaching for him, sweaty and aroused. She curled around herself and thought, *It's just sex. It's been a long time. Don't be stupid.* He wasn't even her type. She liked her men edgy and artistic, with long hair and suffering eyes. Not overgrown Eagle Scouts.

She had half a million things to do, but she wound up spending most of the day swinging on the front porch, drinking lemonade and watching bumblebees flit from the peonies to the sunflowers and back again. She called in, once, to get word on the chief. "No change," Harlene said. "Still unconscious, still on a ventilator. But the doctor's real hopeful."

Hopeful of what? That he dies before he wakes up and realizes how bad it is?

She rocked and rocked on the narrow porch, one bare foot braced against the railing, a notebook propped against her thigh. Writing down pros and cons of staying on the force. PROS: Good pay, great benefits, only six weeks more of Basic. CONS: Could die or be disabled (insurance?), no natural ability, ugly uniform. That last was small change, but she thought she ought to put it down, to keep honest.

She wrote *co-workers* under CONS, then thought for a minute and included it under PROS as well. She wrote Flynn's name between the two lists. She added an arrow pointing to the CONS side, then another pointing to PROS. Then another, and another, until his name radiated dozens of sharp-tipped lines in every direction.

She wrote FEAR beneath Flynn's well-armed name. She wrote PUNTA DIABLOS under that. Then HUMVEE/HUMMER? Then 5. She slashed out the 5 and replaced it with 3.

She stared into the heat shimmers rising off Burgoyne Street. Across the way, one of her granddad's elderly neighbors waved. Hadley absently raised a hand.

The crunch of tires rolling into their drive snapped her out of her thoughts. It was an Aztek. *Oh, no.* She glanced into the window behind her before recalling she was alone for now. She held out the hope that he was just returning something she had left behind until he rounded his truck and she saw his face, shining like the sun.

He bounded up the steps, Romeo in baggy shorts and a MILLERS KILL MINUTEMEN T-shirt. He held a small wrapped package in one hand. *Oh, hell, no.* He tossed it onto the swing's cushion and squatted in front of her, crowding the space between the swing and the railing. He grinned, half-pirate, half-moonstruck. "Hi," he said.

Oh, shit. This was going to be like shoot-

566

ing a puppy.

"Hi," she said. "Uh, I see you got the day off, too."

"We're supposed to if we've been involved in a shooting. According to the regs, MacAuley should get a week off while the state investigates, but I guess nobody expected the chief and the deputy chief to both exchange fatal fire with suspects in the same incident." The whole time he was talking like one of her instructors, he was looking at her lips, her neck, her cleavage, as if he were picking which dish on the buffet line he would dig into first.

"Oh," she said.

"Are your kids here?"

"No. Nobody but me until Rec Camp gets out." Wrong answer. Heat flared behind his eyes. Against her will and good sense, her body responded. *Maybe it wouldn't be such a bad idea,* some part of her that wasn't her brain suggested. *Maybe just once — or twice — more?*

"No. No, no, no." She pointed to the empty seat beside her. "Sit."

He scooped up the package and sat down. The swing creaked beneath his weight. "I got this for you," he said. He handed her the paisley-wrapped gift. She took it reluctantly. It was just the right size for a bracelet or a necklace. Heavier, though. He liked books. Oh, my God, maybe it was a collection of love poems.

"You shouldn't have," she said.

He smiled, pleased with her, with himself, with the whole world. "It's not anything."

"No, I mean it. You shouldn't have." She tucked one foot beneath her leg and turned toward him. "Flynn, I think you misunderstood what was going on last night."

"I was there. Believe me, I remember everything that happened." His cheeks reddened. "It was the most —" He shook his head. "*You're* the most amazing thing that's ever happened to me."

"Flynn. Thank you, that's really sweet. But it was just sex. It was" — *achingly good* — "lovely, but it was just sex."

He was shaking his head. "Don't underestimate yourself." He took her hand.

Oh, Christ. This wasn't going to be shooting a puppy. It was going to be slowly hacking it to bits with a rusty saw.

"This can't lead to anything," she said, grasping at the easy way out. "You know what the chief said. Absolutely no fraternizing."

"I've been thinking about that," he said. He brought her hand to his mouth and kissed her knuckles, sending an electric jolt to the base of her spine. "I think if we go to him together and explain our relationship, he'll be okay. He's worried about somebody hassling you, not about two people — you know . . ." He blushed again.

She withdrew her hand. "Flynn. Kevin. Look. We don't have a relationship." She took a deep breath. "Yesterday, the whole thing at the Christie farm was like a horrible nightmare for me. I needed some human warmth and comfort, some . . . proof that I was alive and whole and that there was still something good in the world." She touched his arm. "And you gave that to me. Thank you. It was wonderful. But it's not a relationship, and it's not going to happen again."

He stared at her.

The ice-cream truck tinkled down the street, spilling calliope ragtime in its wake.

"I don't —" He stopped. Inhaled. "Okay. Wait. How do you feel about me? Now?"

"I — uh, like you. You're a nice guy. I thought you were a nice guy before."

He looked at her, baffled and desperate. "I'm a *nice guy*? But we made love! It was transcendent! It was passionate! It was — it was *everything!*"

She closed her mind to the images his words conjured up. She did not want a

569

relationship with this young man. "It was sex, Flynn." She forced a smile. "You can't fall in love every time you have sex."

His face changed. Flattened, maybe. His eyes took on a trapped expression.

"Flynn?" A dreadful possibility wormed into her brain. "You weren't — you *have* had sex before. Right?"

He sat there, silent.

"Oh, shit." She slapped her hand over her forehead. "Don't tell me you were a *virgin.* Oh, my God."

"You don't have to say it like that."

"A twenty-four-year-old virgin. I didn't think it was possible." She looked at him. "Wait. If you were a virgin, how come you had condoms?"

His face was bright red. "I'm inexperienced, not hopeless."

"Oh, my God." She stood up. "Okay, that explains everything. You're not in love, Flynn, you're just pussy-struck. Get up." She tugged at his T-shirt and he stood. "Go home and take a cold shower. This weekend, go out to a club, pick up a girl your own age, take her home and everything you did to me? Do it to her. I promise you, she'll follow you anywhere and want to have your babies." Her voice sounded brittle and shrill in her own ears. She shut up.

His handsome, open face was stiff. "I'll go home," he said. "But I'm not picking up a girl my own age because I don't want a girl my own age. I want you. And I may not know much about sex, but I know how I feel, and I don't try to lie about it or cover it up or ignore it because it doesn't happen to coincide with some sort of preprogrammed image I've got in my head." He turned away. Thudded down the steps to the walkway. Turned around. Came back up four steps. "If you're still thinking about quitting the force, don't. You're a good cop, and we need you." He turned. Went down the steps again. Stopped. Turned around and came back up three steps. "I love you." He stomped down to the walkway and was pulling out of the drive before she could begin to think of what to say to that.

She climbed back onto the swing, crisscrossing her feet beneath her. She stared at her half-empty glass of lemonade. The notebook. The package. She picked it up and ripped the paisley paper off.

FRACTION FLASH FOR FOURTH GRADE, the box said. *Help your child master fractions in a flash!*

She tipped her head back. Struck the porch rail with her heel and set herself rocking. *Oh, Flynn.* She held the flash cards tight against her chest. *What am I going to do about you?*

XX

Just before leaving to pick up the kids, she looked at her lists again. Read over the notes. Thought about what Flynn had said, not today, but way back. About putting on the suit. Becoming The Man. She went into the kitchen and called the station again. She waited while Harlene bellowed for Lyle to pick up the extension. She wondered if he was sitting in the chief's office, at the chief's desk.

"There's no change," he said.

"It's not about the chief," she said. "It's about the Punta Diablo guys. The ones at the Christies."

"What about 'em?"

"They didn't have a vehicle there. Did we pull any prints from the CFS caseworker's car?"

"No-o-o."

"So they must have been dropped off. By their friends in the Hummer."

"Don't worry. There's a warrant out for that car, and a BOLO on all the guys we think are linked to Punta Diablo. The First District AGTF is looking for 'em down in the city."

"Did the Christie brothers give up the list?"

"They lawyered up. Wouldn't say anything except they didn't know nothin'." He paused. "Neil's still in county lockup, though. He'll be there until he gets his hearing on assaulting an officer. Maybe we can cultivate a snitch." MacAuley's voice had taken on the considering tone she'd heard him use when he and the chief bounced ideas back and forth.

"It was just a thought, and maybe I'm off base, but as long as that list is somewhere up here, won't the Punta Diablos be around looking for it?"

MacAuley's voice was grim. "That's what I'm afraid of."

XXI

The congregation was standing to hear Elizabeth de Groot read the Gospel when the teenager walked into St. Alban's.

"And he called to him the twelve, and began to send them out two by two, and gave them authority over the unclean spirits."

The great double doors were open to a dazzling patch of sunshine, and just inside the sanctuary, a man-high industrial-

573

strength fan oscillated north to south and back again. Clare, trying to focus on the reading, almost missed her in the movement and glare.

"He charged them to take nothing for their journey except a staff: no bread, no bag, no money in their belts."

The girl halted, glanced around, clearly unsure of what to do. Frank Williamson, one of today's two greeters, went over to her.

"But to wear sandals and not put on two tunics."

She said something to him. He nodded. Gestured toward one of the rear pews. The girl gazed about, wide-eyed, taking in the altar, the flowers, Clare, standing before the bishop's chair. She said something else to Frank, then turned and walked back into the square of light dividing St. Alban's from the outside world.

"And he said to them, 'Where you enter a house, stay there until you leave the place.' "

Frank Williamson walked up the north aisle in shining leather shoes that never made a sound. Clare watched him, dread squatting like a toad in the pit of her belly. It had been four and a half days since Russ came out of surgery, and he was still in a profoundly unconscious state no one wanted to call a coma.

" 'And if any place will not receive you, and they refuse to hear you, when you leave, shake off the dust that is on your feet for a testimony against them.' "

Frank disappeared around the side of the organ. A moment later he reappeared, quiet, self-effacing, headed back to his post.

"So they went out, and preached that men should repent."

Betsy Young rose smoothly from her bench. She glided across the choir, crisp in red cassock and white surplice, bowing before the crucifix at the high altar. She stopped next to Clare.

"And they cast out many demons, and anointed with oil many that were sick, and healed them."

"Russ Van Alstyne's niece brought you a message," the music director said in a low voice. "He's woken up and he's responding to stimulus."

"The Gospel of the Lord," Elizabeth concluded.

"Praise to you, Lord Christ." Clare's whisper was lost in the congregation's response.

XXII

The CCU waiting room was wall-to-wall by the time Clare got there. She was trailed by Mrs. Marshall and Norm Madsen and Dr. Anne, who squeezed in with Janet and Mike, their three daughters and Roxanne Lunt — "You know we're both on the board of the Historical Society, don't you? I don't know what we'd do without him." Margy Van Alstyne's cousin Nane, several elderly Miss and Mrs. Bains, his high-school friends Wayne and Mindy Stoner. Jim Cameron and his wife, Lena — although Janet whispered, "He's just here to see if they're going to have to pay out on Russ's short-term disability insurance." Noble Entwhistle and Paul Urquhart, and Harlene Lendrum, escorting a potato-faced man with the biggest, hairiest ears Clare had ever seen. "Have you met my husband, Harold?"

Eventually, Margy Van Alstyne came into the waiting room, looking as if she, and not her son, had returned from the dead. People straightened, stood, smiled as she glanced from face to face, looking for the next visitor to be allowed in the CCU. Her eyes came to rest on Clare. "There you are," she said. "Don't just stand there. He's been asking for you."

"Wantin' to confess his sins, no doubt,"

Harlene said.

Clare could feel her face heating up as she threaded her way through the crowd, but the smiles around her were generous, whole-hearted. If she was destined to play out her life center stage in a small town, at least she had a forgiving audience.

The room seemed larger without the ventilator apparatus. Russ still had an IV running into one arm, but his nasogastric tube was gone. He was pale, with deep purple shadows beneath tired eyes. Bits of adhesive stuck to his five-day beard, and his hair badly needed washing.

She stood at his bedside, so full she couldn't speak.

"Hi," he said. His voice was weak, raspy.

"Hi," she said. She smiled. Brushed his forehead. Touched his cheek. "I thought you'd left me."

"No."

"You scared the crap out of me."

He smiled faintly. "Turnabout . . ."

"I'm sorry. I'm so sorry for those horrible things I said to you. I didn't mean it. Not any of it."

"Liar."

She laughed a laugh that was very close to a sob. "All right, I meant some of it. But not that I hated you. I love you. I've loved you from the very start. I will always love you."

"I know." He inhaled slowly, as if it hurt to breathe. "I knew."

"Let's not ever fight again."

He closed his eyes, still smiling. "Fat chance." He shifted, a small movement, and his lips went white.

"You're in pain. Let me get the nurse."

"Not yet." He opened his eyes again. Held up one hand, taped and tubed and bruised.

She took it, gingerly. "Holding on."

He squeezed. "Not letting go."

XXIII

Clare ran into Hadley Knox when she went for coffee. She had kept to her five-minute limit in Russ's room, turning her spot over to the Stoners, then huddled with Margy, who gave her the doctors' latest prognosis.

She didn't expect another chance to see him — that would be selfish, considering how many were waiting to go into the CCU — but she wanted to hang around, to talk with other people who cared for him, to see her relief and happiness reflected in other eyes.

But happy or not, she needed her caffeine fix. Apparently, Hadley did, too. She was standing in front of the lobby coffee-tea-hot chocolate dispenser as Clare walked by. "Don't do it," Clare said.

Hadley looked up. "What?"

"That stuff is to real coffee as Cheez Whiz is to good English cheddar. Come to the cafeteria with me, they have a couple of decent grinds down there."

Hadley fell into step with her. "Have you seen the chief yet?"

"Yep."

"How's he doing?"

"He looks like hell."

Hadley laughed. "Then why are you grinning like that?"

"Because it feels like Christmas and Easter rolled into one?" Clare pushed the cafeteria door open. "He is risen, he is risen," she sang. "Tell it out with joyful voice!" She dropped back into normal speech. "Actually, it'll be some time before he rises. The doctors say he's facing a long period of recovery and rehab. But," she stressed, "he shows no sign of brain damage. And the bullets missed his spine, so he should recover all normal physical functions."

"All normal physical functions."

"Yep."

Hadley's lips twitched. Clare led her to the coffee urns. She found herself humming, "The Day of Resurrection," as she loaded her Sumatran Dark with sugar.

"Can I ask you a question?" Hadley snapped a thermal top over her milkless, sugarless cup.

"You sure can."

"You're a — I'm not trying to get personal here, but there's a pretty big age difference between you and the chief, isn't there?"

"Thirteen or fourteen years. I guess some people would call that a pretty big difference." She blew across the top of her coffee. "My parents would." It hit her, then. Sooner or later, Mother and Daddy would have to meet Russ. Ugh.

"Doesn't it bother you?"

"What, that he remembers the Beatles and I don't? Not particularly."

Hadley frowned. Clare set her cup down next to the napkin dispenser. This wasn't just curiosity. For some reason, Clare's answer was important to Hadley. "Okay. Seriously." She thought for a moment. "I wish I could have known him when he was young. To see who he was then. And I wish I hadn't missed so many of the events that shaped his life. I turned five during his tour of duty in Vietnam. That's . . . a little daunting. But for the rest of it?" She smiled. "We have so many differences that have nothing to do with age that I don't spend much time thinking about it."

Hadley pulled a plastic stirrer from the rack and began to fold it into small pieces. "But what about the future? Don't you worry you'll be, you know, turned off when he gets old and saggy?"

Clare laughed. "Hadley, we all get old and saggy sooner or later." She sobered. "If we live that long." A possible reason for this odd line of questioning popped into her head. "Have you — are you and Lyle —"

"No! Oh, my God, he's older than my father. Oh, yech. Besides which he's, like, my boss. Double yech." She patted her pockets. "Let's pay for these and get back. I'm sorry. Sometimes my curiosity gets the best of me."

"Sounds like a good trait for a police officer." Clare handed the cashier a five. "This one's on me."

"Thanks."

"Can I ask *you* something?"

"Not if it's about Lyle MacAuley." Hadley shuddered.

Clare took her change and gestured toward the door. "The vestry's agreed to pay for the mortuary expenses and the cost of returning Amado Esfuentes's body to Mexico." After considerable arm twisting.

"Kilmer's Funeral Home can take care of everything, but I need to know his next of kin and how to contact them. Do you guys have that?"

"No. We didn't take it when we questioned him. There're a stack of official forms that need to be filled out, but we haven't tackled them yet."

"Would you come with me to the Mc-Geochs, then? Tomorrow? I want to ask his friends if they want a memorial service here, but I don't speak Spanish." She held the door open and sprinkled a little sugar in her voice. "We could both get the information we need."

"I'm on patrol tomorrow."

"After work? Or lunchtime?"

Hadley sighed. "Okay. Lunch."

"Thanks." Clare winked. "I promise I won't tell Lyle about your mad crush."

"Oh, my God! Reverend Clare!"

XXIV

This time, Clare arranged the visit with the McGeochs first. "Oh, yes, please." Janet flapped the stack of forms she'd gotten from the financial office. "I know they've all been sick with worry and grief, but I've been so caught up with everything going on here" — she waved at the CCU waiting room —

"I haven't had a chance to think about what the men might want to do. I'll talk with Octavio. He'll have them ready for you."

When she pulled into the deserted barnyard the next day, Clare realized she should have asked *where* he'd have them ready. The noonday heat buffeted her when she got out of the car, making her converted-to-clericals sundress — a loose linen shift falling from dog collar to ankles — feel like a burka. She retrieved a sack of deli sandwiches and a small cooler of drinks from her backseat. Shut the door. Turned at the sound of tires and saw Hadley's squad car swinging into the barnyard. Dust tumbled behind her wheels as she rolled to a stop next to Clare.

"I don't suppose the barn is air-conditioned," Hadley said, by way of a greeting.

" 'Fraid not."

"Here, let me take one of those." Hadley hoisted the cooler. "You brought lunch?"

"I didn't want anyone to miss out because of the meeting." Clare took a step away from Hadley. "*¡Hola!*" she shouted. "Octavio?"

There was a faint sound of voices in response. "That way." Hadley pointed. They headed for the far side of the barn. "God, it's hot. I don't remember it being this warm when I summered here as a kid."

"You weren't in a uniform and boots when you were a kid."

"Yeah" — she sounded disgruntled — "well. . . ."

They rounded the corner. The men sat at the far end of the barn, in the double shade of its three stories and its silo. Behind them, a two-rut lane ran past a cornfield and disappeared down a slope toward the old farmhouse. Clare could see its roof, floating above the sheaves.

"Hola." The workers were clustered in a ragged semicircle, bagged lunches spread out on the lush grass. Clare set her offering in the middle and plopped down, facing them. Decided the coolness of the spot made up for the smell of manure pervading the air. Hadley opened the cooler, took out a bottle of water, and lowered herself carefully, wrestling the bits and pieces of her gun belt out of her way.

"Go ahead," she said, twisting the top off the water. "You talk, I'll translate."

Clare took a deep breath. "Amado's death is a great loss," she began.

One of the men cut her off with a sharply worded question. Hadley answered him. He said something else, angry, accusing. Hadley replied at length, measuring out her words, her voice patient.

It was Octavio, Clare realized. The foreman. She had noticed his resemblance to Amado the first time she met him. Had thought then they might be related. "What's going on?" she asked Hadley.

"He wants to know what's happening with the investigation. How come we haven't caught Amado's killers yet."

"Ask him if he's one of Amado's family."

"*¿Sois parientes?*" Hadley said.

"*¿Emparentado? ¿Emparentado?*" He sprang to his feet. "*Yo soy Amado Esfuentes. Mí.*"

What in the world?

Hadley's mouth opened. "He says —"

"I got that. Who was my Amado, then?"

Octavio — the real Amado — didn't need that translated. "*Mi hermano. Mi hermano, Octavio.*"

"Brothers," Hadley said, before rattling off another question. Amado's face twisted as he answered her. He spread his hands. His tone, his pain, translated for him. *I thought I was doing the right thing.*

"He was the one with the employment papers," Hadley said. "He swapped them with his little brother the night of the accident, so Amado — Octavio — wouldn't be deported."

"Oh, dear Lord." She had been there, just where Amado was, eating the bitter fruit of good intentions. It was a meal that lodged in your throat and never went away. *"Lo siento, Amado.* I am so, so sorry."

Hadley asked him a question. Clare caught the words *"Punta Diablos."* Amado frowned. Said something. Clare caught the word "Christies." Hadley replied to him.

"What?" Clare asked.

"I'm trying to find out if he knew why the Punta Diablos were interested in his brother. He's confused. He was under the impression the Christies killed Amado — Octavio. Damn, I'm never going to keep the names straight."

"Nobody told them?"

"We had other things going on!"

"What about Isabel Christie?" Clare wondered. "Did she —"

Amado tensed. *"¿Isobel?"*

She had said to Russ, *He can't say boo to a woman.* She had said to Lyle, *So there was something there.* Clare met Amado's dark eyes. "You." She pointed to him. "It was *you* and Isabel."

His gaze shifted away. He glanced at the men sitting around them, their faces divided between worry and interest. Hadley stood. "Amado," she began. Clare got to her feet as well, wishing like hell her languages weren't limited to written Greek and Hebrew. With dictionaries by her side.

She was good at reading faces, though. As Hadley spoke, Amado's altered, from stony to pained, to horrified. He was hearing how his brother died. Clare laid her hand on Hadley's arm. "Go easy," she said.

"I want him to understand what's at stake. There are more of those guys out there. If he knows *anything,* we have to have it."

Amado straightened. He looked at the sky, the blue leached away in the heat of the sun. He looked at the other men. He looked at Hadley. "Come." He turned and strode toward the bunkhouse.

"What?" Clare said, hurrying to catch up.

"I don't know." Hadley hustled after her. The grass in the lane was brittle, the strawflowers and Queen Anne's lace already dry. The corn was stunted, with dull, cracked leaves.

"Tell him what I say, okay?" Clare lengthened her stride. "Amado. I met Isabel in the hospital. Did you know she had been wounded?"

Hadley spoke. Amado stumbled. Glanced over his shoulder at her. Resumed walking. "She is okay?"

"She was released on Friday." She paused,

just long enough for Hadley to translate. "She thinks you're dead. It hit her hard. Very hard." She thought of the young woman's blank face while Hadley spoke and Amado replied in a low voice. The sense that Isabel had gone beyond caring.

"He says it's just as well." Hadley skip-hopped to keep up with them. They crested the rise. Below them, a thread of water trickled across the lane through a stony streambed. The bunkhouse baked in the sun beside it. "He says she's not for him and he's not for her. I dunno. Maybe she spun a romance out of a few meaningful glances?"

"I don't think so." Clare plunged forward and grabbed Amado's arm before he could enter the old farmhouse. Tugged him around to face her. She touched the silver cross hanging beneath her collar. Hoped the black and white would have an effect on him, even if she was an Anglican woman, and not a Roman man. "What if she's pregnant?"

Hadley copied her authoritarian tone.

Amado's mouth opened. "*¿Embarazada?*" He looked terrified and hopeful.

"Oh-ho," Hadley said. "You nailed that one on the head."

"Tell him I don't know. But he needs to come with me and let her see he's still alive.

588

If he wants to break it off with her after that, fine."

He smoothed over his initial shock and listened to Hadley's translation with an impassive face. He looked at Clare. She stared back. "Okay," he finally said. "I go with you. For good-bye." He nodded stiffly and disappeared into the bunkhouse.

"Huh." Hadley propped her hand on her hip and fanned her face. "Methinks the lady doth protest too much. Or the man, in this case."

"I'm not trying to play Cupid. I was worried enough about Isabel's state of mind to put in a word with the hospital counseling folks. She blames herself for Amado's death — Octavio's death. You know what I mean. I think seeing him alive and well will let her forgive herself for accidentally setting her brothers on him. On his brother." She batted away a buzzing fly. "Whatever."

"Speaking of brothers, have you considered they might not be too thrilled if you bring yet another Latino guy to their farm?"

"I'll burn that bridge when I come to it."

"Don't you mean —" The sun-blistered door creaked open. Amado stepped out.

"Here." He thrust something at Hadley. *"Esto es lo qué deséo el Punta Diablos."* He sounded like a soldier at last laying down his arms.

Hadley stared at the black-and-white composition book in her hands. She flipped it open. Ran one finger down a handwritten page. "Holy shit." She looked up at Clare. "The chief was right. It's the distribution list."

XXV

Clare eased her car up the Christies' drive like a woman easing her way into the haunted house at the county fair. She knew there was nothing to be afraid of. But the sights, the smells, her sense of what-might-have-happened made her heart pound as she parked on the dusty grass and approached the porch steps.

Amado was an indistinct figure in her Subaru, waiting behind tinted windows. She had left the engine running, as much for a quick getaway as for the air-conditioning. She was lucky she had him with her — Hadley had been all for dragging him back to the station for formal questioning. Amado dug in his heels, saying only that he had found the notebook nearby and that he'd tell the police everything he knew after he had seen Isabel. Hadley had been torn between accompanying him and Clare and delivering the list to the station — so torn she had shifted back and forth, back and forth, on the balls of her feet, poised at her cruiser's door.

"I promise," Clare said. "I'll bring him in to you as soon as we're done at the Christie place." Which would also give her time to call Sister Lucia and set her to find a Spanish-speaking lawyer. Russ would have never gone for it, but Hadley, flushed with triumph, her fingers leaving damp prints all over the MKPD's biggest haul of the year, was an easier touch.

Now, approaching the weathered mahogany door she had last seen flung open for cops and EMTs, she wondered if it might not have been a better idea to wait, to have come up here after he was questioned, with Hadley and Kevin Flynn and maybe even Lyle MacAuley in tow. Too late now.

"Fly or die," she said to herself, pressing the bell.

The shirred curtains in the window shivered. The door opened a handbreadth. A thin teenaged girl peered out. "Yeah?"

It wasn't what Clare had been bracing for. "Um. I would like to see Isabel."

"How come?"

"I'm Clare Fergusson. I" — the specter of Pastor Bob caused a midcourse correction

— "am the chaplain who spoke with Isabel at the hospital. I wanted to see how she was doing."

"She's fine." The door swung.

Clare stuck her foot in the jamb. "I'd like to hear that from her."

"You can't." The girl pushed the door a few times, but Clare's lug-soled sandal didn't move.

"Are you Porsche?" The girl looked more like a Chevy Nova, but Clare hadn't named her.

"Yeah."

"Porsche, your aunt told me that Christies stick together. That you help each other. Is that true?"

"Yeah."

"Then please let me speak to her. I promise you, you'll be helping her."

The girl looked at Clare's foot. She released the door, letting it drift open. "She's not here. I'm" — she checked behind her, as if someone might overhear — "worried about her. Dad and Uncle Bruce and Uncle Neil took the van and drove off, and as soon as they were gone, Izzy was on the phone with somebody. Then the next thing I know, this chrome-flap Hummer pulls in the yard and Izzy's out the door."

"And that worried you because — ?"

"There were Mexicans in it! I almost went and grabbed a gun, 'cause Dad said we ever see another Mexican on our land, we better shoot to kill!"

"But she went with them? Voluntarily?" Could they be some of Janet's men? No. That made no sense. There was only one group of Latinos interested in the Christies. "When was this?"

"Just a bit before you showed up. That's why I was being so careful and all."

"Do you know which way they went?"

Porsche stepped onto the porch. She leaned over the railing and pointed to where the open pasture rose into a stretch of woods. It was just visible in the gap between house and barn. "Up that way. There's a sort of a road up into the mountain, leads to the high meadows. Same way Dad and the others went."

"They're *all* up there? Together?" *Jesus wept! This mental midget is who Russ almost died for?* Clare passed her hand over her face. That was unworthy. "Porsche." She tried to project patience. "Do you have a phone I could use?"

XXVI

"Chief? You awake?"

"Mmm? C'mon in, Kevin." He opened his eyes. He'd been drifting, not dozing, wrapped in a warm Percocet-flavored cloud. He wanted to dial down the dosage this morning, to take back some small measure of control over his life, but by the time the nurse got around to him, he needed those two little pills rattling around in the plastic cup more than he wanted any sort of self-sufficiency.

Kevin's face came into view. "Hey." The kid smiled down at him like a proud dad looking over a newborn. Which, until he got the okay to get up to pee, wasn't too far off the mark. "Wow. It's sure great to see you."

None of the hospital staff had told him, yet, how close he had come to checking out. The heart surgeon and the orthopedic surgeon and the internist had gone over the technical aspects; *right lung, pericardium, hip joint;* the bottom line was he was going to be lying here, hurting, for a long time. After that, he'd be in rehab, hurting, for another long time. But no one said, *You nearly died.* He was learning that from his visitors' faces.

"Not as great as it is to see you," he said, getting a laugh. "What's happening at the station?" Kevin obliged his weak lungs by taking over the conversation at that point, rattling on in his usual Energizer Bunny way, allowing Russ to float in and out of awareness, until he connected the words *twenty-two* and *ballistics test* and *confirmation.* "What?" he said. "Go back."

"The ballistics test matched up one of the Christies' twenty-twos with the bullet that killed John Doe number one."

"We didn't have a warrant for their twenty-twos."

"Since there were multiple shootings from several firearms in the incident where you . . . you . . ."

"Got shot."

". . . the state required ballistics tests on all possible weapons. MacAuley figured that ought to include all the available guns in the Christie house."

"Did he, now?" It hurt to smile, but in a good way.

"Well, as he said, how did we know the Punta Diablo guys didn't use one of the Christie guns and then replace it? Of course, there's no way of telling who might've used it, but it gives us something to hang our hats on." That last phrase was pure Lyle.

There was a knock at the door. Kevin turned, and from his prone position in the bed, Russ could see the slice of his face where his smile cut out.

"Oh," the kid said. "Hi."

"Am I interrupting?" Russ could hear Hadley but not see her.

"No, I was just —"

"Because I can —"

Russ hoisted one hand to a ninety-degree angle with the bed. His exercise for the day. "I think I can stand the excitement of both of you."

"I don't know if you can stand this excitement." Hadley replaced Kevin at the bedside rail. "Look at this." She dangled an 11-by-14-inch evidence bag over his bed. It contained a kid's composition book. "I know I should've taken it straight in, but I wanted you to see it before it goes to CADEA."

Kevin got it first. "Is this it?" He leaned over her shoulder. "The dealer list?"

Hadley looked at him, lit up like the Fourth of July. "It is."

"Oh, man. CADEA will be shining their noses on our backsides for this." Kevin grinned at her. They bumped fists together, something Russ would look like an ass doing; then there was a confusion of looking down and stumbling around, and next thing Russ knew the notebook had dropped onto his bed and his two youngest officers were a good five feet apart, so he had to crane his neck to see both of them. Hadley launched into an account of how the thing came into her hands, word-spinning as much as Kevin was prone to do. The part about Amado-Octavio-Amado clicked for him — *that* was why the boy had been so nervous during questioning — and he brushed past her apologies for handling the notebook without gloves on — "I didn't have them in my pocket, Chief, because I was just there to translate." He threw the brakes on when she said she let Amado — the real Amado — go. After he'd just proven he'd been in possession of the Punta Diablo's distribution list.

"I thought it would be okay, Chief. Reverend Clare promised to bring him to the station after they'd spoken to Isabel Christie."

Clare. Godamighty. He was going to have to get out of this hospital a lot faster than predicted, or she'd be running the damn force.

Kevin's phone rang. "Sorry." He checked the number. Flipped it open. "Kevin here." *Harlene,* he mouthed. "No, I'm visiting the chief." Hadley shut up. "What?" Kevin said. He glanced at her. "Yeah. I will. Hadley's right here with me, I'll tell her."

He closed the phone. Looked at Hadley. "Reverend Clare called from the Christies'. A group of Latinos in a Hummer just picked up the sister and went up the mountain after the brothers. We gotta hurry. She said" — he looked at Russ for the first time, as if he just remembered he was lying there — "she's going up after them."

XXVII

Branches twisted and whipped at the windshield. Clare gripped the steering wheel and eased off the acceleration as her Subaru humped over another kidney-jarring tree root. How far did this goat path go? How far did they dare drive? The last thing she wanted to do was burst onto the scene like a clown car driving into a circus ring. "Amado . . . ?"

He leaned forward in the passenger seat as if the extra inches would help him see their destination. "Isobel," he said, in an unarguable voice. "We go help."

From the moment she had conveyed, in Spanglish and sign, who Isabel Christie was with, Amado had been dead set on following her. She couldn't let him go alone, she argued to a mental tribunal consisting of her bishop and Russ. It wouldn't have been —

Consistent was the bishop's word.

Stupid enough, Russ said.

"Stop." Amado raised his hand. She braked, pitching them forward. "I think . . . close." She inched the car as far off the trail as she dared and killed the engine.

Amado opened his door. "You stay!" Shades of Russ. God, she wished he were here.

"Sorry, no." She stepped out, latching her door with a click. The decaying leaves beneath her sandals had been compacted into two tire tracks leading upward, disappearing from view as the old road twisted behind a clump of beech trees. Amado frowned but waited for her to catch up. He gestured, hand flowing over the ground, finger to his lips. *Slowly. Silently.* She nodded.

She toiled upward, through shafts of sunlight and patches of shade, listening for a sound other than the song of warblers and the cry of jays. A decayed stone wall, tumbled by frost heaves and oak roots, showed the overgrown track had once been a real road. She spotted small, burly apple trees among the maples and red spruce; an orchard overgrown centuries ago, or the accidental fruit of farm boys playing Apple Core.

Apple Core!
Baltimore!
Who's your friend?

She heard a sound. She and Amado both stopped. It came again, muffled by leaves and misdirected as it bounced from hardwood to hardwood. Voices. Men.

And then a shot.

She hiked her skirt and ran. For a dozen strides, maybe two, Amado outpaced her, but the Guard didn't give pilots a pass on PT, and her conditioning kept her moving, churning up the leaf-spumed road, reaching Amado, drawing past him, leaving him behind.

The voices were louder, even over her sawing breath and pounding heart. No more shots, thank God. The road curved past a chunk of bedrock granite and she made the amateur mistake of rounding it at top speed, only to see the trees peter out, a sunlit meadow, a barn, a white van, a Humvee.

She threw herself behind the nearest maple with enough force to jar the air out of her lungs. *Try not to be dumb, Fergusson,* Hardball Wright said. *You might live longer.*

She dropped to the ground and crawled forward. Between the trees and the open field, a massive rhododendron flourished. She took refuge behind its glossy, impenetrable leaves.

There were three of them, dressed in urban gear so foreign to these woods they might as well have been from another planet. One, half visible around the uphill corner of a pole barn, held a gun pointed toward an unseen opening. Another guarded the downhill side, his weapon steady on a wide second-story door. The third stood at the narrow end of the barn. With Isabel Christie. She was seated on one of many bales scattered near the barn's foundations like cornerstones. Evidently the brothers had been pitching hay when the Punta Diablos arrived.

A flicker of movement in the corner of her eye caught Clare's attention. Amado, leaning against a tree, taking in the scene in the meadow. If he moved a few inches in either direction, he'd be spotted. She gestured for him to join her. He shook his head.

"So where is it?" the third man asked. Clare could just hear him above the insects droning over the field grass. Isabel's answer was indistinct. She got up, walked to the barn wall, and pulled a graying clapboard away from the foundation. The man who had been speaking to her craned forward, his gun drifting down toward his foot, the bad habit of someone who carried a weapon but was never trained to use it.

Isabel's shoulders moved, then moved again. She flattened herself against the narrow opening, as if she could stick her face instead of her hands inside.

"Where is it?" the man demanded.

Isabel whirled around. Said something. Spread her hands wide in bewilderment. Clare heard a moan beside her. She looked away from the drama for a moment. Amado's mouth was a perfect O of despair. And Clare knew, at that moment, what had been hidden that Isabel couldn't find.

He closed his mouth. His face set in lines of terrible determination. Ready to — what? Confess? Lie? What would they do to him to get the truth?

Clare, he was tortured.

Amado stepped out from behind the tree.

"No!" she whispered. She lunged forward, awkward on her hands and knees, and tackled him around the ankles. It was sloppy, but it worked. He went down with a crash into the rhododendron bush, setting a pair of crows cawing into the sky. From near the barn, someone shouted, *"¿Qué es eso?"*

She heard dull thuds, the swish of legs scissoring through tall grass. They had sixty seconds — maybe less. Clare knotted her hands in Amado's shirt and dragged him to her. She pointed to herself. *"I say I have the book. El libro."* She pointed at him. *"You stay with Isabel."* She rolled to her knees. "Wait. Be smart. Um, *inteligente.*" She clambered to her feet and smashed through the bush before her nerve could desert her. The third man was halfway across the field, dragging Isabel behind him, waving his weapon like a machete, a .357 Taurus, just like the one she'd seen in the church kitchen, but holy God, this one looked twice as big, pointed at her.

"Don't shoot!" Clare threw her hands up.

The guy jerked to a stop. "Who the hell are you?" He stared as if her clerical collar and cross were as bizarre as the three studs sprouting from his upper lip. Maybe they were.

She had four heartbeats to figure how to play it. Looked like Isabel had the lock on terrified, and she didn't think the gang-banger would respond to ecclesiastical authority as well as Amado had. That left crazy.

"Hey!" She converted her upraised hands into a cheerful wave. "I'm Reverend Clare! I came to see Isabel!" She smiled wide enough to display her eyeteeth.

The guy's mouth formed the words *What the . . .* then he jerked the .357 up. "Get over here." He had a trace of an accent.

"Isabel, how are you?" Clare sauntered through the timothy and clover, smiling as if Isabel wasn't wide-eyed and trembling, as if there wasn't an enormous gun swinging like a compass needle between them. "Is there anything I can help with?" She hugged the startled girl. The guy opened his mouth again, but before he could order them back to the barn, she said, "Are you looking for the list of distributors? The one that belongs to these gentlemen?"

Isabel gaped at her. Then clicked her mouth shut. She nodded.

"Bitch, you said you had it!" The gangbanger lifted a fist.

Clare flipped one hand up. "I have it." She smiled at him. "Isabel didn't know." She looked into Isabel's eyes, letting her mask fall away. "Amado took it. For safekeeping. He's alive, Isabel. He wants you to be safe."

Isabel's mouth opened. Her eyes filled with tears and a desperate, dawning hope.

The Taurus stopped its movement, finding true north against Clare's rib cage. "How do I know you're telling the truth?"

"It's a hard-covered composition book, black and white. The entries are written in blue ink."

"Shit," he hissed. Clare kept a smile

pasted on her face. Finally, he narrowed his eyes at her. "Where is it?"

Isabel clutched at her arm. Clare squeezed her hand, still smiling at the man. "I'll take you."

He poked the gun into her flesh. "You tell me. I'll go get it."

She shrugged. "It's locked in my office at St. Alban's. I'm afraid one of the seven or eight people working there today would phone the police as soon as they see you going in there." She brightened. "Maybe you can have a car chase through town! Now that would be something for the tourists to talk about." She turned to Isabel. "Do you think that would make people more interested in checking out our church? Or less?"

The faint hope that had lit in Isabel's eyes went out, quenched by Clare's obvious insanity.

"Shut up," the man said. He ran his tongue beneath his lip, frowning in thought. The studs rose and fell like buoys. He gestured with the .357. "Back to the barn." Clare linked arms with Isabel and strolled toward the angular structure. She could feel the gun behind her as if it were still pressed into her skin. If she could just put a little more space between them and the gunman, she could let Isabel know that the police were on their way. That all they had to do was survive for the next half hour.

The man said something in Spanish to his two buddies. One of them asked a question. Their captor answered. The he grabbed Isabel's thin arm, jerking her away from Clare. The girl stumbled and went down. Clare tensed. The Taurus swung back to her.

"You and me will go get this book. She stays here. If I don't come back in an hour, they'll kill her and her brothers. Got that?"

Clare nodded.

"Let's go."

She twisted her head around as she walked back to the entrance to the road. "Be brave, Isabel," she shouted. "Remember Revelation! God will wipe away every tear from their eyes."

Mr. Personality shoved her. She stumbled, trotted forward, righted herself. "Are you a druglord?" She tried to sound like a teeny-bopper meeting a member of the latest boy band.

"What the hell is wrong with you, lady?"

They passed out of the sunlight into the shade of the forest.

"Do I get to keep the ten thousand dollars? You know, as a reward?"

"What? What ten thousand dollars?"

"The money that was with the notebook and the Ta— the gun. It was a big gun, like yours. I wouldn't know what to do with the gun, but I could sure use the money." She kept her voice loud and singsongy, copying a very sweet, very bipolar woman she had met during her clinicals in Washington.

"You got all that? Rosario's stuff?"

"Yep." She needed some way to remove him from the scene. A rock? A tree branch? She stepped over a fragrant pile. Sheep dung? The road was too wide and too clear for her to vanish into the underbrush, too twisting and uneven for her to lead him on a chase. *Pick your ground real carefully,* Hardball Wright said. *It might be the only advantage you've got.*

The car, then.

They rounded a bend and there it was, nose first in a stand of ferns, its rear quarter hanging into the lane, like a cow content to block the road while she grazed. The man circled around the back of the Subaru, pointing the gun toward her as he approached the passenger door. "Get in," he said.

She braced her hands on her hips. "What about my reward money?"

He laughed, a sound like a heat gun stripping paint. "I dunno. That was the rednecks' payment for taking out the garbage. You think you could be a garbageman for us? Take out our trash?"

Oh, God. The bodies in the shallow graves. She ducked her head, fiddled with the handle on the door. She couldn't think about that, couldn't think about Octavio, because if she did, she was going to lose it, and then she'd be just another terrified victim at the wrong end of his gun. She opened the door. Slid into the driver's seat. Keeping her face averted, she busied herself with the seat belt.

He knew fear. He expected it. Her only chance of doing this was keeping him off balance — by giving him something he didn't expect. She clicked the belt into place. He bounced into the seat next to her, sidesaddle, the better to keep the .357 aimed at her midsection.

She thumbed the audio controls from her steering wheel at the same time she fired up the car. Loud music bounced through the interior, cheerful and springy. She threw the transmission into reverse.

"Turn that off!"

"I can't!" she yelled.

He stabbed at the controls. The stereo fell silent. She shifted into PARK and turned the car off. "You crazy bitch." He jabbed the gun into her ribs again. "Go."

"I can't drive without music. Sorry. It's this thing I have."

"What the hell are you talking about?"

"Well, it all started when I went to summer camp in third grade. The bathrooms had these really thin plywood barriers, you know the kind, and you could hear everything that went on there, everybody doing her business, and I found out the first time I tried to go that I just couldn't, not when anyone could hear me, and —"

"Shut up! Shut up!" He punched the power button. "Just drive," he said, almost drowned out by Dar Williams singing.

She started the Subaru up again. Reversed, went forward, reversed, went forward, scribing that perfect sixteen-point turn. *Maybe I can just do this until the MKPD gets here.* But even a narrow road will be navigated. She found herself nose down, rolling through the woods, past the stone walls, past the echoes of the old farm, thinking, *When? Where's my ground? How do I fight?*

He wasn't wearing a seat belt. A stomp on the gas, steer into one of the great old oaks or maples — but could she get enough acceleration before he stopped her? Bashing into a tree at fifteen miles an hour wasn't going to cut it. Beyond the forest, the pasture, descending in a wide bowl to the farm. Then the drive, then the road, then — what? He wouldn't blink if she whizzed down Seven Mile Road at fifty miles an hour, but her goal was to disable him, not kill them both.

Branches tapped the windshield. Dar sang, *I stole a Chevy and I wrapped it round a tree.* She couldn't let him get as far as the town. Collateral damage wasn't in this guy's vocabulary. The thought of what he could do with innocent bystanders around made her stomach churn.

She bumped, slowed down, bumped again. Ahead, the forest opened onto the field. Sheep grazed over the grass. She felt like one of them: woolly-headed. She knew there was an answer. There was always an answer.

The Subaru picked up speed as the road-bed evened up. She was driving, out of time, out of her chance.

The answer fell into her lap. *Fly or die.* They burst out of the woods into a wash of sunlight. The pasture spread out below her. She rammed her foot to the floor, jerking the wheel hard to the left, felt the sick skid, the strap biting into her, the loft as she broke gravity, and over the gangbanger's howl and Dar singing *Alleluia!* the tires left the earth and with a spine-shattering *crunch* they rolled, and rolled, and rolled, and rolled.

XXVIII

Every muscle in his body tensed as Amado watched one of the men force Isobel around the corner of the barn. He couldn't see what was happening there, and he was too far away to stop it even if he could. He inhaled. The lady priest was right, he needed to be smart. The gunman was going to imprison her in the barn.

Unless he was going to rape her. Or kill her.

He waited for a scream. A shot. He didn't realize he was holding his breath until the gunman reappeared, taking up his guard position. He exhaled. She was in the barn, then.

"Hey!" The man yelled in Spanish. "Victor!"

"Yeah?" Victor was the downslope guard.

"You ready?"

"Hell, no. How are we going to do it, anyway? It's a stupid idea. We should just wait until Alejandro gets back."

"I'm not risking him getting mad. I have an idea."

"What, wave your lighter under the barn?

You're full of shit, Ferdo."

"Set the hay bales on fire."

Victor paused. "That might work." He sounded surprised.

Amado waited for a protest, a plea, some movement from the barn. Nothing. Then he shook his head. *Idiot.* The Christies couldn't understand a word. They had no warning. What should he do? How could he save Isobel when there was an open field and two men with guns between them?

Ferdo snagged one bale by its cord and set it on end. He picked up a second and a third, balancing each on its square end. He dug into his pants pocket. "If you see anybody moving in there, shoot them, okay?" A small flame sprang from his fingers. Amado knew it was a lighter, but from this distance, Ferdo looked like a devil summoning fire to torment the damned.

"I've got a better idea." Victor swung his arm up and shot into the wide shadowed rectangle of the second-floor door. Amado heard yells and shouts from the interior. Victor squeezed off another shot.

On the other side of the barn, the tops of all three hay bales were smoking. Small pennants of flame fluttered, danced, then unfurled into sheets of red and orange. Ferdo grabbed one by its lower half and pitched it into the barn. Yells and screams were cut off as Victor put another bullet through the door. Ferdo tossed the second bale in. Then the third.

Victor's gun blasted one more time. "I think that'll do it."

"Should I get my cell phone? To take pictures? Out here in the boonies, who's going to know what they got?"

"Don't worry. Word will get around." Smoke roiled away from the side of the barn where Ferdo had thrown the hay in.

"Should we let the girl out?" Ferdo asked. "We could bang her."

"That cold-blooded bitch? Forget it. I could find a hotter lay in a convent."

"At the end of your right arm, you mean."

"Better than some of the dogs you do."

Over the increasing roar of the fire, Amado heard a distant metallic scrunch, wrench, smash, repeated over and over. He whirled around. Birds twittered and cawed. Nothing moved along the road or among the trees.

"What the hell?" one of the men said.

Amado spun back. This was his chance. He sprinted from the rhododendron bush to the roadway, staying out of sight of the meadow. He cupped his hands around his mouth. *God, make me a mimic.* "Victor! Ferdo!"

"Alejandro? Is that you?"

"Get over here and help me, you stupid sons of whores! She's getting away!" He jogged a few feet down the road and shouted, "She's running toward the farm! She'll call the police! Follow me!" He ran another five yards. "Hurry, you fools! Help me catch her!" He spotted the huge granite stone and dove behind it. Seconds later, Victor and Ferdo thundered past, already panting as if they'd run a mile. For a moment he was tempted to run after them, to smash into their backs and roll them into the dirt, to batter their faces until there was nothing left but blood and bone. *Octavio. Oh, my brother.*

But Octavio was dead. He had to help the living. He rose and ran for the field, for the barn, for Isobel.

XXIX

She opened her eyes. The windshield had cracked into a hundred pieces, diffusing blue and green and white over the airbags, deflating like emptied bladders. She hung upside down from her shoulder strap and seat belt. The roof, the doors, the floor looked like the inside of a tube of toothpaste after a series of good squeezes.

She looked to her right. The gunman was crumpled between the dashboard and the passenger seat. Parts of him were at odd angles, and blood from a gash on his head sheeted over his face. She swallowed. Tried to feel some stirring of compassion, but all she could see was Octavio sitting in that now-empty seat as she told him, *You're safe. Everything's going to be okay.* Another failing to add to her many failures as a priest.

Her door wouldn't unlatch and her window wouldn't roll down. She braced her back against the seat and planted her feet on either side of the steering wheel. She reached down with one hand to support herself against the roof. It took her three tries to unbuckle her belt. When it clicked open, she jammed herself in place, muscles screaming, and hand by foot by foot let herself down.

She inched forward along the inside of the roof and, twisting sideways, kicked out the remains of the windshield. She crawled past the steering wheel, beneath the slab of the car's buckled, battered hood, chunks of safety glass embedding in her palms and catching in her dress. She squirmed through the narrow space between grass and steel and then she was free, rolling onto her back, breathing deep, looking at the dazzling sky arching over her.

Finally she said, "Thank you, God," and staggered to her feet. It felt like she'd been worked over with a lead pipe. Her poor car was totaled. Another one. She lifted her eyes to the hills. *From whence my help cometh.* USAA was going to cancel her. Her parishioners would start calling her the Reverend Stephanie Plum.

She had been staring at a column of smoke for a while before she snapped to and realized it marked the location of the barn. She shuddered. *Call the fire department.* She glanced at the wreckage of her little red Subaru. Her phone was in there, somewhere. Walk down to the house and call? Hike up and tackle the next two bad guys? Lie down and wait for help? That last was appealing. They could send an ambulance for her. Maybe she could get a bed next to Russ.

Damn, I'd like a happy ending for a change. She smiled a little.

Now let's go deal with the unhappy ending.

"Sure. You're flat on your back in the hospital. Easy for you to say." She started back up the slope toward the forest, stepping over the deep gouges her car had scraped into the soil. She was almost to the tree line when a rumble and whine made her turn around. A yellow Aztek was jouncing across the field. It skidded to a stop next to the wreckage of her car. Hadley Knox leaped out.

"Hey!" Clare shouted. "Leave him! Up here! Up here!"

Hadley said something to the driver, then jumped back in. The SUV roared upslope and braked next to Clare. She grabbed the back door handle and hauled herself inside. Kevin Flynn and Hadley were twisted in their seats, staring at her. "Up this road," she said. "Two more of the gang. And something's on fire."

"Shouldn't you wait for the EMTs?" Kevin said. "You look like hell."

"Go," Clare snapped.

"Yes, ma'am," Kevin said, and the Aztek surged forward.

Hadley unhooked the mic from the radio and switched it on. "Harlene, this is Knox, do you copy?"

"I copy you, Hadley."

"Our eighty is a road behind the Christie pasture, heading up the mountain. We have two injured, two reported suspects at large, and a remote fire. Please send Fire and Rescue."

"Copy that. Fire and Rescue on their way."

Kevin motioned for the mic. Hadley

handed it over. "Be advised non-four-wheel-drive vehicles will have very slow going." They hit a root and bounced in their seats, emphasizing Kevin's point.

"Will advise."

Kevin handed the mic back to Hadley. "Knox out — holy shit, Flynn, watch out!" As they came around a bend, the two remaining gang members appeared, stumbling down the rutted road.

Kevin stood on the brakes. Hadley's door was open before they skidded to a stop inches from the wide-eyed pair. She leaped from the vehicle, gun drawn. "Police!" she yelled. "Get down on the ground!"

The men looked as if they wanted to resist but were too winded. They flopped their arms toward their waists, bending over, sucking in air. Kevin jumped out of the Aztek. He and Hadley advanced on the gang-bangers, weapons ready. "Down . . . on . . . the . . . ground!" Hadley shouted. The two men fell onto the dirt. Hadley trained her gun on them while Kevin cuffed them and removed their weapons. He twisted one man's hand up, showing cryptic symbols tattooed on his fingers.

Clare got out. Through the screen of leaves and pine boughs, she could see the black smoke rising. "We need to hurry.

Amado and Isabel Christie are up there with her brothers."

Hadley and Kevin looked at each other. "Plastic strap their ankles," Kevin said. "Leave 'em at the side of the road to be picked up later."

Hadley nodded. Removed a narrow white plastic loop from her belt. In less than a minute, both men were trussed like turkeys and safely out of the path of traffic. Hadley and Kevin climbed back into his truck. "Who's The Man?" Kevin said, starting up the engine. "Who's The Man?"

Hadley made a noncommittal noise.

They ascended the mountain much faster than Clare had in her Subaru. Kevin jounced through gullies and roared over washboard ridges that sent the Aztek airborne, evidently much less worried about his suspension than Clare had been.

They blasted through the forest fringe into an upper meadow obscured by a heavy haze of white smoke. Clare could see fire and a trace of the outline of the barn, but nothing else.

"Careful," she said. "There's a Humvee and a white van around here somewhere."

Kevin inched toward the barn. A noise split the air like the clap of doom, a twisted mix of snapping wood and screaming metal.

"What in God's name was that?" Hadley pulled her gun again.

The barn appeared out of the smoke as they rolled closer: first the outline, still holding against the sheets of flame roaring out the two doorways, then the texture, paint bubbling, wood charring, and finally —

"What the hell?" Kevin hit the brakes. The Humvee Clare had warned them about was backing away from the lower edge of the barn. Its grill was crumpled. One light hung from its socket like an eyeball in a horror comic. As they watched, the Humvee sped forward and rammed into the side of the barn. Burning clapboards toppled onto the hood. "Holy crow. That idiot's going to blow that car up." Kevin backed the Aztek away and turned off the engine. "Come on," he said. "Reverend Clare, stay here."

"You know, everyone always says that to me." She tumbled out of the SUV. The smoke stung her eyes and burned in her throat. She tried to take shallow breaths. "I'm going to find Amado and Isabel."

She didn't wait for a reply. "Amado," she shouted. "Isabel!" She struck out toward the uphill side, coughing, eyes watering. The smoke was everywhere, thick, sweet-smelling, not sooty like a wood fire, not green-scented like hay. Her head spun.

It's pot, you idiot. The barn wasn't for stor-ing hay. Holy God. Her freshman room-mate, who had arrived at UVA with twenty ounces of Acapulco Gold, would have been in heaven. She was stumbling around the world's biggest joint. "Isabel! Amado!" She tottered up the gentle rise, keeping well away from the barn. Chunks of timber were crashing down into the interior. Clapboards peeled away and tumbled to the grass. Sparks showered through the air like dande-lion seeds. They had to get out of here. The forest was dry. If the wind picked up, they could be trapped like animals in one of those Discovery Channel specials.

Where the animals were trapped by fire. Not one where they mated. She giggled. Thought of Russ. Thought of Hadley repeat-ing, *All normal physical functions.* Giggled again. She was laughing when she stumbled up to the edge of an oval fire pond, and there were Amado and Isabel, chest deep in water, cradling an unconscious, bloody man between them while streams of marijuana smoke curled around them.

"Reverend Clare!" Isabel waved. Amado smiled a huge smile. They both looked very, very happy. "He is alive! He really is!"

"Oh, my gracious Lord," Clare said. "It's a big bong."

You are stoned out of your gourd. Shake it off and think straight or you're all going to die out here.

"What are you two doing in there?"

"My brother Bruce got shot. He's knocked out. When we couldn't get him away, Amado thought of getting into the water." She looked at him with adoring, dilated eyes. "He's my hero." She turned back to Clare. "I wanted to leave Bruce to roast, but Amado wouldn't." She turned to him again. "You're the best person I ever met. Did I tell you that?"

"Oh. That's beautiful." Clare waded into the water. "And it's good, because you're not supposed to leave people to die. You two are beautiful. You wanna get married? 'Cause I can marry you. Legal and all."

There was another boom. The Humvee trying to batter its way into the barn. The sound sobered Clare for a moment. "What's going on over there?"

"Donald. And Neil. They figgured if they could get to the stuff underneath that hadn't burned yet, they could save some. They been hiding it ever since they stole it. 'Sworth a lot of money. There's a lot in there."

Clare filled her lungs. "I can tell." She laughed. "Okay, this is serious. We brought a four-wheel-drive up here. Come with me. Let's all get in and get the hell away from here."

"You said hell." Isabel tugged at Amado's sleeve. He smiled amiably and followed her, dragging Bruce Christie's limp form behind him.

"Yeah. I used to swear a lot. I had to give it up when I became a priest." Clare ducked beneath the water, drenching herself, then led the happy pair toward where she thought the Aztek was parked.

She found it, after several more deep breaths of smoke. She helped Amado wrestle Bruce inside. Isabel clambered over the two men.

Clare looked around the interior. It was a lot smaller with three people in the back. "I dunno how we're going to fit your other brothers in here."

"Oh, let 'em burn and die," Isabel said cheerfully. "Burn and die, burn and die."

"Be nice, now," Clare said. "Okay, I'm going to find Kevin and Hadley." She turned on the Aztek's engine and cranked the AC and blowers on high. "I'll be right back."

She slammed the door shut and staggered toward the downslope side of the barn. "Hadley! Kevin!" A flash in the corner of her eye made her turn so quickly she staggered and fell down. A wall of flame had exploded at the edge of the field, clawing up into the trees, racing along the grass. Toward the narrow mountain road. "Lord a-mercy. That's not good."

There was another boom. She stumbled toward the sound. "Hadley! Kevin!"

"Here! Over here!" She followed Hadley's voice, to find the woman tugging on Kevin's arm. "Come *on,* Flynn. You aren't going to stop them."

"I can do it," he said. "I'm a good shot. I'm a really good shot." He swayed.

"He wants to shoot their tires out," Hadley said. "Like the kid in the movie. 'You'll shoot your eye out!' " She giggled.

As Clare watched, the Humvee backed up for another run at the barn. She had to hand it to them; those things were built like tanks. Then Kevin brought his gun up and dropped into a shooting stance. Which would have been more impressive if he wasn't listing like a sinking ship.

"No!" Hadley yelled.

Clare rammed her shoulder into Kevin's arms as he squeezed the trigger. His shot went off overhead. He staggered upright and looked at Clare reproachfully. His eyes were dilated black. "You shouldn't have done that."

"Kevin, you can't aim. You're stoned. You're under the influence of illegal drugs."

"Am not!"

"Are so."

"You guys." Hadley shook her head, trying to stop laughing. "The whole damn mountain's going to go up in a minute."

The Humvee roared forward. Flames shot out from beneath the hood. It hit the barn. Cracked stone crumbled, battered beams fell, and bale after bale of shrink-wrapped marijuana tumbled out of the broken wall, like the payout from an enormous slot machine.

"Whoa," Kevin said.

The Humvee blew up.

The pressure wave knocked Clare and the officers to the ground. A fireball shot into the sky, chewing and charring the remains of the barn, and an irregular skirt of fire ripped across the grass from the inferno of twisted metal and glass.

"Holy shit." Hadley pushed up from the ground. "C'mon. Let's get out of here."

They ran for the Aztek. Kevin scrambled into the driver's seat, while Clare and Hadley wedged into the passenger side.

"You sure you can drive?" Hadley said.

" 'Course I can," Kevin said, throwing his SUV into gear. "I'm a good driver. I'm a very good driver."

"Nobody's a good driver when they're high."

"I'm not high! I've never gotten high in my life." He hit the gas.

"God, Flynn. I don't think anyone could be more vanilla unless they were Amish. I'm sorry I debauched you, now."

"Okay, everybody? Hold on. We have to drive really really fast through this fire here." He accelerated toward a wall of flame.

Isabel screamed. "No!" Clare shouted. "You idiot!" Hadley yelled. Then they were in it, and then they were through, jouncing and plunging, careening down the narrow road, bouncing like popcorn kernels inside the SUV.

"We're gonna die," Isabel said tearfully. "We're gonna die." Amado recited something over and over. Clare thought it was the Hail Mary. She dug her hands into the sides of the seat and hung on for dear life.

"That wasn't debauchery. That was love." Kevin's voice softened, although his foot was as heavy as ever. "Love, love, love," he sang.

"Aw, Flynn. I'm sorry. I was harshin' you. You're a good man. You're too good for me."

Clare felt tears welling up in her eyes. "You guys are beautiful. You wanna get married? I can do it, you know. Just say the word."

XXX

Lyle MacAuley rolled his cruiser to a stop between Flynn's Aztek and the crumpled remains of Clare Fergusson's car. Beside him, one of the responding EMT crews worked to extricate someone from the upside-down wreck. Christly hell. If he had to tell Russ she was — he wouldn't do it. He'd go home, get his things together, and leave for Florida.

He got out of his unit. Behind him, the last of the Millers Kill Volunteer Fire Department trucks screamed uphill toward the mountain road. The Corinth and Lake Luzerne departments were on the way.

"Whaddaya got?"

"One guy. Broken collarbone, two broken legs. Concussion, probably." The EMT leaned back so Lyle could get a glimpse. "Know him?"

Lyle looked at the studs and tattoos. "Not as well as I'm going to." He straightened. "Was there a woman inside?"

"Nope."

Thank God for that. So where the hell was she? And where were Kevin and Hadley? He heard a noise. Circled, slowly, trying to pinpoint it. Coming from Kevin's Aztek. He walked closer. It was . . . what the hell? . . . voices. A bunch of 'em. Singing "All You Need Is Love."

The Transfiguration of Our Lord

AUGUST 6

Amy Nguyen was leaving Russ's hospital room as Clare arrived. "Amy! Hi. Are you here on business?"

"Catching him up on the Christie/Punta Diablos prosecution." The assistant district attorney pointed to Clare's BDUs. "You recruiting, or what?"

"Oh, this? I'm in the Guard. I just got back from Latham. I serve off-weekend so I can get in more flying time."

Nguyen smiled behind her hand. "You're a very unusual priest."

"I get that a lot, yeah."

Inside, Russ was propped up, shuffling through the papers spread across his bed. He smiled. "Hey, darlin'. How was training?"

"They squeezed the truth about my day job out of me."

"And?"

"And now everyone on the crew calls me

Preacher." She made a face. "Better than my nickname when I was regular army. Charlie Foxtrot."

"For . . . Clare Fergusson?"

"A different C.F." She ignored his grin. "What's all this?"

"A paper trail. Or what we've been able to make of one." He held up a sheet. "Donald Christie did time in Plattsburgh. Along with Alejandro Santiago, a member of the Punta Diablos. Apparently, they struck a deal while behind bars. Donald and his brother would dispose of the PD's business rivals, underperforming sales representatives, et cetera, for ten grand a pop. The idea being that no one would find the bodies up here in the Adirondacks."

"Not an incorrect assumption."

"No." He picked up another paper. "The agreement held for two years. Then a truckload of pot arrives on the scene. Very valuable. High THC level."

Clare rubbed the palm of her hand against her forehead. "Don't remind me."

He snickered. "We don't know exactly what went down. Did the PDs want to store it up here because things were getting hot in the city? Did the Christies turn the driver? Whichever, they were suddenly in possession of ten million dollars' worth of weed. And a load of trouble. The PDs started cruising around, taking potshots, breaking into Bruce's trailer. I suspect they didn't move more directly because they didn't know if their driver had taken off with the goods or if the Christies had stolen the shipment. They sent their accountant up here to check it out. Neil Christie whacked him."

"That was the first body?"

"Yeah. Isabel was out with some of the family, searching that night, and saw the whole thing. She took the guy's bag and hid it, thinking to protect her brother. Then, of course, the PDs got desperate. The merchandise was one thing, but they'd lost their distribution list."

"So what did Amy Nguyen say?"

"Alejandro Santiago and his compadres will be going away for a long, long time." He grinned, showing his canines.

"And the Christies?"

His grin fell away. "We don't have anything on Bruce. He claims he had no idea about any of it and was shocked — shocked! — when his brothers revealed their stash in the barn that day."

"Maybe —"

He shook his head. "Donald and Neil between them only had half a brain. Just look at how they died. No, he was behind it. We just can't prove it."

"That's not right."

He smiled a little. "We've had this talk before." He held out his hand. She took it. He tugged her closer. "When I get out of here —"

"You're going to the Rehabilitation Center at the Glens Falls Hospital. Maybe you can have Sister Lucia's old room. She's been released."

"Okay, when I get out of rehab —" He stopped. "You know, you were right."

"I was?"

"About it taking time. It's going to take five months of hard work to come back from this." He rested his free hand on his bandaged chest. "Losing Linda was worse. It hurt me more than this did. I do need to give it time. A year's not too long." He tightened his grip on her hand. "So when I get out of the hospital, and when I get out of rehab, and when I make it through the anniversary —"

She smiled. "What?"

"We'll have a talk."

ALL SAINTS DAY
NOVEMBER 1

Clare wished Janet and Mike hadn't lit the fire. She and Father St. Laurent stood with their backs to the foliage-bedecked hearth, and while she was sure they looked picturesque, she was roasting in her cassock. She sighed silently and waited for the priest to finish translating the last part.

"Le requiero y cargo ambos, aquí en la presencia del Dios, que de cualquiera de usted saben cualquier razón por la que usted no puede ser unido en la unión legal, y de acuerdo con la palabra del Dios, usted ahora la confiesa."

The only response was Mike McGeoch, honking into his handkerchief, and the rumble of the furnace kicking in. Father St. Laurent smiled at her. What a hunk. Such a shame.

She looked at Isabel, who clutched Amado's hand. "Isabel," Clare began, "will you have this man to be your husband; to live together in the covenant of marriage?"

ADVENT
DECEMBER

I

"Careful, Chief, careful." Noble hovered over Russ, making his way up the marble steps with the help of his much-loathed cane. He'd already decided he was going to burn the damn thing for the winter solstice.

"I'm not going to fall, Noble." He tried to keep his voice even. "If I couldn't walk, they wouldn't have let me come back to work."

"Well, it might be slippery." Noble bent to study the hallway floor. "Might be some melted snow we didn't get up."

He limped into Harlene's dispatch center, Noble at his back. It was empty. They were in the squad room. He could hear muffled laughter, someone shushing. He sighed. Limped through the door.

"Welcome back!" The shout was deafening. Someone — Harlene, probably — had gotten everyone in, all shifts, the full-timers and the part-time guys, every one of his people. His people. Young, old, men, women. They smiled at him. Waiting for him to give a speech. Not his strong suit.

"So," he said. "This morning would be a good time to rob a bank in town." They laughed.

Lyle came up beside him and faced the small crowd. "There oughta be a nice ceremonial way to show I'm beatin' feet away from the chief's chair, as fast as I can run, and turning it back over to the guy who actually belongs there. I thought maybe I could take the chief's insignia off my collar and pin it on him, except I never put it on." He glanced at Russ. "So I figured I'd put something on myself to indicate I was resuming my life of leisure." He reached back and pulled the grungiest Day-Glo orange hunting cap Russ had ever seen out of his rear pocket, snapped it open, and squared it on his head. He held out his hand. "Welcome back, Russ."

Russ pumped his hand, and everybody cheered and the next thing he knew he was hugging Lyle, who was pounding him on the back and saying, "Don't ever scare me like that again," in Russ's ear.

They broke apart, Lyle shifting from foot to foot, Russ banging his cane on the floor. "One hug every eight years," Russ said.

"That's my limit."

Then Harlene and Knox hugged him, and Kevin lugged in boxes of pastries from the Kreemie Kakes diner and he thought, *I'm the luckiest sonofabitch in the world.*

II

Hadley was helping Hudson and Genny decorate the tree when the doorbell rang. Well, maybe "refereeing" was a better word. Hudson had to place every ornament in a particular place, and God help them all if one of the frosted bulbs got too close to a flying reindeer. Genny, on the other hand, was free-form. Right now she was tossing handfuls of tinsel at her side of the tree. Some of it was even landing on the branches.

"Be good," Hadley told them, as she crossed to the door.

It was Kevin Flynn, taking a break from patrol. He was in uniform, his unit idling curbside. He took off his hat and beat away the snow that had fallen on the shoulders of his coat.

"Flynn?"

"Hi," he said. "I know you have the rest of the week off, so I wanted to wish you a Merry Christmas."

"Thanks. Uh, Merry Christmas to you, too."

"Would you like to join the Flynns for our traditional Christmas dinner?"

"Thanks, but we've already made plans."

He glanced past her to where the kids had fallen silent. Undoubtedly taking in every word. "Sledding?"

She stepped onto the porch and closed the door behind her. "No. Flynn, you have to stop asking me out."

"I will. If my feelings change. Until then?" He shrugged, his coat rising and falling.

She stared up at him. "What *is* it with you?"

He took a step toward her. *Stop him,* she told herself. He slid his hands along her jaw-line, her cheekbones. *Do something, woman.* He bent his head. *Just say no. Oh. Oh, my God.* He held her as if she were a breakable ornament and kissed her as if she were the only warm thing in winter. "Merry Christmas," he whispered. She was still catching her breath when he bounded down the stairs. She listened to the thump of his cruiser door. Watched his rear lights dwindle in the falling snow.

"Oh, Flynn." She wrapped her arms around herself. "What am I going to do with you?"

CHRISTMAS
DECEMBER 25 THROUGH JANUARY 5

I

She got the call she had been expecting on Christmas Day, at the Ellis house, after dinner but before the pie and cake had been cut. The kids had fled to the family room, leaving behind a litter of china and adults with elbows propped on the table, finishing off the wine.

Clare's cell rang, a number she didn't recognize. Maybe a wrong number. Maybe a parishioner who had bottomed out on the hardest holiday of the year. "I have to take this," she said, rising. Dr. Anne waved her away.

In the living room, she flipped open her phone. She listened to what the man on the other end of the line had to say. She said, "Yes, sir," and, "Thank you, sir," and hung up. She stood there a long time, staring at the Ellises' tall tree, heavy with children's homemade ornaments.

"Clare?" Gail Jones stuck her head in the door. "If you need to go somewhere, I can drive you."

Clare shook her head. She walked past Gail, back into the dining room. The chatter fell silent as they saw her face. "Are you all right?" Karen Burns stood up. "Is everything okay?"

"My Guard unit's being called up." Clare didn't know where to put her hands. She settled for wrapping them around her arms. "We're going to Iraq."

II

She refused all offers to drive her home, although she agreed to let Geoff Burns notify the rest of the vestry. She walked through the darkening streets of Millers Kill, past windows framing twinkling trees, past strings of fairy lights and illuminated plastic Santas, past closed-up houses whose inhabitants had fled to Florida or Arizona.

She walked past her own house, around the square, beneath fuzzy candy canes and reindeer hanging from the old-fashioned-looking streetlights. She walked past stores closed for the day and galleries closed for the season and old mills, closed for good. Walking is prayer, someone had told her, and she believed it.

Eventually, exhausted and numb from the cold, she turned around and headed back. Before she reached the rectory, she stopped at St. Alban's and let herself into the chilly, dim space. On the deep stone sill beneath the nativity window, she had set a *retablo* she had found with a single votive. She lit the candle, and Our Lady of Refuge sprang to life in hot pinks and blues, a motherly smile on her face, welcoming all into her sheltering arms. Clare thought Octavio Esfuentes might like it. She thought about him, dying terrified and alone in an alien land. Thought about herself doing the same thing. "Holy Mother," she whispered, "Be with us all when we're frightened and far from home."

The rectory was scarcely warmer than the church. She cranked up the thermostat and lit the fire she had laid this morning. Russ had told her a fire sucked heat out of a house, but you couldn't prove it by her. After she had gotten it going, she felt warm enough to shuck her parka and make some hot cocoa. She had just retrieved the pan and was assembling ingredients when a banging at the kitchen door nearly caused her to drop the milk carton on the floor.

The door opened before she could get to it. Russ came in, stomping his boots, clutching a hideous arrangement of red and green carnations and gold-painted holly. "I thought you were locking up nowadays." He shut the door behind him.

"What are you doing here?" She accepted the ugly flowers while he took off his parka. "I thought you were working all day."

"I asked Paul to finish up my shift. He only had his kids until noon. Then his ex got 'em." He nodded toward the carnations. "These are for you. Sorry. The only place open was the Stewart's out by 117, and they didn't have a big selection." He finished untying his boots and kicked them off. "I thought I ought to bring flowers when I asked you to marry me."

Clare, who had been mentally inventorying her pantry for things she could offer him, stared. "What did you say?"

He relieved her of the flowers and set them on the pine table. He took her hands. "Marry me. I'm sorry, I don't have a diamond." He squeezed her fingers. "It feels like you need a pair of gloves more than jewelry."

"I was out walking." She pulled her hands away. "What do you mean, marry you?"

"We can get a license tomorrow at the town hall. Judge Ryswick can waive the waiting period and do the thing right in his office. We can be husband and wife by lunchtime." Russ ran his hand through his hair. "No, that doesn't take into account buying rings. We'll have to go to Glens Falls for that."

"I don't want to get married by Judge Ryswick tomorrow. That's —" The light went on. "Somebody told you I'm being deployed." She shook her head. "Good God. I knew the town grapevine was fast, but I didn't know it was that fast. I only found out myself two hours ago."

"Geoff Burns called me." Russ smiled a little. "I guess I'm going to have to stop calling him a dickhead."

"And so you what, thought you'd rush over here like a swabbie in *On the Town* and marry me before I shipped out? Thanks, but no thanks."

"Clare —"

"I have to see to the fire." She went through the swinging doors into the living room. He followed her. He stopped by the sofa as she knelt and jabbed the poker at the inoffensive logs.

"I don't want you to go." His voice was low.

"I don't want to go either." She didn't look at him. "My whole life is here." She inhaled. "But I knew what I was getting into. Which is more than I can say about becoming a priest." She got onto her feet and turned toward him, a big man in khaki and stocking feet, hands jammed into his pockets.

He looked at the floor. "When I say I don't want you to go, I mean I don't want you to die."

She went to him then, wrapping her arms around him. He folded her into his embrace and rested his chin on her head. They rocked together.

"You're cold."

"It was a long walk. And I'm a little scared."

"Burns told me it was Iraq. He didn't say how long your tour is going to be."

"A year. I've got two weeks to report."

His arms tightened. He breathed in. In the quiet, she could feel him silently enumerating everything that could happen over the course of a year in a war zone. When he finally spoke, he surprised her. "I went to Linda's grave this morning."

She looked up at him.

"I had this idea of — I don't know — talking to her. Like people do in the movies? So I got there, I stood around in the cold, I felt like a posturing fool: then I realized; I don't need to do this. She knew the truth. About how I felt about her. She was headed back. Headed toward me. She forgave me before she died. I just had to — I don't know — forgive myself the same way." He ran one hand through his hair. "It sounds stupid when I try to say it."

Clare shook her head. "No."

He smiled, one-sided. "There were already fresh flowers against her stone when I got there."

"Ah."

"Much nicer than the ones I managed to get for you."

She laughed.

He tightened his arms around her. "I don't want to spend another year kicking myself for what I should have done or not done. So tell me what I can do for you, love. You want me to go away? Help you pack? Take care of your house while you're gone? What do you need from me?"

No more waiting, she thought. *No more time.* She smiled slowly. "Make love with me."

He stared into her face for a heartbeat, then let her go to strip off his shirt. "Ma'am, yes, ma'am!"

She was still laughing when he hauled her against him, bare-chested. He kissed the corners of her mouth and her jaw and her neck, yanked her sweater over her head and flung her bra across the room; kissed her shoulders and breasts and nipples until she was gasping and incoherent. She trapped his face between her hands and brought him back up to her mouth, exchanging deep, drugged kisses that made her head spin.

She tried to tell him, *The bedroom's upstairs,* but he was tugging at her skirt, saying, "I want you naked," and the fire was hot against her back, and his hands were running between her legs and she thought she was going to die if she didn't have him right now.

He kicked away his pants and shorts and there they were, face-to-face and skin to skin. Everything stopped. His hands were shaking. Hers were, too. She touched the fading pink lines and puckered circles marking the violence that had nearly killed him.

"Not very pretty," he said.

"No." She looked into his eyes. "But it's you."

"Yes."

She didn't smile. "Yes." She stepped into his arms, listened to the hiss of his breath as they pressed together, his skin hot against hers.

"Oh, God, you feel good." He buried his face in her neck.

"Um." His hands were moving over her again, making it hard to think. "I should let you know I'm on — oh, God — birth control pills. To regulate my cycle." He moved down her body, using his tongue and teeth now, as well as his hands. "But I don't have — oh, yes, do that again — any condoms or anything."

He looked up at her. "Clare, the last time I was with someone new I was twenty-three years old. I'm not worried about diseases, I'm worried I've forgotten what to do."

She laughed, then gasped. "That's okay. I've forgotten what you're supposed to do, too."

He laughed against her belly, a low rumble that sank into her bones. He got off the floor and half sat, half sprawled onto the sofa. She climbed onto his lap. Leaned forward. Kissed him. Teased him, with her mouth and breasts and hands, until he was clenched and trembling. "Now, please." His voice was heavy. "Please, now."

He looked into her eyes as she took him inside her. "Oh, God," he breathed. "Clare . . ."

"With my body I thee worship." She didn't know if he recognized the words.

"I do," he said. "I will." Then she moved, and he moved, and every thought fled like sparks up the chimney as he kissed her and licked her and stroked her with his long, clever fingers, over and over and over again. Her slick-wet skin felt taut, fever-hot. She clutched at him, closed her eyes, opened her eyes, watched his face glazed with pleasure, a face she knew like her own and had never seen before.

He slid down, braced his legs, thrust hard into her. She cried out.

"Tell me." Rough and hard.

"I love you." She didn't recognize her own voice.

"No. Tell me you'll come back."

"Russ —"

"Promise me. Promise me you'll come back."

He battered at her. Fingers moving. So good. "I can't —"

"Promise. Me."

"Oh, God!" She broke, snapped, arched, tore open to him. "I promise, I promise, I'll come back to you, I'll come back to you, I'll come back. . . ."

Epiphany

Russ woke up in his lover's bed alone. He sat up. She was at the other end of the spartan room, kneeling at her prie-dieu. Morning prayers.

"I was that good, huh?"

Without looking at him, she raised her voice. "Bless, also, O Lord, the aged and infirm, especially your servant Russ Van Alstyne. . . ."

He threw a pillow at her. She laughed but continued on silently. He tossed the covers back and padded downstairs to get the coffee going.

Her duffel bag was already by the door.

After he put Clare's fancy French press to work, he went back upstairs, hip twingeing as it always did these days, and got dressed. Her shower was running. He cracked open the door, letting out a rush of steam. "I'm going to get my truck," he yelled.

"Okay."

For the past two weeks, he had parked his truck overnight in Tick Solway's lot across from the church, in the driveway of a couple of snowbirds, and on Washington Street, two blocks up and one block over. He guessed more than one of Clare's congregation had an idea she hadn't been spending these last nights alone, but no one seemed inclined to judge a woman headed for a war zone.

His stomach twisted.

He brushed a dusting of snow off the window as the engine warmed up and then drove the three blocks to Clare's. He left the truck running. Kicked off his boots and entered the kitchen. "You ready?"

Her hair was seal-slick from her shower, already pinned up. She was going to get it cut at Fort Drum, she'd told him. She poured the coffee into a travel mug. "Ready."

They were quiet on the drive to Latham. The sky was sheet-metal gray, promising more snow by noon. She looked out the window, watching the Northway roll by, and it felt like she had already left him.

"I'd like you to just drop me off at the depot," she said, as he threaded his way through the Albany traffic.

"Okay."

"They're going to have one of those send-offs, with a band, and the young wives dressed up in red, white, and blue, and parents trying not to cry. I hate those."

"Okay."

She rubbed her hands along her BDUs. Past Albany, now, coming up on Latham. Had Linda felt this way when he had deployed to the Gulf and to Panama? How did she stand it? He shot a fierce apology to the place where he kept her memory.

Clare turned to him. "What are you thinking?"

"I've changed my mind. I don't think women should be anywhere near any combat zone at any time."

She laughed.

And there they were, at the gate, showing her ID, pulling onto the tarmac outside the depot. Gunship gray buses were lined up nose to tail, waiting to take the battalion to Fort Drum. They both stared at them.

He moved first, getting out of the truck, hoisting her rucksack, opening the door for her. She jumped down. "Thanks."

She looked up at him, like she wanted to say something but didn't know where to begin. He knew how she felt. He was afraid if he started talking they'd be there all day, he had so much stuff in his head. Instead, he pulled her into a hard embrace. They stayed like that for a long time. She pulled away first. He had always suspected she was stronger than he was.

She dug into her pocket. Pulled out something silver. "I want you to keep this for me until I get back." She placed it in his hand. It was the cross she always wore with her clericals.

He tipped a one-sided smile. "I can see it now. I'm going to wind up going to your church just to be where you were, like some old dog circling back to an empty chair."

"Well." She shouldered her rucksack. "They did want me to increase attendance. Old dog."

He caught her hands. Squeezed hard. "I'm holding on," he said. "No matter where you are, no matter what you're doing. Don't ever doubt it. I'm holding on."

She ducked her head. Leaned against him for a moment. Took a deep breath. Stood straight. Her eyes were liquid-bright, but she managed a smile. "Not letting go," she said.

Then she did just that, releasing his hands. She turned and walked toward the depot. He watched her cross the tarmac, an average-sized woman in desert camo and army boots. He watched her until she disappeared inside. She never looked back.

He dropped the silver cross over his head. Tucked it beneath his shirt. Climbed into his truck. By the time he reached the Northway, the snow had started. He flicked on the wipers and turned on his lights. A lot more winter to get through, he thought. A long, long year to go.

ABOUT THE AUTHOR

Bestselling author **Julia Spencer-Fleming** is the winner of the Agatha, Anthony, Macavity, Dilys, Barry, Nero Wolfe, and Gumshoe Awards, and an Edgar and *Romantic Times* RC Award finalist. She was born at Plattsburgh Air Force Base, spending most of her childhood on the move as an army brat. She studied acting and history at Ithaca College, and received her J.D. from the University of Maine School of Law. She lives in a 190-year-old farmhouse outside of Portland, Maine, with three children, two dogs, and one husband. Visit her Web site at www.juliaspencerfleming .com.